The Sky Is Red

The Sky Is Red

A novel of World War II by Giuseppe Berto

A new translation by Julia Purdy

LitPrime Solutions
21250 Hawthorne Blvd
Suite 500, Torrance, CA 90503
www.litprime.com
Phone: 1-800-981-9893

Published by LitPrime Solutions   08/23/2021

ISBN: 978-1-954886-99-5(sc)
ISBN: 978-1-955944-00-7(e)

Library of Congress Control Number: 2021917871

When it is evening, ye say, It will be fair weather, for the sky is red. And in the morning, it will be foul weather today, for the sky is red and lowering. O ye hypocrites, ye can discern the face of the sky; but can ye not discern the signs of the times? A wicked and adulterous generation seeketh after a sign; and there shall be no sign given unto it, but the sign of the prophet Jonas. Matthew XVI, 2, 4

1

The river was a slow-moving and not very long waterway that rose from the marsh just where the big plain began. From that spot you could see various bluish mountain chains that reared up behind the line of hills that took different forms, some high and conical, others low and rounded, like mounds. And on the hills were fields and houses and chestnut trees and rows of grapevines, and the distance gave all things a faint and even somewhat unreal appearance, almost as if not made for humans.

Where the hills ended, the big plain began. At first it was narrow, closed in between the mountains and the sea, but then it broadened out toward other mountains even more remote, so that you could barely make them out. Looking from the hills on clear days, you saw the whole extent of the fields, which on one side were limited in the distance by the edge of the sea, and on the other appeared limitless. Still, rarely could the view reach as far as the sea, as a light mist almost always lay over the plain and blotted out the landscape.

Up to the feet of the hills, the soil in the plain was fertile. People had partitioned it with ditches and rows of mulberries and poplars and cultivated it intensively, with an ancient devotion, and perhaps an even more ancient fatalism. Then the vineyards and fields came to an end at the edges of the marsh.

The marsh was a broad area of bogs covered with reeds and tall grasses, and the unexpected change of vegetation quickly created a sense of dreariness. There were no houses in the interior, and one lonely road, narrow and not well-trodden, struck off across the bogs, traveling on the tops of a series of dikes connected by old bridges built of brick. Solitude and light and silence lay upon the marsh.

From there the river arose. Between the bogs there opened a number of small and not very deep springs, with clear water that continuously welled up from the grassy depths and joined in channels, soundlessly finding their way toward the sea. The river had been busy for years—centuries, in fact—with finding its path to the sea, because the terrain it had to traverse was level, and the sea lay only a bit below the marsh. For this reason, the river course had become uncertain and slow, and in fact for a long stretch the newborn river kept the appearance of a marsh, although the waters developed two distinctly different qualities, one stagnant and covered with the mosses of the bogs, and the other, limpid and flowing because of the springs and the channels.

Proceeding into the plain the channels joined and little by little assumed the aspect of a river, even though two broad, marshy strips of reeds and grasses lingered along its banks, creating a lonely and almost secluded, yet always melancholy and sweet, impression, while the view remained of the hills and the chain of mountains beyond.

This river did not produce floods. Even in the event of abundant and continuous rain, such as happened in springtime, it rose only a little, since the water collected in the marshy zone, from which it flowed, unhurried. Sometimes, when the rains were especially violent, the water became turbid and arrived at the sea yellow, with a stronger odor of muck and moss.

The river continued to flow in this way, hemmed in by marshes, for about six more miles; eventually, little by little, the riverbanks became more solid, and rows of willows alternated with the reeds, and at last the occasional humble house appeared, facing the river, with its stucco discolored and eaten away by damp along the base of its walls.

But the current remained sluggish, and the water was not very deep, so that at a certain spot people had confined it between two banks, in order to narrow it and assist it to reach the sea. And here the big seagoing boats were able to overcome the current to the point where the banks began.

Closer to the mountains, the city had arisen in ancient times. The main river and two of its tributaries passed through the city, and two additional canals had been excavated, so as to encircle the walls with a moat. So you could say that the city had been born from the river, because the river provided three indispensable things in those times, water and safety and a way to communicate with the coast, where the world opened up.

You saw immediately that the city was centuries old. Viewed from the outside, it appeared, huddled within the circle of walls, as a multitude of rooftops from which rose the towers, the churches, and the old city hall. Outside the walls stood the railway station, the broad asphalt streets and the orderly houses. Inside, everything was different. Indeed, there were the radio tower, the cafés bright with chrome, and even a transit bus line. But the squares and streets retained an almost medieval atmosphere.

The streets were for the most part narrow and contorted and the squares crooked, austere, hemmed in by the huge walls of some church, by the irregular rows of closed and gray houses, or by the low porticoes, each one different from the others.

Two of the more important streets connected the monumental gates in the walls and divided the city irregularly into quarters, which were named San Tommaso, San Francesco, San Sebastiano, and Sant' Agnese. Each quarter had its own principal church and various smaller churches.

Since earliest times a kind of hierarchy had been established among the quarters, according to the people who lived in them. The quarter of Sant' Agnese found itself occupying the lowest position. It was as if wedged between the two branches of the river, and it had, even more than the others, kept its medieval aspect. An ancient brick church reared up in a vast square, the only place where the quarter was open to the sky. All the rest was an intrigue of alleys, where the pavement still consisted of stones laid slightly concave, so water could flow down the middle and empty into the river. Via Sant' Agnese, only slightly larger than the others, became known as the "grand avenue."

The houses rose serrated one above the other, for the most part dark and distressed looking. But there were, as well, mansions that retained a certain graciousness in the proportion of their construction or in some window or in the remains of frescoed stucco, where the design and the colors were by now faded. But the old noble families had abandoned them long ago, and poverty had invaded. Small doors had been cut in the great portals, and in the interiors, the spacious salons were subdivided with partitions, so they might accommodate large numbers of people. Thus were the houses and the mansions all similar on the inside, small and dark places where the odor of filth stagnated.

The things and the people of the quarter seemed to share equally in the squalor, which they both still bore with not a little pride – the things, for their antiquity; the people, out of who knows what dignity or contrariness.

From time to time there appeared a polished doorway, framed with colorful tiles, with a door-plaque of bright metal. That was a brothel. All the brothels of the city were located in the Sant' Agnese quarter.

The inhabitants belonged to the lowest levels of society. The women were almost all washerwomen or, if they weren't ugly, prostitutes. The men were itinerant peddlers and ragpickers, even thieves. In general they moved easily from one occupation to another, taking extended periods of rest in between. The old people and the children furnished the city with a considerable number of beggars. It was a populace that accepted its own situation. Whoever wanted to live differently moved out of the quarter.

There had been a lengthy discussion in the city about the rehabilitation of the Sant' Agnese quarter. And at last the work began. It opened up a broad, straight street that connected the cathedral square to a new portal in the walls, cutting through only one district, at the margin of the quarter. A few ancient mansions remained standing to the side and were scraped and cleaned and then covered with fake antique frescoes, following the suggestions of scholars. Ultimately, they appeared very interesting. Alongside them would be constructed some house of five or six floors, which the populace accepted with enthusiasm and immediately dubbed "skyscrapers." Not knowing where else to go, the poor people, chased out of the demolished houses, took refuge in the intact center of the quarter.

The city had also begun another project, at the opposite end. An old mansion had already been selected and restored and repainted. Then the war came, and everything was suspended.

The war did not change many things. Even if things to sell became scarce, at the same time money became inflated, and vendors charged more for their merchandise. And so a little more poverty was added to those who were already poorly off.

People doubtless believed that war was evil. But this war was going well and was being fought elsewhere, and so people said that it was holy and just and necessary. But otherwise they did nothing. They only held onto the vague hope that it would end soon.

And, naturally, many of the boys of the city left and went to fight, and of one or another the news would come that he was dead. But this happened in faraway places, in Greece or Africa, and eventually even farther away, in Russia. The people were unable even to imagine places so far away and different, and they never thought about the suffering of the soldiers or of those civilians. Each person worried only about himself, trying to get by as he always had done.

That was how things were at the beginning, when the war was going well and was far away.

But then the war began to go badly, and got closer, and the danger and the inconveniences increased. The populace was manifestly unhappy. They said the war was a horrid, beastly thing, and they wished for peace, any kind of peace. The government and national order collapsed, and people were divided against each other. Almost everyone lived in expectation that the war would be over some day, perhaps even soon.

Nevertheless, the inhabitants of the city thought themselves safe from danger. It was a small city, with no industry. Not even the railroad station was very big. The railroad had one main line, to which other shorter lines connected. No one would come to bomb a city of such minor importance to the war, where its people lived in anticipation of peace.

Every day at ten the siren on the tower of the city hall blew, as a test, and perhaps to remind the citizens that there was a war going on. Frequently the siren sounded at other times as well, now that the war was close by. The inhabitants were not terribly impressed. Some went down into the shelters and the underground cantinas just in case, but the majority stayed at their occupations or their recreation. Still, uncertainty and trepidation crept into everyone's heart and lasted until the alarm ended. And when it did end, they thanked God that this time it had been intended for someone else.

Some of the more important cities in the interior had been struck and devastated by bombardments, and many refugees had sought shelter in the small, peaceful city. These people brought with them pain and destitution, because they had lost everything they owned. The people of the small city did not regard them with sympathy. The refugees constituted a nuisance that everyone would have preferred to keep away from themselves, or at least to ignore. By now everyone was withdrawn into himself, as if disoriented, and men were divided and without compassion for one another.

So the people went on living as best they could, as long as someone gave them enough food to keep them from dying. They anticipated that the war would end. This was essential—to survive until then. Then, someone else would help them to stay alive in a world that they believed would be better.

2

The taxi driver arrived in the square in his dark green automobile and parked it in front of the exit doors of the train station. He covered the radiator to keep it warm, then walked across the square, toward the trolley stop. It was an interurban that came from another city, twenty miles away.

The wind was blowing from the east, coldly and steadily.

Arriving at the stop, the driver looked around on the ground, where the streetlamps projected the shadows of the trolley wires onto the asphalt. The wires were vibrating, a sign that the car was approaching. So he decided to wait outside, in spite of the cold. No one was waiting to board because that car was the last one of the night and would be returning empty to the trolley shed.

He began to pace back and forth, stamping his feet hard on the pavement. Meanwhile the wires vibrated even more, and then the trolley car burst from the top of the overpass, descended clattering, and stopped with a squealing of brakes.

"Taxi, taxi!" he called to the few who got off.

The driver of the trolley observed that the taxi driver was left without a fare. "Slim pickings this time," he said, spitefully.

The taxi driver ignored his tone. "Lucky for you that you're done for the day," he said. "I have to wait for still another train."

"What about me?" said the trolley driver. "I still have five miles by bicycle to get home."

"Some trip, with this cold," said the taxi driver, returning the attitude.

"Five miles, from the depot to my house," said the trolley driver, and immediately he shifted a lever, and compressed air hissed as it passed through valves, and the doors closed.

The taxi driver watched the trolley slowly and jerkily make the curve and then swiftly climb the ramp of the overpass with the rumble of wheels on asphalt and the wires shooting out sparks.

Then he recrossed the square, making for the café. The lighted clock high on the front of the station read twenty minutes to two. It was the end of January, 1931.

The station café stayed open until late at night for the arrival of the last train, and inside there was a total of five or six people. The taxi driver went straight to the counter. He wanted to order a cup of coffee and initiate a conversation with the counter girl. "It's cold as a bitch tonight," he said.

"Be patient," said the counter girl. "By now we're almost done with it."

"Hey, we can't talk about being done with it just yet," returned the taxi driver. He had pushed his hat back onto his neck, and he stood with one elbow propped on the counter. The girl wore her bleached hair in a permanent with tiny curls.

The coffee began to gurgle in the spout, and they both watched it in silence.

"Shall I put in a little *grappa*?" the girl asked.

"Sure," said the taxi driver, and his face squinted with concentration. "I don't know if you remember," he said, "but two years ago the cold spell came right in February."

"Oh, you could tell right away that it had to turn colder, that time," said the counter girl.

"You never know," said the taxi driver. "A cold wave might turn up from Russia or who knows where. These unexpected cold snaps happen, right? And it suddenly drops to twenty below. I say the worst is yet to come."

The girl at the counter made no comment. She admired the taxi driver and his black leather coat tremendously, but she was sleepy, and in the meantime she warmed her hands on the coffee urn.

The taxi driver drank his coffee with the *grappa* in it, with slow sips.

"I feel sorry about the figs," he said. "We had lots of fig plants in '29 and they died from the cold. Now we have only two, in front of the house. They should produce fruit this year. I would be sorry if they died."

The bell at the station started to clang for the arrival of the train, and the girl at the counter cheered up a bit at the thought that soon she could go home. She looked at her reflection in the gleaming espresso machine and adjusted a curl here and there with languid gestures. One by one the customers approached the counter to pay and then went away. These were people who were meeting someone on the last train.

The taxi driver had previously invited the girl to his house to eat some figs, and now he boringly resumed his discussion about the cold. Then he heard the sound of the train approaching and even he left to cross the square and position himself by his car.

A few people passed in front of him, all in a group, heading for the city center. No one asked for a taxi, but the taxi driver wasn't unhappy about that, because he was thinking of taking the counter girl home. Instead, at the last minute there emerged from the station a girl with two big suitcases, and she stopped in front of him and asked if he was available.

"Yes," he replied, and looked attentively at the girl, then at the suitcases, then back at the girl.

"All right," said the girl indifferently and got into the taxi.

The taxi driver loaded the suitcases into the back, and before closing the trunk he suddenly asked, "Want to go for a drive, Beautiful?"

"Take me to Via San Bernardo," the girl responded curtly.

The taxi driver shrugged his shoulders and feigned great indifference as he uncovered the radiator and sat down behind the wheel. Still, he was miffed and stayed in a bad mood for the whole trip. He liked the girl well enough, but she was surly, and it would have been better if she had not come along if she was going to be that way. With the counter girl, something might have come of it.

He stopped the car in Via Sant' Agnese, on the corner of Via San Bernardo.

"Where do you want me to go?" he asked.

"It's all right, here is good enough," said the girl.

The driver turned around. "But there are no houses here," he said.

"It doesn't matter," answered the girl, getting out. Since the taxi driver did not move, she unloaded her suitcases herself.

"That's seven plus twenty," said the driver. "There's the nighttime surcharge."

The girl found the money in her purse and handed it to him without speaking. Then she stood still, expecting the car to pull away.

"Okay, Beautiful," said the driver again. "Don't you want to tell me whose house you're going to? I'll come find you, if you tell me."

"It doesn't matter," said the girl again.

Grumbling, the driver engaged the gears and left. Then the girl picked up the suitcases and walked along Via San Bernardo, which was located on a gentle slope toward the river. She stopped in front of a small, plain door and knocked loudly several times.

The girl was impatient. As soon as she thought she heard sounds from inside, she left the steps and stood in the middle of the street, looking up at the floor above. The house was low, just two levels.

A window opened noisily, and an old woman looked out. "Who is it?" she shouted.

"It's me," answered the girl in a low voice.

"Oh, how come?" said the old woman. "We weren't expecting you." She spoke too loudly, and her words echoed all the way to the end of the silent street.

"Hurry up and let me in, please," said the girl. "It's cold out here."

The old woman closed the window and took from the bed her black shawl to cover herself. As she reached the landing of the stairs, a man's voice asked from the other room, "What is it?"

"Giovanna's here," answered the old woman, descending the stairs.

As soon as the old woman opened the door, the girl entered with the two suitcases. It was cold indoors also, but at least the cold was not biting, as it was outdoors. There was the smell of a burnt-out fire and rotting garbage, but right away every other smell was masked by the girl's perfume. It was a heavy, almost thick fragrance.

Her face was garishly made up, and she was wearing good silk stockings and a very showy fur-piece. She removed the fur with care before sitting down near the table, under the harsh light of the lightbulb. The old woman sat down as well, waiting. Overhead there was a sound, and a baby began to scream.

"How are they?" asked the girl, nodding with her head toward the stairs.

"Fine," said the old woman.

"The little one too?" asked the girl. Her voice sounded deep and tired, and it could have been she was talking just to pass the time.

The old woman answered, "Yes, well enough."

"She's crying," said the girl.

"She woke up," said the old woman. "She must be hungry, I guess, that's why she's crying. Usually she's good, she doesn't cry much."

There was a silent pause, and the old woman waited.

Suddenly the girl said, "I've come home to stay, Mamma. I'm going to have a baby."

"You?" went the old woman.

"Yes," said the girl. "I think I've got three months to go." As she spoke, she did not look at the old woman but at a peeling pattern of red roses in the oilcloth table cover. With a finger she scratched absentmindedly at it.

"And you don't know who the father is?" asked the old woman.

The girl smiled bitterly. "How do you expect me to know, in my profession?" she said.

"But don't you even have someone in mind?" the old woman asked, sourly. "Someone who thinks he might be the father? You women always have someone."

The girl made a gesture of annoyance with her shoulder. "Yes," she said. "Someone who paid."

They lapsed into silence again, caused by the resentment and lack of understanding that existed between them. The child upstairs continued crying. Soon footsteps were heard on the wooden stairs, and a man came into the kitchen. He was at least thirty years old, unshaven, and wore a threadbare overcoat the color of tobacco.

"Oh," he said in the direction of the girl.

She said, "Hello, Augusto," giving him barely a glance.

"She started crying and hasn't stopped," said the man. "A person can't sleep."

Then he fell silent and fixed the old woman with an inquiring look.

"She's come back," said the old woman. "She's going to have a baby."

"A baby, a baby!" said the man, looking in amazement at the girl. "What's got into you?"

"You heard it, didn't you? It seems to me that Mamma spoke clearly enough."

The man's voice sounded mean. "You must be out of your mind, to make a bastard."

"What do you care?" said the girl, almost in tears. "It was convenient enough for you that I took on this work, right? And so now that I'm going to have a baby, I'll have it."

The man was getting more furious by the minute, and he moved toward the girl to give her a smack. But the old woman jumped up and blocked his way with her arms raised. "No, not this, for the love of God!" she shouted.

The man turned away slowly and went to sit in front of the girl, without taking his gaze off her. She sat with her head lowered, and her fingers stopped moving on the oilcloth.

The old woman paced a little around the room, then moved closer to the girl again.

"Listen, Giovanna," she said. "Augusto should not have spoken to you that way, but when all is said and done, he is right. A bastard is always a big mistake. There are always so many unfortunates in the world that there is no need to add another one. And then, how will you work at your trade? You need to think carefully. You would not be able to work carrying a baby on your back."

The girl listened attentively to the words of the old woman but did not reply.

So the old woman continued, "In my opinion, there is only one thing to do. With a little courage, you can free yourself up right away. And it doesn't cost much. Here there are some safe people, who do it for not much money."

The girl obstinately kept her head down and did not reply.

"How long has it been?" asked the man.

Still the girl did not respond, and the old woman quickly said, "She says six months. It could be done."

"Sure, it could be done," said the man. "So that's that, do it right away. It's a business that only takes a few days."

"Yes, yes," said the old woman persuasively. "She'll sleep on it tonight, and you'll see that tomorrow she will have decided. It's the only thing to do."

Finally the girl raised her head. "Listen, Mamma," she said. "At the beginning, as soon as I became aware of it, I didn't want it. I've done everything to free myself up. I've taken so much of that stuff that anyone else would have been rid of it."

"You must not have done things the way they're supposed to be done," said the old woman.

"No," said the girl. "It's just that he didn't want to go away. And then I began to feel him move inside me, and to love him. And now I want him. I may be stupid, but I want him. I don't care if he's a bastard."

The man became infuriated again and jumped to his feet, knocking over his chair. "You wretch!" he shouted. "A bastard, and she still wants it. She has no shame!"

The old woman tried to calm him down. "Be nice, Augusto," she said. "Be nice. Don't let yourself be heard in the street. It's better that they don't know."

But the man was more enraged than ever and shouted, waving his arms at the girl. "I'll give you the bastard!" he yelled. "I'll give you so many blows that I'll force you to abort, as sure as there is a God!"

The girl angrily raised her head and she also began to shout.

"Oh, yes," she said. "You want to make me abort, right? Do you think I don't know why? You shout bastard and shame, but it's the money you're thinking about. Up to now I have supported you, all of you, including that slut that you married. And now you're afraid for the money. You think that if I have a child, I'll care only about him and I won't give anything more to you. This is what you think, isn't it? Out with it, at least have the guts to say what you are thinking."

"But no, no," said the old woman. "It's not what you think."

"What do you mean, it's not?" shouted the girl. "You think I don't have a brain to reason with? I already understand too much. But now I know what I need to do. I'm going away from here. I have enough money to live until the birth, and if it's not enough I'll work. And I'll go to the maternity ward to give birth. There they're not on the lookout to see if it's a bastard. Don't think I came here out of need! I came because I thought that this was still my home! I thought that someone besides me would love him."

The voice of the girl was rising with emotion, and finally she put her head on the table and began to sob, hard and desperately. "I'll go away, I'll go away," she said, repeatedly.

The man now wavered indecisively, and he only mumbled some unintelligible words. Gesturing with her arms and head, the old woman signaled him to go back upstairs, and he went off. In the kitchen there remained the girl, crying, and the old woman who watched her cry. The wailing of the child could no longer be heard.

Gradually the weeping of the girl became less desperate.

Then the old woman put a hand on her head, caressingly, and spoke to her with a voice that she forced to sound affectionate. "You don't have to take it that way, Giovanna," she said. "We're advising you in your own interest."

"I'll go away," the girl said again.

"But where will you go? Don't think that you'll find a better spot than your home. Here everyone loves you, even your brother, even though he's so rough. And we are insisting only so that you'll think about it, while it's not too far along. It's above all *him* that you need to think about, how he will fare in this world after you've brought him here. Look, I had you two, I raised you however I could, and you grew up. Now I don't know if you two are happy to be alive, we never speak of these things. But maybe you are not happy, it's not possible to be happy in our poor condition. I as well have felt bad many times, and I've thought maybe it would have been better if I had not been born. It's better to be nothing than to be poor."

"My child will not be poor," said the girl. "I will not let him lack for anything. I want him to be happy to be alive."

"Happy to be alive," said the old woman, and her voice was now low and pensive. "We think that in order to be content to be alive, all that is necessary is to have things we've never had, enough to eat and wear, and a nice house. And maybe it's not even that. But even if it were that, what are you sure you will be able to give your child? If work goes well, you can give him enough to eat and wear for a few years. And then what? And do you think that even eating well he would not feel the shame of not having a father, and of being born to someone who works at your trade? He could never be happy to be alive. The world is too wicked for such a thing."

The girl raised her head with a jerk.

"It's useless for you to insist, Mamma," she said. "Before I came home I thought it over, for so many months. And I have decided he must be born. He and I want this, of that I'm sure. And if you or my brother don't like it, I'm taking my stuff and going."

The old woman heard the hard resolve in the words of the girl. She had this idea in her head, and no one was going to get rid of it.

And so she replied, almost meekly, "There you go getting mad again. You shouldn't get mad that we are advising you to think it over. We give you our counsel, but you can do what you want, at your age. It's your business, bringing this child into the world and supporting it, we're not going to interfere."

The girl said nothing for a long time. She was gazing with a fixed stare at the oilcloth, and silently a few tears slid down her already smeared cheeks. She was no longer so sure of herself, nor of the one who wanted to be born, nor of what would happen afterward. For long months she had carried her pregnancy in the brothels, amid indifference and sneers, and always it had given her courage to think that at home she would find a refuge and even a little comfort. Home, instead, was worse than anywhere else, a matter of calculating money and convenience. Without a father to pay for him, a child was not convenient and should not be born.

The old woman watched the girl and in the silence she thought hard to find something to tell her, anything, and found nothing.

Finally she said, "Maybe it's better if we went to bed, Giovanna."

"I thought of calling him Giulio, Mamma," said the girl. "And I thought that if he were to resemble any man, he might resemble just *that* man."

"Who knows," said the old woman. "If *he* had lived, many things would be different."

Both of them remained quiet for some time.

Then the old woman asked, "Where have you come from?"

"From Parma," said the girl. "I left early this morning."

"You must be hungry," said the old woman. "And just now we have nothing. We weren't expecting you."

"It doesn't matter," said the girl.

"There's a little milk for tomorrow morning," said the old woman. "You can have that. We'll buy some more."

"I don't want to, Mamma. I'm not hungry."

Just the same the old woman moved to get the milk, and she prepared a bowl on the table with bread.

"Eat it cold," she said. "It will do you good. Meanwhile I will go upstairs to make a place for you to sleep. You'll have to content yourself with a place on the floor, for tonight. Augusto took over your bed for the child. But tomorrow we'll find something else for the child. She is so small she could sleep in a basket."

"I'd like to sleep by myself," said the girl. "I can set things up down here, if there's a spot over there."

"Yes, yes," said the old woman. "Tomorrow we'll see. Over there it's a big confusion of stuff, but tomorrow we'll put it to rights. We'll put everything to rights."

She moved toward the stairs and mounted the wooden steps, trying not to make noise.

The girl listened to her footsteps on the stairs and then overhead, crossing the ceiling. And meanwhile she looked at the peeling walls, and the old kitchen range, and the dirty plates piled to one side, the whole aspect of squalor that her home offered. And in her mind were only random and slow thoughts, because her head was empty and feeble from so much weeping.

Then, when she no longer heard the footsteps moving overhead, she went to the kitchen sink and washed her face in the basin. Finally she pulled from one of the suitcases some garments for the night, and a mirror. She looked a long time at herself in the mirror. Her face was pale, too pale now that she had washed, and there were two dark circles under her weary eyes. This might also have been a result of her pregnancy, perhaps.

So she turned off the light and climbed the stairs, she too trying not to make noise. She left the bowl of milk and bread on the oilcloth with the red rose pattern. She couldn't eat anything. Always, whenever she suffered from the misery of living, pain took over, from her mouth to her stomach, and she was not able to eat.

But now she became a little calmer, as beneath the blankets she waited to warm up in order to fall asleep. She touched her belly with her hands, tenderly, and it seemed she was already caressing the baby that would be born. Once more she felt secure. She wanted him at any cost, for herself, so she could continue living.

3

The main street of the city extended from the cathedral to the station, crossing the city hall square. In that area were the hotels, the cafés, and the more modern shops.

At fixed times, twice a day, the main street filled with people who walked back and forth and appeared to have nothing to do. They just walked back and forth, chatting placidly together, admiring or criticizing each other. This was not a thing of minor importance for the little city. It was the elegant life that emerged on the main street twice a day, at fixed times.

Two little girls came out of Via Sant' Agnese and turned toward the main street, and began to stroll in a more leisurely way, because now there were lots of things and people to see. Well-dressed people, who didn't give off bad smells.

Even so, the little girls soon got tired of watching the people, as the people paid them only enough attention necessary to avoid them. So then the little girls turned their attention to the things.

First there was a bicycle shop, then a shop for optical devices, and the little girls didn't stop there. Those things were beyond their curiosity and their desires. They stopped before the window of a third store, a large fashion store. Things in wonderful colors were on display—neckties, handkerchiefs, scarves.

"These are things for men," said one of the little girls, who was called Carla.

They looked a little while into the display window, keeping a step or two away, then, unconsciously, they approached the glass until they were pressing their hands on it, and finally their faces. They were only able to look for a short while, because a sales clerk came to the door of the shop and shooed them away. As they left, they left on the glass greasy spots where they had pressed their hands and faces.

Right away there was another display window of the same store, with colorful things even more alluring, because it was merchandise for women. The little girls walked slowly, with their heads turned slightly. At the door there was the same sales clerk, who glared menacingly at them. Then Carla took the other little girl by the hand and led her to the other side of the street, in front of the principal hotel in the city.

The principal hotel in the city interested them, but not very much. Not as much as the displays in the shops, anyway. Still, passing in front of the entrance, they threw curious glances into the big lobby, where glass chandeliers were lit up, and people were seated in red armchairs, not doing anything. Perhaps they would have stopped here too, had it not been for a man in a uniform with gold buttons.

Having passed by the hotel, the little girls stayed well away from the uniformed man and recrossed the street, toward the perfume shop.

This had a wonderful display window, with boxes and bottles of various shapes and colors, and the little girls admired them almost with trepidation, holding their arms stiffly behind their backs.

"Carla?" said the other little girl, whose name was Giulia.

"Eh?" went Carla, without tearing her gaze away from the window.

"If you were a lady, what would you buy?"

Carla replied on an impulse, "This one," she said, looking toward a green bottle that stood just inside the glass, in front of her.

"I'd buy that one," said Giulia, nodding with her chin to an almost round lavender bottle that cost twenty *lire*.

"And I would buy *that* one, then," said Carla, and pointed to another, larger bottle full of transparent yellow liquid.

Giulia saw her point her finger and said severely, "Get your hand down so they don't send us away."

"Oh," went Carla loftily, "nobody is going to send us away from here."

But she gave a worried look toward the shop door, and drew her hand back behind her, but slowly, so that Giulia wouldn't think she had made her do it.

Giulia eyed her cousin suspiciously, but then kept searching the window. There in the middle was a faceted and sparkling little bottle, inside a case of red silk. She hesitated a second, because it cost fifty *lire*.

Then she said, "I'll buy that one in the middle."

Carla looked at the bottle and the price label attached to the case and made a little contemptuous sound with her mouth. "You will never have fifty *lire*."

"What do you know about it?" Giulia answered spiritedly.

"You're too poor," said Carla.

"*You're* poor," said Giulia, vexed. "If you only knew, my mommy had a suitcase full of bottles like that one."

"Liar," said Carla.

With a red face, Giulia insisted. "I've seen it myself, I remember when she came home," she said. "My mommy had money, as much as she wanted, and she wasn't even a housemaid."

Carla pressed her lips together angrily, and said, placing emphasis on each word, "Better a housemaid than a prostitute."

Giulia hushed up, this time. With a pale face and a mortified expression, she gazed back at the bottles, maybe without even seeing them. Carla should not have spoken that way, since her mother was dead.

For some time the little girls remained in front of the perfumer's window, but they had lost the pleasure of looking, because that word weighed heavily on them.

"Let's go," said Carla, moving away, and Giulia followed a few paces behind.

At the flower shop Carla stopped. Giulia joined her and stood by her side, downcast and silent.

The flower shop window was also marvelous. A thin cascade of water flowed down the glass on the inside, like a veil before their eyes. Inside were the flowers, great vases of yellow, pink, and red roses, and splendid carnations, and enormous chrysanthemums, and so many other flowers whose names they did not know. It was beautiful, although they didn't understand how there could be such a thing as a shop of flowers or people who spent money to buy them.

They lingered to look, but with little pleasure, because the feeling of tension that had come between them was hard to shed.

Then Carla said again, "Let's go," and took the other little girl's hand and led her in front of the big pastry shop.

Everything was nicely arranged in the display window of the pastry shop. There were enormous sweets in the center, with lovely designs, and vases full of little chocolates all one color, or different colors, and heaps of candies, and so many boxes that must have been full of good things, maybe even better than the little chocolates and the candies.

They gazed with big eyes, and little by little their desire overcame their awe, and the tension between them was forgotten.

"Giulia, which one would you like?" asked Carla.

After thinking a moment, Giulia answered, "I don't know."

There was a short pause, then Carla said, "I would like the candies."

"All of them?" asked Giulia.

"No, not all," said Carla. "Five. Five for me and five for you."

Giulia didn't answer. She appeared to be thinking, with her hand covering her mouth.

"I bet one *lira* could buy ten candies," said Carla.

Giulia suddenly seemed embarrassed.

"Let's go home, Carla," she said. "I have to do my homework."

"What homework?" asked Carla.

"A problem," said Giulia. "It's hard, it's fractions."

"Oh, are you already at fractions?" asked Carla. "Well, you can do it after you eat."

Giulia said nothing and continued to gaze into the window, thinking.

"If you want," said Carla, speaking slowly and with emphasis, "if you want, we could buy ten candies."

Giulia regarded her seriously. "What are you saying?" she said. "We don't have any money."

"If you want, there's a quick way to make a *lira*," said Carla, still with the same slow emphasis.

Giulia kept standing silently, fascinated with the candies.

"What, have you lost your tongue?" said Carla.

Giulia turned her gaze to her. "I don't have the courage to ask for charity," she said. "I'm too ashamed. Even the other time I felt ashamed."

"You're stupid," said Carla. "Why should you feel ashamed? They have pockets full of cash, and they'll give you some, because you have none. Even if they gave you one whole *lira* all at once, they wouldn't even notice it."

"You do it," said Giulia.

"You think I'm scared?" said Carla, irritably. "I'll do it, but with the money I get I'll buy the candies for myself. Watch how it's done."

She looked carefully around, and no sooner did she spy a man leaving the pastry shop than she attached herself to him, holding her hand out. After two or three steps the man gave her a coin, and she returned triumphantly. "Did you see how it's done?" she said.

"How much did he give you?" Giulia asked.

"*Twenty centesimi.*"

"Show me."

Carla furtively opened her fist, and Giulia was able to see for a second the small, shiny coin.

"Now you try," said Carla.

"No, no, I'm ashamed," said Giulia quickly.

With an air of supreme indifference Carla said, "Well, I'm going."

Giulia let her get some distance away, but then darted among the people until she was again at her side. "Wait," she said.

"What do you want?

"Wait."

Carla stopped and fastened her eyes on Giulia. "Now will you ask for money?"

Giulia nodded her head yes.

"You always take too much time to do things," said Carla. "Get going, now. I'll look out for the cops."

"Stay near me," said Giulia. "I'll have more courage if you're nearby."

"Be quick," said Carla. "Don't stand there like a goose. And don't quit until you've made a *lira*."

She took herself outside the stream of people walking by, and began to look around, as if distracted by something.

Giulia remained alone and began to observe, perturbed, the faces of the people that passed by. They were all walking along unconcernedly. It must be because they ate well and had good clothes and for sure did not lack for money in their pockets, that they were so unconcerned. And they did not notice her. She had thought that if they were to see her as she was, with worn-out shoes and clothes, they would give her a handout even without her asking. But it seemed that no one was paying attention.

Carla made signs to hurry up, and Giulia felt confusion growing inside her. Sudden thoughts came into her mind. She needed to have courage, because no one was paying attention to her. She would ask money of just five people, and she would begin with a lady. It seemed easier to begin with a lady.

A well-dressed lady passed in front of her, and the little girl made a timid gesture, and immediately pulled her hand back, and the lady passed on without giving her anything. Maybe she had not even seen her.

She tried with another lady, and this one stopped and started searching in her purse, for very long time. In the end she gave her a copper coin.

"Thank you," said the little girl, and her voice came out in a croak, she was so discouraged from waiting so long.

She thought of asking a gentleman, then. She waited for one who seemed nice, but she was completely mistaken about the generosity of that gentleman.

"Off with you!" he said, miffed, and she retreated quickly and ended up tangled in the legs of another gentleman.

The new gentleman stopped to look down at the scruffy little girl that had run into him. He saw that she felt abashed, almost to the point of crying. "What do you want?" he asked.

The little girl, who in the first moment had raised her head, now lowered it, focusing her gaze on her hands that she held out in front of her. From her came no response.

"Begging?" the man asked.

The little girl stood obstinately with her head lowered, and the man was not able to see anything but her blondish hair, gathered into two clumps with black ribbons, and her shoes below, misshapen and scuffed.

Meanwhile the people continued to pass close by them, and the little girl thought that now she would be thrown in jail and that she would prefer to be in jail than in her present situation. Instead, the gentleman opened her hand and put a coin into it.

The little girl took a long time to realize what had happened, and when she tried to look for the gentleman he was no longer there, nor could she pick him out among the people who were walking along. She didn't even remember his face, nor the color of his clothes, and still she searched among the people, dazedly, with her heart pounding, because she had met with goodness in the world, for the first time in her life.

She heard Carla calling to her, and she ran over to her, still in a daze and bright-eyed.

"What did you get?" Carla asked.

"Nothing," she replied, and with a slow gesture she turned over the shiny coin that the gentleman had given her, and then also the copper coin that she had hidden in her pocket.

"Only one person gave me fifty *centesimi*," she said.

Carla took the coins and studied them.

"You don't have a *lira* yet," she said.

The joy in Giulia's heart at having discovered good in the world was now a bit dimmed. "It's enough for today," she said.

Carla made a disdainful face, but she got control of herself and said bluntly, "Well, this means we'll buy fewer candies, that's all."

Together they returned to the big pastry shop and discussed the relative qualities of the candies that they would buy. It was Carla who would go and buy them. And so, when they had made their choices, she walked toward the door, but passed it without going in. Then she turned around, looking toward the door, and still did not go in.

She came back to Giulia, trying to hide her embarrassment.

"I thought," she said, "I thought that until there is one *lira* it would be useless to go in here, because they cost so much. They might cost more than ten *centesimi* each. It would be better to go and buy in another place."

Giulia wanted to protest. More than anything she wanted those candies, the candies in the big pastry shop. Still, she followed Carla without saying anything. Now she knew what Carla would finally have done, and not even she had the courage to enter the big pastry shop.

They hurried along then, without taking an interest in the people or the shop windows. They turned into the street from which they had come. There, there were other shops, dark and humble, where it was easier to go in and make them give you whatever you wanted.

Later, sucking carefully on candies, and with slow steps, almost as if trying to dawdle, the two little girls went off to their house on Via San Bernardo. They arrived as evening was just beginning.

In the kitchen the light was off and the faint glow that entered from the street gave everything the color of ash. The old woman should be inside, but they did not see her. The little girls stopped hesitantly by the door.

Only after some moments was the old woman's voice heard. It was unpleasant, deep and rasping, like the voices of old people. "Ah, are you there?"

"Yes," said Carla.

"And where have you been up till now?"

"Around," said Carla.

"Around, eh, you tramps? And now you'll want to eat, right?"

Carla didn't know how best to respond. "Yes," she said, without conviction.

"Well," said the old woman. "There's nothing to eat. Until your mother gets back, there's nothing." She seemed quite pleased about it.

The two little girls stood still, lined up along the wall. They were not too worried about the old woman's tone and not even about eating.

They knew that Carla's mother would come back, bringing something to eat. She always brought something, if only the bread and milk that she bought with the vouchers of the charity society, or food saved from the household where she was a maid.

After some time had passed, Giulia closed the door and turned on the light and took from her schoolbag the arithmetic notebook, to work at the table. Seated as always in the corner the old woman said nothing, and the little girls understood that the awkward moment was now past. Carla came to sit in front of Giulia and began to watch her idly.

"Don't you have anything to do, Carla?" asked Giulia.

"No," said Carla, "I don't feel like it."

Giulia didn't feel like it either, and yet the thought of going to school tomorrow without having her lessons done scared her. She wasn't able to do as Carla did. She bent her head over her notebook, and she pondered at length a problem with fractions that she didn't understand. No one spoke in the kitchen.

One night Carla's mother came home from her job. She was a woman past her prime, soft and fat, with a suffering face that never changed expression. She dumped onto the table the milk and bread—a lot of bread—and cheese, and a big piece of meat.

The old woman came out of her corner and looked first at the things the woman had brought, and then looked curiously into the woman's face. "Did they pay you?" she asked.

"Yes," the woman answered wearily.

"So, you're done?" asked the old woman. "You're done there too?"

The woman lifted her shoulders and began to set the table. "Let's put the meat away until tomorrow," she said.

They began to eat in silence, sadly. Even the little girls understood the reason for the unexpected abundance.

The woman began to talk, in an almost expressionless voice.

"They let me go this time too," she said. "I don't know what I'm supposed to do, when they let me go. As soon as they find out, they fire me."

The old woman and Giulia focused on their food. Carla, instead, raised her eyes every so often to her mother, trying to grasp if behind the words there was something she was not saying.

"I can't find work in this city," said the woman. "Already three houses have sent me away, and it wasn't my fault. So I'm thinking of going away."

"Where?" asked the old woman.

"I don't know yet," said the woman. "Maybe to Naples. The people in the agency told me that they're looking for maids in Naples, because of the bombardments. They'll do the job of writing. They also pay for the travel."

"Why do you want to go so far away?" said the old woman. "You won't be able to go see Augusto, and when he gets out—"

"When he gets out—" repeated the woman, interrupting her.

The old woman didn't continue her statement.

The woman said, "I don't have the strength to stay here and wait five years. You can't live here, there's no work. And I'm fed up—fed up—with him and with everything. I ruined my life with a man who did nothing but abuse me and get drunk, and never has any motivation to work, and when he started to steal he made himself look like a fool."

"Then it's because you don't want to hear anything more about him, that you're going away," said the old woman.

The woman didn't answer.

"And your daughter?" the old woman persisted. "You won't really want to leave your daughter with me, would you? I have enough with the other one. They're two tramps, with no desire to do anything. You'll see how it turns out, in two or three years. I don't want the responsibility."

"Relax," went the woman. "I'll send you money."

Later the little girls went up to their room and listened to the women still arguing below. Finally, the women also went up to sleep, and there was only silence in the little house.

While they remained awake, the little girls thought over all the events of that day. They had passed a new threshold in life; they were richer in new experiences and sensations, both glad and sad, that would persist in their awareness for some time, and that in some way would help to shape the way they must exist in the world.

Carla's father was in prison and would be released in five years, in 1945. A time frighteningly far off. And Carla's mother would go to Naples, perhaps, also a place frighteningly far off, where the war was, and airplanes went sometimes to drop bombs. And the problem with fractions couldn't be solved. And in the main street, among the wonders and desires and things and people, one of them had met with goodness in the world, a nameless gentleman who had given her fifty *centesimi*, without her even asking for it.

The thought of tomorrow, made up of minor events, barely touched them. A piece of candy that each of them had saved to eat as soon as they awoke, and then school, and then . . . who could know?

Footsteps pattered along the street, and the sound reached them. It was the people who were passing along Via San Bernardo, going to some brothel. Something that, if it entered their awareness at all, entered only dimly. Still, they knew where those people were going, and what they were going to do.

4

In the bedroom the light, which hung from a cord in the center of the ceiling, was on. Giulia could not get to sleep because of the light. Turned to the wall, she tried to remedy this somehow with her arms and the blankets, but all the same she could not sleep. And outside it was raining.

It often rained those days, because it was the beginning of spring, and the old walls of the Sant' Agnese quarter were encrusted with saltpeter because of the dampness. The waters of the river flowed past with almost no sound, but yellow, with a strong odor of muck and moss, that you could smell in the streets and even inside the houses.

Carla was seated at the dressing table, in front of a cloudy piece of mirror, and she was trying out various ways to do her hair. Each evening she did her hair before going to bed, but she had never spent so much time looking at herself in the mirror.

Giulia had watched her for a time, the way she moved her hands and arms, and the waves she put in her hair. Then she got tired of watching her and tried to go to sleep by turning toward the wall and was unsuccessful because of the light. She heard the muffled sound made by the rain on the roof tiles. From time to time people passed beneath the porticoes on the street, talking loudly, or even singing. It was perhaps already eleven o'clock.

At a certain moment she heard Carla push the chair aside and move softly through the room. She turned to watch her.

Carla was standing up near the light, with her overcoat over her shoulder and bare feet, and in her hand she held her beautiful dress, a red one. For a while she examined the dress carefully, then with a satisfied air she draped it on the chair and brought the chair close to the bed.

Then she became aware of Giulia watching her. "Oh, you're still awake?"

"I can't fall asleep because of the light."

"God, how sensitive you are," said Carla, a little teasingly.

They spoke in low voices, almost whispering, so the old woman asleep in the other room would not hear them.

Giulia watched Carla admiringly. She had not gotten ready for bed but had made herself up in a really becoming way. She had drawn her hair back, leaving her ears uncovered, and it was held with a ribbon that passed around the nape of her neck and tied at the top of her head. It was a red ribbon to match her dress, and it set off her black hair. She seemed taller with that new hairdo, and less of a child.

"How good you look, Carla," said Giulia. "Turn around, let me see the back."

Carla let the overcoat slide to the floor, and she turned slowly with the studied grace of a model. She looked good even from behind. Her hair fell loose and swinging to her shoulders, and her shoulders were round, and nude, because Carla was wearing only her nightgown.

"Beautiful," said Giulia. "But why are you doing this tonight?"

Carla did not reply. She was kneeling on her own bed and was laughing—her mouth, her glowing eyes, her whole face, full and happy. She rubbed her thighs with her hands and puffed up her chest to push up her breasts, which were still not well developed.

"I'm beautiful, aren't I? Tell me I'm beautiful," she said, and Giulia nodded her head yes, and she too was glad.

"I'd like to have a big mirror," said Carla. "I'd like to see all of me, without a nightgown."

"Get under the blankets, silly," said Giulia, laughing. "Don't you feel cold?"

Carla tossed her head and her hair rippled around her. Her excitement illuminated her face in a wonderful way. She was truly beautiful.

"I'd be happy if I got to be as beautiful as you," said Giulia.

"If you're good!" said Carla, with mock seriousness. But then she said, without joking, "You're a little backward in your development, Giulia. But some day you'll be beautiful too."

Giulia studied her a moment. "You're different, tonight."

Carla started laughing again, as if hiding something.

"Tell me why you did yourself up like this," said Giulia, too loudly.

"Quiet!" said Carla with sudden harshness and ran to the door to turn off the light.

"Tell me, Carla," Giulia insisted, lowering her voice. "You've even got your new dress out."

"Oh, how boring you are," said Carla. "It popped into my head to do it, that's all. No other reason."

Giulia remained in silence, wide awake in the dark. She heard Carla get onto the bed, and then some quick movement, but she did not lie down. She must have been sitting up in bed, and she did not move again. Maybe she didn't want to muss her hair. In any case she could not stay in that position all night, just to avoid mussing her hair. Giulia began to see better in the dark and had the impression that she saw Carla's shadow sitting there.

"Carla?" she called.

Carla replied at once, in a curt tone, "I'm tired. Let me sleep."

Giulia was certain that she was sitting up, and her curiosity made her earlier desire to sleep vanish. She wanted to see what would happen.

Much time slowly passed, and outside it was raining lightly. Carla didn't move, and Giulia couldn't even hear her breathe, and this meant that she was awake. You always heard Carla breathe when she was sleeping.

From time to time someone passed below the portico, so it was not yet one o'clock.

Then someone in the street whistled twice, the same notes.

Then Carla moved with caution. She got off the bed and began to dress in the dark. From the street the whistle repeated two more times, more loudly. In her haste Carla knocked over the chair and froze, listening. The whistle repeated again. On tiptoe Carla left the room and ran down the stairs. The street door opened with too much noise.

Until now Giulia had been holding her breath for fear of being heard, and now she sat up, her heart pounding. So Carla, too, had come to this. All girls arrived at that point sooner or later, as she well knew. But that Carla had, was a thought that particularly disturbed her. She thought Carla was too young for such things.

Suddenly the light went on.

Giulia threw herself down and pretended to be asleep. But already the old woman was there in the doorway, and she glanced briefly at her and then at Carla's empty and unmade bed.

"Where is she?" she demanded.

Giulia could not reply.

"Did you understand me?" the old woman asked again. "Where's Carla?"

"I don't know," said Giulia. "I thought she was sleeping."

The old woman wore an expression both hard and hateful, with her face all wrinkled and her eyes sunken and her lips disappearing into a straight line. Still, she seemed calm.

"Oh, yes?" she said. "We'll see."

She left the room but returned right away with her black shawl. She sat down on Carla's bed, turned toward the door, and said no more.

Outdoors it was starting to rain harder, and the water beat on the roof and made noise in the downspout.

Giulia could not take her eyes off the old woman. She observed the bowed back and the yellowish hair, all askew. She wanted to picture Carla, where she was at that moment and what she was doing, and she could not, because the old woman was there, waiting. Something bad was about to happen.

Time seemed to stand still. And it might have been good if it did stand still, to give the hate and fear time to fade away. The old woman stayed immobile, without speaking. By then no one was passing by on Via San Bernardo.

They waited, and started a little when, finally, the street door opened and closed again, too loudly.

On the wooden stairs they just heard the final footsteps and then Carla appeared, holding her shoes in one hand, and her face showing surprise at the lighted room. Her hair was plastered to her head, miserably straight.

She looked and stopped at the threshold, letting her shoes fall to the floor.

The old woman got up from the bed and advanced slowly toward her and planted herself in front of her. "Where have you been?"

Carla didn't respond. She looked the old woman in the eye, with a stiffened expression that revealed no emotion. Maybe she was far, far away in her mind.

"Where have you been?" the old woman demanded once more.

Nor did Carla reply this time, and the old woman felt her anger growing and slapped Carla in the face.

Half out of bed, Giulia looked on with fright. She thought Carla would rebel, and she would certainly get the better of the old woman, since she was stronger. Instead, Carla leaned against the wall and began to stare at the floor, all the while with that frozen expression.

Then the old woman flew into a rage, yelling and waving her arms.

"I should have known you would finish this way, with your character," she shouted. "You've started in right away. You're taking advantage of your mother staying in Naples and she's not here, eh? And you think you can do whatever you want with me, is that right?"

Carla stayed still, as if she didn't hear, and the old woman screeched even louder. "Your mother is somewhere else and your father's in jail, and you start walking the streets. At least tell me who it is. Is it a gentleman?"

This time Carla raised her eyes to the old woman, and right away lowered them again, making a face.

"Ah!" shouted the old woman, exasperated. "A wretch, then. A wretch like you. And what do I do with you now? Tell me what I should do. I'm ruining my life to keep you fed, and you repay me this way. Oh, but you are mistaken if you think you can do whatever you want. Since your mother has sent not more than four *centesimi*, you are under me now. And things will change, starting tomorrow. You will find a job, and you will be home at the hour I tell you. And if you don't like it, you can leave. Go to your wretched boyfriend, we'll see how well he feeds you."

"Better than you," Carla said angrily.

The old woman stood silent for a moment, wordless between wrath and shock. Then she shouted, "Better than me, you said? That's gratitude!"

And she hit Carla in the face again.

Carla did not move. Only when she felt the blood trickle from her nose did she take a handkerchief from her pocket and try to stop it.

And when the old woman saw the blood, she left Carla and turned to Giulia, who had stayed to watch.

"And you didn't know anything, right?" she yelled.

"No," said Giulia.

"Don't think you can fool me with your innocent air," shouted the old woman. "You're worse than she is. You also are like your mother."

Giulia felt a bad feeling inside that she allowed to surface. "Leave my mother out of this," she said sternly.

"I'll leave out whoever I please and whoever deserves to be left out," shouted the old woman. "And don't permit yourself to make comments about me, if you don't want to feel the weight of my hand."

She had raised her arm threateningly, and Giulia watched this and a deep hate was born in her, and even a need to get thrashed.

"Try it," she said defiantly.

"Take this!" screamed the old woman. "Take this!"

Giulia wanted to wait for the blows, to feel the evil on her open face, as Carla had done. But she didn't have the strength. She twisted her body around and tried to protect herself with her arms.

The old woman landed more blows, screaming all the while. But Giulia didn't even feel them. She was seized by a sadness that did not come from the blows, or not solely from them. The old woman had committed a wrong against her and perhaps also against Carla, and it was this that gave her the greater sorrow. In any case the old woman should not have done that.

Giulia wanted to cry, and she wept silently, and was then ashamed of crying. Now that there was silence in the room, the sound of rain on the roof and in the downspout was heard once more.

With an effort Giulia got up. The old woman had left, and Carla remained in the same spot, staring at the floor, and seemed expressionless. With distracted movements she dabbed beneath her nose with the handkerchief, now soaked in blood.

Giulia got off the bed and went to her. "Get into bed."

"Oh, leave me alone," said Carla.

"Come on, Carla, come on," said Giulia kindly, and led her toward the bed, and helped her get undressed and stretch out. She arranged two cushions under Carla's shoulders, so her head would fall back, and she gave her a clean handkerchief. Carla let her do this, almost absently.

"Has it passed?" Giulia asked after a little while.

Carla signaled no with her head.

"Stay like that," Giulia said. "I'll make up a cold pack for your forehead."

"Let it go," said Carla.

Giulia went to wet a towel in the water of the jug in order to put it on Carla's forehead. Then she put on her overcoat and sat down on her own bed.

"Carla?" she called in a low voice.

Carla's eyes were closed, but she wasn't asleep. "What do you want?" she said.

"Has it passed?"

"Yes, go to sleep."

Giulia waited a little while, thinking. Then she said, "You didn't tell me anything, Carla. You never tell me anything. Were you afraid I'd tell?"

Carla made a dismissive gesture.

"What did you go out to do?" asked Giulia. "You should at least tell me this."

Carla gave a listless smile, without opening her eyes. "How stupid you are. Don't you know what a person does with a man?"

"Really? A man?" Giulia asked.

"He's seventeen," said Carla.

For some moments Giulia stayed quiet, meditating on this. Then she said, "I'd like to meet him. Will you point him out, if we run into him?"

"No," said Carla.

Once more Giulia stayed a bit without speaking. "Don't you even want to tell me his name?" she asked then.

"Tullio," said Carla.

It was a nice name, Tullio. A boy named Tullio. She didn't know him.

"And have you actually been together?"

"But of course," said Carla. "What do you want me to say?"

Giulia's face wore an odd expression, thoughtful and dreamy, as she watched Carla, who lay with her eyes closed.

"I don't know if what you did was good or bad, Carla," she said. "I don't know much about these things. But now that you've done it, and if you love him, I don't think you did a bad thing. I'd do the same if I found someone to love. I feel that I would do anything."

Carla didn't say anything, and then Giulia asked, "Do you love him a lot?"

"Yes," answered Carla.

"And he loves you, right?"

"Yes," said Carla. "He tells me so all the time. And then I myself understand that he does love me."

"So he might also marry you, right?" asked Giulia.

Carla lost, for an instant, her empty expression. "Sure, he might. Not right away, that's understood. When we're older. Right now, he's learning a trade. He wants to be a mechanic."

"You must be happy, then," said Giulia.

"For that matter," said Carla, "it isn't important to get married. He says it's not important. And it doesn't even interest me very much."

Giulia did not know what to say, and remained in silence, following her own thoughts. Carla was motionless, and with one hand she held the handkerchief under her nose.

"How are you feeling now?" said Giulia.

"My nose?" said Carla.

"No," said Giulia. "All over."

Carla smiled. "Fine."

And then she said again, "Get to sleep, Giulia."

Then Giulia went to turn off the light, and she got into bed, and notwithstanding her weariness she was not able for some time to fall asleep, because of the multitude of thoughts that swarmed through her head. She had a swollen lip that was cut inside, and she continually passed the tip of her tongue over the cut. But she didn't think about that, nor about Carla, nor the old woman, nor about all the wicked things that had happened. She thought of herself.

With her hands she felt over her body, her long, too-thin legs, her small and tender belly, her flat chest, like a boy's. Still, her time would come, and then she would do it. It was one thing in life she was eager to try; she felt it within herself as an urge, pushing against the misery and suffering of everything else in life. She would certainly do it. She had only to find someone to love.

5

The hour of curfew had come, and the city appeared deserted. The screened lamps, suspended on wires above the streets, swung a little in the wind, and the spots of blue light on the cobblestones shifted continually back and forth, in a gentle movement. In the gardens and in the outer streets, lined with trees and shrubs, that slight wind also made a sound in the new foliage. A train at the crossing whistled now and then.

Distributed in the different quarters were military servicemen, in pairs. As they walked along, their footsteps could be heard in the streets for a long time, and also their conversation. No light shone in windows or doors.

Then, suddenly, the siren on the town hall tower started up. It was a sound both strong and deep, that filled the streets and houses and reached many miles into the countryside. The servicemen stopped, looking toward the sound, even those who could not see the tower.

The siren sounded once, then quit for a few seconds, then began again, then quit and began once more. When the siren stopped for the third time, there were a few moments of silence in the city. Then the servicemen began walking again, and their footsteps echoed in the streets.

Now everything had an even more indistinct appearance, since the streetlights were turned off. People could barely make out the dark arches of the porticoes, or the row of houses beneath the projecting roofs, or, if they looked down, their own feet, planted on the ground like shadows.

Still, as little by little they grew accustomed to the darkness, it seemed to them that a greater light came from the serene sky, and they were able to see many other things.

It was a perfect night for an attack. Somewhere there would be terror and death and destruction.

They heard new sounds around them. Some windows were opened here and there in the houses, and a face appeared, looking out, and then spoke loudly to those inside. The train stopped at the crossing, whistled again, then moved, but it did not stop at the station. It continued on, and after a while it could be heard crossing, with a louder noise, the iron bridge over the river and heading off into the countryside.

More people came out into the street. They were soldiers who were coming back to the barracks, and members of the civil defense who hurried toward their muster places. A fearful man came down with some blankets under his arm and went to get settled in the air raid shelter.

Wherever it reached, the sound of the siren robbed people of their rest and caused apprehensiveness. Everyone's thought was of what could happen, even if they were fairly certain nothing would happen. The siren had gone off so many times before and nothing had ever happened. Still, they could not sleep, and anxiety drove them to listening to sounds around them. They jumped if a window banged, or if they heard the sound of an engine. And the apprehensiveness persisted in them until the siren stopped, announcing that the threat of death had passed.

Giulia suddenly woke up, full of fear because of the alarm. It was the same every time the siren went off at night. Her heart would thud irregularly and breathing became difficult. There was nothing to do but stop and wait and try to think of other things, not of bombs or death, and in this way some part of her unreasoning fear left her.

But while she thought, she remembered what she had promised to do, and dismay seized her, greater than the fear of the siren.

"Giulia," Carla called softly.

"Yes," she answered, and didn't move, waiting to see what Carla would do. It might be that she had changed her mind, or that even she lacked courage.

Giulia heard Carla moving quickly over the wooden floor in her bare feet, then checking the light switch to see if there was electricity, and finally moving toward the window. The cool night air and a faint glow entered through the open window.

"All quiet," Carla said, and she was glad.

But she didn't stay long to gaze at the sky and the stars. Hurriedly she turned back to the chair by the bed and began to dress.

Then she became aware that Giulia had not moved.

"What's the matter? Aren't you getting up?"

"No," answered Giulia, uncertainly.

Carla stopped dressing and went near her. "Why don't you want to get up?"

"Because."

Carla made an angry gesture. "You said you would come."

"Yes, I said that," said Giulia meekly. "But I thought the siren wouldn't go off again. I don't want to, Carla. I don't have the courage."

"Get up, don't play games. You have to come, since you said you would."

Giulia made an effort to produce a firm voice. "Leave me be. "I don't like this. Go by yourself, if you want. I won't say anything."

This childish obstinacy exasperated Carla.

"Ah!" she said with disgust. "You're scared to get stained, right? Even you, a bastard. A bastard, that's what you are."

She expected a reaction from Giulia, but Giulia said nothing. Then Carla went off to finish dressing, and she combed her hair in the dark, and she even put on her shoes.

Then she waited in indecision. "Well? You really don't want to come?"

Giulia didn't answer.

"Look, I'm going anyway," said Carla with some ire. "But if anything happens, you're going to pay for it, right? I'll give you a fat lip with my fist!"

She waited a bit for Giulia to reply, then she went closer and heard her weeping. "Look at you," she said. "When you don't know what to do, you cry. Want to tell me at least why you're crying?"

Giulia began to cry harder, snuffling through her nose.

"Is it because of the word I used?"

"No, no," said Giulia quickly.

"Yes, it is. Admit that it's because I called you a bastard."

"It's not only because of that. You cannot know why I feel so unhappy."

She continued to weep loudly, but Carla saw now that Giulia would go. She sat down on the bed and began to stroke her and speak to her kindly.

"I didn't want to call you that word," she said. "It just popped out of my mouth, because you said you wouldn't come. But you'll come, right? You must come. Now, we've agreed, and he's waiting for me, and I don't want to miss him. He might think I don't love him so much, and he won't marry me. And you would be sorry if he didn't marry me, right?"

Giulia had to swallow before she nodded yes.

"Then you have to go, understand? I can't go alone. The old woman would guess for sure, and you've seen what she did. She even attacked you, who didn't do anything wrong."

"Yes," said Giulia.

"For me, it's good enough that we go outside together. After, you could stop in the shelter and wait for me there. I'll be quick, I'm going only so he can see me. Then we'll come back home right away, even if the siren hasn't stopped. You'll come, won't you? Come on, get your clothes. I'll help you put them on."

Giulia got off the bed and felt a shudder throughout her body.

"It's cold," she said reluctantly.

"That's only at first. When you start moving you won't feel it anymore."

Giulia began to dress, but after a moment she stopped. "And Granny?"

Carla felt a great desire to hit her. "I'll worry about Granny," she said.

"You need to tell her we're going out. If you don't, I'm not coming."

For an instant Carla neither spoke nor moved. Then she said calmly, "I'll go and tell her something so she won't worry. In the meantime, get ready."

She left the room and Giulia heard her speaking with the old woman. Every so often she caught a word, but not the subject of the discussion. The old woman must be asking a lot of questions. Maybe she wouldn't let them go, and Giulia hoped so, because she had no desire to go with Carla. She continued to dress slowly.

Nevertheless, she was ready when Carla came back. "What did you say to Granny?"

"Nothing," said Carla. "Let's go, quick. Try not to make noise."

They each took a blanket and went on tiptoe toward the stairs. But the old woman heard them just the same and called to Carla. They stopped on the first steps, waiting.

"Carla," called the old woman, more loudly.

"Damn," said Carla. She gave Giulia her own blanket and gave her a push to make her understand she was to go down. Then she went back to the landing and put her head in at the old woman's door.

"What do you want?" she demanded, harshly.

"Are you going off?" said the old woman, anxiously. "Going without me?"

"Well, yes," said Carla. "I told you before we're going down."

"I don't know why you're going down. We haven't been to the shelter for a long time."

"Yes," said Carla. "But this time I'm scared. And even Giulia's scared, so we're going down. But you can stay here if you're not afraid."

"No, no," said the old woman. "I'm coming too. I don't have the courage to stay alone in the house."

"Get dressed then, hurry up," said Carla and made as if to move away.

The old woman saw this. "You'll wait for me, right, Carla?" she asked, suspiciously.

"Sure, we'll wait below in the kitchen. As long as you're quick about it." She hurried down the stairs so the old woman wouldn't have time to ask any more questions.

Giulia was waiting in the kitchen, in the dark. "Why did she call you?" she asked.

"No reason," said Carla.

"What do you mean, no reason? I heard you talking for a long time, and before that you talked for a long time too."

Carla had already opened the door. "Let's go," she said. "I'll tell you in the street."

They went out, leaving the door ajar, and started walking toward the main street of Sant' Agnese. Outside they could see better. The damp cobblestones took on a little of the glow of the night sky. And where the houses weren't very tall, they could even see some stars, through the arches of the porticoes.

"So then, what did Granny say to you?" asked Giulia.

"Are you asking me that to annoy me?"

"Why?"

"You don't mean to tell me that old woman matters that much to you, now?"

"Yes, she matters to me."

Carla took a few steps in silence. Then she said, "All right, she wanted to know where we were going, that's all. I didn't even go into her room. I don't like the smell in there. She's filthy, you know. I've never seen her wash herself down there."

"And what did you tell her?" asked Giulia.

"I told her that we were going into the shelter because we're scared, what did you want me to say?"

She was walking with great haste, and at a certain point she took an alley to the left. She did not want to pass by the shelter on Via San Bernardo.

Giulia struggled to keep up with her. "And did she say that she was coming too?"

"Who?"

"Granny."

"You're still thinking about that old woman!" said Carla, impatiently.

"But did she say that she would come?" Giulia demanded again.

"Yes, she said that. But she won't come, of course. She's too lazy to hurry."

They came out in a street a little bigger than the alley and passed below the porticoes.

"And what if she really goes to the shelter and doesn't find us there?" asked Giulia.

"Oh, you're always thinking of her," said Carla impatiently.

"But I want to know."

"All right," said Carla. "If she really goes to the shelter and doesn't find us there, we'll tell her some story or other. She also needs to change, now that we're working."

Giulia didn't speak, because they were approaching some people. She noticed their figures up ahead, under the porticoes.

Carla slowed her pace, to appear casual.

They were three soldiers, who were chatting with an old lady near the doorway. The door was open, and inside they saw a bright corridor, with a bit of yellow light that shone from an inside room.

The soldiers quit talking and watched the two girls as they went by, with curiosity but without saying anything. Then they came off the portico and took up a position in the middle of the street to observe the strip of sky between the two rows of roofs.

"Do you see anything?" the old lady asked, who had stayed by the door.

"Scared, eh?" said one of the soldiers.

"That would be something, to present yourself to the Eternal Father with all your girlfriends," said another soldier, laughing.

The other two laughed heartily too.

Then the third one said, "Let's go, boys. They'll throw us in the lockup if we arrive late."

They left together in the direction of the cathedral square, where there was a large artillery barracks, and the street filled with the racket of their cleated boots. They walked outside the porticoes, looking up at the starry strip of sky, not out of fear, but because it was so beautiful.

The girls began to hurry along once more.

"They were having some fun, those guys," said Carla, thinking of the soldiers.

Giulia said nothing.

They turned onto the big avenue of Sant' Agnese, toward the city wall. And suddenly they saw two shadows, which came slowly toward them. More soldiers, but these were on active duty, since they were wearing helmets and carrying guns on their shoulders.

Carla took Giulia's hand and tried to pass by as if she had not seen them.

"Hey," said one of the soldiers, "where are you going?"

"To the shelter," said Carla, stopping. Behind her Giulia came to a halt, all afraid.

"How is it you're going to the shelter in this section?" asked the soldier. "Don't you have a shelter on your own street? Everyone must go to the shelter on their street."

"But we're going to the shelter beneath the wall," said Carla. "It's safer."

"Ah," said the soldier teasingly, "how frightened the little misses are."

Carla took Giulia's hand again, and they passed beyond the soldiers.

The soldier who had spoken to them watched them walk away and smirked. "Chicks!" he said to his companion. Together they walked on.

A bit later, the soldiers heard someone coming along in a leisurely way, whistling. When he was closer, they stopped. It was a boy with a bicyclist's cap on his head.

"Where are you going?" the soldier demanded.

"To the shelter."

"Oh, you too."

"Well," retorted the boy, "when the alarm sounds people go to the shelters, don't they?"

"What an attitude. Where do you live?"

"Near here, on Via dei Ferraioli."

"Then turn around and go to the shelter on your street."

"I can't go to any shelter I want?"

"Turn around, get it?" said the soldier. "After the curfew no one can go anywhere they want."

The boy knew that it was no use to insist. He turned around and began to whistle again, walking more briskly, however. When he was far enough from the soldiers, he turned into a side street, made a quick detour, and came out again onto Via Sant' Agnese a little farther along.

He passed in front of the shelter without going in and got up onto the wall that lined the broad avenue of horse chestnuts. Then he whistled a couple more times, not too loudly, and right away he saw, emerging from the darkness and coming toward him, the small figure of a girl.

6

The man was startled awake just as the warning siren began to sound. He heard the three blasts of the siren from the nearby tower. He had the impression that the sound was something fluid that undulated a long way, like concentric rings in still water.

He made every effort to stay still. Absurdly, he hoped that his wife had not awakened.

But the woman spoke almost right away in the dark. "It's the air raid alarm, isn't it?"

"Yes."

They remained still and silent for some time, listening to the sounds outside. They heard a train in the direction of the station, and it whistled once and then again, more prolonged. Then the engine puffed heavily.

"Hear how slowly it puffs," said the woman.

"It's because it's putting itself in motion," said the man. "It must be a freight train."

The puffing of the train increased in tempo and then receded in the distance and finally ceased to be heard.

Still the man and the woman remained motionless and silent in the dark, waiting for some noise and not hearing anything. There were the usual sounds, of course, the creaking of furniture and the gurgling of the plumbing and so forth, but these didn't enter their minds, because they weren't the kind of sounds they were waiting to hear. Something might come from outside, and they were alert for it, although they didn't think it would.

Then the man rummaged on the bedside table, around the lamp that was off. He lit a match and looked at the clock.

"It's not even one o'clock," he said.

"Let's hope it doesn't last long," said the woman, "otherwise tomorrow you'll be tired at the office. You've always been tired for several days now."

"There's a lot to do now," said the man.

Before the match went out, he lit a cigarette. He tried to focus on the play of the glowing end every time he inhaled. Even that could not distract him from the thought of what might be about to happen.

The woman was unable to stay still for long.

He heard her get out of bed and move around as if looking for something.

"Do you want me to light the candle?" he asked.

"A match is good enough. I can't find my robe."

He struck another match and was able to see the woman in her long white nightgown. She found her robe right away. From the way she moved, he could tell she was tense.

The match went out, and they remained once more in the dark.

"You're always tense when the alarm sounds," said the man. "You shouldn't be so nervous. Here there is no danger."

"It's not for ourselves that I'm afraid," said the woman. "You know I'm thinking of him in moments like this."

The man smiled. "Be reasonable, darling. We sent him away to school for our peace of mind, and instead you're always worrying over him."

"I understand," said the woman, "but it's stronger than I am, and I don't know what to do. I'm not exactly scared, you know. I don't even know what I'm feeling. I wish we could all be together when there's danger, that's all I want. That way if something happens to him it also happens to us."

The man did not respond to this. He only said, "Let's also hope this war will end."

"Let's hope so," said the woman.

She approached the window and pulled hard on the cord of the window blind. In going up, the blind shrieked in the silence, and perhaps somewhere nearby someone jumped because of the sound.

The apartment where they lived was up high, on the fifth floor of one of the new "skyscrapers." From the window the woman could see far across the plain, toward the little town where her son was in high school. Thank God, that area was all dark and peaceful. One would have to be a downright fool to be afraid. They were never going to bomb such a small town.

From below, sounds reached her of people walking along, talking loudly. She heard them clearly, notwithstanding it was so far below, and thought they must be soldiers, because they made a lot of noise with their boots. She watched below and saw nothing, naturally, only darkness, but she imagined the soldiers that were walking and talking there. She imagined they were merry—poor kids.

Then the soldiers passed behind the house toward the cathedral, and she heard them no more, and yet she continued to watch.

The Sant' Agnese quarter was all dark, many roofs piled on top of each other, always with some new tile amid the old ones, and between the roofs the openings, narrow and contorted, made by the streets. Farther along was the church, so tall that it seemed all alone in the midst of the houses. She couldn't see it, but she could picture it in her mind. And after that were the walls, and the station, and still farther the houses on the periphery that bit by bit mixed in with the greenish-gray of the countryside. And farther yet was a little town that no one was quite aware of even by day, being so far away. There, her son certainly slept, because the siren didn't reach out that far. And above everything were the stars and a calm night.

"Come back to bed, darling, you'll catch cold," said the man's voice behind her.

She turned her head slightly. "Let me stay a while longer. It's so beautiful."

She was calm now. She felt only a slight exhilaration in her blood and her head, a good feeling that came from the air that smelled of the river and of springtime, from the night and from that light breeze, and from her own thoughts that were in harmony with all these things.

Again a sound reached her from below, beginning far away. It was a motorcycle that was moving slowly because of the darkness, but making a lot of noise. It spread a great racket throughout the space all around it. And the people inside the houses trembled, and even after they recognized the sound it still was hard to calm down.

It must be a military motorcycle, without a muffler. And who knew where it was going, at that hour. The sound slowly came nearer. The motorcycle passed the house and continued on, and its rumbling lingered and fluctuated as it bounced off the houses.

The sound lasted perhaps three minutes and then hovered in the air, but differently now. The woman wasn't aware of it, because she wasn't paying attention to it. At each moment the new sound became stronger, and different. Then the woman looked up at the sky above the city, and she thought it was coming from up there. Certainly, it must be a friendly airplane, all alone like that, but meantime she shivered all over and could neither move nor speak. All she was able to do was to watch. And then right away she saw, igniting and remaining suspended in the sky, a cluster of white lights. They seemed to dangle gently in the air.

And the man, who was looking toward the woman, suddenly saw her figure become a dark silhouette against the light outside. Then he lunged to the window. He caught sight of the illuminated city, and in the sky a cluster of white lights, and then another, were descending. Engines droned high above. From a rooftop in the San Sebastiano section an antiaircraft gun began to launch red projectiles toward the clusters of lights. The projectiles rose, one after the other, slowly it seemed, ever more slowly, and died out with little bursts.

"Let's go, let's go," said the man, breathlessly.

But the woman stared and could not move. Actually, she felt her legs would not move. Through the whole sky the light grew and so did the drone of engines.

"*Move!*" shouted the man, shaking her, and he grabbed her by the arm and dragged her out to the stairs. The elevator cage was empty and useless.

They started down the stairs. On some landing below a woman shouted a name repeatedly, in a frightened tone, and then fell silent. They also heard footsteps below, and doors slammed. From the skylight came a white glow like the moon, but more intense and diffused, a light that did not produce shadows. Everything appeared faded-out and unearthly in such a white light.

They went down a few steps. The woman moved haltingly, and the man was at her side, holding her up. Meantime the noise from outside grew louder. Hundreds of engines were in the skies over the city. Then were added the sounds of the bombs that were falling, like something that was sucking up the air, horribly.

The woman knew right away they were bombs, although she had never heard such a sound before. They seemed right overhead and became ever more terrifying. She felt the first burst of wind in her face, and heard glass breaking, and then the impact of the bomb obliterated every other sound. The house shook and the staircase bucked under their feet. She stopped, leaning back against the wall with her arms outstretched. She looked at the man, as if imploring him, with wide eyes and an open mouth that appeared to be screaming.

The man shouted something that was lost in the tumult and shook the woman and slapped her. She leaned against the wall with all her strength and kept looking at him, pleadingly.

The man tried to lift her up but he couldn't, because now the house was rocking underneath them. Then he also leaned his back against the wall and pulled the woman into his arms. In a second, she became limp and abandoned herself to him, gasping, with closed eyes.

There, it was better that way, she would not feel anything. He squeezed her tight, feebly trying to protect her, and he felt peaceful, because he had never loved her so much.

The last thing he was aware of was a hot wind that rose from below and pushed them up the wall, and the wall behind his shoulders yielded . . . yielded . . . and no longer supported them.

7

There must have been other people at the back of the shelter, since every so often they exchanged words under their breath. But Giulia had no desire to approach them, nor to listen to them. She sat on the ground to one side, with a blanket over her shoulders. Inside there it was cold and damp. It was a pedestrian tunnel, solid and narrow, with a vaulted ceiling. In front of the two entrances they had constructed some protection against flying debris, not very high, and the arch of the vault remained covered.

They had to be prepared to spend who knew how much time there. They drew their knees up against their bodies and rested their arms on their knees and their heads on their arms. Giulia felt drowsy because of the interruption halfway through her sleep, and sorry for her grandmother who was alone, and for Carla, who was outside and would not return very soon, and for everything that had happened before at the house.

She kept her eyes closed, thinking, and so she did not become aware of the light that came from outside. But suddenly a woman began to scream, and then Giulia lifted her gaze.

She saw a few faces, all the same and pale in the shadows, and the arch of the ceiling lit up with a vivid, white light, that was increasing.

Then there reached them, weak and throbbing, the sound of an airplane. Next, shooting began from some location.

She had an instant of bewilderment, but as soon as she understood what was happening, she got up and ran outside. The streets and houses appeared clearly under the light, and she saw no one.

"Carla! Carla!" she called around her, at the top of her lungs.

She stayed to watch the sky in a kind of stupor. Three clusters of lights were suspended above the city, and red lines of projectiles rose, and the air slowly filled with an immense roar of engines. It was almost beautiful, but it sent a chill up her back.

A boy arrived on the run. He saw her standing by the entrance and started to push her inside.

She tried to get free. "Carla's around here," she said. "Carla!"

"She's coming right now," the boy said, and forcibly pushed her in.

Carla arrived right afterwards, running. Now they could hear the bombs falling. It was a sound that went on and on for those who were waiting, almost as if the bombs would never reach the ground.

Then the impacts followed, one after the other, joining in a single explosion, and the air and the earth shook. Some plaster fell from the vault of the shelter, giving those inside the impression they were about to be buried alive. Everyone screamed in terror, and no one paid attention to the screams of others.

Giulia felt her heart and her breath stop, and she leaned against the wall, afraid she would faint. She held her hands over her ears and closed her eyes.

It lasted a few minutes, then all seemed to return to calm. One heard only a low and muddled sound, like something that was panting, but rather far off. A woman began to appeal to God, and repeated that word over and over, compulsively.

Giulia reopened her eyes, and it was as if she had been reborn; in those moments of terror she had lost all power of thought.

In front of her stood a soldier, who must have entered during the bombardment, because he hadn't been there before. He was on his feet, breathing hard, with a hard expression on his face, and he stared straight at her, or rather at something behind her, that he saw passing through his mind. She felt herself shudder again and turned her gaze to look for Carla.

Carla was there beside her, limp against her boyfriend, hiding her face in his shoulder. And Carla's boyfriend wore some of the expression of the soldier, hard and lost, and he too fixed his attention in the same vacant way on some point on the wall in front. Maybe they were all dead! She also was dead, and so was the woman who called upon God in the same voice. Here they were in a different world, like the living and yet not living, each one inconsolably for himself. It was a sense of aloneness, that felt bad.

She tried once more to look at the soldier, and he was still absent-looking, but suddenly he shook himself. A sad, distant smile flickered over his lips.

Then he asked, "Scared?"

She wanted to answer, but she could not find her voice. She nodded her head.

The soldier took a step forward and held out a hand to stroke her face. "It's nothing, it's already over."

The light from outside diminished rapidly, but the deep and muddled sound grew. The siren began in short, repeated bursts that sounded like laments.

"They're calling for help," said the soldier. "I have to go now."

She gathered up her strength. "Where?" she asked.

"I don't know. I'm military. I think I have to go to some location."

She followed him with her gaze in the dim light as he went off, and when she could see him no longer she once more felt the anguish of being alone. Carla was nearby, and it was as if she weren't there. And Carla's boyfriend and the other people, all of them were useless to her in her anguish. Maybe she should go over to the woman who was calling upon God and be with her just to be with someone.

Now the clusters in the sky had gone out and inside the shelter you couldn't see anymore, but there flickered across the archway a reddish and murky glow that was not the glow of nighttime.

She kept watching the entrance where the soldier had gone out. And all at once she saw the sky once more, illuminated by a white and vivid light like before. They must have turned back to bomb again, and she was there alone, and the soldier was outside, she didn't know where. She wanted to run and call after him, but she was paralyzed in every part of her body, and she seemed also to be suffocating. She closed her eyes with a great wish to die.

After what seemed like a long time of waiting, a confident voice shouted to the people in the shelter to stay down and remain calm.

She opened her eyes and it was *that* soldier who shouted. She looked toward him for help, and he saw her and came over, smiling.

"Let's sit together," he said. "It's better that way."

She let herself slide down the wall, and he sat by her side. He replaced the blanket that had fallen from her shoulders and stayed with an arm around her neck.

He felt her shaking all over. "You don't need to be afraid. Here we're safe. If they don't make a direct hit we're safe."

"Yes," she said, but all the same she felt a great fear, although it wasn't the desperate terror she had felt when she was alone. Now she might hope to live, or even to die, and it was no longer such a scary thing.

She heard the drone of engines that drowned out every other sound, including the laments of the woman who was calling upon God. Then they heard the bombs' sound, that throbbed as they fell.

She huddled convulsively against the soldier, and the soldier held her close, and leaned her head against his.

There was an immense explosion, and again the air and the earth shuddered, rocking and tossing. This one also lasted a few minutes. She still clung to the soldier, even after it was over. She felt the good warmth of his body, and the good smell of his jacket, the smell of the barracks. It was enough, then, not to think about anything.

Little by little darkness returned to the shelter. The siren began to sound, lamentingly, again.

The soldier removed his arm from her shoulder and lifted her face with his hand. "Courage. You'll see, they won't be back."

But she turned the soldier's hand away and pressed her face against his chest and began to weep. He let her cry. He held her close while she cried. It was good also for him, the closeness of that small, frightened person. At least it was only one sorrow to worry about.

He let her cry for a while, then he lifted her face again. "Come on now, enough crying. By now it's all over. Can't you tell that it's over?"

She tried to calm herself. She continued to shake with dry sobs that rose out of her chest, and with her hands she clung to the soldier's jacket.

"I felt your heart beating," he said. "It was pounding. You were very scared, weren't you?"

She nodded her head yes, and the soldier remained silent for a bit, perhaps thinking, or perhaps trying to come up with something nice to tell her.

Then he said, "I have a little girl at home. We live in Piemonte."

"Yes," she said.

"She's young, my little girl," said the soldier. "She just turned three this last month. But she'll get big one day. Big like you."

"Yes," she said again.

"What's your name?" asked the soldier.

"Giulia."

"My little girl's named Mita."

"Mita . . ."

"Mita, like in Margherita," said the soldier.

She understood that the soldier was talking to her this way only to comfort her, but all the same she was happy he was talking.

Two or three people entered the shelter from the other entrance, and one of them began to shout, recounting what he had seen, and repeated the same thing over and over, stupidly. Outside something frightful must have happened. She grasped this, yet she did not think or grieve over it. One human being to love protected her from grief and desperation.

But the siren continued to sound, summoning aid, and the soldier suddenly said, "Now I must go."

She didn't speak, only pressed against him harder, and he didn't move.

"Are you by yourself?" he asked.

"No, my cousin's in here."

"And outside, don't you have anyone? Do you have family?"

"There's my grandmother," she said. "She stayed home."

The soldier asked again, "Where is your house? Inside or outside the walls?"

"Inside. In the Sant' Agnese quarter."

The soldier remained silent for a while. Then he asked, "Did you love your grandmother?"

She thought of lying, but she couldn't because the soldier was being so good to her. "No," she said. "Not very much."

"That's good," said the soldier. "It's better that way." And suddenly he stood up.

He went to the back of the shelter where the woman was who kept frantically calling upon God, and the man who wanted to tell his story but unsuccessfully, since he kept repeating the same thing. But the soldier didn't know what to do for those people. Soon he came back to the girl.

"Now I'm going," he said. "It would be better for you to wait until the alarm ends."

"Yes," she said.

The soldier stood still, almost uncertain if he should go or not. At length he said, "See you later, then, Giulia."

She felt her voice fail her. "Thanks," she said, with effort, and wasn't able to say more.

Besides, she would not have known what to say to him. It would be absurd to say she loved him, or hopefully to tell him to stay a while longer. Maybe he would stay if she asked. But she did not have the courage for those things. It already felt shameful and in a way debased to feel so abandoned.

She realized he was going away, and she didn't know what to do, whether to scream or hold it in. At least there had been enough light to see him one last time. But it was dark, and he was gone, and she could not see him except as a shadow.

And she was alone once again. The anguish of being left alone assailed her anew, more strongly now, because she loved that soldier, and he had gone away, and this time he would not come back again.

The archway above the protective barrier appeared to brighten with a reddish and indistinct light, which didn't penetrate the shelter. It was the light of fires. And it was the noise of fires that she heard, low and muddled, along with the sudden crash every so often of something collapsing. Maybe the entire city was burning, after being struck.

More and more people arrived in the shelter. They came in the dark without paying attention to anything, terrorized, desperate. They began to weep or to yell, or else they simply stood there, dazed by it all.

She got to her feet. The anguish she was feeling was increasing to an unbearable level. There must be someone for her also, among those people around her.

"Carla!" she shouted frantically. "Carla!"

"What do you want?" asked Carla, close by.

She didn't know how to answer; she wanted nothing. Carla could not help her in her distress, and neither could the other people there. Not even her grandmother could help, if in fact she was not dead.

"What's wrong with you, shouting that way?" asked Carla.

"Nothing," she said. "Nothing." And then, almost right away, she asked, "What are we going to do, Carla?"

"What do you want to do? We have to wait until the siren finishes."

"No, no," she said. "What are we going to do later, when the alarm is over?"

"I don't know," said Carla. "We'll do what everyone else does."

She stayed silent. Carla was cold, distant in her heart, and made no effort to comprehend her pain and console her.

It was useless to talk of other things. Perhaps it was her destiny to stay so inconsolably alone, becoming a drag on the others. By now she would be nothing but a drag on Carla.

She thought of leaving, going away, she didn't know where, in the destroyed city or anyplace else, with none of the people she had known before. It could be that in the world there might be good people. She had already met someone who took pity on her. An unknown gentleman, when she was still a little girl, had given her fifty *centesimi,* without her even asking. An anonymous soldier had known how to comfort her and made her love him. They had done so because they were good people. It could be that in the world there might be many people like them, and that it would not be difficult to live.

"Carla, I'm going outside. I can't stay in here any longer."

"Why?"

"I need air. I feel like I'm suffocating."

Carla's boyfriend reached for her hand. "Are you sick?" he asked in a voice that was not unpleasant.

"It's nothing," she said. "It will pass as soon as I get outside."

"If you want, we will come with you," said Carla's boyfriend.

"No, it doesn't matter," she said quickly.

"Go and sit on the wall," said Carla. "We'll come too, later."

She left and right away looked around for the soldier, and the soldier wasn't there, naturally. It was stupid to think he might be there waiting for her. Yet she had hoped he would be, because without him she could not go on. It should have been enough that he had helped her even a little, with his kind voice, and she could have gone on. But this way she couldn't go on, she didn't have the strength.

She went up onto the walls right above the shelter and gazed toward the city. She didn't see much, on account of the smoke and dust. Everything was covered with a great cloud that was red below and dark above and invaded every part of the sky. The wind was pushing it south, and in the north, toward the periphery, some fires appeared more distinctly.

She sat on a park bench with her face in her hands. She would have to wait for Carla, to stay with her, enduring the anguish of solitude. There was no other way to live, because everyone was turning inward, toward himself, and didn't think of anyone else, unless occasionally, like the good soldier. They would have to be alone and gain strength and not entertain many hopes about life.

The roar of the fire arrived more clearly, there on the wall, with the smell of things burning. From time to time a truck passed by, fast and noisy, on the outer road. And the sound of human suffering also reached them, with groans, cries and prayers.

She paid no attention to them. She only raised her head every so often, when the sudden sound of a collapse made her look toward the city that was burning.

8

Hundreds of airplanes have flown long and far through the night to reach the little city. Inside each is equipment and every man with his assignment. Pilots, spotters, radio operators, gunners. Well trained personnel, reliable and competent.

The men think, flying through the night. Below is the dark earth, nothing can be seen. Above are the stars, and the stars help their thoughts. Flying through the night this way, the men have thoughts of faraway things, towns in another part of the world, where they belong and where they hope to return one day. There is in them an inexorable anxiety to go home, which makes them a little depressed, but it's also their refuge against the difficulties of life. Always, whether in boredom or in sadness, they think of going home, of what they were doing or who they were, before.

Nearing the city, the men abandon their thoughts of faraway things. The planes array themselves for the bombardment. Formation, altitude, direction for the assault. All are calm because it's an easy action that will not take away the chance of going home.

A light plane had gone before and dropped clusters of parachute flares. The others aim toward the lights. From the ground some automatic weapon begins to shoot at the flares, absurdly. The shells rise one after the other and die in midair.

The spotters look below and recognize the places they have studied on the maps, during the preparation for the mission. Now they are following the railroad line. Up ahead the station is visible, the size of a pack of cigarettes, with the strips of railroad track and the overpass. A little farther on will be the iron bridge over the river.

Ready. All on board assume a tense attitude. The instruments are trained on the target.

The targets are a station, an overpass, strips of railroad track. From above, everything looks like children's toys. They must strike those things so the enemy can't use them to conduct its war. But around and beside those things are also other things, equally as small as children's toys. These are the houses of the city, that are not marked on the maps with special symbols that highlight the objective. Since they are omitted, it is as if they don't exist.

And omitted as well is the fact that inside the houses live people, many people. The little city has perhaps more than one hundred thousand inhabitants, now that so many refugees have fled there from nearby cities. More than one hundred thousand people are plunged into terror. They have seen the lights and heard the engines, and they have understood.

But those up in the sky don't think about that. They know nothing of the people they are preparing to kill. They don't know how they might speak and how they might live, with what hopes and what sorrows. They have never seen even one of those one hundred thousand people.

Those are people who speak with an ancient gentility, who aspire to a comfortable and tranquil life, who no longer have much to do, either for hate or for love. For now, they are glad merely to have survived, reaching the end of the war alive, so that afterwards they may live better. And many are pinning their hopes for a better future on those very people who are just then about to pull the levers.

The men in the sky know nothing of that, and they don't think about it. Yet even they, when they picture the good life, imagine it as comfortable and tranquil, a nice home and honest work and living in peace with those around them. Indeed, a universal evil has offered them the chance to kill people they don't know, yet people so like themselves. A very great evil, by which they bring terror and death and destruction without thinking about it, with only the awareness of completing an assignment.

Their hands move the levers in simple gestures. The hatches beneath the fuselages open and the bombs slip into the air. The men can't hear the sound the bombs make as they fall.

The planes release their bombs in formation, and each formation is wide, it covers the station and many things around it. Intently, the men who have pulled the levers watch below and observe the sudden flashes of the explosives and the luminous bursts of the incendiaries. The strikes are well placed in the vicinity of the objective.

The formation executes a wide turn and returns over the city. By now even those pathetic antiaircraft guns have stopped firing. Below, there is a cloud of dust and smoke in the midst of which can be barely observed the fires and the continuous exploding of bombs. The station, the tracks, the overpass, all are covered by the cloud that the light of the rocket flares cannot penetrate. They drop the bombs into the midst of the cloud. With such a great number of bombs, with such a vast bombing area, the target is certain to be hit.

Now they are on their way back. Over many miles they observe behind them the glow of the city that is burning. The men feel satisfied. No antiaircraft, no nighttime pursuit, and a mission well executed. For some time the enemy will not be able to use the station, the tracks, maybe the overpass, if it has been hit. And if, to accomplish this, they have produced a totality of human sorrow that nothing can erase, with no benefit at all on the ground, this doesn't matter. They don't think about it, and they are not to blame, because of the universal evil.

In a short time, the glow of the fires is lost in the distance, and the men fly on beneath the stars.

Even the stars fly at a phenomenal speed toward the places where the men belong, on the other side of the world. In barely a few hours—

where the men already are in their own minds—the stars will be over Kentucky, Missouri, California. And each one of those men who destroyed houses and human beings can think with fondness of other houses and other human beings.

9

All around them the numbers of people grew. People shoved to make space for themselves and others protested, and still others despaired or wanted to tell about something. Every so often someone lit a match, and the tiny light revealed for an instant the great confusion. Then they were plunged once more into darkness, where the confusion seemed even worse. These were the people who were only frightened, who had not suffered harm from the bombardment.

They remained sitting on the ground, with their legs drawn up, as if isolated from the others. Carla felt stunned. Pressed against her boyfriend, she pursued slow thoughts, but not sorrowful ones. The people were strangers, and a thousand bombs had fallen on the city, and from outside came the sound of the fires. All this was jumbled together in her awareness. It wasn't hard to tolerate, pressed as she was against him and loving him.

But the boy's mind was outside, on the stricken city and on his house. "Let's go outside too, Carla," he said suddenly.

She moved her head slightly. "The alarm still hasn't stopped," she said.

"That doesn't matter. I want to go and look."

She sensed in his voice a new determination. "Is it for Giulia that you want to go out there?"

He smiled and detached himself from her. "Let's go."

Carla followed him out of the shelter. The houses along the peripheral road inside the city wall appeared intact and black against the red smoke of the conflagration that rose behind them. Toward the station, toward the city center, toward the cathedral, the fires were everywhere.

They climbed up on the wall and stayed for some time, staring in silence. From that height they saw the glow reaching farther above the houses; nevertheless, their gaze couldn't penetrate much farther than that. The fires in front of them were all in the Sant' Agnese quarter. Beyond that point they could not see what was there, but in their minds they pictured a vast destruction. Perhaps nothing was left standing, in the whole city.

Finally the boy made a violent gesture but calmed down at once. "My God!" he said.

Carla was too confused to speak. She had taken his hand and could do nothing but squeeze it with unconscious movements of her fingers.

"Who knows what has happened there in the center," the boy said again. He pronounced the words in a flat tone of voice, as if he had said nothing at all. Meanwhile he could not stop staring.

There in the center were flames and ruin, and he imagined the living and the dead burning up together, and people under the masonry, who still must perish. And he could assume that therefore, dead or dying, they might also include the people he had left at home. There was not much hope for their rescue. Even so, his particular misfortune, having lost his home and family, did not strike him with sorrow. Nor did that even greater destruction, of the whole city and all the people. What he experienced was a different feeling, euphoria and agitation together, because, as horrific and spectacular as what was happening was, he was standing there and watching it—a man who had survived.

Little by little his emotion rose into his throat, and he did nothing to suppress it, because he seemed to feel better that way. But then he came to the point of weeping, and he looked for Giulia and went to her. She was seated on the park bench, with her face in her hands. He touched her shoulder.

"I'm Tullio," he said.

"Yes," Giulia said, without moving.

The boy took her by the arms. "Come on, let me see you," he said. "I still don't know you." He spoke with an intentionally expressionless voice, preoccupied with conquering that stupid emotion that was almost making him weep.

Giulia raised her head, docilely. The reflection of the fires softened the pallor of her face, but in her expression and in her eyes there was anguish and resignation, and he thought he saw fear there.

"Are you still unwell?" he asked.

"I'm feeling better now," Giulia replied.

"But your teeth are chattering."

Giulia clamped her jaws so her teeth wouldn't chatter, and her lips drew up in a smile.

"Are you cold?" he asked.

"No."

He let go of her arm. He felt in her something that was hard to penetrate, and he couldn't find words to say to her. He turned again to the city that was burning. The collapses were following each other now with greater frequency, and right after each collapse the flames in some spot would shoot higher in the sky.

"I'm afraid nothing will be left of our homes," said Tullio.

And Carla, who was listening, asked him, "What are you thinking of doing?"

The boy looked at her almost wonderingly. "I don't know," he said. "Something must be done, but I don't know what, yet." He turned to look at the fire. Surely something must be done. What was happening was too overwhelming, one could only stand and watch it, without doing anything.

So he said, in a muted voice, "You two wait for me here. I'm going to look, and I'll try to be quick."

"You're going right now?" Carla asked, worried. "The alarm is still going."

Her boyfriend shrugged his shoulders. "Who knows where those planes are now?" he said and made a movement to leave.

"Wait," said Carla resolutely. "We're coming too."

"But aren't you scared?"

"No. Not if I come with you," said Carla in a low voice.

A hard expression appeared on the boy's face. "It's better for me to go alone," he said. "It won't be easy to get through. And in any case, I think there might be something that girls shouldn't see."

"That doesn't matter," said Carla.

"But we'll need a place, if we're left homeless," said the boy. "You two get set up in the shelter somehow and hold a spot also for me."

"No," said Carla. "We're coming with you. We'll think later about a place."

The boy was getting irritated. "But what do you want to come for?" he said. "I'll go by your house to see what is left. And if your grandmother is there, I'll bring her here."

"I'm coming with you," said Carla. "You can't leave me alone."

The boy made a gesture of displeasure. Then he turned around to Giulia and asked, "Do you want to come?"

Giulia raised her head and looked at him, and then looked at Carla. "Let's go," she said, standing up.

As soon as they arrived at Via Sant' Agnese, they saw the destruction. The sides of the streets were clogged with debris fallen from the houses, and in the air was an odor of smoke and dust and old things. At intervals the smoke from the fire reached that area, and it burned in the throat and in the eyes. The red light in the sky often got absorbed into a cloud of dust, and they couldn't see very far ahead. The few people who were about appeared and disappeared quickly. They were different from the people in the shelter, in the sense that they were not agitated and spoke only when necessary. These went along the street or worked to pull their belongings out of the houses and and appeared to be completely absorbed in what they were doing, whether walking or working. Even when calling or lamenting, they made sobbing and panting sounds, or at least it seemed that way, because the roaring of the fire was now quite close.

Tullio went ahead in silence, and the two girls followed him, also without speaking. At times Giulia stopped because she had a fit of violent coughing, perhaps caused by the dust and smoke.

They walked in the middle of the street, to avoid the danger of debris that still could fall from above. The wreckage was everywhere evident. In certain houses entire sections of walls had collapsed, and in certain others the roof had caved in and through the upper windows you could see the reddish sky on the other side. All around the people were struggling to pull their possessions out.

They walked in silence, each one with different thoughts. Tullio had hoped to be alone and free, and took every opportunity to make his ill humor obvious. Perhaps he hoped the girls would turn back if he did this. Carla felt bitter and vexed at this, and she was not responding, but would not turn back. Giulia understood she was excluded from them.

They were together but not united, and they walked on in silence.

They came upon a wounded person stretched out in the street, under a blanket drawn up to the chin. He appeared to be seriously hurt, for he lay as if dead and was not moaning. Only every so often he moved his mouth, mumbling, and so it was apparent he wasn't dead. They stopped to look at him with feelings of respect and pity. He was the first wounded person they had seen.

"But why don't they carry him away?" asked Carla.

A woman who happened along by the wounded man heard her. "How would you want them to carry him?" she said, harshly. "On their shoulders?"

Tullio started walking again right away, and they followed him. "You need to mind your own business, Carla," he said.

Carla pressed her lips together and said nothing.

A little farther along the road was blocked, because the collapsed houses had formed a solid mass of masonry. Some soldiers were working to open a passage. They could be heard hammering and shouting amid the stones and plaster. A soldier that was working higher up on the mound was loudly singing a song, and he kept time with his pick. But no one else followed his example.

They tried to pass through by taking the cross streets, but everywhere the houses were down, and you couldn't move forward. They returned to Via Sant' Agnese, where the soldiers were working.

"Will it be long before we can pass through?" Tullio asked a soldier.

The soldier was working to load a wheelbarrow at the foot of a pile of masonry. "It'll be a week," he replied, and laughed loudly.

"Don't say that," said the boy. "I have to go look for my house."

The soldier quit working and fastened his gaze curiously on them in the flickering light. "Well, I don't know when we'll finish this accursed work. The order is for eight o'clock, but if no one comes to help us, it'll take a week, seriously."

He took up his work again with the shovel, but as they didn't leave, he stopped again right away. "I've never seen a disaster like this. And no, it isn't the first time I've been in a bombardment. Once I found myself in one at Genoa, once at Milan, and twice in Germany. But it's never happened like it's happened here."

"Did they do a lot of damage?" asked the boy.

The soldier listlessly shoveled up another load of masonry before he responded.

"Oh yes," he said importantly. "Big bombs, that spare nothing when they strike. And they ended up right where people were living like ants. And also, what is missing here is organization. Oh, in Germany, yes, there was organization, but here it's been almost two hours since it ended, and I still haven't seen an ambulance. If I were in charge, I would shoot whoever is heading up this business."

Someone who was sitting on the ruins, doing nothing, shouted toward the soldier, "Hey, you! You want me to come over there and put you to work?"

"Right away, sergeant," replied the soldier and put another shovelful onto the wheelbarrow. Then he stopped working to talk.

"And they left us to supervise ourselves, as if this were our trade. Four worn-out tools, and a mountain of rubble, and they tell us that at eight o'clock the firemen have to go through. Who knows, maybe they're convinced that we can work miracles. And anyway, where are the firemen?"

"There are firemen . . ." said the boy.

"Firemen?" scoffed the soldier. "They put the firemen's barracks right next to the railroad station, and so they screwed themselves. I heard that some others will be coming, but in the meantime here it's burning up. Even the belltowers will be on fire before the firemen arrive."

The soldier said these things in an odd tone of voice, between scornfulness and indifference. And the boy stood in consternation in front of the rubble. He listened to the other soldier who, on top of the pile, labored as he sang, all alone, a verse from an old love song, *"And thus our youth will end."* Sure, for them it would be different. They came from elsewhere, they were not from this city.

"But I must go and see," said the boy, violently. "It's not possible to get over the top?"

"I don't know what you want to go and see," said the soldier. "If it were me, I would rather go for a walk—as far away as I could. But if you really want to look, try to get through there to the right. Everyone got through there, those who have gone ahead."

Tullio turned to Carla. "I hope you'll go back, now."

"No."

The boy looked at her with disgust. "There's all this mess to get by," he said. "How do you expect to get by it?"

"If you get through, that means we can get through too," said Carla, obstinately.

He said no more but turned and began to climb the mound of debris at the spot where the soldier had indicated. He went ahead as if he were alone. Carla followed him closely, but Giulia soon fell behind. She was less sturdy than Carla, and not brave, so she encountered a lot of difficulty in moving in the midst of the rubble. The beams slid at every step, and she didn't know where to place her feet, and there were great pillars to climb over without seeing where you were going to end up on the other side. The others continued on ahead, and she began to be afraid. She called to Carla to wait. Then Tullio turned around and helped her over the difficult places, without saying a word.

Farther ahead they found a stretch of open street, and then another obstacle of rubble, where more soldiers were working. They passed through the second blockage with greater ease, because it was neither very long nor high, and right away they came out into the big square of Sant' Agnese.

They stopped to look around.

At the far end, where the street continued, there was a large fire, and they saw others a little farther away. The air was filled with light and noise. From time to time the smoke passed low over the square, blocking the light and the view of things. Then it lifted again and permitted a view of the ruins and people that were laboring at a tall pile of rubble where previously a belltower had been.

But the great church was still standing. The thick old walls had resisted and even the roof, supported on enormous beams. And yet even the church looked different, with that red light flickering on its bricks.

They stared, frozen. First, they had experienced the terror of dying and then that strange euphoria and the uncertain sense that it was over. But now they saw in detail how things had changed. They remembered well the square as it had been before; they knew every stone and every structure. Since birth they had seen it as it used to be. There they had played and had spent many hours in the sunshine on winter afternoons, and it had seemed to them that the square would never be any different than it was then, with the houses placed in just that way, and the belltower placed in that spot, in just that form. It was the square for their quarter, ancient. For the old-timers as well, and for those even before the oldest old-timers, as far back as anyone could remember, that square had always been the same. And now it was no longer the same, and never would be.

"Let's go," said Tullio.

They went off toward the rear of the square, where the fire was. People moving in the red and confused light had a fearful appearance. There were military men and civilians alike, and everyone was carrying something, or else stretchers with the wounded and the dead on them. From a distance they were like dark blots, with no sound of footsteps or voices. But close up they appeared transformed, with eyes sunken and dark, and faces that stood out too starkly.

A soldier with a rifle and helmet stopped them at the edge of the square and did not let them go ahead because the area was dangerous.

They realized that they were about to go, stupidly, straight to where the fire was. But also, at the outlets of other streets, the soldiers with guns and helmets kept guard and weren't letting people pass.

"Our houses are up ahead," Tullio said to a soldier. "Maybe someone is still alive. We have to go and see."

"Only rescue teams can pass," said the soldier. "You cannot pass."

Tullio tried to insist. "We know the streets," he said. "We're able to get everywhere."

But the soldier did not let himself be persuaded. "If you're looking for someone, go look in the church. Those they find, they take them all to the church."

They turned back, toward the church.

They entered by a doorway on the long side. In the middle of the main nave, on top of a chest, was an acetylene lamp, with a strong and harsh light and a sharp odor and a weakly fluttering flame. People moving around the lamp cast shadows that reached onto the walls and the ceiling, monstrously huge.

Near the lamp the wounded lay stretched out on the floor, half-naked children, women, and men. Their flesh was dirty and in some parts bloody, or else white in those parts where it was neither dirty nor bloody, and then those parts appeared too white, like wax. Almost all had their eyes closed, and an absent or submissive expression on their faces, and they moaned in an exhausted way, continuously. Only when the doctors bent over to touch their wounds did they utter a cry, and their cries filled the vast church.

There were few medicines, and the doctors couldn't do much. They tried above all to conserve the supplies. Sometimes they only looked at the wounds without touching them, and they limited themselves to injecting something into the flesh, so that those people might have an easier path to death. They carried them a short distance away, to wait in the shadows.

"Let's go, let's go outside," said Giulia.

"I did tell you, didn't I, to stay in the shelter," said Tullio.

But then he turned to look at her, and he saw her face, pale and drawn, and her eyes, wide with pity and horror. Then he took her tenderly under the arm. "Let's go," he said. "There's nothing for us to do here."

They went to find a spot by the front door. The big door was closed, and the deep archway of the entrance offered a good shelter from the smoke. Some other people had found refuge in that spot, but there was still a little space in the midst of them. They sat down, packed in together with their backs against the portal. The others were also sitting with their backs against the portal, and they rarely spoke. It seemed that a great weariness, too great to react against, weighed on everyone.

"Is it passing?" asked Tullio.

"Yes, it's gone away," answered Giulia.

They stayed for some time sitting without speaking. Every so often Giulia's cough returned with violence, although there was not much smoke where they were.

Tullio was restless; he could not stay seated. "Now I'm going to try to get through," he said, and yet he didn't move.

"You really don't want to stay with us?" said Carla.

"I'm going to try to get through," said Tullio, emphatically. "I'll mix in with one of those rescue teams. They should let us through."

Carla looked at him but said nothing.

"Are you mad at me?" said Tullio. "I told you to stay in the shelter. Now I have to go and look."

Carla kept looking at him, but she couldn't see him well because the fires were on the other side of the church, and little light reached their position.

He stood somewhat still, waiting for her to say something. Then suddenly he said, "Well, if you want to wait for me, I'll come back."

And he ran down the steps and disappeared around the corner, without turning to look back.

10

They remained seated close to each other, wrapped up in their blankets. They had nothing to say to each other, because each one's pain was not the other's pain. They had to wait, both of them, and for this reason they stayed sitting close together.

While they were seated like that, the siren sounded the all-clear, but it brought no relief to anyone in the stricken city. This time it had been for them, and there was no thanking God for the blood and the destroyed houses and the scattered families. No one moved among the people under the entrance archway, and they remained still. Perhaps sleep would come. They felt their brains heavy, and their eyes burning, and nausea in their empty stomachs.

Giulia began again to cough now and then, and when the fit was over there remained the pain in her head and the urge to vomit. Perhaps sleep would liberate her from the evil that was in them and all around them.

Gradually they fell asleep.

Giulia awoke first. The surrounding air was gray, and the houses gray, and the sky gray. She recalled vaguely having seen stars during the night. Perhaps even above the grayness of the smoke there was sunlight and a serene sky. She didn't want to sleep any longer. She felt a little better with her headache and the nausea, but her body was cold and sluggish. She constantly thought of getting up and instead continued to stay sitting down.

Carla slept stretched out on the stones, completely wrapped in the blanket, including her head.

New people came to take refuge in that spot and were seated or stretched out on the steps. Some slept, and others kept their eyes open, with a spellbound or glazed expression in their eyes.

There arrived a little girl who might have been nine years old. Her arm was tied to a stick of wood, and she was barefoot and clothed only in a nightgown, with a military jacket over her shoulders that hung down to her knees. She was very dirty.

With a long, distrustful look the little girl observed the people sheltering in the entrance, perhaps searching for a spot for herself. Giulia signaled to her to come up. The little girl stayed where she was for some time, undecided, then she carefully climbed up among the people and went to sit down in the place Giulia made for her. She sat there curled up in a ball, shaking.

"Are you cold?" asked Giulia. "Do you want to get under my blanket?"

The little girl didn't answer. Just the same, Giulia put half of the blanket around her and covered her feet. Then a little of the child's cautiousness lessened, but she didn't stop shaking. Maybe she had a fever.

"Does your arm hurt?" asked Giulia.

The little girl shook her head. "Before," she said.

"When, before?"

"When he took care of it," said the little girl. She pronounced her words in a kind of singsong, and it seemed to be an effort to speak.

"And they didn't take you to the hospital?"

Again the little girl shook her head. "It's not broken," she said. "It's only out of place."

"So you aren't going to the hospital?"

"He said no," said the little girl. She always replied a little belatedly.

Giulia distracted herself by gazing toward the area of the square that was visible from the church entrance, and she didn't ask any more questions.

"I don't have any complaints at all, you know," said the little girl suddenly.

"Yes," Giulia said, mechanically.

In the square the soldiers had begun to do something. They carried the dead and lined them up on the ground, with their faces to the sky. They placed the men in one area and the women in another, all in rows, and the little babies they placed together with the women. The people watched without speaking. The little girl looked on without expression.

"Are you by yourself?" asked Giulia.

The little girl shook her head no.

"Where are your people?"

"They've gone ahead."

"Where?"

"I don't know," said the little girl. Then she screwed up her mouth, as if it was an effort to think. Then she said, "They were up ahead, and the bomb fell behind them and threw me on the ground. And then I got lost and the soldiers found me."

"But where are your people?"

"I don't know."

They remained in silence for a bit; then the little girl said, "They should be coming here."

"Perhaps they will," said Giulia, and eyed the corpses.

Many of those seated at the entrance had left, and others arrived and sat down to rest, and then they also left.

Later Carla awoke and immediately uncovered her head. "Is Tullio back?" she asked.

Giulia gestured to indicate no.

Carla sat up and became aware of the little girl who was inside the blanket with Giulia. "Who's that?" she asked.

"I don't know. She was cold. She's hurt her arm."

Carla didn't say anything. She watched the work the soldiers were doing in the square.

"Carla," said Giulia, "I don't have the courage, but if you feel like it you should go there in the middle to see if they found Granny."

"Later," Carla replied thoughtfully. And then she asked, "Do you think he'll come back?"

"Tullio?" asked Giulia.

"Yes."

"Sure, he'll come back," said Giulia, and she got up to move around a little. By now it wasn't so cold, even though there was no sun.

They kept waiting for a long time, and then Tullio returned, with a big load of something under a blanket on his shoulders. With him were two smaller boys, each loaded down with something. They appeared weary and dirty, but remained lively, in an almost cheerful mood.

"I've brought you a bunch of stuff," said Tullio.

Carla regarded him with an attitude both sullen and rebellious, and he turned serious.

"Are you still mad?" he said. "You can see I came back."

She did not reply and looked off somewhere else.

Tullio then turned to Giulia.

"I've also brought these two boys," he said. "They're alone, like us. One is named Antonio and the other, I don't remember. You, what's your name?"

"Mario," said the boy that was not called Antonio.

"See," said Tullio, "he's Mario and he's Antonio. Two smart kids."

They all sat together on the steps, except Carla.

"Have you been to our house too?" asked Giulia.

"Yes," said Tullio, and seemed not to want to say more.

But then he said, "I was over there, but you can't make out anything. Everything has gone down, you can't even see any sign of the streets. And what's more, it's burning. They told me that they're letting everything burn that will, because it isn't worth it to get the firemen to come. And anyway, they wouldn't do it in time. Too much work to get them through."

"The houses of the losers," said a man nearby who heard him.

"When the firemen get there, they send them to work in San Francesco and San Tommaso," said Tullio. "And near the cathedral too there are some who are already working. But here and around the station there are too many ruins. They say it's not worth it."

"It's because we're the losers," said the man.

"And your people?" asked Giulia.

"I don't know," said Tullio. "I think it's the same for everyone."

He again looked sadly toward the square. The rows were already quite long, and the soldiers continued to bring more bodies.

"Tullio," said Giulia, "we should search among these dead to see if any of our people are there. Carla could go to look for Granny."

Tullio made a face. "If she's dead she's still back there," he said. "No one has gone to get any of them."

"Losers!" repeated the man for the third time.

"And what if she's alive?" demanded Giulia.

"If she's alive we'll find her," said Tullio. Then he made a face again. "But she's not alive," he said, and suddenly he stood up. The others also got at once to their feet.

"Are we leaving?" Giulia asked.

"It's best if we relocate to look at the stuff," said Tullio. "Too many soldiers around here."

"Here's a little girl," said Giulia then. "She's by herself and has hurt her arm. Her people are dead, maybe."

"They went on ahead," said the little girl.

Tullio looked closely into the child's face that poked out of the blanket. "Do you want to come with us?" he finally asked.

The little girl shook her head no. Once more she wore the same wary expression she had when she arrived.

"Come with us," said Giulia.

"We'll take you to the Institute of Sant' Anna," said Tullio. "All the lost children must go to the Institute of Sant' Anna. Your mother will come to look for you there, if she's still alive."

"They went on ahead," said the little girl with conviction.

"All right," said Tullio. "Then we should find them for sure in the streets."

The child looked hesitantly at Giulia.

"Come on," said Giulia. "If they went on ahead, we should go ahead too."

The child stood up with the aid of her good arm. "Are there nuns there?"

"Where?" asked Tullio.

"At the Institute of Sant' Anna," said the little girl.

"Hey, I don't know who in the devil is there," said Tullio. "We'll see later."

They began to walk along the Via Sant' Agnese, toward the walls. The slight barrier of rubble near the square had been already moved to make enough space for a truck to pass through. Meanwhile, soldiers and workmen were still working together on the other barrier.

A soldier helped them carry the little girl across the rubble. Then they proceeded along the open street. The sky cleared at moments, as if low clouds were flying past. One moment a hint of sun might appear, pale and smoky, but was right away covered over.

Tullio started to walk alongside Carla. Ahead of them went Giulia, holding the hand of the little girl, and even farther ahead walked the two boys, bent under their loads.

Tullio said, "I think it would be better if you all went to the Institute of Sant' Anna, Carla. There they'll give you something to eat, and maybe also a place to sleep."

Carla was walking with her head down, but her attitude of rebelliousness vanished from her face. "Why, are you fed up with me?" she asked.

"It's not that," Tullio said. "But you're being stubborn and you don't want to understand that everything has changed now. I can't be always tied to your skirts. I have too many things to do. Some ideas came to me during the night, while I was going around through all those ruins. It's important to take care of things, right away."

"All right," said Carla simply, and continued walking with her head down.

Tullio said no more to her. He shouted loudly to the two who were walking ahead, "Hey, boys! We need a cart. It wouldn't matter even if it were a big one."

The two boys turned their heads briefly. One of them grinned and shouted, "All right, chief!"

Up on the walls they were able to find a spot, because the avenue was full of people evacuated from the stricken zone. Many had brought as much as they could find of their belongings up there and were encamped like gypsies. Some bonfires had been lit in various spots, and the people stood around to warm themselves and especially the children. Almost all had escaped from their houses half-naked, just as they had left their beds.

Tullio chose an available space on a low wall at the foot of the city walls. Stretching some blankets between a tree and the ledge, they fashioned a kind of tent, low and lopsided. Under it the boys opened the bundles that they had carried and drew out things to eat. During the night they had taken a lot of things to eat from the bombed-out shops.

They all ate, seated in a circle on the ground. Then the two new boys went to sleep under the tent, and the little girl began to watch the people around them, with a long and distrustful stare.

Tullio and Carla were seated near each other, but they did not speak. There was obvious tension, although they tried to conceal it. Tullio had gathered a stick and was making doodles on the ground. Carla gazed at them thoughtfully. Now something must happen between them, either with each going his own way, or staying together. But the moment of decision had come, and neither of them was ready to speak. Giulia stayed seated together with them, waiting.

"Tullio," Carla finally said.

He did not reply, but made a slight movement with his head, to let her know he was paying attention.

"If you want," said Carla, "we can stay with you. We don't need much. We can enlarge the tent with our blankets."

Tullio didn't stop doodling on the ground. "We have plenty of blankets," he said.

"We can also help you," said Carla. "We can put your things in order, and prepare things to eat, if they can be found."

"Tonight they will be handing out hot soup," said Tullio. "For you at the Institute of Sant'Anna, and for us at Balilla House."

"Will they keep us in there?"

"I don't know. I think that if someone wants to leave, they let them. There must be, also, too many other people who would want to stay inside."

"So will you take us with you?" Carla persisted.

"If you wish," said Tullio.

Carla fell silent and sighed deeply.

Giulia had followed their conversation attentively. "Will we keep the little girl with us?" she asked.

He considered the child at some length. She continued to be absorbed with watching the people.

"Maybe it would be better for her to go to the Institute," said Tullio.

"Maybe," said Giulia.

"Why? Wouldn't you like her to stay with us?"

"I don't know," said Giulia. "I want to do what's best for her."

Tullio smiled at her way of saying things. "In any case," he said, "try to get from her what she wants to do."

Giulia approached the little girl, kneeling in front of her. "Do you want to stay with us or go to the Institute of Sant'Anna?" she asked.

The child did not respond, but stared at Giulia with a surprised, even stupid, expression.

"Don't you want to go to the Institute of Sant'Anna?" Giulia asked again.

A crease appeared at the corner of the little girl's mouth, perhaps because she was thinking. Then she asked, "Are there nuns there?"

"Yes," said Giulia. "There are even nuns."

The little girl seemed to be still in thought. "Aren't you going to the Institute?" she asked.

"I'll accompany you there, but then I can't stay."

"Then I don't want to go to the Institute," said the child.

"All right," said Tullio, and tossed the stick away that he still held in his hand and got up to walk away a few paces. He moved with a calm weariness, swaying his body. He went to sit on the low wall, with his legs dangling above the canal that ringed the walls. He began to stare down, intently or distractedly.

He saw the grasses swaying on the bottom like slow water snakes, and upon the water insects, floating with long legs, that seemed to be spiders or big mosquitoes. They let the current carry them a short way, then they darted back, always to the same spot. He did not understand why they did this. And the embankment on the other side was all green and white, green with the new grass and white with the many daisies that grew among the new grass. The plane trees on the edges of the peripheral road already had fairly large leaves. And farther away, at the limits of the suburb, there was sunshine, and it crept forward as the wind, a bit changed, pushed the smoke to another area. He could see the sunshine creeping slowly forward over the houses.

At length, also on the walls, there was a diffused glow, and a little afterward the full light of the sun warmed everything and created shadows on the horse chestnut trees and the tents and the people. Then the sunshine moved on, and Tullio turned his head to follow it over the caved-in roofs, over the piles of rubble, to the first fires of the quarter of Sant' Agnese. Any farther it could not go because the smoke continued to rise, dense, and covered everything. The great mass of the church of Sant' Agnese was barely distinguishable.

Tullio turned his head back toward the canal and again began to watch that insect that was floating on the water. Then the sunshine struck his head and his hands. He took his cap off and crushed it into a ball that he put in his pocket. The sun was good, as one of the things that were unchanging in the world.

Carla came up next to him, leaning against the low wall. For a while she watched the canal, with her eyes narrowed, as the sunlight reflected up into them. Then she looked into his face. He appeared exhausted and sad. Even underneath the dirt she saw the signs of fatigue and anguish that the previous night had left on his face. And Carla felt a tenderness so profound that her voice trembled when she spoke.

"I love you more than ever," she said.

His face put on an expression that was not quite a smile, and he placed his hand on top of hers and kept it there for a bit, without speaking. And Carla's heart filled with even greater tenderness and gratitude.

Then he swung his legs over the low wall and dropped to the ground. "Oh well," he said with indifference. "I'm going to try to sleep a little, before evening."

Upon his face was now an earnestness that she had not seen before. His sweetness of moments before was gone, when he had put his hand on hers, without speaking. Perhaps he had struggled within himself to conquer that sweetness that made him weak. He was a man, after all, and he wanted to be strong, and free also, even while staying with her. And she bent her head once more to watch the water, and accepted this, as much as it saddened her. From now on it would be always like this, a little fleeting tenderness, and many other things on his mind, which he kept to himself. He was becoming like a boss, and perhaps not a good one. Already she could tell from his voice, how it was cold and confident, that he wanted to be boss.

"You two go to the Institute of Sant'Anna and take the soup and whatever they give you," he was saying. "They'll give you some bread, too, for sure. Go right away, because you'll have to wait who knows how long in line. Try to be back by six. Wake me up at six."

"All right," said Carla.

Suddenly he drew forth from a pocket an object and pushed it toward Carla with a brusque gesture.

"Keep this," he said. "This will let you know when it's six o'clock."

Carla turned to look at the object in his hand. It was a small wristwatch, of white metal. She made a vague gesture and then stopped. She raised her eyes to his face, without deciding to accept it.

Tullio also looked at her, directly into her eyes, and slowly his mouth twisted in bitterness. "No," he said. "Be assured I did not take it off a dead woman."

Without looking at him any longer, Carla reached out her hand and took the watch. "Thanks," she said.

"A lady gave it to me," said Tullio. "She gave it to me because I helped her get out of the ruins." He paused for a long time and then said, "But you need to learn to have trust. Without trust we can't stay together." And abruptly he left her and went over to Giulia.

Giulia was not aware of him. She was doing a difficult job, working with a razor blade over a blanket folded in two and spread on the ground. She worked with great concentration, and the tip of her tongue protruded childishly between her teeth.

"What are you doing?" asked Tullio.

She raised her head, then, and flushed. "I'd like to cut out a dress," she said. "A dress for the little girl."

Tullio's eyes smiled and he didn't frighten her, so she continued to work with the razor blade.

"Look," she said, "the head goes through this hole, and then it hangs down like this, like the robe of a friar."

"And how will you sew it?"

"Sew it, nothing," said Giulia. "There's no thread. We'll fasten it with twine. It won't be pretty, but she has nothing, you know, except the nightie."

"We need to get her something," said Tullio, softly.

"Shoes would be good," said Giulia. "I can't make a pair of slippers if there's no thread."

"We'll get something."

Then he began to watch the child, his face grave. She was sleeping stretched out on the ground, and her bad arm lay outside the cover, resting on her chest, and the other hand formed a fist by her temple. She breathed through her open mouth, regularly, and it gave her a peaceful look. The sun made patterns on her face with the moving shadows of the horse chestnut leaves.

"Poor little one, she must not be quite right in the head," said Tullio, again softly. And he went to stretch out under the tent, beside the other two boys, who were by now asleep.

11

That day, and for a long time afterwards, the cars of the interurban had to stop in the suburb. Because of the bombing, it could no longer travel the final stretch of road and mount up the overpass and arrive at the station square.

Notwithstanding, the cars were unusually full, and the people got out in the suburb and then proceeded on foot toward the city. They were almost all curious about what they were going to see.

Late in the afternoon, from one of the cars there stepped down, among the other people, a boy and behind him, a priest.

The boy was wearing a peaked cap, the kind that railroad men used to wear, with letters embroidered in gold. The rest of his clothing was dark in color, with black shoes and a blue suit without any distinguishing features. Still, the suit was styled in such a way that you knew right away that the boy was a student.

The priest was not very old but had a dignified manner and was dressed as priests commonly dress, with a fur cap and a lightweight, well-worn overcoat that fit him poorly.

As they walked, the boy remained silent, and the priest talked without a break of this and that. Perhaps he intended to distract the boy.

They arrived at a point on the road where soldiers and uniformed guards were stopping people. They were asking everyone where they wanted to go and why, and they only let through a few people.

The priest went to speak to a guard, and the guard told him that no one could go through that area and they had to go around.

Then the priest turned to the boy. "We can't go through here, we have to go around."

The boy said nothing. He was staring toward what he could see beyond the guards: collapsed houses and great uprooted plane trees and the ramp of the overpass that rose up to a certain point and then broke off. Farther away, dense and dark smoke rose up from the fires and moved toward them, blanketing the whole sky.

"We need to make haste, my son," said the priest. "There are almost three miles to cover on foot."

"Yes, sir," said the boy.

They took a road through the suburb. Walking along, the priest continued to talk, always about something or other. At times his voice rose in a happy note, especially when he admired the flowers in a garden or the colors of a house. The boy remained silent and looked around.

The road was very busy. People were walking in the same direction, and other people walked in the opposite direction. Many of them coming toward them were in groups, loaded down with possessions on their shoulders, and many pushed wheelbarrows or handcarts or even baby carriages with their belongings inside. Rarely, wagons pulled by horses passed, or automobiles, with trunks and mattresses on top. They were going far away from the city.

At a certain point they also encountered a truck, that came along very slowly. A soldier was driving it, and another soldier, mounted on the running-board, threw a glance behind every so often, because the truck had no sides, and he was afraid of losing something from the load.

The people drew apart while the truck passed, and they watched it in silence. Some women from the country knelt on the sidewalk. The priest arranged his face in an expression of great dignity and made the sign of the cross in the air. The boy fixed his gaze on it. But he didn't want to look at the load, there was just something about that truck. It was a very old truck, and from the bed dripped some fluid that left a long dark mark along the road. And from the exhaust pipe came blue smoke, with a smell of burnt petrol, different from all the other odors of burnt petrol that he had smelled before. The truck went on, bouncing over the holes in the road.

"Let us go, my son," said the priest, and began walking again.

They were able to enter the city through the gate of San Francesco. That quarter had been struck very lightly. Only two or three bombs had fallen, and they had blown holes among the houses, and the rooftops for a large radius around had fallen in. But there were only small fires, and in the main streets, paths had been opened through the rubble.

Farther ahead, though, toward the city hall square, the destruction was greater, and at a certain point the guards stopped them again and obliged them to take another detour in order to reach the cathedral square.

Coming out in the square, the boy stopped, and his gaze went immediately to the far end of the square, down the perspective of the new avenue toward the walls, where he should have been able to see the three skyscrapers. And the three skyscrapers were no longer there. Only one could be seen, the farthest one, that one also partially fallen. But in place of the others there were only heaps of ruins.

The priest let the boy stare for a bit, then he asked, "Where did you live?"

The boy did not answer. He didn't even know what the priest had asked, and for this reason he didn't respond. But something must have struck him, perhaps the empty sound of the words, because he pulled his gaze away from the heaps of ruins and looked around the square.

The cathedral had been hit and appeared all caved in on the end by the apse. Another bomb had perhaps fallen behind the dais, and the façade of the building hung off the outside, and sawhorses had been placed under it so people would not get close. All the houses were missing shutters and window glass, and the rolling blinds of the shops were knocked down or twisted from the force of the blasts. Inside the artillery barracks there had been a fire, now burned out, but some whitish smoke still rose from the ruins.

There was a sad solemnity in the square, and absence of human voices, even though there were many people. You could hear the muddled growl of a big fire just beyond the square, in the Sant' Agnese quarter, and the sound of a truck parked with the motor running. What was missing was the sound of human voices.

Finally the boy got up the courage to look into the square itself. He looked first at a parked truck, onto which some men were loading bodies. Then he saw the long rows of dead, many hundreds of dead stretched out there on the pavement, side by side in order by gender.

Among the rows of dead, people circulated silently, looking or searching. Some men with red armbands offered their services. And if someone happened to find what he was looking for, the men went to see and wrote the name of the deceased on a registry and attached a number to the body. They attached the number to the right wrist, or else the left wrist, if the body was missing a right arm, or else to the neck. And following that, men with stretchers passed by and carried the bodies with numbers to the truck, where there were already so many other bodies, many without numbers but reduced in such a way they could not be recognized. And whoever had happened to locate a body stayed there to wait until they had loaded it onto the truck and even then, sometimes, lingered until the truck departed.

"Where did they live, your people?" asked the priest once more.

This time the boy responded. "There at the end," he said, and indicated the ruins of the first skyscraper.

The priest removed his hat and wiped his forehead with a big white handkerchief. Then he put his hat back on. "Courage, my son," he said. "You will see that the devil is not after all as ugly as he has been depicted."

The boy remained absorbed in staring.

"And now what do you want to do?" asked the priest.

"Let's go to see if they have been found," said the boy.

"There among them?" said the priest, gesturing broadly toward the rows of dead. "It's horrible, my son. Do you feel strong enough?"

"Yes, sir," said the boy. And he made his way at once toward the rows of dead women, and the priest followed closely but unwillingly.

There were dead women of all ages, some lying by the children with whom they had been found. Almost all of them had on some garment reduced to shreds, that allowed you to glimpse their nakedness. And all lay facing the sky, many with eyes fixed and open, or half-open, where the whites of the eyes gleamed like porcelain. There was a disgusting odor, of blood and dirty bodies and cadavers.

The boy went around searching, and the priest kept following him, but he avoided looking at those supine corpses. The priest was saying some prayers, his lips moving visibly.

They progressed in this way, up one row and then down the next. Both were a bit pale, and they struggled with nausea.

"Perhaps it would be better to ask for information from someone," said the priest.

The boy began to walk along another row, without responding.

But when they came to the end of the third row, the priest put a hand on his shoulder, affectionately.

"Wait for me here, my son," he said. "I'm going to get information. We won't have time if we must look at these cadavers one at a time."

"Yes, sir," said the boy.

The priest sought out a man with a red armband, and then he stepped up into the vestibule of the cathedral, where other men with red armbands were seated around some tables, writing in their registries. The priest spoke first with one and then with another, who appeared to be their captain.

Finally he returned to the boy, with an apologetic and relieved demeanor. "It's useless to search here, my son," he said. "Unfortunately, the rescue work is not adequate for such an enormous job. As for your house, they haven't been able to arrange for the removal of the bodies."

The boy stood resigned, with his head bowed, and said nothing.

The priest again placed a hand on his shoulder.

"Do you want to return to the school now?" he asked.

"Let's go and see the house," said the boy.

"The house?" went the priest. "Of course, my son, let's go. But my heart bleeds to see you so grieved by the sight of this disaster."

Around the collapsed skyscraper many people were standing and looking. It was a curious phenomenon, that such a large building should be reduced to a pile of ruins. Where the bombs had actually landed couldn't even be seen, and from the mass of rubble there rose only some twisted pylons of reinforced concrete. People standing around commented on the solidity of modern houses.

The boy stepped in front of the people and began to look with a mournful expression, the corners of his mouth downturned. At his side the priest waited, meditatively.

Time passed, and the priest sighed and looked at his watch, because there was a lot of road to cover, and he needed to be home for the supper hour.

"That's enough now, my son," he said. "It's a spectacle that works evil."

The boy neither moved nor spoke. "They're underneath there," he said.

"No, my boy, you should not despair," said the priest.

"They're underneath there," the boy repeated, obstinately.

The priest waited a moment, then looked at his watch again and sighed again. Finally he put an arm around the boy's shoulders to pull him away from the people with gentle force.

On the way back, before they left the cathedral square, the priest walked in silence next to the boy, perhaps preparing in his mind some appropriate thing to say. It was indeed necessary to say a kind word to that boy, so stricken with such a great calamity—some word that would help him move forward in life with hope once more.

As soon as they were a few paces away from the square, the priest began to speak.

"I understand your sorrow, my son," he said. "Certainly, there is no misfortune greater than that of losing, at your age, the guidance and support of your parents. And especially in your case it's a great misfortune because I know you loved them with immense affection, equal to the affection they had for you."

Talking and walking, the priest watched the boy from time to time, and he saw his approach wasn't going well.

So he said, "Besides, my son, it's premature to think they are really dead. One must never lose faith in Divine Providence. Consider the case that they might not have been at home when the bombardment came. They might very well have been at the home of some friends. They must indeed have had friends, your parents, isn't that true?"

"Yes, sir," said the boy.

"They could have saved themselves, then, if they were at the home of friends," said the priest. "Hopefully at this moment they are at the school waiting for you. Think with what anxiety they would be waiting for you."

"They would have come this morning, if they were alive," said the boy.

"Of course," said the priest, "of course. But they could have also been slightly wounded. There is a large number of wounded. They've taken them even into the churches and schools, because there's no more room in the hospitals. Tomorrow the school director himself will come to carry out the search. He has more skill in dealing with the world. He may turn to your father's friends. Without a doubt your father had very influential friends in the government."

The boy said nothing during the pause.

The priest continued: "In these difficult times, good friends are a precious help. And beyond that, fortunately you have relatives that can take care of you. They live in Rome, is that correct?"

"Yes, sir."

"The director will telegraph your relatives, and they will come to see you. They will certainly come for such a serious reason. They're relatives on your mother's side, right?"

"Yes, sir."

"And on your father's side you have no relatives?"

"No, sir."

For a while they walked in silence, the priest struggling between weariness and the wish to make haste. And the boy was filled with a desperate sadness, that made him see things with dry eyes and appearing not to see them.

Almost no one, now, traveled toward the city, but many people were leaving it, the curious ones who had lingered and the refugees, who were carrying as many things as they could. Where they were walking it seemed to be evening already, because of the great cloud of smoke that covered the sky.

And in a little while the priest began again to talk.

"My son," he said, "I have counseled you to hold onto hope, and I will raise to the Lord my most fervent prayers and vow, that your parents might have found a miraculous rescue. But on the other hand, we must also expect that the misfortune that we fear might be true, and that you might now find yourself a poor little orphan. I want you to understand in this moment that we are close to you in your sorrow, that we feel your loss as you do yourself. You see, we have left our families and our homes voluntarily, called to the service of God. And we have formed among ourselves a big family, according to the intentions of our founding saint. All of you are yourselves part of this big family, in a certain way, during the time that you spend with us to receive instruction and moral religious direction. If now by misfortune you might have lost your family, you must feel more intimately connected to us. With our affection we will try to replace the affection of your parents. And on the other hand, it is necessary to accept with a serene spirit all that comes from God, and to understand that whatever He causes to happen on earth is not without motive. Very often our mind does not succeed in comprehending His wisdom. He Himself has said to me that His ways are infinite. One cannot know what means He chooses to reach us and speak to our hearts."

He made another long pause, then began again to talk with a trembling voice.

"My son," he said, "I exhort you to pull yourself together with a hope so much more elevated than what might be found in this world. Solely in faith will you find the comfort necessary for your tremendous sorrow. And it is faith that teaches us that beyond this miserable life there is another, the true and eternal life, the only one that counts. There, you will be able to rejoin forever the people you love."

The boy said nothing, and so the priest continued, with an even more inspired tone of voice.

"And who knows," he said, "perhaps all this is nothing but a warning from God. I wish that every man would pay attention to His voice.

But for you it could be something more, an impetus towards a pious existence, perhaps even of sanctity, for the means by which you can win true, eternal bliss. You will spend some days in meditation, now. We will be near you, we will seek to sustain you during this difficult and sensitive time in your life, but we will also take care not to disturb your grieving. You will be able to look deeply into yourself. And if by chance you should hear a voice that calls you, I implore you to heed that voice, my son, and to follow the path that the Lord points out to you, because only by doing so will you be able to achieve happiness and eternal salvation. You will do it, won't you?"

The boy walked along and did not reply.

"You'll think about it, won't you?" asked the priest again.

"Yes, sir," said the boy.

12

The survivors walked around among the rows of cadavers and the heaps of rubble and the fires. Their faces were distraught, or without expression, or dazed. They searched for their dead and their belongings. They were sent away from some places, and they returned to keep looking. There must have been a deep motive in their stubbornness to keep searching. They rummaged among the ruins, moving aside every kind of object, with equal care for the useful and the useless. Perhaps there was just one particular thing they wanted to save from their house, whatever it might be. They would take it somewhere else, to a new place, wherever they might happen to live.

Some of them went away, either after finding something or becoming weary of searching. They took only a few possessions, whatever they could carry on their shoulders, and left to go far away. It was necessary for them to go far from the city. They did not want to end up in such an unpleasant place, and beyond that, they were still fearful. They said that the planes would return to bomb in the night, guided by the fires.

Others, instead, took themselves barely beyond the stricken zones, onto the walls, into quarters distant from the station, or into the suburbs. They reunited with whatever was left of their families and their possessions, and tirelessly returned to the destroyed houses to recover ever more belongings.

Still others didn't go far away. They remained amid the rubble and did not search for anything at all. They wandered numbly, and when exhaustion finally overcame them, they dropped to the ground and rested. They did not know where else to go. They had no desire to go anywhere else.

The first day passed, then came nighttime, and the next day, and the trains began to run again along the rail line. The station no longer existed, but the tracks were pulled up and replaced. Workers and soldiers had worked without a break to repair the damage, and now the trains were running. And the fires invaded the sky with flames and smoke, and the dead accumulated in the square.

For two days the rescue teams continued to line up the cadavers in the squares of Sant' Agnese and the cathedral and the city hall. Over five thousand bodies were lined up in the squares. Then they carried them all away, even those whom no one had come to identify. They had dug long trenches near the cemetery precinct, and there they buried the dead. Five thousand, dead. And others, perhaps seven thousand, remained under the rubble, and no one looked any longer for them. One might occasionally come to light during the cleaning of the streets and the demolition of sagging houses.

But there were areas where they neither cleaned the streets nor demolished the houses. In those areas it had been difficult to bring even the most urgent aid, and only a few of the dead had been collected. The rest remained where the bombardment had left them. And in those areas the fires lasted until they burned themselves out, and when at last they were spent, a few men walked through the rubble and spread abundant lime and disinfectant.

Then they enclosed the areas with barbed wire and stakes, and on wooden signs they wrote in large letters, "Infected Zone," and painted huge black skulls on them. People called those precincts "the zone of the dead." Inside that zone remained groups of houses half tumbled down, and also the bodies and the precarious walls behind which there was nothing, and expanses of irregular ruins, turned black and white by the smoke and the lime dust.

The biggest of the fires took almost a week to go out, and even then the smoke continued to issue from the rubble for another few days, but there was no longer any sound. There was finally silence in the city. Vehicles passed only slowly, now, along the peripheral road. Many people had left. All those who were able had gone into the countryside, or into the hills, or even farther away.

The others remained in the houses, in public buildings converted into shelters, or in the squalid shacks that were erected more or less throughout the city. And the remaining people were all the same. In the beginning they had wept or prayed or cursed. They had cursed the foreigners who had held the country under occupation and were waging the war, or the other foreigners who had passed over in the sky, raining down destruction and death. Or else they cursed God, which was the most appropriate thing to do, because it was a way of cursing themselves and the evil in all men.

But now it appeared that they understood the futility of cursing or weeping or yelling, and also of praying. They all existed in a dull weariness, even the desperate ones, even the indifferent ones.

Still, they felt more free. Regarding all that slaughter, it remained in their consciousness that it was an unjust thing. Even without knowing exactly who was at fault, they were able to say that it was an unjust thing. And that awareness liberated them from the laws that bound them to God and man. They were forced into being what they believed themselves to be for the most part, either better or worse, each according to his own nature. Pity and charity increased, and also wickedness and egotism.

And yet there was still a blessing to hope for, that the war would end.

Each day it seemed it must end, the war, and instead it did not end. Months passed, and the leaves on the trees grew large and then dried up and fell to earth to decay, and the war did not end. In fact, it came closer. One of the foreign armies that were fighting in the countryside advanced slowly toward the city.

There were more days of terror for the remaining people. Tanks fought in the outskirts, and groups of soldiers entrenched themselves in the houses of a suburb and held on for days, waging their war. Shells flew haphazardly, to land among the houses, but they took few victims. Now the people were living in the underground canteens and inside holes they dug in the ground.

Then one foreigner yielded his place to another, and the people emerged out of the ground to see this new foreigner. They regarded him with hatred, or with love, or merely with curiosity. But they all felt relieved. Whoever this new stranger might be, whatever law he might bring, he was strong and banished forever the terror of war. There would be no more battles in the outskirts, nor air raids.

The people returned from the countryside and the hills and the places where they had taken refuge, and began to greet and chat with one another, passing back and forth along the stretch of the main street that had not been completely demolished by the bombs. It was as if the war was over, and they had made it through to that point, and yet they were not the same as before. And hard as they might try, the people were no longer able to be as before.

And it was not only from misery and hunger, hate and revenge and fear, that they were not able to be as before. They themselves did not know the reason why they felt, deep down, always exhausted and withdrawn, and unhappy with themselves and with life. Perhaps that part of the universal evil that had touched them had gathered inside them and remained, without ever going away. Perhaps it was the finality of losing everything forever, on the part of all of them, that they had overlooked at first. They had been ruined in the big war, and they were unable to find themselves again.

13

When he spotted the white shape of the kilometer marker, the American corporal, John, pulled the cargo truck as far as he could to the right and turned on the big headlamps. In spite of that, the marker went by without his being able to read the number on it. Then he switched off the headlamps and he steered back into the center of the road, which was broad, between two rows of big plane trees. He could see the red taillight of the truck that was proceeding ahead of him.

The corporal yawned a couple of times, then he began to sing as he waited for the next kilometer marker. He sang at half volume, "*Da-de-da-da down the street, down the street, down the street …*" He didn't know the words very well, but he went on anyhow, whistling the tune. The motor was running well. The road had some gentle curves and long, straight stretches.

The headlamps of the truck that followed him sent out a beam of light, and the corporal got to a point in the song where he remembered the words. So he began to sing, "*Mama, Mama, let me dress up tonight, dress up tonight, dress up tonight …*"

In the meantime, he never stopped watching on the right, in search of a new kilometer marker. Some of those stones had been bashed and pushed into the ditch to the side of the road, and at times it happened that not even one could be seen for miles at a time. The asphalt was quite ruined and full of potholes.

As soon as he glimpsed a new marker, the corporal quit singing and turned on the headlamps and got ready to maneuver close. He proceeded down the center of the road until a few yards from the marker, then swerved hard to aim the headlamps, but he did not succeed in reading the number this time, either.

Then it occurred to him to wake Roy Supina. "Roy … Hey, Roy!" he called.

In spite of the bouncing of the truck, Private Roy Supina had been sleeping for some hours, bundled up in his trench coat. "What do you want?" he asked when he was sufficiently awake.

"I'd like to know where we are," said the corporal.

Roy blinked his eyes a few times and snorted with disgust. "I don't know where we are," he said. "I was sleeping."

"Christ, did you ever sleep! It must be fifty miles you've done nothing but sleep."

Roy stared sleepily at the road and the red taillight of the truck up ahead. "Why did you wake me up?" he grumbled.

"Now let's both watch the kilometers. Pay attention to the first stone."

Roy forced himself to stay awake, even though the sound of the engine was pulling him back into sleep. Fortunately, the corporal wasn't making a great effort to avoid the potholes in the road. But in general their trip down the big road across the plain was monotonous.

"Sometimes I need to talk to somebody," the corporal said. "If only to help me stay awake. These roads seem made just to put people to sleep. They're so long and straight, and you fall asleep, and end up crashing into one of these trees. Look how big these are."

Roy looked at the trees with indifference and said nothing.

"Gonna dance by the light of the moon …" the corporal sang.

Suddenly he said, "There's a marker, Roy. Look sharp."

Roy lowered the window on his side and the cold wind came into the cab. The white stone was a few yards ahead. Again the corporal lifted his foot off the accelerator and made the same maneuver as before to aim the headlamps. Roy leaned as far as he could from the window to see better, then he sat back down and raised the window. His eyes watered in the cold air.

"Well, did you see the number?" the corporal asked.

"I think it was fifty-seven," said Roy.

The corporal pressed the accelerator once more. "What does fifty-seven mean?" he said.

"Fifty-seven kilometers," said Roy.

The truck moved along through the great plain, down the road with its gentle curves and long straight stretches, between the two rows of plane trees.

"Roy," the corporal said, "fifty-seven kilometers is thirty-five miles."

Roy made a mental calculation, then he said, "More or less, John."

"Well, I already knew *that*," said the corporal. "But thirty-five miles from where?"

Roy didn't feel like engaging in small talk. He said, "From some spot behind us."

"That city we passed before?" asked the corporal.

"I didn't see the city," said Roy. "Maybe the number refers to some place up ahead."

A stone house appeared on the left side of the road, and then a hedge of evergreens, and then the row of plane trees resumed.

"Still, I'd like to know how long before we get there," the corporal said. "The sergeant said we should get there before midnight. Isn't that what he said?"

"Maybe it's not midnight yet," said Roy.

The corporal hit the horn three times with his fist. "Roy," he asked, "what was that damn city called?"

"Dunno," said Roy.

The corporal hit the horn again, for no apparent reason. "Christ," he said, "you don't know nothin'. I thought you knew everything about these towns."

The rows of plane trees broke up on both sides, and the road became a long and narrow square. There were houses with porticoes, and ruins, in various places. The war had passed through there too, and a little town had been half destroyed. The noise of the engines and the tires was loud as the trucks passed through the square. The windows in the houses were closed, and there were no lights and no one about.

Roy opened his eyes just in time to make out the shape of someone who was walking along the side of the road, wrapped in a dark cloak.

"Did you see that?" said John. "Going around on foot in this cold!"

"Obviously there's no other way to get around," said Roy.

Hitting a pothole with its left wheel, the truck jolted hard. The corporal became alert. He went in search of another pothole and the truck pitched hard again. Then the corporal swore angrily, dropping the truck out of gear.

Roy opened his eyes and asked, "Grounded again?"

"It's the left one," John said. "It must have blown out."

The red taillight of the truck up front pulled farther away as they slowed down and came to a stop.

"Of all the times," said Roy, wide awake now.

The corporal cursed again. Then he got out and Roy did also. Their legs were stiff.

The left front tire was extremely low. John hit it with a tire iron and listened to the hollow sound of the deflated rubber and swore again. Behind them the other trucks in the convoy were stopping. Someone blew the horn in hoarse and insistent blasts.

The corporal turned his head and said disgustedly, "For the love o' God, go tell them to pull ahead and go to hell. And look for someone who has a spare wheel, this way we can at least wait for the sergeant."

The stopped vehicles got under way again and went past, one by one. At length Danny Golden's truck stopped behind the corporal's vehicle. Danny put his head out of the window. "Are you the one that's grounded?" he shouted.

The corporal was pulling out the tools. "The third one," he said, and cursed, but without conviction, because he was already resigned to the need to change the wheel.

Danny just laughed.

"Do you have a spare there?" demanded the corporal.

"Roy's looking in the back," said Danny.

The corporal put the tire iron on the asphalt, next to the deflated wheel. "If you can wait a minute, get into position to give me some light," he said in Danny's direction.

Danny moved the truck a bit sideways on the street, then killed the engine, keeping the headlamps on. There was silence all around, but the engines continued to grind in the ears of the men.

Danny's companion, Ralph, got out of the cab and stretched noisily. Roy could be heard rummaging through the load in the back.

"Want me to give you a hand?" Danny shouted to him.

"No," said Roy. "I found it already."

Ralph stared rather stupidly at the corporal, who was working with the jack. "It would have to be right now, when we're almost there," he said.

Without lifting his head, John answered with a kind of grunt.

"Let's go make some coffee in the meantime," said Danny.

When the last lug nut was off, the corporal worked the wheel toward himself and it came off. "Roy," he said, "take this and bring me the good one."

He had said this in a low voice, thinking Roy was there watching him. He saw his shadow, a bit to one side. But no one came to take the wheel.

"Hey, Roy," the corporal said again, turning his head, and then he saw the boy. It was a boy with a quiet demeanor, who was standing where the corporal thought Roy would be. With the boy was also a suitcase, set down near him.

"Hey, Roy," shouted the corporal. "Come look at that son of a bitch we noticed a little while ago."

Roy came from the place where Ralph was making coffee and looked at the boy with the quiet demeanor. He must have been the same person they had seen earlier, as they passed in the truck. He had a dark cloak that reached below his knees and dark pants and a woolen scarf wound around his neck and head.

"Who is it, Roy?" asked John.

"Why," said Roy, "it's a kid."

"Christ," said John, "don't you think I can see that? Ask him what he wants."

Roy asked the boy what he wanted and had to ask several times because his Italian was bad, and the boy didn't understand him.

Apparently, the boy didn't want anything because he rolled his eyes in an odd way, almost in jest. But then he asked, "Will you let me warm my hands on the radiator?"

Roy turned to the corporal. "He says he wants to warm his hands on the radiator."

The corporal looked from the boy to Roy.

"Tell him he can warm anything he likes," he said, as if irritated. "And you can take this wheel and bring me the good one."

"All right," said Roy, and he brought the good wheel. Then he approached the boy who was waiting and indicated to him to put his hands on Danny's radiator. The boy's hands were red, with darker blotches because of the cold. He watched attentively as the boy placed them against the radiator.

"It's bad luck that I lost my gloves," the boy said.

"Lost your gloves?" Roy repeated mechanically, in Italian.

"Yes," said the boy. "I had them, and then I couldn't find them at the moment of leaving. So I've frozen my hands, carrying the suitcase."

"Ah," said Roy.

The corporal had got the wheel onto the axle and was working once more with the tire iron and the lug nuts. Nevertheless, he was listening to the boy's words.

"Roy," he said after a while, "what's that damn son of a bitch saying?"

"He says he lost his gloves and his hands are cold," said Roy.

"Oh," said the corporal. His hands were cold too, even though he was wearing leather gloves.

Roy studied the sky between the rows of bare trees. "Maybe it'll snow," he said in Italian.

The boy also looked at the sky. "It usually never snows until Christmas," he said. "Some years it doesn't snow at all."

Roy continued to keep his gaze on the sky and saw the wires

stretched above the road. "There's a trolley line here," he said, indicating the wires.

"There was one, before," said the boy. "Before all of you arrived."

Roy said nothing.

Ralph and Danny were talking, standing around the fire where they were making coffee, and their voices carried faintly. Three trucks passed in file on the road, then another came, which stopped. The sergeant stuck his head out of the cab.

"Almost done, Sergeant," the corporal said. "How much farther is it?"

"Five miles, I believe."

"Then you can go on ahead," said the corporal. "I'm almost done."

"Check that no one's still behind," said the sergeant.

"All right, Sergeant."

"I'll wait for you, going into the city," said the sergeant. "Follow this road straight ahead and try to hurry."

"All right, Sergeant."

The sergeant's truck left, and for a little while they could still hear its sound in the silent night—the grinding roar of the engine and the rumble of the wheels on asphalt, getting fainter and fainter.

The corporal looked at the boy for a second before returning to his work. He was almost glad that the sergeant had not noticed him, although it didn't matter to him very much anyway.

Danny shouted to Roy to bring cups for the coffee.

The boy stood apart from them. He continued to wear a patient, even melancholy, expression, that made you feel sympathy for him in a certain way. After a while he put his hands in his pockets and turned around, leaning his back against the radiator. He watched the corporal, who finished mounting the wheel.

The corporal tightened the final nut, then he took off his gloves and went to warm his hands on Danny's radiator.

"It's not very hot anymore," said the boy.

The corporal smiled, not understanding.

"How old are you?" he asked in English.

The boy shook his head no.

For a moment the corporal thought of explaining with signs, but it was too hard to explain such a thing with signs, so he smiled, and the boy smiled.

"*Je parle français*," said the boy, hesitantly.

The corporal signaled no with his head and smiled again, and they stood in silence.

Then the others came with the coffee, and Ralph gave a cup to the boy. He inhaled over the cup and smiled at Ralph and looked around for Roy.

"It's too much," he said in Italian. "It might make me sick. It's been years since I've had coffee."

Roy shrugged his shoulders. "Drink it," he said.

The cups of coffee smoked in the cold air.

The boy drank a few sips, then he said, "My mother kept a little coffee, even before the war. But she didn't want to drink it. She said that if someone fell ill, it would be good to have a little coffee in the house."

"Roy, what's this damn son of a bitch saying?" asked the corporal.

"He's asking if we'll give him a ride in the truck."

The corporal sized up the boy with authority. "He might be a spy," he said.

"In my opinion, he doesn't look like the spy type," said Danny.

"You can never be sure," said John. "Try asking him where he wants to go."

"Where are you going, on foot like this?" Roy asked the boy in Italian.

"Home."

"Very far?"

"No. I still have to do eight kilometers."

"He has to go home," Roy said in English. "Five miles ahead."

"All right," said the corporal, thoughtfully. "All right."

Still, there was no need to make a decision, in his mind. Turning to Roy, he said with mild irritation, "Take the jack and stow the tools and the wheel. We're wasting time."

Roy knelt on the asphalt to turn the handle, then he reached under the truck to pull out the jack.

The other three men watched the boy with continued interest.

"You might say he resembles my brother Bill," said Danny. "I have a brother named Bill."

"How old do you think he is?" asked John.

"Dunno," said Danny. "My brother will be sixteen in January."

"What does this have to do with your brother? I'm talking about this one here."

"Oh well, I dunno," said Danny.

The boy listened attentively to their words. He fixed his gaze on their faces while they were talking, and in the glare of the headlamps he saw their breath forming vapor. But he understood nothing of what they were saying.

Suddenly Ralph had an idea and said, "Let's look in the suitcase, John. We can tell if he's a spy or not from what's inside."

"Sure."

Again Danny said, with indifference, "In my opinion, he doesn't look like a spy."

The corporal paid no attention to him. He took the suitcase and carried it closer to the light and signaled to the boy to open it. It was a yellow suitcase, frayed on the edges.

The boy appeared surprised, but just the same he sprang the latches of the suitcase and lifted the lid. Inside was a tangle of underwear, books, and grooming articles. John lifted up the things a little to look underneath, and underneath were the same things in the same confusion. He took up a book and began to thumb through it. The boy observed this, preoccupied with trying to understand.

"Leave it," said Danny. "Your hands are all dirty."

"I'll do what I like," said the corporal and continued to leaf through the book a little longer. Then he put it back and closed the suitcase again.

Facing Danny, he looked rather puzzled. "Maybe he's not a spy," he concluded.

Danny limited his reaction to a smile. The boy still observed the corporal without understanding anything.

Roy came up and said, "We can go now, John."

Corporal John made a move to get into the truck.

"And this kid?' asked Roy. "We're not taking him?"

John paused, irresolute.

"I'll give him a ride if you want," said Danny.

"What does it have to do with you?" said the corporal. "He asked us, not you. Tell him to get in, Roy."

"Do you want to come with us?" Roy asked the boy in Italian. "We'll carry you as far as the city."

"In the truck?"

"Yes."

"Oh, thanks," said the boy, and picked up his suitcase.

Up in the cab the three were squeezed together and uncomfortable, but the remaining road was short, and the truck moved fast.

The plane trees flew by one after the other, fading behind in the night. The boy remained a bit flattened against the door, with his suitcase under his feet. He ate some candies that Roy gave him, and meanwhile watched the road and the plane trees that he was flying by now, without having to expend effort walking. From time to time he quickly turned his gaze to Roy, who was seated in the middle.

The corporal drove with the accelerator to the floor. He saw, in the rearview mirror, Danny's headlamps, which got farther and farther behind them. On a curve the headlamps disappeared, and it was some time before they reappeared, even farther away.

"Ask him how old he is," said the corporal at a certain point.

"How old are you?" Roy asked the boy.

"Almost sixteen," answered the boy.

"Sixteen," said Roy to the corporal.

"Like Danny's brother," said the corporal. "Danny has a sixteen-year-old brother. He talked a little while ago about his brother named Bill. This one here, what's his name, Roy?"

The boy called himself Daniele, and the corporal repeated it a few times as if satisfied, then drove in silence.

The plane trees appeared more sparsely along the side of the road, replaced in places by houses and rubble.

"How much farther until we get to the city?" Roy asked the boy.

"Now it's the road to the cemetery," said the boy, "and then it's one kilometer to the railway."

"Roy," said the corporal, "it might be better if we make him get out before we get there. I wouldn't want the sergeant to say something because we've brought this kid."

"He won't say anything," said Roy.

The corporal then drove very slowly along the rough road. Danny's headlamps were lost in the distance. The boy looked around attentively. In that suburb there had been a battle, and it wasn't easy to recognize places now, at night.

"There's a curve there," said the boy, "and after the curve you'll see the overpass."

Roy waited for the truck to round the curve. "John," he said, "it's time to make him get out if you're scared of the sergeant."

The corporal didn't respond but continued to drive. The ramp of the overpass appeared, with a wooden plank barring the access to it. Many wooden signs with letters and arrows indicated the road to take, to one side of the overpass.

The corporal turned onto the detour and slowed down, because the road there was in even worse condition. Up ahead he noticed two soldiers stopped at the point where the road crossed the tracks. They wore helmets and carried guns and had armbands on the sleeves of their overcoats.

"Push him down, Roy," said the corporal. "It's the MP."

When the truck came closer, one of the MPs stopped it by holding up a hand.

The corporal had to lower the window.

"You with the convoy?" asked the MP.

"Yes."

"All right, turn immediately left as soon as you cross the tracks."

The corporal hurried to leave. "There's another one behind us," he shouted to the MP.

The truck bumped over the tracks, then turned left.

"You can get up now," said Roy to the boy.

"If they didn't notice him, we just avoided a big mess," said the corporal.

"All right, now we can let him out," said Roy.

Still the corporal didn't stop. The two MPs were still too close and would have been able to notice him. The road suddenly opened into a big square.

"This is the the station square," said the boy. "It was very beautiful, at one time."

The other cargo trucks in the convoy had stopped there, arranged in different rows. The sergeant came forward and indicated to the corporal where he was to put his truck.

"Now, make him beat it," said the corporal.

The truck stopped behind a row of other vehicles, at the far right. The corporal turned off the motor.

"Now take off," Roy said to the boy. "And try not to be seen."

The boy made to open the door, but suddenly Roy held him still and tried to conceal him with his own body. The sergeant had stepped up on the running-board, on the corporal's side.

"Where's the other one?" he demanded.

"Danny?" said the corporal, trying to look innocent.

Then the sergeant noticed the boy. "Don't you know you can't transport civilians in the cargo trucks?"

"He's a kid, Sergeant," said Roy. "We found him five miles from here, on foot."

"Why did you let him get on?"

"He was tired, Sergeant," said Roy, "and cold."

The sergeant paused uncertainly for a moment. Then he said, gruffly, "All right, where's Danny? Why aren't you answering me?"

"He'll be here before long, Sergeant," said the corporal. "We left together."

The sergeant stepped off the running-board, muttering, but immediately got back on it and said, "Make that kid disappear, Corporal. I don't want to see him again."

"Go—now," said Roy to the boy.

"You all have been very kind to bring me this far," said the boy, as he opened the door. "I don't know how to thank you."

"What's he saying, Roy?" asked the corporal.

"He says do we by any chance have an extra pair of gloves," said Roy.

"Gloves, hell," said the corporal. "Why should we give him a pair of gloves?"

The boy got out and was putting his suitcase down.

"He has to carry that suitcase in this cold," said Roy.

"What do I care if one of these godforsaken sons of bitches freezes his hands?" said the corporal. "That's his problem. I should give him my gloves so my own hands will freeze?"

"If I had two pairs of gloves, I'd give him one pair," said Roy.

"Hell," said the corporal. "These people would take your shirt if they could."

Still, even while he was saying this, the corporal began to rummage through his pockets and finally pulled out a pair of woolen gloves and threw them out the door, where the boy had gotten out.

"Now close it, it's cold," he said.

"See that you don't let the police catch you," said Roy to the boy. "And if they do catch you, don't tell them you came with us."

The boy gathered up the gloves and his suitcase and headed toward the far end of the square. There had been gardens there once, but now the flowers were gone, and there remained only some half-shattered trees. He sat down on the suitcase to wait. He still had two candies the American soldier had given him. He put one in his mouth.

Danny's truck arrived and stopped behind that of the corporal. Farther on in the square the engines started once again to rumble, and the cargo trucks began to leave, one after the other, along the peripheral road, until after a short time all of them had gone and the square was empty. At the far end there remained the ruins of the station and the small wood structure that now served as a station. Farther away there was the red glow of a semaphore. The sky was cloud-covered, the color of ash. Above the clouds perhaps there was a moon.

14

The boy was seated on the suitcase, appearing to have arrived too early. He put the last piece of candy into his mouth and began to suck on it, taking care not to chew it. He tried the gloves on and they proved to be too big, naturally, but they kept him warm nonetheless. The square was silent and empty. No one was about at that hour. Perhaps there was one person or at the most two, and there were still many hours before daylight. And he didn't have anything to do, having arrived too early. Still, he could not stay sitting there like that for the whole rest of the night. It seemed to him that the cold had become more raw. Then he decided to move.

He took his suitcase and began walking along the street by the station, toward the center of the city. All that he was able to see around him was destruction and solitude. The suitcase was heavy with all those books inside it. At brief intervals he stopped to change hands. He walked along one side of the road, keeping close to the ruins.

He entered the city. He no longer recognized that part of the main street, because there were so many ruins in place of the houses. At certain points the street resembled a trench, excavated out of the rubble.

As soon as he found a street off to the left, the boy turned toward that section, passing on into the Sant' Agnese quarter. He was able to move forward only a hundred yards or so, because he found the street barricaded with boards. He went around through other streets, all of them dark and deserted. It seemed to him he was walking in a city where the people had suddenly died, all together. His footsteps made a scary sound, and his heart contracted with anxiety.

Finally the boy came out onto a larger street that had to be the Via Sant' Agnese. He stopped a moment to rest. It would be better to reach the walls and go around the outside of the quarter. He began walking toward the walls, but not far along he found himself once again in front of another barrier of boards. He was no longer sure he was on the Via Sant' Agnese. He turned and began to walk back. The thought that he was lost among the ruins gave him a fresh worry, even when he made every effort to remain calm. It seemed that the gloves were worthless and the hand holding the suitcase went suddenly stiff, from the cold and the weight. By going in that direction he must certainly come out onto the main street, unless that street was not Via Sant' Agnese but some other street. His mother had always warned him never to go through that quarter.

He remained alert to everything he was able to see. Some houses were standing, but not many, with ruins and open spaces between one house and another. On the left side of the street, the empty places were closed off with a barrier of barbed wire, taller than a man and wide at the base. That must be the forbidden zone.

Suddenly the boy heard himself being called to, in a barely audible whisper. He stopped, and the call was repeated. It was a few steps behind him, but from the other side of the barbed wire. He felt an initial, frightened impulse to start running, but he couldn't move his legs. The dead were there, inside.

"Hey, you, where are you going?" asked a voice.

Since it was quite impossible for the dead to speak, his fear began to pass. Still, he trembled, however he might try to control himself.

"Where are you going?" the voice asked again.

The boy made an effort to reply. "I don't know."

"Why are you walking around, then?" asked the voice.

"I don't know. I'm afraid of getting lost here in the center."

"You know that if they catch you at this hour, they'll throw you in jail?" asked the voice.

The boy felt calmer then, although he didn't know how to respond. He stared at the place where the voice was coming from, and he saw nothing but darkness, and the shadow of some pile of rubble, darker than the rest.

The person inside the barbed-wire barrier waited a bit for his reply, then demanded in an irritated tone, "Are you willing to go to jail?"

"No," the boy replied.

"Then you're being stupid. Don't you have a home?"

"No," answered the boy.

The voice could not be heard for some minutes. Then it said, "Look around well and see if you see anyone."

The boy looked around but there was no one. "There's no one," he said.

"Then turn around, quick."

"Where?"

"Behind you," said the voice. "Walk over here, by the fence."

The boy walked back about fifty paces, until the voice told him to stop. Whoever was talking had followed him on the other side of the barrier.

"Look around again and see if you see anyone."

The boy looked around but there was no one. "There's no one," he said.

Then a shadow came silently out from the ruins and slipped halfway through the barrier.

"Pass me the suitcase," it said.

The boy paused uncertainly. "Are you the police?" he asked.

"What do you mean, police?" said the voice through the barrier. "Pass me the suitcase, quick."

The boy decided to do it but didn't know where to hand it over.

"Underneath, underneath," said the shadow. "Can't you see that the barbed wire lifts up?"

The boy raised the barbed wire and pushed the suitcase forward. The other took it and drew it toward himself. "Pass me the cloak, too."

The boy took off his cloak and passed it under the barrier. The shadow crawled back, carrying the suitcase and the cloak. The boy waited. He couldn't see the shadow on the other side.

"Are you waiting for the soldiers to come by?" demanded the voice. "You come too, quick."

"Under?" asked the boy.

The other was losing his patience. "Unless you want to fly over. But make it fast."

The boy stretched out on the ground and slid under the barbed wire, at the place where he was able to raise it. He crawled forward a yard or so, then stopped.

"What are you doing?" asked the voice.

"I tore my pants," said the boy.

"God, you must really be stupid," said the other, and again approached the barrier in order to help the boy get through. Once through, the other took the suitcase and cloak that he had set on the ground and began to hurry away, carrying the things with him.

The boy followed him closely, struggling a bit on the uneven path, which wound tortuously between the rubble and the remains of the houses. The one going ahead of him was also a boy, coatless and with a strange cap on his head.

They walked perhaps a hundred yards in silence, then the one in front asked, "Who are you?"

The boy could not think of a reply right away. "My name is Daniele," he said after a bit.

"What are you doing around here?"

"I don't know. I'm afraid I'm lost. It's difficult to guess the streets, with all these changes."

The other made an unintelligible sound and didn't ask anything more, until they stood before a house with its walls still in place. Then he stopped and deposited the suitcase on the ground and gave the cloak to the one who was following him.

"Keep it," he said. "Take your stuff."

So saying, he looked closely at Daniele and saw how he was dressed. "What are you wearing?" he asked.

"It's a uniform," said Daniele. "The uniform of the boarding school."

"You are in a boarding school?"

"Yes."

"And you ran away?"

"Yes."

"Ah," said the boy. "And what's in the suitcase?"

"My stuff," said Daniele. "My grooming things, and underwear, and books."

"Books?"

"Yes. Books for studying."

"Ah," said the boy again. "And what do you study?"

"Lots of subjects. Italian, and Latin …"

"Latin too?" asked the boy. "What for?"

"I don't know. They make us study it, also Greek."

"Are you studying to be a priest?" asked the boy.

"No. I'm going to be a doctor when I grow up."

Once more the boy said, "Ah," but this time he seemed lost in thought. After a moment he asked, "Why were you walking through these parts?" His voice had changed its tone suddenly. It was calm and almost affectionate.

Daniele seemed to hesitate before responding. Finally he said, "They told me to watch out for the police, so I came into the center of the quarter, in order not to pass along the main street. I wanted to go to the area of the cathedral."

"You should have known no one can go through this quarter anymore," said the boy. "Where have you been all this time?"

"At school," said Daniele.

The boy wasn't annoyed. "Why did you want to go to the area of the cathedral?"

"My house was on that side, before. It went down in the bombardment."

"And your people are dead?"

"Yes," said Daniele.

"You have no one in the world?"

"I still have relatives," said Daniele. "They're on my mother's side. But they aren't here, they're in Rome."

"And do you want to go them?" asked the boy. "It's not easy to get to Rome these days."

"I don't want to go to them," said Daniele.

"Ah," went the boy, for no particular reason.

Then he came nearer, face to face with Daniele, and studied him intently, as well as he could in the faint light. Finally he asked, "What sort of person are you?"

"What?" Daniele said.

"I'd like to know what job your father did in this city."

"He was a government official."

For a moment the boy fell silent, then he said, "I'm a communist."

He said it with an air of importance, as if he wanted to impress the other. But Daniele said nothing.

"You have nothing to say about it, that I'm a communist?"

"Nowadays a person can be anything they want to be," said Daniele. "Even the priests at school have formed a Christian political party."

"Leave the priests out of it," said the boy. Then he asked suddenly, "Why don't you want to go to your relatives in Rome?"

"Because," said Daniele stubbornly, "I don't want to go there."

"Aren't they rich? Wouldn't they have something for you to eat?"

Daniele made a gesture of disdain. "Why are you asking me all these questions?" he said. "And why did you make me come in here? I didn't want to come in here."

The other boy did not reply. He was leaning against the wall as if in thought. It was cold, and he was going around without a scarf and overcoat and appeared not to feel the cold. Daniele's feet, on the other hand, were freezing.

"Why did you make me come in here?" he asked again.

Instead of speaking, the boy laughed, as if Daniel's persistence amused him.

"Oh, don't laugh, if you please," said Daniele.

The boy quit laughing and asked seriously, "Can I sit on your suitcase?"

Daniele was tempted to give a rude answer, but instead he just said, "Yes."

The boy placed the suitcase on the ground and sat on one end of it. "Sit down yourself," he said. "It can hold both of us."

Daniele sat down in the place the boy had left open. They squeezed together and their shoulders touched.

"Listen up, now," said the boy. "I could help you, maybe, but first I have to know what you want to do, and why you ran away from school, and why you don't want to go to your relatives in Rome."

Daniele thought for a moment. A moment before, he wouldn't have said anything, but now the boy seemed different toward him, the way he left him a place to sit and above all the manner in which he had asked to talk. His voice had a steady and understanding tone, and it was clear that he did not intend to trick him.

"Do I have to tell everything?" Daniele asked.

"Anything you want to tell."

"I will begin with after the bombardment. All right?"

"Yes, all right. But make it quick. We'll freeze, staying still."

"My mother and my father died in the bombardment," said Daniele, "and I stayed alone at school. Then the director telegraphed my relatives in Rome, and my grandfather came. I had never seen my grandfather before. He didn't get along with my mother and father, I don't know why. I sent him a greeting card each Christmas and Easter, because my mother told me to, but he never responded. I don't know why it was like that. They never told me."

"Leave off these stories," said the boy. "They're not important."

"So then he came, and I saw him for the first time," said Daniele. "He said he had paid for my schooling and I needed to continue to stay there. Then he returned right away to Rome and left money for the term. Meanwhile I was waiting for vacation. I hoped he would have me go to his house in Rome, but he never said that. I wanted very much to go to Rome, because I couldn't stay all the time at school after my mother was dead and no one was coming to find me.

"So I waited to go to Rome, and instead, before vacation began, the Americans took Rome and I couldn't go there anymore. So I had to stay at school all summer, and I was alone, because the other boys had gone to their homes, and the priests treated me differently, now that there was no one to pay for me. There was one who wanted me to become a priest, too.

"And then, when the new year began, they wanted me to become a spy. Every time some disturbance happened at school, they wanted to know from me the names of those who did it. This, because I couldn't pay, and they said I would have to compensate in some way. But I didn't want to be a spy, nor did I want to become a priest. So they punished me, and I was committing more transgressions all the time. They kept threatening me with expulsion, but in the meantime, they didn't know where to send me. They must have thought the Americans would come and take me away. And I also anticipated the Americans, because I was sure I would go to Rome then. Then, when the Americans arrived, the director wrote to my grandfather that I had bad conduct and merited expulsion. I also wrote my grandfather, telling him the truth. But he replied only to the director and wrote to him that he had found a spot for me in another school. So I ran away."

Daniele fell silent for a bit. The other boy stayed motionless, as if expecting him to continue.

"I don't want to go to school anymore," said Daniele. "And by now I don't even want to go to my grandfather's, either."

"What do you want to do, then?"

"I want to live on my own."

The other smiled. "How do you plan to live?"

"I could find work. I thought of going to some friends of my father. Maybe they would hire me."

The other was still smiling, bitterly.

"You have no idea what the world has become," he said. "You think someone will give you a job, in these times? And in any case, are you sure they are still friends of your father? He has been dead for six months, and so many things have changed in six months. Even the officials will have changed. They've sent almost all of them away."

"One is still here, for sure," said Daniele. "I know there was, until a few days ago. He's one who always came to our house."

"All right," said the boy. "The only thing he will want to do will be to send you back to school. You're a minor, and you must do what your relatives want you to do. If they want to keep you in school, you have to go there. That's the law."

"I don't want to," said Daniele, obstinately.

"Well, that's the way it is," said the boy. "If not, you must stay hidden, because the priests will have them searching for you. It would be sufficient to stay in hiding for a week. The police have other things to think about these days. But you'll have to find another suit of clothes, because with what you have on, they'll catch you within the month, as soon as they see you around."

Daniele stayed in silence for a bit, thinking. Then he said, "But I can't stay hidden for a week. I must find work right away so I can eat. It doesn't matter even if it isn't an office job."

"What do you know how to do?"

"I don't know. I could be an errand boy or any other kind of job. One learns fast, when one is willing."

"You don't know how to survive in the world," repeated the boy. "There is no work, in these times. The only thing you should do is to go back to school and follow that path. You're luckier than so many others."

"I don't want to," said Daniele.

The other boy seemed distracted. He pulled his hands out of his pockets and tried to see the time on the watch he wore on his wrist, but there wasn't enough light. "It must be late," he said.

Daniele didn't speak. He was suffering from the cold and wished the situation would resolve itself somehow.

All at once the boy said, "I could give you work, if you wanted. Are you willing to do anything?"

"Yes."

"Even steal?"

"No," said Daniele. "I wouldn't want to steal."

"Then nothing doing," said the boy. He got up and took a few steps, stamping his feet on the ground. Then he asked, "What did you want to do around the cathedral?"

"My home was there. I lived in the first skyscraper towards the square."

"But it's all fallen down. Nothing is left standing."

"I only wanted to go see it because it was my home," said Daniele. "They didn't pull out the dead at all, isn't that true?"

"No, they didn't pull out the dead," said the boy. "Why would you want them to pull them out? They're better off where they are."

He had begun again to walk around, stamping his feet. Then he stopped in front of Daniele and spoke with harshness in his voice. "Now I'll take you to the area of the cathedral, and you can go your own way, whether to jail or to school or wherever the devil you want to go. But don't tell anyone you met me or that you went through the barrier. All right?"

"All right," said Daniele, standing up. "I won't tell anyone."

The boy left first, walking quickly. Dark or light patches and the remains of houses were revealed suddenly and quickly disappeared into the night. The sound of their footsteps was the only sound in the great silence.

Then the boy stopped again, suddenly. "Do you know how to keep a secret?"

"Yes."

"I could have you spend the night under cover," said the boy. "So meanwhile you will be able to think carefully about what you should do. You need to think carefully, because all the ideas in your head are stupid, and will not work in a world like this. If I let you go tomorrow, they will send you back to school, or to those relatives of yours in Rome. Besides, I think it would be better if you went and got support from somewhere. You don't know how to live alone in the world, you don't."

"I would die of hunger, rather than let myself be kept by them."

"That's your business," said the boy calmly. "I'll help you this one night, so you can think about it. It only matters to me that you do not tell anyone where you have been and who you have seen."

"All right."

"You must vow that you will say nothing to anyone," said the boy. "You must swear on your father and your mother."

"I swear," said Daniele.

"All right," said the boy. "Let's go." And he set off again, walking ahead.

They entered a zone where the remains of houses were more numerous, and in certain places there was evidence of streets and porticoes. But all was silence and solitude.

Then the boy stopped in front of a doorway and opened it cautiously, without making any sound. The wall ended a little above the doorway, because the upper part was collapsed.

"Go ahead, and try to go softly," said the boy. "People are sleeping inside."

Daniele entered and the boy closed the door again. It was all dark and there was a smell of dampness and also of a fire, but there was no heat. It was as cold inside as outside. The boy pulled a flashlight out of his pocket and turned it on. Only a thread of light shone from the screened reflector.

"Hold this and give me light," said the boy.

Daniele put his suitcase down and held the flashlight between his hands.

The boy searched in the pocket of his jacket. He brought forth a packet of tobacco and rolled a cigarette. "Do you smoke?" he asked.

"No."

"Give me the flashlight," said the boy. He took it and turned it off and they were once more in the dark. Right away, though, the boy lit a cigarette lighter and held the flame close to Daniele's face. They studied one another for a moment. Then the boy lit his cigarette and closed the lighter. In the light of the cigarette ember he looked at his wristwatch. "It's late," he said.

"Will I stay here?" asked Daniele.

"Now I'll take you to the bed," said the boy. "Try to be quiet."

"Should I bring the suitcase?"

"If you want."

Daniele picked up the suitcase. The other boy grabbed him by an arm and led him forward two or three steps, then made him turn into another area. He couldn't see anything except the ember of the cigarette. When they arrived there he smelled a strong odor of perfume.

"The bed's behind you," said the boy.

Daniele felt for the bed with his hands and found it down very low, just a few inches from the floor.

"You can get undressed," said the boy. "It's enough just to take off your cloak and your jacket."

Daniele took off the cloak and scarf and jacket and draped them on the suitcase.

"Also your shoes, you should take them off," said the boy.

Daniele sat down on the bed and made a slight sound, although he was trying to be quiet.

The other boy, however, said nothing. He puffed continuously on the cigarette, as if in a hurry to finish it. For some time Daniele remained bent down, untying his shoes.

"But can't you even take off your shoes?" demanded the boy impatiently.

"I made a knot. I can't see to undo it."

"God!" said the boy, fairly loudly. He looked for the cigarette lighter to make a little light. "Hurry up," he said, "I've already wasted enough time on you."

Daniele hurried to undo the knot, and while he was doing this someone turned in the bed and, in turning, emitted a big sigh. The springs creaked. Daniele turned to look. It was a large double bed, and someone was sleeping on the other side; he saw long hair spread over the pillow.

He jumped to his feet in alarm. "Do you see that?" he said. "There's a woman in the bed."

The boy extinguished the lighter. "Think about going to sleep," he said. "You're going to be here too."

"Here with her?"

"Unless you want to sleep on the floor, it's all the same to me. There aren't any other beds."

"She won't say anything if I sleep with her?"

"What do you want her to say?" said the boy, moving around by now.

"Don't go," said Daniele, pleadingly. "Who is this woman?"

"It's Carla, don't worry about it."

Daniele heard footsteps as the boy left, and then nothing more, except the breathing of the woman who was asleep in the bed. Now that he was alert, he could hear her heavy breathing clearly. And in the meantime, he stayed on his feet and didn't dare move. When he quit school, he had resolved to have the courage for anything, but he hadn't thought of something like this.

It was very cold in the room, and he shivered without his cloak and his jacket, and his bare feet froze on the floor. He searched with his hands for the suitcase and his things, but they were no longer where they had been put. Maybe the boy had taken everything away. And he was no longer able to bear the cold. He listened to the woman's breathing, regular and deep. Then, softly, he lowered his hands to the blankets, lifted them, and lay down under them. The woman's breathing stayed the same, and all the rest was silence. For a long time he remained awake, shivering at the far edge of the bed, listening to the woman's breathing.

In some tower, bells began to ring while it was still dark. Then it became day, cold and gray under a uniformly overcast sky. In the houses and the shelters people awoke and saw light between the slats and felt the sorrow of a new day.

The people woke up, and for the most part stayed in bed or on their piles of straw, because there was nothing to do but remain lying down. Stretched out under blankets, one could stay alive, even with the little strength left in one's body because of the lack of food.

But those who had something to do got up in the dim light and went out into the streets, toward the places where they had to go.

There were those who went in search of food, and they were many. Drawing their rags close around them, they formed long lines to wait in front of the bakeries. They waited with a resigned patience. At any moment the doors would open, and someone would hand out bread for that day. Others set themselves to going through the streets and the squares, in search of something else, aside from bread. Whoever had enough money could find anything.

And there were those who went to work—not many, because work was scarce. Small shopkeepers, workers in shops that repaired war machinery, street sweepers whose job it was to clean the city, office workers who converted into numbers and formulas the misery of the people—even they went forth joylessly in the gray morning, and their footsteps were like those of the people who went out in search of food with little hope of finding any. There was in everyone the same weariness, because each was dimly aware of the futility of whatever he was doing.

A bit later the air became less cold. At that time those who had remained idly in their houses went out to loaf around in the streets and squares. Poorly clad, with worn-out shoes or with rags in place of shoes, they walked around the city or sat on the ground beneath the porticoes and in the shelter of the houses. If someone better dressed or better fed than they passed by, they discussed this at length. They talked also about news of the world and people. Something was always happening in the world and to people, and they discussed it, for whatever might come out of it for them, for better or worse.

But they discussed these things without much conviction, because it was difficult to maintain a great deal of interest in such things, when everything that happened brought so few changes in their misery. They might change some man in the city government, or else the representative of a political party might make a speech, or even some major event might occur in one of the many places where they were carrying on the war. But for the people, it was always the same misery. Perhaps it just required waiting until the war ended, until men should quit destroying so many of the good things of the world, just in order to kill each other.

Every so often a quarrel broke out among those who were conversing, or who waited in the lines, or who went about in search of food. The people ran over to look and listen. Then the quarrel ended, and each went his way.

Early in the morning, at the hour when he had been accustomed at school to get up, the boy stirred a little in his sleep, nevertheless without gaining consciousness. He continued sleeping for some hours. Then he opened his eyes in a faint light, as if the room were under water. There was only one window, where paper had been stuck up in place of window glass. The entrance to the room was covered with a blanket.

No outside sounds reached into the house, and in that huge silence the boy felt lost in inertia, devoid of energy and of will. Weariness from the night before weighed on him. He felt a desire to sleep more, or perhaps he had slept even too much and for this reason was sluggish. He had no idea what time it might be.

Suddenly he heard the sound of clogs, barely two or three footsteps. Then he remembered the woman in the bed, and he turned to that side and saw the shape of a body under the blankets. But it was a man, because it had short hair. It must be the boy who had brought him to the house. And the woman was perhaps the one who was moving around in another room, wearing clogs on her feet.

Now fully awake, he looked for his suitcase and spotted it in a corner. The cloak and jacket were now, instead, on a chair near the bed, the cloak folded and the jacket well spread out on the back of the chair, without a trace of dirt. But the shoes were missing. He couldn't see them on the floor where he remembered leaving them. It was a tile floor, with an alternating red and white pattern. Perhaps the boy had hidden the shoes to prevent him from leaving.

There came again the clatter of clogs, just a few steps.

The room was painted bright yellow, with a colored frieze high on the walls: a chain of naked babies bearing garlands of flowers. At least that's how it appeared in the dim light. A crack ran from one side of the ceiling to the other, and he could see large, damp stains.

The bed was a box spring placed on the floor, and it had no sheets but only gray blankets such as soldiers used. Near the door was a small table with a basin on it and a mirror attached to the wall and two candlesticks with almost new candles. On the floor was another basin and a German fuel oil canister, a jerry-can. On the other side of the door he saw a radiator, with a towel hanging up to dry. Nevertheless, the heat certainly was not on. Perhaps it had broken in the bombardment, or else those people did not have coal to burn. It was very cold. The boy drew the blankets up to his chin and lay with his eyes open, staring at the ceiling. Now he saw many other cracks, other than the main one that ran from one side to the other. Together they formed curious figures, and so did the damp stains, like animals and trees and even heads. He was no longer sleepy. He was rather hungry, with a sensation of emptiness in his stomach.

Time passed and he stayed there, visualizing the figures on the ceiling and alert to every sound. But in the silence he heard only the noise of clogs from time to time, and this produced disquiet in him each time. He did not even know what he wanted to do exactly, but perhaps it would be good if the boy were to awake and escort him out, without seeing the woman.

Then the church bells began to sound, some nearby and others farther away, and after a bit they ceased. The person with the clogs was moving around more frequently now, and he also heard sounds as if things were being handled and shifted around. They were nevertheless vague sounds, from which he could not guess what that person might be doing. Often, too, the boy turned his head toward the one who was sleeping. That one continued to sleep, and from the blankets peeped only the top of his head, with short, black hair.

Then he heard the sound of the clogs closer by, just outside the room, and they paused for a second. The boy sat up to look toward the door, and in his nervousness his breath failed him. The blanket at the entrance moved, and she came in, making no sound with her bare feet. The boy caught his breath again, but in a spasmodic way, because his heart was pounding so hard. The person who entered was only a girl, who might have been fourteen years old, tall, and disheveled looking. She had his shoes in her hand. She came forward, and as soon as she saw he was awake, she hesitated and after a second continued toward him. Now she kept her eyes fixed on the shoes that she held in her hand.

When she was close, she said in a low voice, "I cleaned them with a rag, because we don't have any polish."

The boy tried to speak, but then he only nodded his head yes, and she wasn't able to see that because she was looking at the shoes instead of at him. She placed them on the floor and continued to stare at them. "If you want to get up, you can come out there," she said. "There's a little fire out there in the kitchen."

The boy nodded yes again.

"Also, if you want to wash, there's water out there," said the girl.

"Thanks," the boy finally said.

She moved to leave, and in that moment she directed her gaze for an instant toward him. She had large eyes, of a light color. She went out, and he heard once more the sound of the clogs.

Now the boy leaned his head back on the pillow again and pulled up the blankets. Bit by bit he calmed down. He would go out there, but not right away. He didn't know what to do or say around her, after they had slept together in the same bed.

More time passed, and then he heard her again, but he stayed motionless under the blankets. She entered as before, without clogs, and came close to the bed. She seemed more sure of herself now, and she had combed her hair. She had on big green wool socks and a gray dress, of the same color as military blankets. "If you want to go out there, there's some hot *caffè-latte*," she said.

"Yes," he answered.

"It's ready, if you want to come," she said again, and went away.

The boy began to get up, and he moved slowly so as not to make noise. The other boy was motionless in slumber. He slipped into his jacket and gathered up his suitcase and cloak and the shoes. He left the room and found himself in a dark corridor, where just a little light entered through the cracks in a door. He put on the shoes and waited. He heard no sound. Getting accustomed to the dark, he saw first some laundry hanging up to dry on a cord. There were other doors on the wall in front of him, all boarded up. It was cold.

On tiptoe he walked toward the door where the light was shining and opened it to look out. There was a kind of courtyard, choked with debris, with half-collapsed houses around it, and a path in the middle that led away from the ruined houses. The sky was grey and cold. The only living thing he saw was a magnolia tree a short distance away, the branches of which sprang up from the ruins, on the side where the path was.

He closed the door again, taking care not to make noise. He walked softly along the corridor and passed the door to the bedroom where he had been sleeping. Farther ahead was another door similar to that one, also covered with a blanket. At the end of the corridor was yet another door, a larger one, boarded up. There on the floor was a small washtub.

The boy waited without moving in front of the boarded-up door. Then he coughed, not knowing what to do.

Immediately he heard the sound of footsteps, and the girl put her head out of the blanket that covered the door to the left.

"Come," she said.

He turned and tried to appear surprised to see her. "May I leave my suitcase here?" he asked.

"Yes," she said, "you may leave it wherever you wish." She spoke in a manner both direct and kind.

He put the suitcase on the floor and folded the cloak with great care and laid it over the suitcase. The girl had retired into the room. He ran his fingers through his hair in an attempt to smooth it. Then he went in.

She was standing in front of the door, waiting for him. He also stopped to look at her as soon as he entered. On her feet, instead of clogs, she had put on a pair of shoes, which were old. And she was not beautiful. The only beautiful thing about her was her hair, light and wavy, that reached to her shoulders. And her eyes were beautiful also, and there was surprise in them, and a hint of a smile, and a sweet expression.

"Come," she said.

But the boy didn't move. An unpleasant agitation had arisen in him under her gaze, so gentle, but then he began to think about his trousers that must be wrinkled and still soiled with dirt, and suddenly he remembered they were also torn in the seat, and then he became rather perturbed with it all.

Hesitatingly he reached a hand behind him and felt the tear. "Oh," he said, shaking his head.

"What is it?" asked the girl.

He was so confused that he was not able to respond right away. "Perhaps – " he stammered, "– perhaps it isn't so warm in here. Perhaps I had better put on my cloak." He snatched the blanket up behind his back and exited without turning around.

The girl didn't understand his confusion, but the hint of a smile disappeared from her eyes. Then, when the boy returned with his cloak over his shoulders, she avoided looking at him directly.

"Sit down next to the fire," she said.

There was, in one corner, a large tin container with embers in it. The boy seated himself on a stool, holding his hands over the fire. The embers were covered with a layer of ashes and didn't give off much warmth, but just enough to warm oneself by standing close to it. Placed on the coals was a small pot containing *caffè-latte*.

The girl moved through the room, but he did not have the courage to look at her, and that was because of the tear in his pants, and because of that other fact, that they had slept together. The room had two windows, with paper in place of window glass, and there were three large upright beams, like columns, to hold up the ceiling. One corner was hidden with blankets hanging on cords; in another corner could be seen on the floor cooking utensils and jerry-cans. A few skillets and pots hung from hooks on the wall.

The girl came over to him with an aluminum cup. She poured the *caffè-latte* and handed him the cup. He accepted it and began to drink with small sips. It was bitter but good, and it tasted like real coffee.

"Is it hot enough?" asked the girl.

"Oh, yes, thanks."

"There's no bread. We only eat bread in the evening, if we don't there's not enough."

She had stopped in front of him, waiting. Her big dress fitted her awkwardly, and he guessed at her thinness underneath it. She had a little woolen shawl over her shoulders, held together in front with a safety pin.

When he had finished drinking, she reached out her hand to take the cup and carried it away, together with the small pot, to the other side of the room. Then she came to sit next to him, to be close to the heat of the brazier. Both of them leaned forward a little, with their hands held out to warm them. She had a delicate face with somewhat hard features and thin, pale lips. Her hands were deformed with large chilblains and chapped cracks.

Every so often they regarded each other, lifting their eyes quickly, and they never happened to look at each other at the same time. But as soon as it happened that they raised their eyes together, she attempted a smile; nevertheless, he did not respond and right away dropped his gaze. Then she also became withdrawn and remained in a submissive, downcast attitude. The silence was profound and all the while became more awkward. The boy began to fidget with his fingers, and then his lips, with nervousness.

"Who knows what time it is," he said finally. He felt his voice tremble miserably.

The girl did not raise her eyes from the embers. "It had just struck noon, when I came to bring you your shoes," she said. "Now it must be one, maybe."

"It's late," said the boy.

Now the girl raised her eyes. "Why late?"

For an instant he searched for something to say. "Because it's one," he said.

"Tullio said that you should not move from here before evening," said the girl.

"Who's Tullio?"

"You know him. He's the one who brought you to the house last night."

"Oh, yes," he said, and suddenly asked, "He's the one who's sleeping in there, right?"

"Yes," said the girl.

A brief silence followed, and the boy fidgeted more with his hands, because the moment had arrived for him to speak of a particular thing. He had the impression that she also was waiting.

"I …" he said, "I must thank you for cleaning my shoes. And also for putting my things in order. You were the one who put them in order, right?"

"Oh, that's nothing," said the girl.

He took a deep breath. "I'm sorry to have disturbed you, last night."

"No, no," she said. "I heard nothing."

"It was the fault of the shoes," said the boy. "I had gotten a knot in the laces and wasn't able to undo it, and then that boy had to give me a light, and you turned over in the bed. I was really afraid you were woken up."

The girl observed him with wonder. "Oh, that wasn't me, that girl," she said. "That was Carla. I'm Giulia. I sleep here, behind those blankets."

The boy felt his face get suddenly hot, and he began to stutter in his confusion.

"I didn't want to," he said. "I thought it was you, but it's not my fault. That woman slept with her face under the blankets, and I could only see her hair. So that's why I thought it was you, but I was mistaken. I didn't intend to say anything that might upset you."

"She'll be back before long, Carla will," said the girl, matter-of-factly.

He appreciated her directness, but he didn't feel capable of saying anything more.

"Carla's my cousin," said the girl, and then lapsed into silence, since he wasn't saying anything and kept his gaze fixed on the embers. Deep down she was hoping something would happen, and nothing happened.

Finally the girl said, "If you want to wash, there's everything you need here."

He thought with terror of the tear in his pants. "Oh, it doesn't matter," he said. "You shouldn't disturb yourself at all on my account."

"But don't you want to wash?"

"Yes, yes," he said, looking around as if he were searching for something. "Look, I can go outside. Would it bother you if I washed in the corridor? My things are there, with the suitcase."

"It's colder out there," said the girl.

"Oh, it's nothing, the cold," he said.

Then she stood up to carry to the corridor a basin and a jerry-can of water. He followed her, intending to help, and did not succeed in doing anything. The girl turned over the little wooden washtub, positioned it above the basin, and filled it with water. Then she went to open the entrance door and a great light shone in, all the way to the end of the corridor.

The boy tried to play for time with his suitcase. He pulled out soap, comb, and towel, each with great deliberateness.

She stood watching him, and when she saw the soap she said, "Oh, that soap's no good. I'll give you a piece."

She went back into the kitchen and right away came back with a piece of white, perfumed soap.

"Thanks," said the boy and remained still, with his cloak on, although everything was now ready.

"Do you need anything else?" asked the girl.

"No, no, thanks," he said hastily. Still, he did not move, and she also stood still, without understanding, and perhaps it didn't even cross her mind that she should leave.

Then he said, boldly, "Look, I'd like you to go inside, please. And don't come out until I'm done."

"Oh, all right," said the girl, and she went into the kitchen.

Quickly he took off his cloak and jacket and began to wash, bent over the basin. The water smelled like the river, but the soap was good and made a lot of suds, with a flowery perfume. It had been a long time since he had used such good soap. These people seemed so impoverished in certain things, and yet they had good soap and real coffee and a house that at one time must have been very nice, with central heat and paintings on the walls.

Still, he couldn't wait to get out of there. The girl was kind, certainly, but the boy had asked all those questions, as if tricking him, and then had made him sleep in a bed where there was a woman! And he understood quite well that the boy was a thief.

He took the basin with the dirty water and went to toss it outside the door and began to rinse himself with the other water. When he finished, he stood up and took a towel to dry himself and then he heard the voice of a woman at his shoulder, a voice that spoke and laughed at the same time.

"Good morning, Reverend," said the voice.

He turned with a start and remained immobilized, staring. This was a new girl, tall like the other one, but not as skinny. He could see her figure against the background of the light from the door.

The girl laughed. "Hey, Reverend," she said, "you have a rip this long in your pants."

All his strength left him at one blow, and he didn't even have the courage to lower his eyes. He was quite a pitiful sight, with his hair stuck to his forehead and his mouth hanging open and the drops of water dripping down his face and neck into his shirt.

"Dry off," said the girl. "Don't just stand there like a dummy, as if you were tied to a post."

"Oh, yes," he said mechanically, and didn't move.

"And don't worry about your pants," said the girl. "Giulia will fix them. She'll fix them so well no one will notice anything."

He continued to stare at her, stunned.

"She's clever, you know," said the girl. "She was working as a seamstress before the bombardment."

Still he did not move, and she laughed in his face, in a particularly saucy manner, and then went into the kitchen.

Then the boy took up the towel in a huge hurry, but he had not finished when the two girls returned together. Both of them bent over to better examine the rip in his pants.

"What a shame," said the skinny one, and the other laughed, for some reason he did not understand.

He stood still, filled with even more confusion and embarrassment.

And the one who had laughed said, "Turn around the other way, Reverend. No one can see anything, this way."

He turned toward the nailed-up door.

The girls examined the rip more closely, and he felt them touch the fabric where it was torn. He had a great desire to scream, or else to weep, but in the meantime he stood still and rigid, holding his breath.

"It's a shame," said the skinny girl again. "And at the moment I don't have thread that color, only black."

He felt a bit relieved at that, because he understood just then that it was not himself but his pants that were important.

"No one will see it very much, black on the blue," said the other girl.

"Yes, but it's a shame because it's nice fabric," said the skinny one, and she promptly left, leaving them alone in the corridor.

He remained facing the boarded-up door.

"Well, aren't you going to move?" demanded the girl.

"Yes, miss," he said, and turned toward her, but kept his head down.

"Get going, then," said the girl. "You tore them going under the barbed-wire fence?"

"Yes, miss," he said.

"Well, quit calling me 'miss'," said the girl. "My name is Carla. And give me yours. We slept together last night, end of story, right, Reverend?"

He sank into an even deeper shame than before. He got all red in the face and breathed in little pants. She watched him, amused and perhaps also surprised.

Finally he felt able to speak and raised his eyes to hers, though respectfully.

"Look," he said. "I wanted to speak particularly about this to you, because I'm sorry to have disturbed you." And he was unable to proceed further.

"Oh," said the girl, simply, and took him by the arm and led him into the kitchen, near the brazier.

"Sit down, for goodness' sake," she said and let go of him abruptly.

He did not sit down but remained standing where the girl had left him, leaning his back against the wall. Now the expression on his face was sulky and stubborn. More than ever, he wished himself away, among different people who did not laugh at such things as the rip in the seat of his pants, or sleeping in the same bed, or at people's feelings. Still, the girls were paying less attention to him, it seemed to him, and after a bit he raised his eyes from the floor to watch them.

One was called Giulia and the other, Carla. Giulia was rummaging in a small cardboard box. Carla, for her part, moved quickly and confidently, doing something in the kitchen. She had taken off her coat and underneath she was dressed in a whimsical combination. She had on a short dress ending at her knees and a striped wool sweater, also too close-fitting. And she wore silk stockings and platform shoes, like those of stylish young ladies, and a yellow wool beret that covered only the top of her head. She also had painted lips.

At a certain point Carla looked at him and their eyes met. "Well, Reverend," she said. "I've never seen such a sound sleeper as you. I made a bunch of noise getting up and you didn't even stir. You were very tired, weren't you?"

He didn't reply. It would have been better if she hadn't used that ironic tone with him, if she hadn't laughed so brazenly every two or three words.

Giulia found what she was looking for in the box and came over to him with the needle and thread.

"It will be necessary for you to take your pants off," she said, with complete innocence.

Once again he felt seized with panic. "My pants?" he said.

Giulia did not understand. "I can't sew them if you have them on."

"Oh, no," he said. "I have no other pants to put on."

Carla looked at him and laughed.

Giulia was still a bit confused. "It's only to repair them," she said. "I'll finish in half an hour, and then you can put them back on."

"No, no," said the boy. "I can't take my pants off."

Carla came over to them with a serious face but the same bold manner as when she had laughed. She reached out her hands to the waistband of the pants.

"Strength, Reverend," she said.

He grabbed his belt so she wouldn't unbuckle it, all the while shaking his head no, and he wore such a desperate expression that Carla burst into a laugh.

But now Giulia understood, and she did not laugh. "Let him alone, Carla," she said sternly.

To the boy she said, "Come," and took him behind the blanket where her bed was. "Get undressed here," she said. "Then pass me your pants. I'll wait outside."

Carla kept laughing, almost hysterically.

"Don't laugh like that," Giulia said, pleadingly. "Don't you know it hurts him? He's not like us."

But Carla didn't stop laughing.

After a bit, he timidly extended his arm from the blanket, with the pants. Giulia took them and went to sit under a window to sew up the tear. She applied herself to her work with diligence, taking up the edges one thread at a time and sewing them together, so the mend would be as invisible as possible.

Meanwhile Carla was seated close to the brazier and addressed her words to the boy hiding behind the blanket.

"Hey, Reverend," she said, "you haven't told me, how are things in the seminary? It looks like they chased you away because you weren't sufficiently virtuous. It is true they chased you away, isn't it?"

The boy didn't reply, and Carla became more cheeky.

"Indeed, you should tell me how this business came about," she said. "I'm sure you'll entertain me. Tullio said you even know Latin, and also Greek, and that next year you'd be dressed in a cassock. It's really a shame that you didn't come away dressed in a cassock. Just think, we could go out on the street together, and everyone would take us for brother and sister, and I'd make a fine figure, with a priest for a brother. You'd go for walks with me, wouldn't you, Reverend?"

The boy didn't respond this time either, and she wasn't having enough fun this way, especially since she couldn't see his face. So she got up and went to draw back the blanket behind which the boy was hiding, and she suddenly began to laugh. He was there in his undershorts and undershirt, seated on Giulia's mattress, weeping. He made no effort to hide but continued to sit and weep.

She continued to stare at him, with an expression on her face that quickly became pained. Then she withdrew and went to get the cloak and put it over his shoulders, covering him completely so he would stop feeling ashamed. And she sat next to him on the mattress and put her arm around his neck, making him lean his head on her shoulder. Holding him close like this, she began to smooth his hair with her fingers, slowly.

He offered no resistance. Abandoning his head on her shoulder, he closed his eyes and wept even more than before, and no longer silently. Long sobs racked his whole body.

"Come on, that's enough crying now," she said. "I'm sorry I hurt your feelings. I was only kidding. You do understand, don't you, I only wanted to have a bit of fun?"

The boy nodded his head yes.

"So it seems I did a wicked thing, without thinking. I'm sorry."

He snuffled spasmodically. "It's nothing," he said.

"But you need to get stronger," said the girl. "You need to be strong to survive in this world. You'll see that a lot worse things than this will happen to you."

He remained leaning on her, but he was only half listening. He vaguely heard the sound of her voice and smelled her strong perfume, and everything seemed fine; the resentment and the pain he had held inside melted away. He kept his eyes closed, and tears continued to drop from his closed eyes. He didn't want to look at her. From his position he could only see her legs, and they were too exposed, since the skirt had slid up too high when she sat down. He preferred to keep his eyes closed and imagine her differently, and meanwhile he let his tears fall with a feeling of release.

Without speaking, the girl kissed his hair and then moved his head, holding it between her hands, and looked at him with compassion and tenderness. Then he opened his eyes to look at her, and she was beautiful. She had hair like Giulia's, but darker, and also darker eyes, and a round face. He gazed at her, so beautiful, and from time to time he saw her image as if in a mist, through the tears that formed in his eyes.

"Enough crying, now," she said. "Don't you forgive me?"

He had to snuff back another sob before speaking. "Yes, miss," he said.

"You don't have to say 'miss'," said the girl. "Say Carla."

"Yes, Carla," he said.

She flashed a quick smile. "There, that's better," she said. Then she took from her pocket a small handkerchief and dried the tears on his face and held the handkerchief under his nose.

"Blow," she said.

The boy blew his nose, feebly.

"Harder," she said.

The boy blew harder. "When I was little, my mamma ..." he said, then his mouth drew up in a smile and the tears came once more to his face, and finally he cried and laughed at the same time, shamelessly.

"Don't cry, don't cry, please," said the girl.

But he shook his head no, and when he could speak, he said, "My feelings aren't hurt, now. I'm glad to cry."

The girl let him cry, and at moments appeared on the point of crying herself. But then she straightened up suddenly and stood up. "Let's go close to the fire. It's too cold here."

She brought him with her close to the brazier and they sat down next to each other. The girl who was sewing by the window turned to look at them with a long, strange stare. Then she returned to her work, moving her small, ruined hands with concentration. She stayed with her head bent, her hair falling over her temples. It was chestnut hair, with lighter tints, that almost completely hid her face. But the part of her face that was visible had lost all hardness in the sweetness of her expression.

Carla did not speak. She had taken the boy's hand, placing it on her knee, and a bit playfully was touching his fingers one by one, as if playing with the hand of a little child.

Suddenly she asked, "What's your name?"

"Daniele," he said.

"Daniele," she said softly, and there was a kind of wistful wonder in her face, as with someone who is thinking of things that cannot be.

P laced on the floor, the gas burner puffed lightly with its flame. The pot of vegetables was boiling, and steam issued from the lid. Now they all sat together around the brazier. The layer of ashes on the coals had deepened and they felt less warmth. Carla often glanced at the little watch she wore on her wrist.

"What time is it?" Daniele asked.

"After four," said Carla.

The day outside had remained cloudy and the paper on the window was gray and not much light entered the room.

"Maybe it's time to go wake him up, Carla," said Giulia.

"Yes, I'll go now," said Carla, but she didn't move at all.

The burner lost pressure. Giulia got up to give a couple of pushes on the pump, then returned to sit down. The puffing of the flame filled the room then, and it was pleasant to hear it in the pauses between their words.

Then Carla looked again at her watch and got up. "I'll go wake him up," she said.

Daniele followed her with his gaze until she was gone.

The two stayed around the brazier. The flame of the burner fluttered, then restarted.

"It doesn't work very well," said Giulia.

Daniele turned his head with the intention of saying something, but then he didn't.

"It must be that the fittings are leaking," said Giulia. "Tullio has said that he will fix it when he has time."

"Yes," said Daniele this time. He was waiting for Carla to get back, and every so often he glanced toward the door, hoping to see her come through it.

Giulia made another attempt to break the silence. "How old are you?" she asked.

"Fifteen and a half," said Daniele. "And you?"

"Me? Thirteen and a half," said Giulia. "Almost fourteen."

"You're young," said Daniele.

She smiled but couldn't find any more to say, and then she got up and did not return to sit down again. She gave another push on the pump of the stove and set about preparing something to eat. She took from the chest a box of meat and some eggs, then took a skillet off the hook on the wall and carried everything to a table that stood against the wall. She opened the box of meat and broke the eggs and turned everything into the skillet. Then she began to mix. She made slow gestures, without thinking about them. Daniele watched her, and he also watched the door, to see if Carla would return. By now too much time had gone by.

Then Giulia took the pot from the stove, without turning it off, and prepared to pour out the vegetables. Then Daniele went to help her, and he picked up a can with many holes in it, that served to drain the vegetables.

Giulia smiled at him appreciatively. "Be careful not to scald yourself," she said.

She carefully poured the contents of the pot into it. The vegetables stayed inside the can with the holes and the water passed through into a receptacle below it. Dense, white steam rose up, filled with the smell of boiled vegetables.

"Shall I go and throw away the water?" asked Daniele.

"No," said Giulia. "It will be useful later, to wash the dishes."

Things were going better now between the two, as if they were already friends. Daniele followed her to the table, where she mixed the vegetables with the eggs and meat.

Then footsteps were heard at the door, and he turned his head to look. But it wasn't Carla. A little girl came in with a bucket in her hands, and as soon as she noticed Daniele, she stopped short and put the bucket on the ground.

"Oh, Maria," said Giulia.

The little girl did not reply. Her stare remained fixed on Daniele with an expression that seemed spellbound and a little dull, as well. She was wearing a dress like Giulia's, of a coarse, dark fabric.

Daniele tried to smile, but she did not change her expression.

Giulia intervened, giving her a caress on her face. "Don't be scared. He's our friend. Say good evening to him."

The little girl still did not speak and remained motionless. Then Giulia took her by the hand and led her to sit close to the fire. The bucket that the little girl had been carrying was full of embers. Giulia moved the ashes aside to make space, then dumped the embers out onto the fire. The little girl continued to stare.

"Don't mind her that she's so dopey," said Giulia, returning to the table.

"Is she a relative of yours?" asked Daniele.

"No, we found her the night of the bombardment. Then she stayed with us because she was all by herself."

"She really has no one?"

"I don't know. We don't know anything about her."

She had placed the skillet over the flame of the burner and continually stirred while the food cooked. Daniele stayed close by all the while.

"She's a child from this quarter," said Giulia. "But none of us remember having ever seen her, before the bombardment. We don't know if she was like this before."

The good smell of the food spread through the kitchen. Daniele had already felt hungry for some time.

"That night," said Giulia, "we saw right away she was a bit odd in her way of doing things. We thought maybe she had been affected by the bombs, and also because she said she had lost her relatives. We were hoping she would get better, later. Instead she seems always worse."

Daniele gave the little girl a sidelong glance. "Is she crazy?" he asked.

"No, she isn't crazy. She is only withdrawn like this, and she takes a long time to comprehend things. She always takes more time."

The food in the skillet was firming up as it cooked, and Giulia got ready to turn off the stove. "Move a little farther away," she said to Daniele.

Daniele took a couple of steps back and stayed to watch. Bit by bit she opened the valve and the flame slowly weakened and died. There was a sharp smell of gas.

"You have to pay attention when it goes out," she said. "It would run on fuel oil, but we can't find any, and so we run it on gas. You have to pay attention when it goes out, and also when it's lit. Once I caused a huge flame, and it almost caught my hair on fire."

Daniele said nothing. Now in the silence they could hear the voices and movements of Tullio and Carla in the other room.

Giulia set their places at the table and put the food all together in the middle. Then she called Carla, and Carla answered.

A bit later Tullio appeared. He wore an old and sweat-stained bicyclist's cap, with the visor all deformed and threadbare so that you saw the cardboard inside it. His clothing was of a heavy fabric, patched in various places. He looked around at everything with a quick and intense expression. He looked at Daniele and barely greeted him, then right away he sat down at his place. Giulia put a serving of omelet on his plate. Without waiting for the others, he began to eat.

The little girl left the brazier and came to take her place at the table, next to Tullio. Giulia turned a serving of omelet onto her plate also, but she did not start to eat.

"Did you take the grass to the rabbits?" Tullio asked her.

The little girl gave a shy look at Tullio, then answered, "Yes."

"Eat, Maria," said Giulia.

Then the little girl began to eat.

Daniele still waited.

"Sit down," said Giulia, indicating the place opposite Tullio. She gave

Daniele an equal serving of omelet and also a piece of bread, because Daniele was not taking one from the center of the table.

Carla arrived late and smiled at Daniele before sitting down near him.

"Where did you go to get the grass?" Tullio asked the little girl.

"Along the river," she answered.

"You must never forget to feed the rabbits."

"All right," said the little girl.

The light was so dim that they could only see each other's faces as pale smudges.

"When the New Year's holidays get here," said Tullio, "we will slaughter the rabbits, and then Giulia will make you a fur collar. You'll be warm with a fur collar."

"There is only a little grass, now," said the little girl.

Tullio did not reply. He had finished eating and was looking toward the window, where the paper had become brown. "The dark is coming earlier all the time," he said.

Daniele wanted to say something, but nothing came to mind. Besides, Tullio had spoken as if talking to himself, and certainly he didn't expect a reply from anyone. Still, he gazed toward the window.

Silently, Giulia stood up and gathered the plates and began to wash them on the floor under the window.

Suddenly Tullio turned to Daniele. "And you?" he asked. "Have you thought about where you're going?"

"No," said Daniele.

There was silence after that. Tullio took out his tobacco and rolled a cigarette. As he lit it, Daniele watched his face, and he didn't know what he might be thinking. But a bit later Tullio spoke, and there was irritation in his voice.

"So you have wasted a whole day for nothing," he said. "You're in the same situation as yesterday. You go out and they scoop you up and ship you off to the priests or to those relatives of yours."

Before Daniele could speak, Carla reached her arm under the table and took his hand and squeezed it. So he said nothing.

But Carla said clearly, "He could stay a few days with us."

Daniele anxiously anticipated the response.

But Tullio said, "Light the lamp, Carla."

Carla let go of Daniele's hand so she could get up. Before lighting the lamp, she attached some pieces of cardboard to the windows, so that inside the room it was completely dark for some moments.

"Do you have only the clothes you're wearing?" asked Tullio.

"Yes," said Daniele.

"You can't go outside dressed like that," said Tullio. "They would catch you right away. You need at least a street jacket."

"I had a street jacket, at school," said Daniele.

"Why didn't you bring it with you?"

"I couldn't," said Daniele. "They kept it in a closet, and so I couldn't get it."

Tullio muttered something incomprehensible, in a voice that sounded irritated.

Carla came to put the lamp on the table and sat down in her former place. The lamp consisted of a tin box with a wick that came out through a hole in the lid, and the flame was short and smoky. Their faces reflected the yellow color of the flame.

Giulia had finished washing the dishes, but she had gone to sit apart, near the brazier.

"And did you bring ration cards so you can eat?" asked Tullio.

"No."

"Ah," went Tullio, sarcastically.

"I couldn't bring them, because they keep them in Administration," said Daniele.

"Bet you haven't even thought about it."

"No. But even if I had I would not have been able to take them."

Tullio cursed. "What a messed-up way to do things," he said. "And how will you manage to eat, now?"

"I don't know," said Daniele.

"We can't go and ask for extra ration cards for you. They will want to know where you're from and why you're without them. There might be at least a ration card for bread. The rest can be found, one way or another."

There was a moment of silence.

Then Carla said, "We'll arrange for bread too, somehow."

Tullio looked at her a long moment, with a strange smile. "Does it matter so much to you that he stays here?"

Carla raised one shoulder instead of a reply. She took from a pocket a pack of cigarettes. "You smoke?"

"Oh, no, thanks," said Daniele.

She calmly lit a cigarette.

"You must be careful not to make stupid mistakes," Tullio said. "He's a bit behind on these things. He already seems to me to be a bit behind on everything. Hopefully he gets used to living this way, this one."

Then he turned to Giulia. "Are you content for him to stay with us?"

She hesitated and became confused, perhaps because she wasn't expecting that question. "It's all the same to me," she said quickly.

"Come here, Giulia," said Tullio.

She moved close to the table, and the candlelight made two great shadows under her eyes, lighting her face from below.

"Are you content for him to stay with us?" repeated Tullio.

Without looking at anyone, Giulia meekly replied, "Yes."

Tullio's face registered a quick smile. Then he turned his head toward Daniele. "Now then, you can stay with us for a few days."

Daniele seemed to hesitate. "Oh, I wouldn't want to be a bother."

Tullio got angry. "It's not a question of being a bother or not being a bother. You're used to hiding your thoughts behind words. But you have to change, if you stay with us. Do you or do you not want to stay?"

"Yes," said Daniele.

"All right," said Tullio, "then you'll stay until you're in a condition to leave. Naturally, if you want to leave earlier, you can do it whenever it seems best. You can leave at any time."

"Don't talk to him like this, Tullio," said Carla.

"You need to understand something well and immediately," Tullio said to Daniele, harshly. "It's understood that by staying here you'll work. You'll help Giulia with the housekeeping, and I'll have you keep the accounts. Are you able to keep accounts?"

"Yes."

"And you will have to adapt to this life. Maybe you're used to being a gentleman, but this is all we can give you."

"Oh, it's already too much," said Daniele.

Suddenly Tullio's voice changed. "It's not too much," he said. "There's not much to eat, and the house isn't a healthy place to live. It's too cold and damp, inside here. It would be better to live in a different house and have more to eat. But one must content oneself and think about people who are worse off than we are. So many can't find anything to eat every day, and they don't even have four damp walls where they can take shelter. Many are worse off than we are, even if it's not fair that some people might be either better off or worse off."

No one responded to his words, and there was silence. Giulia had returned to sit by the brazier. Carla lit another cigarette.

"Good," said Tullio after a bit, and he stood up.

"Are you going out?" asked Carla.

"Later," said Tullio. "Now it's necessary to go and get a mattress and some blankets for him. We can arrange a spot for him inside here."

"Oh, I can also sleep in the corridor," said Daniele.

"It's colder in the corridor," said Tullio. "Air gets in everywhere."

"It's nothing, even if air gets in," said Daniele.

"All right, as far as I'm concerned you can set yourself up where you want," said Tullio. "But now we have to get the things. It must be dark by now."

He and Daniele went out. Outside, the sky was overcast and the night was dark, as the moon had not yet risen above the clouds. Tullio went off to the left, and Daniele followed him, staying as close as possible so as not to lose him.

While they walked, Tullio began to talk in a low, steady voice.

"They say diseases can break out, staying in here with the dead," he said. "But we pay no attention to these stories. For that matter, we're here because no one knew where else to go, and also because this place is more comfortable and safer than any place else. If we don't let ourselves be seen moving around, no one comes to look for us. I'll bet that they know there are people inside here. There's us, and a couple of old ladies over by the church. But they don't come to look. It's enough to not let oneself be seen, and then no one comes."

"Is it necessary to stay inside the house all day?" asked Daniele.

"No, one can go as far as the house of the shoemaker, and from there go out to the street. At city hall, we all appear to be living in the house of the shoemaker, which is outside the zone. But there's no room for everyone at the shoemaker's house, so we've sent only the little one there. In the end, the important thing is that we appear to live there, because of the ration cards, and also because we're minors and not supposed to be on our own."

"Sure," said Daniele.

Tullio was speaking as if they were already friends, and it gave Daniele pleasure to find himself with Tullio and with a house to return to later. A house where Carla was, and Giulia.

Tullio stopped in front of a dark blotch that must have once been a house. "Wait here," he said, and disappeared.

A little later he came back with some blankets that he put in Daniele's arms. "It's stuff we gathered after the bombardment," he said. "There was a lot of it around in those days, and you could take it."

He went off again and when he returned he had a mattress on his shoulders. They started on the way home. Daniele walked more confidently now, with the pale blob of the mattress going ahead of him.

When they arrived at the house, Carla was not in the kitchen. The little girl was waiting, seated in her place. Giulia had moved the brazier into the middle of the room and was hanging a cord between the walls and one of the beams that held up the ceiling.

Turning to Tullio, she said, "We'll make a shelter with the blankets, and he'll sleep here. It's better than the corridor."

"Yes, it's better," said Tullio, without much interest.

He went to the corner where the jerry-cans were and chose one with a white cross painted on both sides. The little girl stood up, watching him pick up the canister.

"You come too," said Tullio to Daniele. "We're going to get drinking water."

They left with the little girl and walked straight ahead out of the door. It seemed to Daniele they were going along the path that he had seen when he woke up, in the direction of the magnolia tree.

"There aren't any barbed-wire barriers in this area," said Tullio. "The zone is sealed by the wall of a courtyard that's behind the shoemaker's house. But there's a hole in the wall and it's possible to go through."

Tullio went ahead, holding the little girl by the hand. They crossed the break in the wall and entered the courtyard.

"Do you want to see the rabbits?" said the little girl.

"They're sleeping now," said Tullio. "It's better to let them sleep."

"All right," said the little girl.

The shadow of the house was visible up ahead. Tullio knocked on the door, not too loudly, and right away the door opened. A tall, thin man with a bald head opened it.

They entered a room lit by a lamp similar to the one in Tullio's house. The room was fairly big but cluttered with a quantity of objects. In one corner, against the walls, was a double bed. A woman seated on a chest was warming herself near a kitchen range. The man and the woman eyed Daniele with curiosity.

"He's a friend," said Tullio. "He's staying with us for a while."

"I don't have to go and turn him in?" said the man. "I'm afraid they might say something, if I go and turn him in. Every time I go to renew the cards, I'm afraid they might say something." He spoke in a whining manner.

"You don't have to go turning him in," said Tullio. "No one needs to know he's with us."

The woman roused herself listlessly and began to undress the little girl.

Tullio went to the far end of the room where there was another door. "This is where we go out to the street," he said to Daniele.

Near the door stood two more jerry-cans, also marked with white crosses. Tullio left his and took a full one.

"These with the white crosses are used for drinking water," he said. "And the others without crosses are for wash water. We get wash water from the river. You and Giulia will go, tonight."

"All right," said Daniele.

"And if sometimes you get cold during the day," said Tullio, "you can come here to get warm. At our house we can't light a fire, otherwise those on the outside will see the smoke."

The little girl climbed up on the big bed and got under the blankets. Tullio and Daniele headed for the door to the courtyard to return home.

"Don't go to bed right away," Tullio said to the man. "I'll be coming through here to go outside."

"All right," said the man.

They went out and took the first few steps carefully until they became accustomed to the dark. The moon had not yet risen.

As soon as they passed the breach in the wall, Tullio stopped. He indicated toward the right, with a gesture Daniele could not see. "Your house was over there," he said.

"Yes," said Daniele.

"It's outside the zone," said Tullio. "Some day we'll go and look at it, when you can go out."

"Thank you."

"Some day we'll also go and get that clothing you left at school. It's yours, it belongs to you."

"Oh, it isn't important, those clothes. I don't want the priests to see me again. They would lock me inside, if I let them see me."

Tullio laughed, but not ironically. "I meant that we'll go without being seen," he said, and began to walk once more toward the house.

Daniele stayed by his side, because the path in that area was sufficiently wide.

"Tullio," he said suddenly, "were you serious when you said you were a communist?"

"Yes. Why?"

"No reason," said Daniele. But a few paces later he asked, "What does 'communist' mean?"

Tullio stopped to answer, and he put the jerry-can on the ground. His tone became heated, as if he were a priest about to preach.

"It means," he said, "that things are not good the way they are. Too much poverty around. And too many people still living well and not giving a damn about others. If some are suffering from hunger, we all should suffer hunger, and if there's something to eat it should be divided equally among everyone. It's not right that some are eating well and have nice clothes and houses, and the rest of us have nothing but suffering."

"No, this is not right," said Daniele.

"And yet there's no other way for us," said Tullio. "Because we are too poor. What we have is so little, that if someone gets something more, someone else goes without and must die, thanks to him. But even if we had much more, even if we were a rich society, we should divide it equally just the same, because that's the right idea. And this doesn't apply just to us, but to all the peoples of the world. There will come a day when all of us on earth are equal and like brothers, and bad and good will be the same for everyone. I don't know when this day will come, but it will come. Perhaps soon, even. Perhaps it will begin as soon as this war is over."

He picked up the jerry-can, and as he walked he said, "This is all I know to tell you, but it isn't everything, naturally. There are so many other things I don't know. When I go to the meetings to hear what they are saying, there are things I understand and things I don't. I haven't studied it, and when they talk theory and ideas I don't understand everything. But what I do understand is enough for me to believe it's the right way."

Arriving at the door of the house, Tullio halted again. "Some day," he said, "I'll take you to a meeting, if you want. You can understand more than I can."

"I don't know . . ." said Daniele.

When they were in the corridor, he put his free arm across Daniele's shoulders, and like that they walked into the kitchen.

Giulia had finished hanging the blankets, and Daniele's place was ready, with the mattress on the floor, and the blankets. There was also a pillow at the head, and the suitcase had been placed nearby. Tullio looked and seemed satisfied.

"The blankets are a bit mildewed," said Giulia.

"That will last just a few days and then it will go away," said Tullio. "For the rest, tonight he can sleep out there, if it makes him feel comfortable."

"No, no," said Daniele. "I'll be fine here."

"I'm going," Tullio said to Giulia then. "He'll help with the water."

"All right," said Giulia.

Tullio went over to her and smiled. "And don't be scared tonight," he said playfully.

Giulia lowered her gaze to the floor. "Oh, no," she said. "I'm not scared."

They listened to his footsteps as he left, and then there was only silence in the room where they were, and also outside, in the vast zone where the dead were buried beneath the ruins.

Only after some time did Giulia speak. "Now we'll go and get the water," she said.

"Yes," said Daniele.

Both of them felt a little self-conscious and avoided looking at each other. They were alone in the house.

"It isn't necessary to get water every evening," said Giulia. "Sometimes one can lasts two or three days. Do you have dirty things to launder?"

"No."

"Perhaps your shirt. It's white and gets dirty fast. If Carla brings soap, tomorrow I'll wash it for you."

She carried the lamp back to the table and began to cough. Perhaps a little smoke from the lamp had got into her throat, making her cough. It was a deep cough, that shook her whole body.

Daniele looked at her with concern, but he didn't know what to do. "You have a cough," he said when she quieted down.

She still had a red face and tears in her eyes, from the coughing fit. Nevertheless, she smiled. "I get this cough every year. Then it goes away in the summer."

Daniele didn't know what to say.

Giulia adjusted the little woolen shawl, closing it up higher with the safety pin, in such a way as to protect her throat as well. "Now let's go," she said. "We'll take two cans tonight."

She chose two jerry-cans without white crosses and passed a stick through loops of wire on their handles. They each took one end of the stick and went out into the open.

17

Outside it was cold, but a little less dark. Perhaps the moon was about to rise, beyond the clouds. They took a long street between the ruins.

"It's necessary to get water a little farther away, upstream," said Giulia. "To get it close by there's danger of contamination."

Daniele didn't say anything. He began to smell the odor of the river, like at his home.

The jerry-cans knocked together every so often and made noise. Suddenly Giulia stopped and moved them farther away from each other on the stick. "Now we're close," she said. "We mustn't make a noise."

Then, right away, they were at the river. It was a side stream, very narrow. They guessed at the current in the dark, and beyond, the outlines of some houses revealed themselves against a lighter sky.

"There are people there," said Giulia, gesturing toward the houses.

At that spot some steps, which at one time had served for doing laundry, led down to the water. They filled the jerry-cans, then stopped on the riverbank to rest a little while. The river flowed slowly, not making a sound.

"Giulia," Daniele asked suddenly, "where were the skyscrapers before?"

"There," said Giulia, indicating a place beyond the river.

Daniele stared far off into the night. "That's where my mother and father are," he said. "They died in the bombardment."

"I know. Tullio told me."

"Did your people die in the bombardment too?"

"No," said Giulia quickly. "My mother died before that, when I was eight."

And right away she went to put the stick through the loops on the jerry-cans. "Let's go home now," she said.

They walked along in silence. The brightness of the sky had increased, and they could see better the remains of the houses and the heaps of ruins. An immense silence weighed heavily upon those things, forcing one to think of the dead who lay beneath. Nevertheless, they walked on together.

They put the jerry-cans down in their place in the corner, and Giulia went to check Daniele's bed again.

"They smell of mildew," she said of the blankets. "Maybe it would be better if you slept out there, tonight."

"Oh, no," said Daniele. "Carla's out there. I don't want to bother her again."

"Carla's not there tonight."

"No?"

"No," she said, curtly.

He looked at her, but she stood with her eyes lowered and would say no more on the subject. Nevertheless, he had no desire to go and sleep out there.

"It's all right," he said. "I'll sleep here all the same. It's better for me to stay in my place, if this is my place."

"As you wish," said Giulia. "Maybe we can divide these smelly blankets equally. I'll trade two of mine for yours."

She was already moving to take up the blankets, but Daniele stopped her. "Don't do that," he said. "Don't do that, please. I'd rather go and sleep out there."

"All right," said Giulia, and she didn't take up the blankets.

She drew close to the lamp, and he watched her. Even with the light on her face, her features were too hard. And even so she didn't seem ugly, perhaps because of her hair, or her eyes, or a gentle, melancholy air she had.

"Giulia," he said, "do you think I'd do well to leave?"

She raised her head alertly. "Why?"

"Just because . . . It's hard to get food and I'm without any ration cards. I don't want to be a burden on all of you."

"You won't be a burden," said Giulia. "This is not something you need to worry yourself over." Her face furrowed a bit and she seemed about to say something important.

But then she simply asked, "Are you sleepy?"

"No. I slept late this morning."

"Let's sit down, then. I'm happy you're here. I was always alone, before, and I never had anyone to talk to."

They sat near the brazier. The lamp stayed on the table, and its faint light reached Giulia's face. But Daniele's face was in shadow.

"This way we can talk for a bit," said Giulia, as soon as they were seated.

Still, she said nothing more. Every so often she raised her eyes and gave a half-smile to show her happiness in being together and not feeling the solitude weigh on her as when she stayed alone in the house amid the immense silence. But she didn't speak.

"You have a nice house," said Daniele.

"Oh, it's all ruined."

"But one can see it must have been beautiful, before the bombardment."

"It wasn't ours," said Giulia. "We lived in another part of the quarter."

Now furrows reappeared on her face, as before when she seemed about to say something important. She resumed speaking, quickly, as if with a sudden resolve. "There were women in this house, women who sold themselves."

Daniele stared at her in amazement. "You mean, wicked women?"

"Yes."

Daniele glanced around the room and then again at Giulia. He seemed perturbed by the thought that previously there had been prostitutes in that house.

The furrows on Giulia's face deepened, and she seemed uncertain whether she should continue. Then she said, in a low voice, "My mamma was one of those who worked like the women who were in this house."

"No," said Daniele, dismayed.

"Yes," said Giulia. "And I don't even have a father. I don't know who my father was, no one knows."

Daniele pressed his lips together hard. "Why are you saying this? I didn't ask you. I don't want to know."

"You need to know," said Giulia, with urgency in her voice. "You need to know everything about us. Tullio's mother worked as a laundress for the soldiers, and his father was someone who went around repairing copper pots, a tinker. This was his occupation . . . when he felt like working. They both died the night of the bombardment. And Carla's father was in prison because he had stolen something. Then he escaped and now he's around, and still a thief and worse. And Carla's mother was a housemaid. Four years ago, she went to Naples, and we don't know anything more about her. Carla could write to find her, but she doesn't want to. Maybe it was her father who told her not to write. So we're all like this, me and Carla and Tullio. You need to know what kind of people we are."

Daniele had been listening with his head down, and he didn't speak during the pause.

Giulia's voice was both calm and bitter. "We were miserable before the war as well. You're different, instead. It's easy to see you're different. So you can leave, if it doesn't suit you to stay with people like us."

Then Daniele summoned the strength to look at her. "Do you want me to go away?"

"No," said Giulia. "Don't misunderstand. I'd be pleased if you stayed, but it isn't important what I think. I only said something to make you know what we are."

Daniele remained thoughtful. "Giulia," he said then, "I'm fortunate to meet good people like all of you."

Giulia tossed her head in amazement. "We are not good! We are what we are, neither good nor bad. We do both good things and bad things, as they happen. Since we aren't paying attention to see if what we do is good or bad, it's enough that things are working for us. But even if we did pay attention, it wouldn't matter, because it's different for us and for you. If you stayed with us, you'd realize that there are very ugly things among the things we do, and you might become ashamed to be with us, and so it would be better if you went away before that. It would be better for you, and also for us."

"Maybe I will go. But it won't be because of what you told me. I just don't want to be a burden."

Giulia's eyes lit up. "Only for that reason?"

"Yes, you must believe me."

"Then you can't leave," said Giulia anxiously. "Don't give any thought to the food. It is always possible to find the little bit needed to stay alive."

"But I'd like to work, at least," said Daniele. "I'd like to earn whatever all of you give me. Do you think I can help Tullio with something?"

"Tullio has said you will keep the accounts," said Giulia. "He always gets mad when he has to do the accounts. It's because he doesn't have the temperament to be steady."

"But that's not work," said Daniele. "Helping to clean isn't even work. I'd like to do something else. Do you think Tullio would let me do something else?"

"I don't know," said Giulia.

He hesitated a bit, then said, timidly, "I'd like so much to work for all of you, Giulia. I'd do anything, but I don't want to steal."

Giulia raised her eyes with a troubled look. "Did he tell you he steals?"

"He let me understand that."

"Well," said Giulia, "Tullio won't make you steal. If you don't want to, he won't make you."

"I'm happier that way," said Daniele.

They kept talking then, about nothing in particular.

But by now Giulia was tired. After a short while she stood up. "It's time to go to bed," she said. "Help me take the fire outside."

Together they dragged the brazier into the corridor.

"At night it's necessary to take it out," she said. "It causes headaches."

Returning to the kitchen, she carried the lamp into Daniele's corner and placed it on his suitcase. "So you can read, if you want. But don't leave it lit all night, so it doesn't smoke us all out."

"Oh, I don't want to read," said Daniele.

Giulia seemed as if searching for a topic of conversation. "Tullio said you've brought a lot of books in your suitcase. I'd like to read books."

Daniele smiled. "They aren't for reading, those books. They're books to study with. If I'd known, I've have brought something to read as well."

"Well, it doesn't matter," she said, but she didn't go away, although she seemed on the point of doing so. Lowering her voice, she added, "I wanted to tell you again how happy I am that you came here among us. I was so lonely before, but now we'll become friends."

"Certainly we'll become friends," said Daniele.

"Thanks," said Giulia, and suddenly she left the shelter to go to her bed.

He quickly removed his jacket and shoes and stretched out under the blankets that smelled somewhat of mildew. The kitchen now had a different odor, of good soap and clean hair, but not Carla's perfume. In the lamp the flame was low and smoky and gave little light. He listened to the quiet sounds that came from the corner of the room where Giulia was undressing.

Then he heard no more sounds, and asked, "Are you in bed, Giulia?"

"Yes."

"Then may I put out the lamp?"

"Yes, if you wish."

He blew out the lamp and it went completely dark, because the colorless light of the night could not penetrate the covered windows and the blankets and reach them. There was darkness and silence. There remained only a tiny ember on the wick and that slowly died, producing smoke and the sharp odor of burning diesel fuel.

Then Giulia coughed a little, perhaps only to be heard.

"Is this pillow you put on the bed, yours?" asked Daniele.

"Yes."

"Then I'll bring it back. I don't want you to be without a pillow on my account."

She replied belatedly, as if she was thinking it over. With a voice that was barely a breath she said, "No, don't bring it, please. I don't need it. I've got another one."

There was a long pause, then Giulia asked, "Do you say your prayers, before you go to sleep?"

"No. Why?"

"Just because."

"Does it upset you that I don't say my prayers?"

"I've never said my prayers."

"I used to say them," said Daniele. "Now it seems pointless."

"Yes."

Then there was another silence, but each of them knew the other wasn't sleeping.

Some time passed, then Daniele asked, "Is Carla coming back tomorrow?"

"Yes."

"Is she out with Tullio?"

"No."

Once more there was a moment of silence, so Daniele asked, "Can't you tell me why she's out?"

Giulia hesitated before responding, and then she said, "For work." And then she added hastily, "Let's go to sleep now." And once more her voice sounded weak and without breath.

18

The weather broke after a few days, because of the wind from the south that brought dense, dark clouds and dreary rain. People had to stay longer inside the houses, either in bed or around meager fires of dry twigs and leaves.

On the floors of the two rooms, Giulia placed basins and empty containers to collect the drops that fell from the ceiling in several places. The damp patches grew larger and darker, and the paper over the windows was gray all day, and the lamp had to be kept lit for many hours. The kitchen was always full of smoke and the odor of burning fuel.

Then the wind from the south stopped, and the fog arrived. It rose almost suddenly one evening, and it seemed it had been born in the river. People walking through the streets felt more alone in the sudden darkness, where things and other people appeared vaguely and disappeared quickly.

This lasted two weeks. The fog rose before sunset and gathered overnight and was slow to go away the following day. It clung to the houses, the belltowers, the trees, not letting the sun burn it off. And some days the sun was not able to burn it off at all and thus never shone on the city. Then, looking out from the height of the walls, you couldn't see anything, neither toward the sea nor the mountains, and the city seemed isolated in a mysterious world of white haze. Noises had a dull resonance that carried a long way, so that the military trucks could be heard along the peripheral road and also the trains that ran across the plain, toward the war.

Then it got colder, and the people were afraid it would snow. The wind now came, instead, from the east and liberated the sky and the horizon. It happened a little after Christmas. From the walls could be seen the mountains that seemed suddenly close, and they were blue at the base and white with snow on the heights. The sun stayed out all day but gave little heat, because its warmth was blown away by the east wind. Still, people were happier for that, and in the afternoon they began to go behind the houses to take the sun.

When the weather was serene like this, you could hold out a greater hope of making it through that winter. Then spring would come.

But every day, many were lost on the journey through winter. It happened especially to the old people and the babies. They became weaker and frightfully thin, and then some illness or other carried them off. No one considered treating them, because there weren't enough medicines. Even with enough medicines, there was little that could be done. These could have been any ailments at all, which many times didn't even have a name.

Whoever died did not leave a great void. People seemed resigned to the idea of death. Sooner or later they would all be dead, so people said. Those seen going to the cemetery were only those who had passed on.

19

Giulia was having a bad day. She had no desire to talk and stayed with her eyes closed and her head leaning back against the wall. She wrapped herself tightly under the blankets, even though it wasn't very cold, there in the sun and sheltered from the wind.

It was their spot for taking the sun, along the side of the house where people outside could not see them. In front were ruins and remnants of houses, all inside the zone of the dead. Far off they could see the roof of the church of Sant' Agnese, where the zone ended.

Daniele held his book closed on his knees, and he turned frequently to Giulia, until he no longer saw her opening her eyes. Then he asked, "Don't you feel well?"

"Just a little headache," she said. But by the way she opened her eyes, he knew she was not well. She had not brought something to sew that day.

"It's better to go inside," said Daniele. "The sun isn't good for you, if you have a headache."

"It doesn't matter," said Giulia, and closed her eyes again.

Daniele tried to read for a while, and then he realized nothing was staying in his head. It was always like this. Before, in school, when he had thought of running away, he imagined he would work all day and study in the evening until midnight. He had felt an extraordinary energy then. Now, instead, he never had any desire to study. Keeping the accounts for Tullio and helping Giulia were simple jobs that required little time, and he could have studied, if he had had the desire. But he didn't have the desire, and meanwhile the sun shone marvelously on Giulia's hair, and ahead the ruins extended to the church of Sant' Agnese, alternating light and dark under the sun. And the great church was as it had been at one time, as he had seen it from the windows of his house so many times. It was missing only the belltower on the side.

At a certain point Giulia got to her feet. "I'm going in."

And even though Daniele was ready to get up, she still said, "No, stay here, please."

She went off with small steps. Her legs showed below the blanket, still slim like those of a child.

Daniele became lost in thought, gazing at the ruins in the sunlight. The winter sun had a weak warmth that stunned you a bit. And he remained inert in that state, without feeling regret for the hours wasted. The days followed one after the other, and it was as if he were passing time, as if he had nothing else to do with his life. He had not spoken with Tullio again about leaving, even though he might go away one day. It was so strange to live in that place, together with Giulia and Carla and Tullio and the little Maria, all of them so different from himself, and different also from every other person he had ever lived with before.

The sound of footsteps reached him, of someone who was entering the house, and it had to be Carla. She was the only one who walked that way, confidently and heavily. She always knew what she had to do. Tullio, as well, knew what he had to do, but walked without a sound.

Carla entered the house and went into her room, just to look at herself in the mirror. She closely checked her mouth, her eyes, her hair. Her hairdo was a bit messy, but it looked all right that way.

Then she went into the kitchen. The two windows were open, and the sun entered with two matching stripes on the floor, and Daniele wasn't there. Sitting on a stool was Giulia, who wasn't doing anything. Carla looked into her pallid and exhausted face, with darker circles under her eyes.

"Again?" she asked.

Giulia nodded.

"What a lovely nuisance," said Carla. "It seemed to me it wasn't that time yet."

"Maybe I'll go to bed," said Giulia.

Carla's lips were heavily painted, as always when she went out. She was standing near the brazier, where the coals were so covered in ashes that they gave out almost no heat. A fine dust floated in the sun's stripes. On the walls and ceiling the large damp stains and cracks were clearly visible, and also the paint that was peeling almost everywhere. The sunlight contrasted with the squalor of all the things that were dying.

"A lovely nuisance," Carla said again. After a long pause she asked, "And Daniele?"

"He's outside," said Giulia. "In the sun."

Carla seemed to be thinking something over, indifferent to everything and to Giulia. Then she lit a cigarette and moved without haste toward the door.

"Maybe I'll go to bed, Carla," said Giulia.

Carla went outside without answering. She went in search of Daniele. She saw him and smiled so she would appear glad.

She didn't want to take the spot left vacant by Giulia. "Make me a little space next to you," she said.

He moved aside to let her sit down, and she sat next to him in silence. Her dress had slid too high above her knees, but she paid no attention to such things. She had an odd way of doing certain things, in a manner that bothered him. Nothing mattered except to sit down and either comb her hair or tie her shoes. Yet she didn't do those things the way Giulia did, for example.

With Giulia, he wasn't even aware when she did those things. But with Carla there was, instead, always something coarse, which stirred his blood and then made him feel shameful and disgusted with himself, at times. It was not a good thing to feel that agitation around Carla. Carla was Tullio's girl, he knew that. So it didn't matter what else she might be.

The cigarette that Carla was smoking had a sweetish odor of

molasses in the tobacco. Thinking about that, he kept his eyes fixed on the cigarette, and on her fingers, which were a little yellow at the tips with nicotine.

Carla noticed him. She drew forth the pack of cigarettes and put it into his hands. "Have a smoke."

He shook his head no. But he still held the pack in his hands and studied it, first one side, then the other. The two sides were the same, with a red circle and words printed in black. He tried to read the words "Lucky Strike" aloud.

Carla gave a little laugh. "That's not how it's said It's pronounced, *Laki Straik*."

"*Laki Straik*," said Daniele. "What does it mean?"

"Don't know," said Carla. "I don't remember anymore. One day it was explained to me by one of those American boys. Then I forgot."

"Can you speak English also?"

"A few words. Just enough to understand." Then she fell silent.

He kept searching for some other topic and didn't find one. "What are the Americans like?" he asked, finally.

"Ah, well," said Carla, "one can't describe them in two words."

"For me, they aren't bad," said Daniele. "They helped me out a lot, that night that I ran away from school. They had me get into the truck, and they gave me coffee and candy, and even gloves, without my even asking for anything."

"Sometimes they're good," said Carla, "and sometimes they're bad, you never know. It's hard to understand people who aren't like us."

The cigarette had burned down to the end and she tossed the butt away among the debris. She did not continue talking. She was restless and withdrawn now, as if turning a thought over in her mind.

"When I was at school the first year," said Daniele, "I was twelve years old, and many times I got up at night, myself and another boy, and went to smoke in secret. I never experienced any pleasure smoking."

"No," said Carla, vaguely.

"I only liked it because it was forbidden," said Daniele. "I'll bet they would have thrown us out if they had caught us smoking. Since then I haven't tried it."

"It's good for you, smoking," said Carla. "It helps you get by."

She took another cigarette and lit it. She had a cigarette lighter like Tullio's, just a bit smaller. She drew the first breaths hurriedly, nervously. Daniele also had stopped talking.

Suddenly Carla called softly, "Daniele?"

He raised his head and waited with his eyes on her face, and he saw that she had changed. Her eyes were darker now, and her face glowed. She fastened her gaze on him with an intensity that made him ill at ease, due to a warmth that was spreading over his body, just beneath his skin.

He suddenly had a desire to go, to return to Giulia. "Let's go in," he said hastily. "It's getting cold staying out here."

"Wait," said Carla, without taking her eyes off him. She moved closer and took him by the shoulders. "Lean your head over here," she said.

Even her voice had changed. It was low and trembled a little. "I'll show you how to smoke."

He found himself with his head resting on her legs and felt uncomfortable in that position. The book had fallen to the ground, and he thought for a second about gathering it up, and then he forgot about it. He heard Carla's watch ticking near his ear.

She smiled, with her head inclined toward him. "Scared?"

He too tried to smile, but only made a grimace with his mouth.

"Don't be afraid," she said. "I'm not going to do anything to you. I'm just going to teach you how to smoke."

Slowly she lowered the hand that held the cigarette to Daniele's mouth.

He saw the end of it, stained with red, coming toward his lips, and he felt Carla's fingers pressing on his face. He inhaled and pushed her hand away and blew the smoke out.

"No, not like that," said Carla. "When you have the smoke in your mouth you must take a breath and send it down into your lungs, or it's no good."

"It burns."

"No, it doesn't," said Carla, and she laughed loudly. "Watch how I do it."

She drew in a big mouthful of smoke and opened her mouth so Daniele could see.

He saw the smoke go down her throat and right afterward it came out her mouth and also her nose, and in the meantime Carla's face lowered ever closer to his, and he watched it, spellbound. He only closed his eyes when Carla's mouth was so close to his as to touch. He felt her mouth, soft and sweet, tasting of smoke.

Carla kissed him with a kind of slow desire. She lingered on his lips, and Daniele was docile and inert, and she didn't want him to be like that, so she began to squeeze and bite, and he allowed her to do it.

But then, suddenly, he pressed his lips together tightly and jumped to his feet with a jolt. He was red-faced and breathing heavily, and he looked at her with loathing and fear.

"What's wrong?" said Carla. "Why are you looking at me like that?"

"Why are we doing this?" he said. "I don't want it – I don't."

Carla pressed her lips together in anger. "Is it because of Giulia that you don't?"

Daniel's expression didn't change, as if he had not heard her. He took a step back. "I don't want this," he said again, and ran toward the door of the house.

Carla watched him go. Her face was still flushed and her eyes were dark, and she was biting her lip. Then the signs of passion faded and sadness took its place, and then her face changed once more, and her features became hard and fixed.

Daniele had stopped at the entrance to the kitchen. He was afraid to enter, because Giulia must certainly be aware. Perhaps it would be better to return outside and possibly go to the shoemaker's house and spend some time with little Maria.

But Giulia had heard him come in. She called from inside.

He went forward into the room but he didn't see Giulia.

"I'm over here," she said from her shelter.

"In bed?"

"Yes," said Giulia. "But it's nothing, you know. I only felt tired and now I'm better, staying in bed."

Daniele stood motionless in the middle of the room. He didn't want her to see him.

But Giulia said, "Draw the blankets aside a bit. I want to see the sunlight."

He made the blankets slide aside on the cord that held them. Giulia looked only at the stripes of sunlight on the floor. One had become slender but the other, from the west window, was wider and longer. "I like to see the sunlight."

"Yes," said Daniele.

Giulia was so calm, and maybe she had not been aware of anything. "Sit down here," she said.

He sat on the mattress, staring in front of him at the narrow stripe of sunlight.

"Turn this way," she said.

He turned and immediately saw that she already knew. But she didn't say anything. She only studied his face and and then drew a handkerchief from beneath the pillow and, extending an arm, she wiped his mouth. Daniele lowered his head and once more stared at the stripe of sunlight. Giulia put the handkerchief back under the pillow without even looking at the lipstick stains. She let her arm fall on top of the blankets.

Time passed without either one speaking or moving. Then she moved her arm again and touched him on the shoulder. "Daniele?"

Daniele spoke without turning. "I'm sorry, I never thought I could do such a thing."

"It doesn't matter, you know," said Giulia. But in spite of her efforts, this was something sad.

"Did you hear what we were saying?" asked Daniele.

"I imagined it," Giulia said vaguely.

After a long pause he said, "Maybe it's better for me to go, Giulia."

"Why?"

"I don't know. I feel so guilty."

"It's not your fault. I know that it's not your fault."

"Yes, it is definitely my fault," said Daniele. "Tullio will be angry, when he gets to find out."

"No, he won't get mad," said Giulia. "Not with you, anyway. And anyway, you don't have to tell him. It's not an important thing."

"It's not a nice thing," said Daniele.

"But it isn't important," said Giulia. "Don't get it in your head to go away because of this. Tullio won't say anything, I'm certain of it."

Perhaps she wanted to say more, but she fell silent, because she heard Carla's step in the corridor.

Carla came in and went straight to them. She was holding Daniele's book in her hand. "Here, I brought your book back."

He took it but neither spoke nor raised his head.

Then Carla placed a hand on his hair and smiled in a mocking sort of way. "He's still hurt, poor baby." To Giulia she said, "He told you what happened, right? A girl kissed him! *Actually kissed*, you understand."

Giulia turned red at her mocking tone. "Let him alone, Carla. You should be ashamed."

"Does he interest *you*?" asked Carla.

"Let him alone," Giulia said again. "Do you really need him for anything?"

Carla looked sharply at her and quit laughing, but her face remained hard and mean. "I do understand, you know," she said. "I've known for some time."

"No," said Giulia. "What have you known?"

But Carla lifted her shoulders and did not reply. She moved away from them, stopping near the brazier.

"It's cold again," she said, casually.

The other two hoped that now she would leave. Instead she sat down and began to shift the embers with an iron rod. She did this lazily, as if teasing, to make the others understand that she wasn't about to leave. Daniele remained in the same position. The stripe of sunlight in front of him had vanished, and the other one had turned almost red.

"Giulia," Carla said after a while, "as far as I'm concerned, you can take him, you know. You could even take him right away, if you didn't have *that* thing. What a pity that *that* should have happened to you just now, this would be the right moment."

Giulia said nothing.

"You should explain to him what you have," Carla said. "He's all worried, over there. I'll bet that he has no idea what this development is."

Giulia didn't speak even now.

"You want me to explain it to him?" asked Carla.

"Carla, quit it," said Giulia. "Don't be like that. I swear to you that nothing you're thinking is true. Don't speak about such things."

"Why?" said Carla. "These things happen to all women. Even those who are good as angels. The first times it hurts a little, but it isn't necessary to be a whiner like you. With me it started when I was littler than you, and I never spent a day in bed. You want people to coddle you, that's why you go to bed. You never tried to coddle her, did you, Daniele?"

"Enough, Carla," shouted Giulia.

But Carla had no intention of stopping. She began to explain what Giulia had and to enjoy Daniele's confusion.

He listened to her for a bit and then no longer wanted to listen and turned toward Giulia. Giulia was hidden with the blankets over her head. He touched her and felt her go stiff and he guessed she was crying.

"Don't keep on, Carla," he said. "You've made her cry."

"It's for you she's crying," said Carla. "Don't you understand that it's for you she's crying?"

"God, how wicked you are," said Daniele.

Then Carla stood up, looking directly into his eyes. "We're all wicked in one way or another," she said. "Even *you* must realize how wicked you are." And right away she left the kitchen.

A little time passed, during which Daniele didn't know what to do. Giulia remained with her head under the blankets and didn't move. The stripe of sunlight on the floor turned pale pink and then disappeared. He got up and went to close the windows.

Then he returned to sit down on the mattress. "Giulia," he called softly.

She didn't reply. Daniele called to her again, and she still didn't reply. Then he uncovered her face but she hid her eyes with one arm, like a child who feels ashamed.

"It makes no difference, Giulia," he said.

She was so weak and wretched that he felt compassion for her and also a great tenderness, which he had never experienced before. He took her arm and moved it aside, uncovering her eyes. Then he put a hand on her forehead. "You have a fever, too," he said. "Is there any medicine to take for this thing?"

Tears flowed from Giulia's eyes, trembling a bit on the lids before trickling down her cheeks.

"Is it true that you're crying over me, because I'm such an idiot?" asked Daniele.

She signaled no with her head. "Now you'll never be able to look at me without thinking of that," she said, "of all the ugly things that are inside me."

"That's not true," said Daniele. Still, he wasn't entirely convinced.

The room was rapidly getting dark. He stood up and attached the cardboard to the windows and lit the lantern on the table. Then he cut up some greens and put them in a pot with some water.

Giulia watched him and was no longer unhappy. He smiled at her from time to time. In this way they were able to forget all those ugly things.

He lit the burner and the sound of the flame filled the kitchen and reached the other room. Then Carla came in with a serious, almost sullen, face. She set to work at the table, preparing something to eat. Daniele stayed near her. Her hands moved surely and quickly, and two or three times she sniffled, and it could have appeared that she had been crying in the time she had stayed outside.

20

They went through the shoemaker's house to get out to the street, and they headed for the main avenue. They walked side by side at a brisk pace, with their hands in their pockets. Tullio had turned up the collar of his jacket and his ears were hidden under his old cap. He had nothing over his clothes, as he did not own an overcoat. Daniele as well was without his cloak. Tullio had made him put on a big, collared bicyclist's sweater and an old jacket that was too big. His pants and scarf were still the dark ones of the school.

Above the street, the narrow strip of sky between the houses appeared, the bright azure of early evening.

On the main street they had already lit the streetlights. They were screened, placed a great distance apart, and they gave off little light. You saw few people about at this hour, almost all soldiers and girls. The soldiers wore good-quality woolen greatcoats, and they walked together with the girls. By the doorway of a popular cinema, a group of people waited, pressed against the wall. They were waiting to go in, since inside it wasn't as cold.

Daniele and Tullio walked toward the station. Before leaving the city wall, Tullio cut to the left through a narrow alley, now filled with shadow. After a few steps he stopped before a darkened door.

"Is this it?" asked Daniele.

"No," said Tullio.

He pushed the spring-door open with his foot and they went in. The place was vast and smoky, poorly lit by two oil lamps attached to the ceiling. There was a strong odor of wine and smoke. Some girls were seated at a long table, together with a few soldiers. The table was cluttered with bottles and glasses and packs of cigarettes. Four men from the town were playing cards around a small table beneath a lamp.

One of the girls watched, spellbound, as they entered, and another greeted Tullio loudly, with an unnatural-sounding voice. Tullio gave her a wave but went straight to the counter that was at the far end of the room. Above the counter hung another oil lamp, larger than the other two. The man behind the counter greeted Tullio like a friend.

Tullio gave him a wink. "*Caffè.*"

"Two?" asked the man, watching Daniele.

"Yes."

The man left through a small door in the end of the room. Behind the counter there were shelves, almost empty, and high up was a round clock that read eight o'clock, but perhaps it had stopped.

The girl who had greeted Tullio got up from the table, bringing with her a soldier. Passing close to them she gave Tullio a slap on the back.

Tullio turned. "Hey, kid, how are you?"

"Fine," said the girl, laughing. She was beautiful and her eyes were bright. Then she went through the small door, leading the soldier by the hand. The soldier was laughing and his eyes were bright also.

The man came back with two cups on a tray. Tullio handed one to Daniele. "Toss that down. It helps against the cold."

Daniele hesitated, smelling the pungent odor of *grappa*. The cup was full to the brim. But when he saw Tullio knock back his *grappa* in one gulp, he forced himself to drink, taking two or three swallows. The alcohol burned in his throat and sent a shiver down his back.

Tullio offered some money, but the man stopped his hand. "Another time."

Tullio put the money back in his pocket and took out tobacco to make a cigarette.

Daniele turned to look around the room. The girls were making a din, talking and laughing with the soldiers. One was around Carla's age; the others were older. They must have been drunk. At the door three more soldiers entered. A young boy accompanied them. He brought them to sit down at the long table, and then he left.

"Why don't you send me that girl anymore?" said the man behind the counter. "She could be making good money now."

"When she wants to come, she knows the way," said Tullio.

"Oh," went the man, "I only said it for her sake. She could make good money."

Tullio didn't reply. He had finished rolling his cigarette, and now he lit it.

"Let's go," he said to Daniele.

They went into the alley and turned onto the main avenue. Closer to the station, the houses still standing were even fewer, and along the edges of the street there were mostly rubble and walls with empty space behind them. Even the monumental portal of San Sebastiano had crumbled and they had removed the ruins so cars could pass through.

Daniele had been on that street two months before, the time he got lost in the quarter and found Tullio. Now Tullio walked by his side, with a thoughtful and serious face. The cigarette that he had lit when leaving the dive had gone out, but he kept it between his lips, in a corner of his mouth. It gave Daniele a feeling of security to accompany him, because Tullio was so sure of himself in everything he had to do. Daniele adjusted the scarf higher on his neck. The *grappa* wasn't helping much against the cold, it only burned in his stomach.

In the square of the station, cargo trucks crossed paths with a great racket. They were going toward the war, or else returning from it, and their headlamps illuminated the dust suspended in the air.

The sky had grown dark in the meantime, but a trace of sunset could still be seen in the west.

They walked along the side of the street, close to the overpass. Many people had gone to live under the overpass after the bombardment, and you could hear their voices mingling with the roar of the cargo trucks.

Some fires had been lit in various places, with the people sitting around them to get warm.

Guards at the railroad crossing said nothing as they watched them pass. A little farther on, Tullio stopped and relit the butt of his cigarette. "We're almost there."

Still, they had a long way to go. They abandoned the grand avenue, heading farther into the suburb. The streets were deserted and dark, as they lacked streetlights.

Gradually the city ended. The houses became fewer, and the fields frequently reached almost to the edges of the road.

Twilight had vanished. In the sky was a multitude of stars. The wind from the east was not very strong, but just enough to maintain a steady temperature.

Then they began to walk alongside a high wall on their left.

"They live in here," said Tullio. "It was a military warehouse, and the Germans set it on fire before they went away."

They passed into the enclosure through a large gap where the wall had been knocked out. They could make out the silhouettes of storage bays, lined up in rows. Even here, people were talking loudly and there were scattered fires. Inside some of the roofless bays, against walls blackened with smoke, people had constructed hovels with blankets and sheets of tin and tables. The odor of the old conflagration still lingered, different from the smell of the fires.

Tullio called at the door of one of the shacks, and a woman's voice answered from inside. Then they entered. In the middle was a kind of large stove, made from a gasoline drum, glowing red. On a chest an oil lamp had been lit. The rest of the surroundings remained in shadow. A woman and a girl were seated near the stove.

The girl, seeing Tullio, stood up, looking happy. She must have been eighteen and was unattractive, with tightly curled hair.

"Andrea's not here?" asked Tullio.

"I'll call him for you right away," said the girl. She left through the door and began to shout loudly for Andrea.

"Sit down, boys," said the woman. She must have been quite heavy at one time, but now the skin on her face was slack and full of wrinkles.

They sat down on some stools around the stove. The heat was strong on the fronts of their bodies, but their backs felt the cold that penetrated the walls. The shack was square and not very large. Daniele took off his scarf. His face began to sweat, due to the sudden warmth after the cold outside.

The girl came back in. "He's coming now," she said and remained standing to stare at Daniele with open curiosity. "Is he a new one?" she asked.

"Almost," said Tullio.

The girl kept staring at Daniele, and he became a bit embarrassed.

Shortly Andrea came in. He was a good-looking boy, with an important demeanor, even elegant, although he was dressed in rags. He had black hair, left a bit rumpled on top.

"Greetings, chief," he said.

"Greetings," returned Tullio.

"Antonio hasn't brought the bicycles yet," said Andrea.

Tullio looked at his watch. "It's still early. Let's wait a bit."

"Meantime there's the one with the trailer," said Andrea.

"Yes, I know," said Tullio.

"I put a different tarpaulin on the back," said Andrea. "The one we had before, you couldn't pull it forward."

"Care should be taken with the tires," said Tullio. "It's always hard to find tires."

Andrea began to study Daniele with interest. "Is he that new one?"

"Yes."

"Young," observed Andrea.

"He'll turn sixteen in May."

"He seems younger," said Andrea. Then he took a seat. "Will it be a long job?"

"No," said Tullio. "Most of it is traveling on the road."

The girl remained standing and continued to stare at Daniele in a way that made him uneasy.

Tullio noticed this and laughed, instead of rescuing him.

"Can you play cards?" she asked.

"No," said Daniel.

"Pity," said the girl. "I can teach you if you want."

Tullio laughed but came to Daniele's rescue. "Here," he said to the girl. "I'll play a hand with you. What will we play for?"

"I don't know," said the girl. "My blouse, if it's all right with you. I don't have anything else."

They moved the lamp onto the chest and began to play with a pack of dirty, worn-out cards. Every so often Tullio reached a hand toward the girl and pinched her in a certain place on her body. Then she laughed without embarrassment, and even a bit stupidly.

The woman remained seated, almost immobile, with her huge legs in the posture of one accustomed to idleness. She appeared not to be interested in anything.

"Is it true that you were once in the priests' college?" asked Andrea.

"Yes," said Daniele.

"Was it all right?"

"So-so."

"Until I was seven I thought of becoming a priest," said Andrea. "Then I changed my mind."

The girl lost her hand, and Tullio joked a little about the fact of the blouse.

"Let's do a return game," said the girl.

"What will we play for?" asked Tullio.

"Well, we'll see."

They took up playing again and she lost a second hand.

"I'll heat some coffee for you," she said. She was free and easy in spite of being unattractive, and she had a pleasant voice. She got up to put a small pot on the stove.

"How are you finding it here?" Tullio asked the woman.

"It's inconvenient because of the water," said the woman. "There's enough wood, but it's inconvenient because of the water. You have to go more than a mile to find water."

"Patience," said Tullio. "You can't have everything."

"But at least they could decide to fix the aqueduct," said the woman. "I've heard that they need to repair it."

"In ten years, maybe," said Andrea.

"I don't know," said the woman. "Before, people were saying that with the Americans things would go better. Everyone said so." She spoke as if Tullio were somehow at fault because they were without water.

"People have to know how to help themselves," Tullio said. "Above all, people have to know how to help themselves."

"Yes, but what's a person to do? We have nothing."

Tullio shrugged. "I wasn't talking about you here. I was speaking of all of us."

The small pot on the stove began to murmur with a low sound. The girl lifted the cover of the chest and took out some military-type aluminum mugs. She passed coffee to everyone. They drank noisily, because the edges of the mugs were scalding. The coffee was bitter and aromatic.

"Will you pass by here, on your way back?" asked the girl.

"Yes," said Tullio.

"Meanwhile Antonio is nowhere to be seen," said Andrea.

"He wasn't sure if he could come," said Tullio. "I'll wait a little longer, but he wasn't sure."

Her coffee finished, the woman got up lazily. "I'm going to bed," she said. She peeled off her dress while standing near the stove, then went to lie down on a pallet. There were three pallets on the floor, along the walls.

"It's always this way," said Andrea, bitterly.

"There's not enough to eat to keep a person on their feet," said the woman.

"She doesn't do anything all day," said Andrea. "She can sleep twenty hours at a stretch."

"Stuff it!" said the girl. "It's the best she can do."

They remained for some time in silence. The small pot stayed on the stove and burbled loudly.

"Don't you even know how to play *briscola*?" asked the girl.

"No," said Daniele.

"I'll bet that you would like to have her blouse," went Tullio.

"If only," said the girl, with a silly smirk on her face.

From time to time, the woman turned over on her pallet, and she scratched her body so hard that the sound could be heard.

"She must be full of lice," said Andrea. "We'll end up getting them too."

"You're too bothered by lice," said the girl.

Already Tullio had checked his watch two or three times. "Antonio isn't coming, by now."

"What will we do, then?" asked Andrea.

"He and I will go with the trailer," said Tullio. "This time, you'll stay home. It's no big deal."

"All right, it's better this way," said Andrea.

"Don't you want a little coffee?" asked the girl.

"After, when we get back," said Tullio. "Now we could use a blanket. It gets cold sitting still on the trailer."

The girl took a blanket from one of the pallets.

"Are there lice?" Tullio asked.

"I hope not!" said the girl. "When will you be back?"

"Between two and three, if all goes well," said Tullio.

"I'll keep the fire burning," said the girl.

They went out together with Andrea. The bicycle with the trailer was right outside, leaning against the wall of the warehouse. Tullio turned on a flashlight and bent to inspect the tires. He pressed each one with his thumb, to check if they were inflated.

"They're in order, relax," said Andrea.

"Are there tools and parts?" asked Tullio.

Andrea touched a pouch behind the saddle. "All here."

He turned toward the way out, and Tullio pushed the bicycle with his hands on the handlebars.

"Chief?" said Andrea.

"What is it?"

"Nothing," said Andrea. "Just that if you won't need anything when you get back, I'm going to sleep somewhere else."

"With that girl again?"

"Another one," said Andrea.

"You waste too much time with girls."

"She lives near us," said Andrea. "She arrived three days ago, I couldn't help seeing her. Her name is Astra. I never heard a name like that before."

Tullio laughed.

"It's because of the cold," said Andrea. "One stays warmer, sleeping together. She's also of our way of thinking."

"All right," said Tullio. "If some order or other comes I'll let your sister know."

"Agreed," said Andrea, and he immediately left them to return inside.

They went on foot as far as the street. Then Daniele got up on the trailer and covered himself well with the scarf and blanket and put on woolen gloves. Tullio mounted the saddle and they left. He didn't have gloves, but the grips on the handlebars were covered with two rabbit skins. The trailer bounced over the potholes, because the street was bad. Daniele clung to the sides of the trailer while seated on the bed. Ahead of him he could see Tullio's back, and the sky full of stars.

"What do you think of that girl?" Tullio asked.

"She doesn't even seem like his sister."

"Because she's so ugly?" said Tullio, laughing. "But she's a clever girl, you know. Maybe in fact just *because* she is so ugly."

"She likes to play cards," said Daniele.

"In these times it's an unfortunate thing for a girl to be ugly," said Tullio. "The other ones always manage, more or less."

They continued on for a piece in silence, then Tullio said, "Andrea wastes too much time with girls. He's always going in search of a new one, and so he wastes too much time. But apart from this, he's a good team player, and when there's work to do, he does it. It's hard to find one with his courage."

They were traveling along a country road that was not flanked by trees and had continual curves, so that Daniele couldn't tell the direction in which they were going. His feet were getting cold, as well as his hands and his nose. His nose felt colder perhaps than the rest of him. Tullio continued to pedal strongly and no longer spoke for a while.

"Aren't we going by the big road?" asked Daniele.

"No," said Tullio. "There could be patrols on the big road. This way we're going the long way around, but it's safe."

They had not encountered anyone yet on that road.

"Are you cold?" Tullio asked suddenly.

"A little," said Daniele.

Tullio stopped the bicycle. "Now you try, pedal hard. You'll see, it warms you up fast."

He took his place on the trailer and Daniele got onto the saddle. "Should I stay on this road?"

"Yes," said Tullio. "And if you meet with people, keep going straight ahead."

Daniele was completely numb with cold, but it was hard work pulling the trailer, and after a bit he warmed up. His nose was the last to warm up, because the air stung his face, but eventually it also got warm.

The countryside was deserted and cold and silent. Rarely did the road pass by any houses; in any case, the houses were closed up and dark, although it wasn't very late. Sometimes a dog barked in the barnyard of a farmhouse, and the boys heard it for a while afterwards, as they rode through the night.

They continued this way for perhaps two hours, changing places every few miles. Twice Tullio detoured through narrower streets, wanting to avoid groups of houses. But as they pushed on, the houses became more frequent, and it was impossible to avoid them.

Daniele, who was on the trailer, recognized places as he looked around. "Tullio, now we're close."

"Yes, almost there," said Tullio.

"Oh, we passed through here so many times when they took us on outings," said Daniele.

"Yes, but don't talk, Daniele," said Tullio.

He proceeded for a brief distance, then turned to the right onto a new street that was worse and narrower than the other one. Soon they were once more in the open countryside. Then a row of poplars rose out of the night, and there they stopped and lowered the bicycle into a dry ditch at the side of the road.

"Remember that the bicycle is here, at the tenth poplar," said Tullio.

Daniele looked up at the leafless tree that reached toward the stars. "All right."

"If some complication should come up," said Tullio, "cut yourself loose without worrying about me, and come here. Then wait half an hour, and if in half an hour I don't come back, go back to Andrea's house. He will tell you what you must do."

"Do you think something will happen?" asked Daniele.

"No," said Tullio, "I'm saying this just to say it. Everything will go well, for sure."

They were crossing a plowed field. The ground was uneven and rough with frost, and they felt it rise and drop abruptly beneath their feet. Two or three times Daniele turned to look at the row of poplars and fix the direction in his mind. At the end of the field he turned again, but the poplars had already disappeared in the darkness.

They passed another dry ditch. Tullio went ahead, following the edge of the ditch, until the outline of a long structure appeared. Then he stopped. "This that we're seeing, it must be the storage building?"

"It looks like it, but I'm not sure," said Daniele.

They continued forward for a bit, then stopped again. Now the outline of the building was more distinct, and they could see also the outlines of the church and, farther away, the main building of the school, which was taller than its wings.

"Yes, it's the storage building," Daniele said.

"All right," said Tullio, "take me to where the courtyard is." His voice was low and steady, as usual.

Daniele guided him across a field, in another direction. They followed the wall of a two-story building. Then the building came to an end, and a surrounding wall began.

"It's here," said Daniele.

Tullio studied the wall to find a place that would be easy to get over. "Let's take off our shoes. It goes better without shoes."

They removed their shoes and left them at the base of the wall.

"Now I'll get up on your shoulders and go over," said Tullio.

He climbed onto Daniele's shoulders and easily reached the top of the wall. Beyond it he could see a large courtyard with some trees and, at the back, the main building, with three stories. All the windows were dark.

"Come on," said Tullio to Daniele below. He reached down to help Daniele up, and both of them let themselves down on the inside. "Now you go ahead, since you know the way."

Daniele turned to the right, very close to the two-story structure that they had followed on the outside. They passed under the arch of the portico into another, smaller courtyard. They heard a cargo truck pass by far off, on the main road. But there inside all was quiet, nor did they make any sound with their bare feet.

Daniele stopped at the beginning of an exterior staircase. "The storage is above, up there."

At the top of the staircase was a closed door.

"You're sure there's no one inside?" asked Tullio. Now he was speaking in barely a whisper.

"It was just an old man, before," said Daniele. "He slept at the back of the first unit to the left."

Tullio began to feel around in the lock with a tool, and he moved his hand slowly. Daniele's feet were freezing and he shivered. He breathed with his mouth open. Another cargo truck passed by on the main road, and when its sound had faded, the lock gave way.

Tullio opened the door barely a crack and then closed it again. "There's a light on inside."

"No," said Daniele.

"Yes, right here over the door."

Then Daniele remembered. "It's the lamp, the lamp of the Madonna."

"Damn, you didn't tell me there was this lamp."

Daniele said nothing. He hoped in his heart that now they might turn back, because of that light.

Instead, Tullio opened the door again and listened. "Come on," he said, and went in first, and as soon as they were inside he pushed on the door, leaving it ajar.

The lamp of the Madonna cast a faint, rosy glow. In front of them they saw the dark passageway that led to the second unit. The storage area was partitioned into four big rooms, one after the other, with a passageway between.

"Wait for me here," said Tullio.

Daniele saw him disappear into the second big room. He stayed with his back to the wall, in the shadow made by the shelf that supported the lamp. The air in the room was warm, but he continued to shiver. Nevertheless, he was no longer scared, now that he was inside. Tullio knew what he was doing, and there was no need to be afraid.

The school bell tolled once. It might be one o'clock, or maybe one-thirty, or even twelve-thirty. The school clock struck also on the half hour, so one could never be sure. A pot of water on a stove made a light sound, like a hiss. His feet began to warm up, standing on the wooden floor.

Tullio came back. "Let's go, there's no one over there."

They walked straight down the passageway. Each time the floor squeaked under their feet, they stopped to listen. Passing the second big room, Tullio turned on the flashlight and ran its beam over the walls. "Quick, let's find your things."

"It's right here to the right," said Daniele. "Number forty-five."

The walls of the unit were completely filled to the ceiling with shelves and cupboards, covered by curtains. They found cupboard 45, but inside it were the belongings of someone else, not Daniele's.

Daniele felt mortified. "We came here for nothing. I should have thought of this before."

"Never mind," said Tullio. "Hold the flashlight and give me some light."

As soon as his hands were free, Tullio drew out a sack that he had kept under his jacket and began to fill it with things from the cupboard. He did this calmly, taking care to select the items. He often paused, motionless, to listen. Daniele followed him to give him light.

"You'll see that something among this stuff will be suitable for you, too," said Tullio.

Little by little the sack filled with garments of all kinds, underwear and clothing. Tullio climbed up to the ceiling to search for what he wanted. And when the sack was almost full, he handed it to Daniele and took the flashlight.

"I'm going to take a look in the fourth unit," he said.

But in the fourth unit there was nothing to take. He opened two huge armoires, and they were full of priests' robes and vestments for the church. It was beautiful stuff, silk, with embroidery and designs and colored stones, but he would not have known what to do with it.

He returned to Daniele. "Want to go?"

"If you want."

"You're not scared?"

"No," replied Daniele.

Tullio turned off the flashlight and hoisted the sack onto his shoulders. They went now toward the glow of the lamp, and it seemed like a great distance, walking in that manner. They heard once again the light whistling of the pot on the stove. In the first unit it was warmer than in the others. It seemed that outside there was greater light and cold air, good to breathe.

Tullio pulled the door closed, and they descended the stairs and went off toward the place where they had entered. "We could go and see if we can find something to eat, do you want to?" asked Tullio.

"No, I don't want to," said Daniele.

Tullio laughed and turned to talk to him. Then he realized Daniele was concealing something white under his jacket.

"What do you have there under your jacket?" he asked.

"Sheets."

"Ah," said Tullio, as if displeased. And after a few steps he said, "Hide them better. At night white can be seen a long way."

They scaled the wall once more and put their shoes back on.

"Put those sheets of yours into the sack," said Tullio. "Didn't you really have anything else to steal?"

Daniele put the sheets in the sack and didn't reply. The clock struck the hour again as they walked along the dry ditch. There were many strokes in sequence. Daniele forgot to count them, but it must have been midnight. A bit later, the clock in the town also struck the hour, and Daniele counted the strokes. It was midnight. They came to the plowed field.

"Tullio," said Daniele, "I didn't take the sheets for myself. I can make do with less. But they're for Giulia. When that ailment comes to her she must stay in bed for two or three days, and then it's good that she should have a pair of sheets."

Tullio pulled ahead without speaking.

"Do you think what I did was really stealing?" asked Daniele.

"It depends how you look at it," said Tullio.

They arrived at the tenth poplar and pulled the bicycle out of the ditch and loaded the sack onto the trailer.

"I think . . ." Daniele began, "I think that they have many sheets, more than are necessary. We, instead, are without and Giulia needs sheets and deserves them. Everyone in the world should have what they deserve."

Tullio laughed. Daniele had assumed that preaching tone that he himself adopted whenever he spoke of these things.

"It's fair, like this, right?" asked Daniele.

"Now I'll have to go find a set of sheets for Carla too, somewhere," said Tullio, and he sounded happy.

They moved fast along the whole stretch of road in the neighborhood of the houses, and it felt better, now, to sit on the trailer on top of the soft sack. Then Tullio yielded his place on the saddle to Daniele and they proceeded at a more leisurely speed.

The frozen countryside slumbered under the stars. The trees that grew closer to the road appeared bare and ghostly. All the rest was indistinct in the darkness.

"Now you'll have a suit of town clothes and you can go out," said Tullio. "Don't go around the city too much at first. It's better that you go along the walls or along the river."

"All right," said Daniele.

They covered a long stretch of road in silence, and then Tullio said,

"Well, I wanted to say one thing to you. Now, as the season goes on, the days will get more pleasant and longer. So then when you go out, take Giulia with you. She is not in very good health, you know, and she's always closed up in the house and it's not good for her. You should take her with you, to walk in the air and the sunshine."

"All right."

"But you must do it in such a way that she doesn't understand that you're going just for that reason. You should find some excuse to take her outdoors. I think she'll come with you willingly."

"All right."

They spoke no more about that for the rest of the way.

When they knocked on the door of the shack, the girl came to open it. "Did it go alright?" she asked.

"Yes," said Tullio.

The woman turned over on her pallet because of the noise and began to scratch herself.

The girl took the small pan of coffee and set it to warm up on the stove. They all sat together around it.

"You were fast," said the girl. She had her only blouse and a blanket over her shoulders, but she did not take care to cover herself in front. Part of her breast could be seen through the neckline of the blouse. Daniele had the impression that she was exposing herself on purpose.

"Now we should find a suit for him," said Tullio, indicating Daniele.

"Where?" asked the girl.

"In the sack. There are different things like that."

The girl untied the mouth of the sack and began to pull things out of it.

"Wait," said Tullio, "let's have some coffee first."

The coffee was hot and strong, but no longer aromatic like before, because it had boiled too long on the stove.

Then the girl emptied the sack and put all the suits in one pile. One by one she held them up to Daniele and made him try on the various jackets that might fit him. She was very hurried in doing this, even though her manner was too intimate. Tullio in the meantime busied himself with the other goods and separated them into piles according to type.

Finally the girl selected the jacket that fit Daniele best. It was of a heavy fabric, the color of hazelnut. "Do you want to try the pants too?" she asked.

"No, no," said Daniele. "It's good enough if they're more or less my length."

Then they checked the articles separated into various piles, and Daniele noted down everything in a notebook.

"You'll make a pile of money with just this stuff," said Tullio to the girl, "leaving out the sheets and suit for him. You'll tell Andrea to send the sheets and the suit to my house. The rest goes to the usual place."

"All right," said the girl.

"Now we can go," Tullio said to Daniele.

"You don't want more coffee?" asked the girl.

"No," said Tullio.

They were ready to leave.

"Stay until day comes," said the girl. "You can sleep here, one in my bed and one in Andrea's bed. It's easier to travel by day."

"Oh, we can travel alright," said Tullio, moving toward the door.

The girl went to him and put a hand on his shoulder. "You really don't want to stay?" she asked. There was a tone of genuine disappointment in her voice.

Tullio gave her a quick caress on her face. "That's for another time," he said. "We've worked hard tonight."

The girl stood in the doorway of the shack. Even when they had already disappeared into the dark, she still stood in the doorway. It was cold, and she felt sad. Then she went back in and closed the door and lay down on her pallet, although she was sure she would not be able to sleep.

Outside, they went thoughtfully through the cold night, with their hands deep in their pockets and the collars of their jackets turned up. Farther on Tullio took another street, different from the one by which they had come.

"Now we need to make a damn detour to cross the railroad," he said. "We can't go right under the noses of the guards."

He was in a bad mood, and Daniele thought it was because of the detour they had to make. "We could have stayed at Andrea's house," Daniele said.

"Did you want to stay there?"

"It was all the same to me," said Daniele.

"But would it have suited you if we had?"

"What?" asked Daniele.

"Never mind," said Tullio, and he kept walking, deep in thought and dropping the conversation.

When Daniele awoke, the ceiling was illuminated by a lot of light, with the cracks and the damp patches standing out clearly. He searched for the figures that were usually there, a house and a head with hair like Giulia's and a man on a horse. A slight weariness remained in his head, but he didn't have a headache. Turning, he saw on his suitcase his new suit and the sheets. It must have been late, and yet he didn't hear any sounds in the kitchen. But he couldn't tell if Giulia was still sleeping.

"Giulia?" he called.

Then she moved. She was wearing her clogs. "You're awake?"

"What time is it?"

"It's past three o'clock."

"And is Tullio still sleeping?"

"No, he went out before noon. He had some business to do with the stuff that he brought in."

"I'm embarrassed to have slept so long," said Daniele. He glanced again at the ceiling, and he felt lighthearted, without thoughts.

Giulia continued to move around, making a lot of noise with her clogs. Then she appeared with a cup of coffee in her hand.

He sat up abruptly. "There's some beautiful sunshine outside, don't you think?"

"Yes. It doesn't even seem like winter."

"There were so many stars last night," said Daniele. "So I was thinking that today would be a beautiful day. And I was thinking, too, that we might take a walk on the wall, the two of us. Now I have a new outfit."

Giulia smiled because he was so carefree. "It's already too late today."

"Tomorrow, then."

"All right, tomorrow," said Giulia.

She waited until he had finished drinking, then left with the cup. But as soon as she was gone, Daniele called her back. And when she returned, he was holding in his hands a pair of sheets, rather bashfully.

"I brought these for you," he said.

"For me?"

"I thought . . ." said Daniele, "I thought that if it happened that you needed to stay in bed some day, then you'd be better off with sheets. Aren't you pleased?"

"Oh," Giulia said, hesitating, "I'm afraid that you'll be sorry for stealing these things."

Daniele's lips tightened in a painful thought. "Because I stole? Well, I'm not sorry for stealing."

Giulia's expression changed. "Then I'm pleased, really pleased."

She took the sheets and held them tight to her chest and with the fingers of one hand she stroked them gently, and perhaps she didn't even know she was stroking them like that. She stayed that way for some time and seemed undecided whether to say something or not.

At last she said, "I was very scared last night, until you came back."

"Did you hear me come back?" asked Daniele.

Giulia nodded and smiled.

"I'm sorry," said Daniele. "I tried to go softly so as not to wake you."

"It was because I had yet to fall asleep," said Giulia. She paused, unconsciously stroking the sheets.

Then she said again, "You know, it was the first time you went out, so I was a bit scared. I'm used to it with Tullio but with you it's different."

Daniele's heart began to thud in his chest, and he lacked the breath to say much. He only said "Thanks," and lowered his eyes to the blanket, and his eyes were laughing, even with the confusion he felt inside. He had not felt so happy as at that moment, for a long time. It was an inexplicable happiness, and the sheets did not have much to do with it. He was not certain what had caused such happiness.

22

I t came about that the ragged people, who had at first confined
themselves to the streets and squares of their quarter, gradually
invaded the whole city. At every hour of the day, the main street and
the squares of the city hall and the cathedral were now full of these
ragged ones. It wasn't clear what they were there to do, since there was
nothing to gain by being in those places. One could neither buy or sell
in those places, and the few stores that remained open displayed goods
that were useless to them and cost too much. And yet they remained
established in those places, and it seemed they preferred to be there
than in any other place in the city. They wandered idly back and forth,
and when it was sunny, many of them sat on the ground, leaning with
their backs against the walls, to soak up the warmth the sun gave to
the stones. They interested themselves a bit in what went on around
them, and they discussed it endlessly.

It could have been that they felt less ill at ease in those places where
the hotels and the shops were now not so elegant, and where ruins were
visible along the sides of the streets every few steps, like in their own
streets and squares.

Or else it might have happened that, increasing in numbers and
poverty, they felt braver, lords of everything, and so were emboldened

to take over the principal areas of the city. Perhaps this was actually the reason, and it explained also their stubbornness in frequenting those places. They wanted to show off the misery of their rags and malnourished bodies in the very places where at one time they had not dared to show themselves because they would have been chased off. It seemed there was some moral force in them. It seemed that something might come out of that effort, in time.

And so, all day long the ragged population lingered in those places, and only towards evening did they go home.

Then a strange change would take place among the people on the main street.

Many of the new arrivals were similarly clad in rags, but they were less dirty, and they obviously felt anxious to keep up appearances despite their poverty. They appeared to cling very much to a kind of decorum, because they had not been impoverished previously, and they intended for everyone to understand that. They had been well off. They had worked all their lives, or their fathers or grandfathers had worked all their lives, to accumulate money sufficient to live decently and comfortably. The money had gone, with the war. If they had any on hand, it was almost worthless and they had fallen into poverty, not having known what to do. Perhaps there was nothing they could have done to remedy the state of things. Perhaps, even if it had been possible to do something, they would not have been capable of doing it. So they found themselves at the same level with the destitute, were it not for better hygiene and decorum, and the different hour when they went out onto the main street.

In this second group were also the new rich, people who, with the coming of the war, had become suddenly enriched by either profiteering or stealing. Although money wasn't worth much, these had millions and were continually making more, so that their women and their daughters could make their appearance on the avenue at the fashionable hour, with furs and jewels and curious hairdos. They were not terribly clean, but that didn't matter, compared with the others.

It was strange to see, promenading together along the avenue, those people, among whom such a rapid transfer of riches had taken place. The new rich and the new poor. A thing you couldn't even know how to judge.

23

They had to go and find an old man outside the San Tommaso gate, Tullio had said, and he had shaved his beard and polished his shoes. He had buffed them hard with a rag, but the shoes had not improved much, being too old. He carried a small basket made of willow twigs, covered with newspaper.

The day was not cold, although the sun was veiled in a bright haze.

"I'm not comfortable with these visits," said Tullio. "You have to say a lot of pointless stuff, and I'm not comfortable with it. I don't get why people have to say some things just to talk. When there's nothing to say a person should shut up."

Daniele didn't say anything.

"This is why I'm having you come too," said Tullio. "I hope you'll help me get through it. You're used to dealing with people like this old man, and you'll have to say all those pointless, silly nothings."

Daniele laughed. "You don't have a very high opinion of me."

Tullio laughed too. "Hey, it's all right that way. This is really one of those silly nothings."

"You'll see," Daniele said. "I'll stand there, pinned, and I won't be able to utter one word."

"He's a strange bird for an old man," said Tullio. "He was a schoolmaster for I don't know how many years, then they pensioned him, even before the war broke out. And now he's in poverty. I'll bet one month's pension isn't enough for him to eat for one week."

They arrived at the main street and went along the opposite side of the street, where it was sunny and there were lots of people. Daniele felt ashamed of his brown suit, which looked too new.

"I don't know how he manages to live, this old man," Tullio continued. "Maybe it's the people he's taken into his house who help him. He must have let out or sold the house and kept just one room. But he's as proud as if he lived in a palace."

They passed the city hall square and Tullio followed the main street instead of going toward San Tommaso. Perhaps he did not want to arrive at the old man's house too early. It was barely three in the afternoon.

"What makes one feel compassion for those people," Tullio went on, "is that they haven't been used to hardship. The old man was alright, before. He had a son who practiced law."

"And he's dead?"

Tullio got distracted looking into the display window of a store and he did not reply right away. Then he started walking again.

"Maybe he's not dead," he said. "I don't know what might have happened to him, but he must not be dead. He was in Croatia when they signed the armistice, then nothing more was known about him, at least so they're saying around town. But the old man must know where he ended up. I know that they wanted to give him an indemnity for this son, and that he didn't want it, and there sure must be some reason he didn't want the money."

Tullio was now stopped in front of a window full of ceramics, and he gazed thoughtfully at the things on display, and spoke equally thoughtfully.

"In my opinion, he went over to the partisans," he said. "And the old man knows it. He's one of those would let himself be killed rather than change his mind."

There was no reason why Tullio should stop in front of a window full of ceramics. But suddenly he asked, "What would you give to a girl who was turning fifteen?"

"Me? Nothing," said Daniele. "I have no money."

"But if you *had* money, what would you give her?"

"I don't know. A book, maybe."

"Why a book?" Tullio asked, and laughed. "What do you think Carla would do with a book?"

"Ah, it's Carla. I didn't think it would be her."

They resumed strolling and passed beneath the porticoes on the shady side, where there were fewer people. They sauntered along casually.

"Well, what would you give Carla for a gift?" asked Tullio.

Daniele had been thinking about it during all that time. "You could give her a bottle of perfume."

"No, not perfume," said Tullio. "She would use it up too soon and nothing would be left. It must be something she would always use, so she would remember that I gave it to her. And she would also remember for a long time."

Daniele did not reply. The pavement of the portico was made of irregular flagstones and while walking he tried not to step on the cracks between the stones. In a certain way, that meant he had something on his mind. Even his lips were pressed tightly together, as whenever he was thinking about something.

All of sudden he asked, "Tullio, do you love Carla a lot?"

Tullio looked directly at him and realized something was worrying him. "Do *you* love her?"

"Me?" went Daniele, and at once embarrassment appeared on his face. "Yes, I love her," he said. "And also Giulia, as if they were my sisters." Now he seemed even more preoccupied in avoiding the cracks between the stones. "But with you it's something different, isn't it?" he asked.

"Yes."

"And you must love her a lot in that way, right? And she must love you very much too, isn't that so?"

"Yes," said Tullio, thinking something over. He knew that something wasn't going well with Daniele. Something was bothering him regarding Carla, he could see.

So he said, again, "Things between me and Carla are not exactly what you think, Daniele. In the beginning, maybe, it was different, when we began and we loved each other. But events happened afterward that ruined everything. It isn't all our fault that those events happened. More than anything else we have been unlucky. But we stay together all the same, even if it's not great to be together in this way. We try to help each other out as good friends. Carla has done a lot for me."

Daniel didn't talk about what was troubling him inside but remained thoughtful. They walked along casually, going toward the cathedral square. Before arriving at the end of the street, Tullio turned around to go back. "Well," he said. "We haven't decided what to give Carla."

Daniele immediately stopped paying attention to the cracks between the stones.

"You could give her a powder compact," he said. "They gave my mother one too, when she was married. She always carried it in her purse. It was beautiful, made of silver."

"That will cost too much, silver," said Tullio. But a bit later he asked, "Where do they sell them?"

"At the jeweler's, if you want a silver one," said Daniele. "If not, the perfumer's, or even in a fashion shop."

They began to watch the shop windows, and right away Daniele found a compact on display in a perfumer's shop. It was round, of some bright metal, and cost a lot of money. Tullio decided not to buy it because it cost too much. And while they were standing still in front of the window, a patrolman passed behind them and continued on a bit, then turned around and came to a halt near the door of the shop.

Daniele wasn't even aware of the patrolman, but Tullio quickly said, "Let's go."

"You're not buying it?" asked Daniele, and then he saw the patrolman and he stood rooted to the spot in fear. The patrolman was staring directly at him.

"Let's go, Daniele," said Tullio, urgently.

Then he was able to move and he followed Tullio. As soon as they came to a side street, they left the main street, pressing on into the San Tommaso quarter.

Daniele was still upset. "I was scared, Tullio," he said. "Did you see how that patrolman was looking at me? He was looking as if he recognized my suit."

Tullio spat on the ground. "I'd give anything to be able to bust the nose of one of those bastards," he said.

"Now I'm afraid to go around the streets," said Daniele. "That one knew about my suit for sure."

"It wasn't because of the suit," said Tullio. "He's a pig, that's all. Maybe he thought we wanted to rob the store. They're pigs that get their kicks by breaking people's balls."

"Maybe they do that so they can eat," said Daniele. "If they didn't do that, they would get rid of them, and then they wouldn't know how to get food."

"Yes," said Tullio, "but too many of them are pigs. And they always take the side of the owners."

They were crossing the quarter of San Tommaso, through narrow, filthy streets. People were occupying the places where the sun beat down.

The San Tommaso quarter had been lucky during the war. The houses were still standing, with the exception of two places near the walls, where they had been knocked down by the bombs. Nevertheless, misery had invaded here all the same, and the homeless had constructed their hovels wherever there was a little space.

It was Tullio who spotted the children. A group of children was gathered in the corner of a courtyard and they all stood bending over something on the ground, something that could not be seen.

Only one of the children noticed the boys who were approaching. He was at the edge of the group, and he was unable to see what was going on in the middle. He looked with amazement at Daniele, and then Tullio, and wasn't scared. He was small and dirty and poorly dressed.

"She's making kittens," he announced importantly.

All the other children were paying attention to the cat. One of them, who was the owner of the cat, was very energetic and pushed against the others, trying to hold them back. The cat was peacefully giving birth to kittens in a cardboard box.

"Seed where it came out?" asked one little boy.

"From its behind," said the owner of the cat, "but you can't see it very well."

Another little boy said, seriously, "If they're in her stomach, you know where they're coming out."

A little girl, who was older than all the boys, lifted her head, laughing, and so she saw Tullio and Daniele. She suddenly got all red in the face and turned very serious.

"Ick, look what she's eating," said a little boy in disgust.

One by one the children noticed Tullio and Daniele and became embarrassed and quiet. Finally they all hushed up. The little girl who had laughed retreated a little from the group.

"How many are there?" asked Tullio.

"Four, for now," said the owner of the cat.

"She hasn't finished yet?" asked Tullio. He asked the question with a smile and a cheerful tone of voice, so the children wouldn't feel so embarrassed.

"At first it seemed she finished, and instead she just had another," said the owner of the cat.

Another little boy plucked up his courage. "It would be better if she kept having them," he said. "Then we'll eat them, when they get big."

"But they also have to eat, so they *can* get big," said Tullio. "What will you give them to eat?"

"The mother cat takes care of the milk," said the little boy.

Tullio chuckled a little. The cat was so emaciated that she would soon die of hunger, if no one found anything for her to eat.

"Be careful that no one steals them," he said.

"Oh, no," said the owner of the cat. "I'll have them sleep with me."

Tullio distributed some money to the children before leaving.

Going out of the courtyard they noticed again the little girl who knew how kittens were born and who had laughed. She had kept herself apart, seated on the ground in a sunny spot. She was six or seven years old, with black hair cut short.

Tullio went up to her and smiled. "Want to walk with me to the gate?"

Without a word the little girl stood up and went off with them. She was barefoot and wore only a dirty dress.

"Don't you have anything else to put on?" asked Tullio.

The little girl repeatedly shook her head "no."

"Not even a blanket?"

"It's not very cold today."

"No, it's not very cold," said Tullio. "What have you eaten today?"

"Porridge," said the child.

"Porridge only?"

"Yes."

"And yesterday?"

This time the little girl did not answer. She suddenly stood still and lowered her eyes to the ground in annoyance. Clearly she would not come any farther. She was so skinny that her bones poked out everywhere, but at the same time her belly was swollen. Even under the dress one could observe her swollen belly.

Tullio rummaged in the basket and handed her two eggs. "These are for you," he said. "How many are at home?"

The child accepted the eggs without raising her eyes.

"How many are at home?" asked Tullio again.

"Three."

"Three others?"

"No, two," said the little girl.

Tullio gave her two more eggs. "One for each of the other two," he said.

The child raised her eyes at last and looked at Daniele instead of at Tullio. Daniele was well dressed and made a big impression on her. Her eyes were too big in her lean face and had an expression of dullness and fear.

"Do you know a boy named Ernesto?" asked Tullio.

"No," said the child.

"He's right close to the church. He has red hair."

"Then I know him."

"Well, go to him. Tell him that Tullio is sending you. Remember the name well—Tullio."

"Tullio," echoed the little girl.

They left her in the middle of the street, holding the eggs in both hands against her swollen belly.

"They have swollen bellies because they're starving," said Tullio, and then they spoke no more, not even after they had passed through the gate.

T hey took an avenue to the left, lined on both sides with two-story cottages with gardens in front. The old man lived almost at the end of the avenue. The garden gate was open and they entered. In one corner grew some evergreen bushes, and in all the rest, only frostbitten weeds.

"Be careful you don't say anything that might make him remember his son," said Tullio, before knocking on the door. There was also an electric doorbell, but the houses had no electricity.

A woman, wearing a clean dressing gown and with her hair done up in a large knot, came to the door. "What do you want?" she asked. She had opened only one side of the door and stood there suspiciously, ready to close it again if necessary.

Tullio held the basket out in front of him. "I've come to find the schoolteacher."

Then the woman recognized him and opened the door wider. "There are certain kinds of people about," she said.

It seemed that inside the house it was colder than outdoors, and it had a not-so-good odor, from some unknown source.

"Please do go up," said the woman. "You already know which room is his."

They mounted the stairs and the woman remained below to wait while Tullio knocked at the old man's door.

The old man let them in, and he seemed happy they had come. He had huge slippers on his feet, and on his head a black hat, ridiculously without a brim, that reached down to his ears. Otherwise he was dressed as if to go out, in his cravat and street coat.

Tullio removed his own cap as he entered the room and stuffed it in a pocket of his jacket. "I've brought a friend," he said. "His name is Daniele."

The old man studied Daniele at a short distance. "Where do you come from?" he asked.

"From home," said Daniele. "I'm at his house."

"He didn't know where to go and we've taken him in with us," said Tullio. "Before, he was at school, he was studying."

"What classes have you taken?"

"I've started the fifth term of high school."

"And you aren't going on?"

Daniele glanced at Tullio before replying. "I ran away from the school three months ago. I couldn't stay there any longer."

The old man sat down in a high-backed armchair upholstered with wine-colored fabric. He said nothing more on the subject of school. Daniele waited, but he said nothing and seemed preoccupied.

He was a lot different than what Daniele had imagined. This man was small in stature, almost scrawny, very thin with age, and the tendons stood out under the skin of his neck when he lifted his head. But now he held his head down, and it seemed as if he had forgotten them.

Suddenly he shook himself. "Be seated, boys."

Tullio showed him the basket. "I've brought you something."

Daniele was afraid of that moment. From the time they had entered, the old man must have seen the willow basket, yet he acted as if he had not seen it. And now that Tullio had spoken, the old man fixed his gaze on him.

"Thanks," he said, and smiled painfully.

Daniele prayed that Tullio would not do something wrong that might increase the awkwardness of the situation.

Tullio began to lift things out of the basket, putting them down on the top of a chest. The old man was no longer watching.

"This time of year is a bad one for eggs," said Tullio, without turning, "but as time goes on there will again be plenty. Spring only needs to come, and then right away there will be plenty of eggs. It will be a big help for everyone."

The old man said nothing while Tullio paused. Daniele had gone to stand near the bed, and he did not dare to sit down, although he wanted to. He felt unhappy to have come.

"It was Antonio who found these eggs," said Tullio. "He's gotten much taller since last year. I'll bet you wouldn't be able to recognize him, if you saw him on the street. One day we'll come together and look you up."

It appeared that the old man would not reply, but instead he said, "I'll be happy to see him."

Now the things were all arranged on the chest: the eggs, and sausage, and a little coffee and sugar in two paper cones.

"Be seated, boys," the old man said again.

Tullio crossed the room to take a chair near the bed. Daniele also sat down. There were two chairs, made of a lovely dark wood, and also the big double bed and the chest and the wardrobe of the same dark wood. The armchair, on the other hand, was ugly and did not match the rest of the furniture. On one place on the high back, just above the head of the old man, there was a hole in the fabric and some stuffing was sticking out.

"Does anyone hear anything of Mario?" asked the old man.

"No," said Tullio.

Once again they lapsed into silence. It was just as Tullio had said, that they had nothing to say to each other and it was better to remain in silence, even though the silence was heavy.

Then it was the old man's turn to speak. "How are things in town?"

"Miserable," said Tullio, and that appeared to have exhausted the subject.

But then Tullio spoke again: "The winter is bad. People don't know how to go on because they are lacking everything. And there are all the time more people here in town."

Tullio expected someone would say something, but neither the old man nor Daniele had anything to say. The old man stayed motionless with his hands on the arms of the armchair. The veins in his hands were very large.

"They're stubborn," said Tullio. "They're the most determined people I've ever seen. At times they take up a position in front of the town hall or the military post, and they wait. They wait from morning to night. No one even asks them anymore what they want and yet they stand and wait all the same. Maybe some day something will shake out, because they're so persistent."

The old man shook his head, which he kept lowered. "Nothing will shake out."

"The bad thing is, they aren't organized," said Tullio. "But all the same, something will come about, some day."

The old man lifted his head to look at Tullio and his voice became unexpectedly excited. "Why are you saying this? How can you know?"

"That's how I see it," said Tullio. "Because it's a misery too hard to bear. No work, no food, and even those who had put a little money aside are reduced to poverty. It would take millions of *lire* to live, but people don't have millions, and they are dying little by little of hunger. Everyone knows that you can't go on this way."

Tullio had also become heated as he spoke, and Daniele watched him. It was strange to see Tullio without his old cap. He had a large head, which created an impression of power.

"And them?" asked the old man. "What are they doing?"

"The Americans?" asked Tullio.

The old man nodded yes.

"They do something," said Tullio, "but it's as good as nothing. As soon as they arrived they had rations of soup distributed. Ten thousand rations per day, for ten days. And they had these rations distributed on Christmas. But what good does that do? People cannot survive eating only at Christmas. Everything needs to change, so people can live.

What's needed is work for everyone, and for everyone to get food with the money they earn by working."

The old man made a movement with his head, but he didn't speak.

"People expected a lot before the Americans were supposed to arrive," Tullio continued. "They said they would bring freedom and things to eat. Instead, the suffering is worse than before. A person can complain about the government now, but it doesn't fill the belly to criticize the government. So they aren't doing anything but increasing the chaos."

"So then, even you think it was better before," said the old man.

A look sprang to Tullio's face as if he was about to challenge the words of the old man, but then he let it drop.

"I don't understand a lot of things," he said. "Because if we take these American soldiers one by one, there's nothing bad to say about them. There are good ones and bad ones, like people all over the world. It can be said that there are more good ones than bad ones, and they help us when they can. But it's no use. Our lives get worse all the time, and they aren't resolving anything, even if they do give candy to the children."

"It's futile," said the old man.

"I don't understand why they could have brought such devastation, if they aren't bad people," said Tullio.

The old man was now facing Tullio squarely, stimulated by the discussion.

"You only see what's in front of your eyes," he said. "The evil is not entirely in these men you see going about in our streets. These men don't bear the greater blame for what happens. They are making war because they have been sent to make war, and they can't wait for it to end so they can return home. I don't believe anyone would voluntarily undertake this job of massacring people and destroying cities."

"If it were up to the peoples of the world, there would be no war," said Tullio.

"There will always be wars," said the old man. "It's enough that people are treated unjustly, or are convinced into letting themselves be treated unjustly, and sooner or later there will be a war, unless others have the will to remedy injustice. But it would be presuming too much of people. No one wants to give someone else what he himself has, only for the love of justice. This will never happen in this world."

"Maybe it *will* happen," said Tullio.

"It has happened rarely between individuals," said the old man. "But it has never happened between groups of people. Maybe because so many individuals, put together, are more wicked than just one."

"No," said Tullio. "It's because the people who rule have never been the best ones. They're the strongest, or most devious, possibly also the most capable, but they are never the best ones."

Tullio had spoken in his sermonizing way, and the old man smiled.

"Has it been the communists who have put these ideas into your head?"

"It's right thinking."

"Yes, it's right thinking," said the old man. "They are never the best. But not even with your system do good people come forth."

"With our system it's the better portion of the people who govern themselves," said Tullio.

"A people does not govern itself," said the old man. "In whatever system, those who govern are few, and the most astute and capable always come forth, no matter whether they are good or not. Up to now, it has been your own system that has provided examples of the greater violence."

"At first, violence is necessary," said Tullio.

"And then there will be yet more violence," said the old man. "So it's useless for them to scold us for what we wanted to do. What they're doing is worse than what we wanted to do, and it's based on the same principle. There are always some groups that must submit to other groups, this is the principle, even if they mask it with fine words. So it serves no purpose whether it's a soldier that gives out candy or a major that tries to govern a city with humanity and fairness. These are not the ones that count. These come and go, and then others come, who could be good or bad, and their conduct doesn't have any great importance, because they all act according to a principle that originates with people we don't even see, and many times we don't even know who they are. They are exactly the more astute and capable men, those in politics and big industry. And if their guiding principle is that of subjugating us, we become slaves . . ."

He continued: "Perhaps we don't deserve a better fate. But they ought to feel the responsibility that they are assuming in subjugating other people. I am not speaking of death and destruction, which also can be a necessary condition of war. But disorder, hunger, moral ruin, are things for which they should provide a remedy. Or else they should let us try to remedy those things by ourselves. That's not how one conquers a people, unless one's guiding principle is to destroy it."

"They won't destroy us," said Tullio. "Sooner or later all Europe will be in the same ruin as we are, three hundred million people. Then our idea will be on the march, and something will happen."

"But what *can* happen?" said the old man, almost shouting. He was very agitated, and it wasn't clear whether he wanted to know what Tullio thought or not. He got up from the armchair and walked to the window in front of him and looked down.

"Anyway, it's fair enough," he said. "This is your form of hope, and you are young, and you need to have hope. But I am by now old and useless. We made many mistakes in what we were doing, I've understood it now, what with the war and all this disaster. However, there are even more mistakes in what they are doing, and we depend on them, on the good will of men who have no good will. So my thoughts always get confused, and I'm not able to see anything right in front of me. Maybe I'm too old, and it seems that no one can do anything, in the condition we're in. But all of you must have hope in something."

Now it was truly a very old and small man that was speaking so despairingly. He moved back to his armchair. He kept his legs rigid and it was painful to watch him walk. He sat down, gazing fixedly at the window.

"I'm weary," he said. "Once upon a time this didn't happen to me, getting tired so quickly."

Tullio stood up from the chair, and Daniele after him.

"I'll pay you another visit some time soon," said Tullio.

The old man looked at him with a sad expression. Tullio went to take the empty basket from the chest, and the old man followed him with his eyes.

"Come when you can," he said. "I'm always by myself, and I'm happy when someone comes to see me. But don't worry about bringing things. It's not necessary, really not necessary."

"Don't give a thought to the stuff," said Tullio. "When I can, I'll willingly bring it to you."

The old man shook his head. "Be prudent. I'm only advising you to be prudent. I, too, would feel much to blame if anything should happen to you."

"Nothing will happen to me, for sure," said Tullio.

The old man smiled sorrowfully and said, "I've spent forty years of my life teaching honesty and tolerance, and now I don't know what to tell you other than to be prudent."

The old man also stood up, since they were about to leave. He approached Daniele and studied him up close, as when he had entered.

Then he asked Tullio, "And him? What are you thinking of doing about him?"

"Nothing," said Tullio. "He'll do what he wants."

The old man threw a look at Tullio, almost as if he didn't trust him. "You need to keep an eye on him. Because he's different, you understand. He's not like the rest of you."

Perhaps the old man wanted to continue speaking, but Tullio interrupted him roughly.

"He isn't different," he said. "We are all equal – we are. It's only a question of habit. When he gets used to us he'll become like us."

The old man wore an apologetic expression. "That's not what I meant."

"All right," said Tullio. "In any case, he'll choose his own path by himself. He's grown up enough to do that."

When they left the house, the sun was getting low, and before long it would disappear in the denser haze that covered the horizon. A light wind blew from the north, and it was cold. Tullio was still irritated. Two or three times Daniele turned his gaze on him and was always met with a dark scowl. "Tullio," he said.

"What do you want?"

"I wasn't a great help to you."

"Don't give it a thought," said Tullio. "The important thing was for him and me not to find ourselves alone together. And anyway, this time it was different. We've never discussed those things before."

25

They passed through the San Tommaso gate and entered the city. Tullio still took to the small streets in the middle of the quarter.

"You got mad on account of me," said Daniele. "You got mad when he said that I'm not like the rest of you. But it makes no difference what he said. I'm happy that you consider me one of you."

Tullio forced a smile, but his expression did not clear up.

"You are *not* like us," he said. "The old man is right when he says you're different. But he thinks the difference is because you might be the son of a lawyer or doctor, and in that he's mistaken. He thinks that when someone is born to a lawyer or doctor he can't turn into a crook or suffer hunger, just because he is born to a lawyer or doctor. It's this that is maddening. We are not the same. Every person is different from every other person, but it doesn't depend on who one's father is, or if one is rich or poor. It depends entirely on oneself, on how one is made: if not, one can't explain why crooks are born to poor and rich alike."

"It also depends on education," said Daniele.

"Maybe," said Tullio, "but education isn't everything. Mario was the son of a vagabond and he grew up on the streets, and yet he was never able to adapt to our life. He tried to do better than he was capable of doing, and he never said anything, but after he had been around he

210

stayed by himself to think it over and he tormented himself because it seemed to him he had never done anything good. Our life wasn't for him. Then he went away. He was sixteen, and he went to war, and he's dead, maybe. He has written two or three times from the front, and that's all. He was a little like you, Mario was. He thought too much."

"Oh, I don't think much," said Daniele.

"Maybe you don't realize it," said Tullio, "but you think too much about things." He was serious now, but no longer irritated.

"And the old man was your schoolteacher?" asked Daniele.

"No," said Tullio. "I got to know him after the bombardment. I was together with Antonio and Mario then, and you had to go to get the soldiers' rations that they gave out at Balilla House. The old man was there helping out and we ended up in his group. He should have reported us, and then we would have finished up in one of the camps that they've created just for boys who were on their own. Instead, he didn't report us. He also knew what we were up to, being on the outside, and all the same he didn't report us. But he was very different, then. These changes that have happened have ruined him. He's too attached to the way things used to be."

"Yes," said Daniele. "He's very confused in his ideas."

Tullio laughed. "They would be our worst enemies, if they counted for anything, but they don't count for anything. Their only song is that it was better before. And someone listens to them, because it really was better before. But then we were at a standstill, while now we are on the move. People must move forward, it doesn't matter what they must go through."

"Yes," said Daniele.

"And anyway," said Tullio, "what does it matter if those before us also did some good things? In the end they've gotten us into a war, and they've ruined everything. We aren't people who make war, and we weren't even prepared. They must have known that we were like this. And they've ruined us in the war."

Daniele did not respond and Tullio also went on a little way without speaking.

Then he said, "But I love him all the same, that old guy. Now that he's so reduced one feels more compassion than ever. And anyway, it was he who helped Carla get me out of prison. Because Carla had found the shoemaker who was ready to pass himself off as responsible for me, and she also found the money to pay him, but it was necessary to do the paperwork, and it was a long business. Then the old man did up the papers and took them around to the offices. He knew different people in the offices, and so I got out almost right away, and we went to live inside the zone. Before that we camped out by the walls, all together."

The streets where they were walking were almost deserted, because it was cold and beginning to get dark. People had already retired inside their houses, and passing near the walls you could hear voices and the cries of children and also the clatter of dishes.

"Tullio," said Daniele, "I'd like to do something for you. Never mind if I seem not so skillful. I feel I'm able to do it."

Tullio gave him an inquiring look. "Even steal?"

Daniele walked along, looking at the ground. "Yes."

"Good," said Tullio, and he clearly felt pleased. Still, a few steps later he said, "It's not necessary for you to steal, Daniele. Also, there are too many of us doing it, and also you wouldn't succeed the way we do, you don't have the knack. You're just like Mario. But there's something you *can* do for us. I've been wanting to talk to you about it for some time."

"What is it?"

"You could help us with a piece of business. I'll explain it to you, some other time."

"Tell me now."

Tullio smiled. "Well, it involves a girl. A girl who must be twenty years old, I think."

"Yes," said Daniele. His expression was all concentration.

"Then there's the father of the girl," said Tullio. "He's a pharmacist, owner of a big pharmacy. The girl is also going to be a pharmacist like her father. I don't know how many more years she'll have to study, but she will become a pharmacist for sure, because she's a smart girl. She already helps out in the pharmacy sometimes."

"Yes."

Tullio was laughing. "Then there are the Americans," he said.

"Oh, Tullio, don't kid around," said Daniele. "Don't you trust me?"

"I'm not kidding," said Tullio. "But you need to pay attention to what I'm telling you."

"All right," said Daniele, and he listened more closely.

"So . . . we had gotten to the Americans," said Tullio. "The girl's father can't stand the Americans. But she, instead, doesn't dislike them. She began to go out in a boat together with a sergeant of the military command post. They went out on the river, where the tall grasses are, and now they have rented a room in one of the streets in back here. Get it?"

"No," said Daniele.

Tullio made a gesture of exasperation but continued. "The girl would give anything so that her father doesn't come to find out about the business with the American sergeant," he said.

"Now I understand."

"Anyone else would have understood it, at this point."

"But I still don't understand what *I* can do," said Daniele.

"Now I'll explain it to you," said Tullio, seriously. "It calls for approaching the girl in the street, and this you must do. If I or one of us did it, dressed as we are, the girl would get scared. She could possibly call the patrol, and we'd get locked up. Instead, you're well dressed, and you have the correct way of behaving with those people."

"And what should I say?"

"Oh, nothing much," said Tullio. "We'll wait for her some evening near the church of San Paolo. She takes that street to go home. Well, you'll go near her and you'll tell her to spend a moment in the church. If she should cause any difficulty, you'll tell her that you need to talk to her about a sergeant that works in the military post, and she'll come right away. I will then be in the church."

"Will you ask for money?"

"No, not money," said Tullio. "This girl will be useful to us for medicines. It's hard to get medicines these days. It requires a doctor's prescription, and the doctors are pigs. When it's about poor people they're all in cahoots to say that medicine does more harm than good.

So it requires dragging it out of them some other way. You'll speak to the girl, and then I'll go liberate the medicines, when the moment is right."

Daniele walked along without saying anything.

"This would be a wicked deed," said Tullio. "They all teach that it's a wicked deed. But I need medicines, and I have to take advantage of this girl. I'm sorry, for her sake."

"I'll do as you say, Tullio," said Daniele.

Tullio clapped him on the shoulder. "Well, there's still time," he said.

Then he walked ahead without speaking, but he was pleased.

Where the main street appeared at the end of the street where they were walking, Tullio halted. "I'm going to have to do that silly thing."

"What?"

"The powder compact. Every so often some silly little thing needs doing. It helps you when you have to get your act together, later. Didn't they teach you that in school?"

"No."

"Well, that's how it is," said Tullio. "At school they never teach anything good."

Daniele felt happy and he laughed. "Maybe they would have taught me that later."

Tullio pulled from his pocket a canvas envelope that served as a wallet. There was a lot of money inside.

"You should go, yourself, and buy that item," he said. "For sure they won't ask you questions. If anything, say it's a present for your sister."

"All right," said Daniele, and he put the money Tullio had given him into his pocket.

"The shop will still be open," said Tullio. "You'll find it on the right, on the other side of the street."

"Yes, I remember."

"And when you're done, head for the cathedral. Take the street to the left, before the clockmaker's. I'll wait for you at the corner."

"All right," said Daniele, moving away.

Tullio watched him walk off, with an expression as if he regretted having sent him. Then he shrugged his shoulders and he also went off, slowly.

The main street was sunk in shadow, because the lights had not yet been lit. People strolled at leisure beneath the porticoes.

Tullio crossed the street and stopped, passing in front of the shop that had the powder compact. The interior of the shop was illuminated by an oil lamp, so he saw Daniele inside. He was near the counter with his back turned, and Tullio saw only the outline of his head, with its blond hair looking a bit unruly. Behind the counter was a woman.

At a certain point Daniele turned his head to the side and then Tullio saw his profile, which was very delicate, almost like that of a girl, and the lips were moving with the slight hesitation that was habitual with him. He wasn't very confident, especially when he had to deal with people he didn't know.

Tullio smiled and went on. For the whole distance to the clockmaker's shop he kept smiling to himself. He loved that boy. He would never pull anything useful out of him, but by now he loved him, sincerely. And it wasn't important if he was so weak and bewildered and didn't know how to do anything if someone wasn't by his side. By himself he would not be able to go forward in life, but that didn't matter. Or perhaps it was just because of this that Tullio loved him.

Before the clockmaker's there was a narrow alleyway. He turned the corner and immediately stopped to wait.

Daniele arrived a short time later, quite pleased with himself.

"Did they give it to you?" asked Tullio.

"Yes," answered Daniele, and went to pull something from his pocket.

"Wait—farther ahead," said Tullio.

They began to hurry through the alleyway, which was already dark.

"Did they say anything to you?" asked Tullio.

"Nothing," said Daniele. "There was a lady at the counter, and she said I resembled her dead nephew, and I told her the compact cost too much. So she gave me two hundred *lire* in change."

"When you grow up, you'll become worse than Andrea, with the ladies," said Tullio, laughing.

"Oh, no," said Daniele. "I always lose my breath when I have to talk with a girl. Two years ago in the mountains there was one I liked a lot, and I was never capable of saying it to her. I always lost my breath."

"Well, you can manage even without talking," said Tullio. "Women understand anyway, when that's the subject."

"Are you saying seriously that they understand even if no one says anything?" asked Daniele.

"Yes, relax," said Tullio. "Let me see that thing, now."

He took the compact in his hands and stopped to examine it better. Inside there was a little round mirror attached to the cover, and a tiny brush. Tullio took up a bit of powder, lifting the brush, and sniffed the perfume. Then he got angry.

"A little bit of nickeled steel and this piece of crap for four thousand *lire*!" he said, starting to walk again. "Ten kilos of bread could have been bought with that money!"

Daniele, until that moment, had felt proud of his purchase. "Did I do a bad thing to buy it?" he asked timidly.

"What's got into you? I told you to buy it, and I already knew it was a silly thing. It's just that right now bread came into my mind, and then I got mad."

Nevertheless, his ire did not last long. "Every so often some silly little thing is okay."

The shadows of evening were even denser in the narrow streets. And Daniele had not until then paid attention to the direction they had taken. But when he did pay attention, he realized they were not going toward home.

"We're not going home yet, Tullio?" he asked.

"No, not yet," said Tullio. Walking, he kept turning the compact over in his hands.

Suddenly he said, "Let's engrave something on the top of this. I know someone that does that kind of work. You ought to come up with an appropriate phrase for Carla."

"Oh, it's better not to engrave anything on it," said Daniele.

"Why? It needs something written on it. Carla is capable of forgetting right away, if nothing's engraved on it. I'd like for her to remember always that I gave it to her."

"She'll remember just the same," said Daniele.

Still, it seemed that Tullio had got it in his head to engrave something. "But really, can't something be engraved on it?"

Daniele stood thinking a few seconds. "You could engrave a date on it. When is her birthday?"

"The twenty-first of this month," said Tullio.

"Then write *Tullio*," said Daniele, "and then, *February 21, 1945.* Make them engrave it on the back, not on the front."

"That's all?" asked Tullio. "Could we maybe write *Tullio & Daniele*?"

"No, not my name," said Daniele. "Why would you want to put that there?"

Tullio looked at him attentively, after he had said those words, but he couldn't see him clearly. The street they were on shrank down until it became a slot so narrow they had to walk single file. Then they came out into an opening by the side of the cathedral. Around the apse there was a high scaffold for masons.

"They leave the people without homes, but they're always ready to fix the churches," said Tullio, ironically.

Daniele lifted his head to look. He saw a profusion of beams and planks of the scaffolding, and higher up a dark blotch, where a hole must have been made by the bombs.

"I remember," he said, "that when I came the day of the bombardment, this hole at the back of the church made an impression on me. And there, at the far end, were some men who were loading the dead onto a truck. They handled them as if they were pieces of meat."

"It happens like that where there are too many," said Tullio.

"And here in front were all the rows of the dead," said Daniele. "And I went into their midst to look for my mother. I have never felt so bad."

They had arrived at the foot of the flight of steps that climbed to the entrance porch, and Tullio stopped. The avenue leading towards the walls seemed much broader without the skyscrapers. On that side the sun had set, and the haze on the horizon still retained a little of its light. But the other side of the sky was getting rapidly darker.

"Go," Tullio said. "I'll wait for you here."

Daniele stared at him. They had never spoken of this further, after that first time.

"Move, be quick about it," he said again.

"Thanks," Daniele said, and left.

Tullio sat down on the lowest step and followed Daniele with his gaze as the boy went toward the pile of ruins that was the tomb of his father and his mother. Daniele attached much importance to those things.

The light wind that was blowing from the north was icy and stung the face. So Tullio hid his ears inside his cap and pulled up the collar of his jacket, and meanwhile kept a steady eye on the square. By now all he could barely make out was a shadow against the haze that still held a little sunset light. A shadow that moved, going towards a certain place. And it was Daniele. So Tullio smiled, as he had before, in front of the shop that had the powder compact. Only, a little more sadly.

26

The boulevard of horse chestnut trees began just outside the walls and continued for almost a mile along the left bank of the river. It ended where the dikes began and the railroad bridge passed over the river.

It was a beautiful boulevard, very long, with four rows of horse chestnuts that formed two lanes for pedestrians and one for automobiles. The automobile lane was of asphalt, and it connected with the peripheral road. The pedestrian avenues had park benches of white stone under the horse chestnuts, and at one time the walks had been covered with fine gravel that then disappeared, swallowed up by the earth. Since the beginning of the war they had no longer put gravel on the avenues of the city.

People greatly loved the boulevard along the river's edge. They loved it especially in summer, when the huge horse chestnuts cast a broad shade and the river was limpid and fresh. But in winter they preferred the avenues by the walls, where there were also park benches of white stone under the horse chestnuts.

That particular winter, people had found living difficult. Food, clothing, the fuel that people needed to survive, were lacking. And the authorities were concerned about that. If they couldn't do anything about food and clothing, at least they could attempt to do something about fuel. So they considered cutting some trees, to provide firewood to the people.

Yet it remained to be seen which trees would be suitable to cut. There were plane trees along the big roads of the plain, but they did not belong to the city, and anyway it would have been useless to cut them down, if a way to transport the wood into the city could not then be found. There remained the horse chestnuts that were closer by, by the walls and along the boulevard.

After long discussions, the authorities decided on the horse chestnuts on the boulevard and sent men to cut them down. When men began to cut down the horse chestnuts, winter had not yet ended, but people were already feeling spring in the air, and they no longer found, each morning, frost deposited on the roofs and gardens. However, firewood was still useful, though less than before. The trees had been felled and then split on the spot, and whoever had a voucher from the city could present themselves to take away some kilos of green wood. The work went ahead slowly. Certainly they would not even reach the end of the boulevard by summertime.

There was always a small crowd that hung around to watch the men as they worked around the trees. Some went only to observe, and they were the old people, and were saddened by what they saw. The old people had a greater attachment to things like trees and gardens and squares and streets. They were fond of those things, independently of their utility. It always hurt to see them disappear. And it would be even more difficult to find oneself in a city already so changed, where one felt always more and more isolated, nor did they have any longer the energy of the young, who were either going far away or thinking about it.

Other people, instead, went carrying sacks with them and waited for when the men should have finished, to gather up the roots and chips of wood off the ground.

In general, no one was happy about that work, neither the ones who could have the firewood nor those who could not. On the other hand, people would have always been unhappy even if the authorities had not made the decision to cut down the trees.

G iulia and Daniele passed by the spot where the men were working to demolish the horse chestnuts, and they continued to walk side by side, without hurry. Now the shadows of the trees fell across the ground, and Daniele seemed absorbed in watching them. There were the dark shadows of the trunks, and the somewhat less dense shadows of the branches, less and less distinct as the branches gradually dwindled higher up, until, for the twigs, the shapes of the shadows blended in with the ground. Then Daniele stopped and lifted his head to see the lacework of twigs against the sun, and his face squinted in the bright sunlight as if he were smiling.

Giulia also stopped after two or three steps. "What are you doing?" she asked.

"Nothing," Daniele said. "I'm looking at the sunshine."

So they began gazing at the sunshine, and after that they watched the sky, which was of an intense azure color, with white clouds that seemed motionless. The expressions on their faces approached a smile.

"Look at those clouds," said Daniele. "Isn't it like springtime?"

"Yes."

"I feel so glad when spring comes."

"Yes, I feel glad too," said Giulia.

They began to walk once more, and the sun on their necks and down their backs imparted a nice warmth. People seated on the park benches were taking the sun and watching the waters of the river. Children played on the other side of the boulevard, far from the water.

"So many times I came to walk here with my mother," said Daniele. "It was shady and cool in the summertime."

Giulia turned her head toward him. "What was her name? You've never told me."

"Lisa," said Daniele, and smiled at a memory that flitted through his mind.

The boulevard of horse chestnuts ended at the place where the railroad bridge was. Farther along, only a dusty and treeless road continued. They passed under the bridge and then followed the river along the embankment.

They stopped to look at the girders of the old bridge. The Germans had blown it up before retreating, and the tangle of bars could be seen, lying on the river bottom, because the spring rains had not yet begun. One side of the collapsed bridge jutted out of the water, and some moss had attached to the bars. The water sped up a bit in passing through it. Above it was a new bridge, also of iron, and it resembled the previous one.

"Let's go a little farther, do you want to?" asked Daniele.

The path along the embankment made continuous bends, following the river. It was a path that the boatmen used to draw the boats along with ropes, when they came up the river against the current. Now there were no boats docked at the pilings along the river's edge, because the brick furnaces and the tile factory were no longer operating. They lacked fuel to feed the fires in the kilns. And the people who had worked on the river and in the furnaces now didn't know what they should do and sat in idleness in the sun. They watched that fairly well-dressed boy and that skinny girl who was still a child pass by, and the women shook their heads because they were plain folk and perhaps had something similar to deplore regarding their daughters.

And Giulia understood, and she was ashamed at the way the women were looking at her and shaking their heads, sitting at the thresholds of their houses.

"I'd like it if it were possible to go over there," said Giulia. "It's prettier without the houses."

On the other riverbank there was no path, not even houses, but cultivated fields and some villa or other scattered among the fields, and a person couldn't walk on that embankment.

"If we continue on from here we'll arrive where the houses end, just the same," said Daniele.

"But we'll be late," said Giulia.

"No," said Daniele, and he turned to check the position of the sun in the sky. It was still high.

"When we're back home," said Daniele, "I will help you prepare the meal. We will do it all in a few minutes."

The houses ended, and now along the stretch of road where they were walking there rose up a high wall that enclosed a park surrounding a villa. They were not able to see beyond, but treetops peeped over the top of the wall, and in some places ivy spilled over the side by the roadway.

When they arrived at a gate they paused to look inside. Giulia stood with her hands against the bars and her eyes were full of wonder. "How beautiful it is," she murmured.

It was indeed beautiful, that park, with so many trees that didn't lose their leaves even in winter, and a small lake, and a shed with a thatched roof on the lake shore, and white statues half smothered in ivy. And the villa as well was large and beautiful, although it was only the rear view, since the front gave onto the main road beyond.

"It's closed up," said Giulia.

"They have another house for the winter," said Daniele.

"Yes," said Giulia. She looked at the windows, which were shuttered because those people had another house. Then she discovered the flowers, and in a different voice she said, "Look at the flowers."

Daniele looked in the direction where Giulia was looking. There was a flowering shrub a little farther on and almost hidden among the trees.

"What flowers are they?" he asked.

"Spicebush, maybe."

"Would you like me to pick some?"

"No . . ." replied Giulia, uncertainly.

"I'm going to pick some," said Daniele, resolutely. He climbed onto the gate, vaulted over the top of the bars, and dropped down on the other side.

Giulia was apprehensive. "Watch out for the watchman. There'll be a watchman at such a grand villa."

Beyond the gate, a small promenade mounted some steps and then proceeded toward the villa, winding among the trees. Daniele began to run in the direction of the flowering shrub.

The park was deserted, and even the avenue along the river was deserted, from one end to the other. Giulia kept watch, a bit on the park and a bit on the avenue, and she was uneasy until Daniele returned with his arms full of blooms. They were leafless twigs with flowers of a dark yellow hue, heavy with perfume.

"Quick," said Giulia. "Pass them through the bars."

"Be careful in case they prick."

"They won't prick. They don't have thorns."

"Well, I got pricked," said Daniele.

He handed the twigs one by one through the bars, then vaulted over the gate and landed in front of Giulia, still out of breath from running, and proud of himself.

Giulia arranged the flowers and held them tight to her chest with one arm. "How many you picked! You must have ruined the whole shrub."

"They were there and they weren't of use to anyone," said Daniele. "Do you like them?"

"Very much," replied Giulia.

"I'm happy you like them," said Daniele. "I picked them for you."

"Oh," she said, and raised her eyes, that were laughing, and in her eyes was a golden reflection of the blossoms. She looked as if she expected something to happen.

But Daniele was mute, and after a moment of standing expectantly that way, she turned and continued to walk.

"Let's give them to Carla," Giulia said. "Tomorrow's her feast day."

"All right, if that's what you want," said Daniele.

"We'll hide them at the shoemaker's house," she said. "And tomorrow, as soon as she wakes up, I'll take them to her."

"We'll take them to her together."

Giulia didn't answer. They walked alongside the wall of the villa in the warmth of the sun. Then the wall came to an end, and you saw the open countryside, with a few houses scattered in the distance. On the river embankment the fields were closed off by hedgerows of brambles or by barbed wire.

Giulia halted.

"Don't you want to go on?" asked Daniele.

"It's late."

"It's not late. If we go on ahead maybe these hedgerows will end, and we can go through the fields."

Giulia looked at the open countryside, full of sunlight. But then she shook her head no. "I'm tired. I'm not used to walking."

"Let's sit down a bit, then. Do you want to?"

"Yes, let's sit down."

"From now on we'll always come here to walk, when the weather is better," said Daniele. "Then you'll be used to it, and we can talk longer walks."

"Yes," Giulia said, without expression. She put the spicebush down on the grass and sat down at the edge of the embankment closest to the river. Daniele sat down next to her.

Looking downstream they viewed again a stretch of road and then the river made a bend, and the road could no longer be seen. Near the bend, a little boy with a stick in his hand was watching a group of ducks that were swimming near the river's edge. On the other side of the river some peasants were working. You could hear their voices from time to time, but you couldn't see them because of the embankment. And the water flowed soundlessly towards the sea, and the long white road also led towards the sea.

It was all so serene, and yet Giulia was no longer at peace, because of a sadness that had come over her.

"Going on from here one would arrive at the sea," said Daniele.

Giulia looked along the stretch of road, and farther, in the direction of the sea. Broken rows of poplars marked the course of the river through the plain.

"I'd like to go to the sea," said Daniele. "Have you ever been there?"

"Once."

"And it's beautiful, isn't it?" said Daniele. "For me, it's the most beautiful thing there is."

"I don't remember much." said Giulia. "I was too small."

"Were you there with your mother?"

"Yes."

"You never talk to me about your mother."

Giulia dropped her head and focused on the river. "I remember almost nothing about her."

Daniele sensed her sadness and seemed about to say something but didn't. Giulia was like an old woman, now, and earlier she had been a little girl, when she had looked into the garden and longed for the flowers. Tullio always said Giulia was like an old little girl, because of the extreme hardships she had endured. She was staring at the river with a bitter curl on her lips.

"Maybe I made you unhappy to remember your mamma," said Daniele.

Giulia's mouth drew up in a strange smile. "You were happy before, when you spoke of *your* mamma," she said. "And I cannot be happy if I think of mine, because her life was so sad, and because of what she did. But I love her even so. And it's not true that I don't remember much about her. I remember everything, how her eyes were, and her hair and her face, and how she stroked me, and things she said to me when she and I were alone together. But we were alone together for too short a time."

Giulia had spoken with almost angry defiance, and when she stopped speaking, Daniele said nothing.

The group of ducks had moved beyond the bend, following the current, and the little boy with the long stick had gone with them. And the peasants on the other side of the river called to each other from time to time, but one couldn't see them. The two of them were alone together, he and Giulia, alone on a place on the earth. But she remained with her head lowered, staring at the river, and the bitter curl remained on her lips, and the sun penetrated her hair, making it shine in places.

And within himself he felt something that was pressing to be said, the most wonderful thing in the world, perhaps; if it were said it would perhaps dispel the suffering that was their lot on earth. But he wasn't able to say it. The more he thought, the more confused his feelings became, and his heart pounded, and he did not have the courage to say anything at all, for fear of being wrong. Although to be silent was worse than anything, he did not have the courage to speak.

Finally one of those clouds, that moved across the sky so slowly they seemed stationary, arrived to cover the sun, and suddenly it got cold.

Giulia lifted her head, shivering. "Let's go."

Without speaking they took once more to the road along the wall. Daniele walked along, looking at the ground. The tranquility of that day was gone, he didn't understand very well how or why, but it had gone, and now Giulia was sad and he was sad, and it must have been his fault. They did not look another time through the gate of the villa. Giulia carried the bunch of flowering twigs tightly in front of her, without caring any longer whether he saw her hands, all red and swollen as they were.

The big bunch of spicebush twigs stood in a bucket of water on the table, and it was fine to see and gave off a lovely perfume. It was a fragrance like in church, and Daniele loved to smell it. But when chicken began to fry on the shoemaker's kitchen range, its aroma quickly overpowered the fragrance of the spicebush.

Then Daniele made another attempt with Giulia.

Giulia always had something to do around the kitchen, and for such an important dinner, she had assumed the bustling manner of "the little woman." She was almost amusing that way.

"Can't a person take a taste, Giulia?" asked Daniele.

"Now? It's almost three hours before it will be ready."

Daniele looked a bit disappointedly at the skillet where the chicken was cooking. Three hours was a long time to wait, and then he was not sure Giulia would even let him sample it before she put it on the table. In fact, he was sure she would not.

"And the dessert? That's been cooking awhile," he insisted.

Giulia made believe she didn't hear him, but when she saw him reach a hand toward the stove door, she promptly pushed him away.

"If you don't leave me in peace, I can't get anything together. Go play with Maria for a bit."

The shoemaker, who was looking on, laughed loudly. He was seated on a chest, smoking a pipe that contained something that was not tobacco, but he was content because he would also have eaten well that day, pasta and chicken and perhaps a bit of dessert.

Daniele tried to talk with the little Maria but couldn't interest her. She was too preoccupied with her own things, such as watching Giulia's movements and continually drawing her head into her shoulders, the better to rub her face against her fur collar. Although the room was hot, she had not wanted to take off her coat, because it had a new rabbit-fur collar.

"You like it, don't you?" asked Daniele, speaking about the rabbit fur.

"Yes," said the little girl, continuing to follow Giulia's movements with her eyes and rubbing her cheeks on the fur. Every so often Giulia turned to smile at her, and then she smiled back, but then right afterward she went back into her serious and somewhat dull expression.

One couldn't talk with a child like that, nor even with the shoemaker. Daniele would have been incapable of saying anything to a man like the shoemaker, whom one had to pay for things that cost him nothing— Tullio's documents and a house in the middle of the ruins. And even then he sent his wife out to get work, and he stayed all day doing nothing but smoking. By now it had been months since he had worked, and it satisfied him to find neither leather nor twine, because it meant he did not have to work.

Daniele waited a bit more, then it seemed to him that it was getting late. "It must be late, Giulia. She might be awake at this hour."

"Then let's go. Meanwhile bring the flowers."

Daniele began to take the twigs from the bucket. He took them one at a time and made up a bouquet on the table as best he could. Before long, Carla would be happy to have those flowers that gave off a lovely perfume.

Giulia called little Maria and showed her how she turned the chicken in the skillet.

"Now I have to go home and I'll come back soon," she said. "In the meantime, while I'm away, every little while you must turn the chicken over with the spoon, like this."

There was a grimace on the little girl's face that showed all her teeth, as she struggled to understand.

"How many times do I have to turn it over?" she asked.

"Ten times," said Giulia. "Turn it over ten times with the spoon, then wait a bit, like going to our house and coming back right away, and then turn it over ten times more, every time like that, until I get back. Understand?"

"All right," said the child.

Giulia gave her the spoon. "Practice the way you should do it," she said.

The little girl turned the spoon in the skillet ten times, then she closed her eyes and the grimace became fixed on her face. After awhile she opened her eyes again and gave it another ten turns, as Giulia had taught her.

"All right," said Giulia. "Every time like that until I get back."

"I'll keep an eye on her," said the shoemaker.

"Oh, that isn't important," said Giulia.

When they went out, Daniele said, "I'm afraid the chicken will get burned."

"No. It's an effort for her to understand things, but once she understands, they never leave her head."

They were very quiet entering the house, and Giulia moved the blanket aside to look inside Carla's room.

"Is she still sleeping?" asked Daniele.

"She seems to be," said Giulia. "Now I'll heat up some coffee for her and then I'll wake her up."

Giulia put the small pot of coffee to heat on the embers. Daniele remained standing with the bunch of spicebush in his hand. Its perfume smelled strong.

"Last year, when we came to this house," said Giulia, "there was a magnolia tree in bloom. Those days I kept the house full of magnolias. I put them into cans with water, and I loved to see them around here."

"Magnolias have a beautiful fragrance too," said Daniele.

"Yes," said Giulia, "and they're lovely. Too bad they don't last long."

When the coffee was hot, Giulia poured it into a cup, and then they went together into Carla's room, walking on tiptoe.

"Will you wake her?" Giulia asked under her breath.

Daniele nodded yes. They were both overtaken by a pleasant excitement. Carla was sleeping on her side, with her face hidden under the blankets.

"Carla," called Daniele, but she didn't move.

"Call louder, if she doesn't hear you," said Giulia. "She's always been a heavy sleeper."

"Carla," Daniele called more loudly.

Then Carla stirred under the blankets and uncovered her face and raised herself up lazily. She still kept her eyes closed. Giulia and Daniele laughed, bending over her. Her movements made them think of a cat.

"Wake up, Carla," said Daniele.

Carla finally opened one eye, just one, because she was rubbing the other with her fingers. She looked at the faces of Giulia and Daniele leaning over her, and Daniele's was half-hidden in the big bunch of yellow blossoms. And then she smiled for joy with her eyes and with her whole face.

Giulia gave Daniele a meaningful look, but he was fascinated watching Carla, and he couldn't decide to say what he should say.

So Giulia spoke. "Today is your feast day, Carla."

Daniele suddenly smacked his forehead. "Oh, yes, and we've brought these flowers with the wish that you'll always be happy."

"Ooh! . . ." went Carla. Extending her arms, she took the flowers that Daniele offered her and she put them up to her face.

"Be careful they don't prick you," said Daniele.

"No, they don't prick," said Giulia.

"Well, they pricked me, yesterday," said Daniele.

Carla had closed her eyes and was inhaling the perfume deeply. "How good you both are," she said.

Now Daniele now found himself in a new difficulty. He kept one hand inside the pocket of his jacket, waiting until Carla finished breathing in the perfume and opened her eyes again. Then, when she moved the flowers away from her face, he produced from his pocket the powder compact and, looking at it, he began to speak, with an air of making an important announcement.

"This is a gift from Tullio," he said. "It'll make you think often of him. Every time you use it, you'll think of Tullio." He paused in case his little speech would not come out right. "He should have brought it to you himself. But he went out suddenly, and I think he did that on purpose."

Carla took the compact and began to examine it on both sides, and finally raised her eyes to them. She was pleased and moved.

"Tullio's name is engraved there, and also mine," said Daniele. "But it was Tullio's idea. It's got nothing to do with us, Giulia and me. And anyway, we have no money."

"How good you all are," said Carla again. She had sat up in bed and had opened the compact. She was smiling into the little mirror and narrowing her eyes to appear more beautiful, and she shook her head every so often to make her hair ripple. Daniele had never seen her so lovely, with all the flowers in her lap.

"Carla, the coffee is getting cold," said Giulia.

Carla put the compact down and took the cup of coffee.

"It's only coffee," said Giulia. "We used up the milk."

"Yes," said Daniele, "we put it all into the dessert."

Giulia gave him a sidelong look. "*Stupido!*" she said. And all three of them laughed, truly happy.

It was a good day. Carla didn't want to go out and Daniele stayed with her in the kitchen, so she wouldn't go to see what Giulia was doing at the shoemaker's house. But it was nice to be together with Carla when she was so happy and unworried, like a little girl. She looked into the little mirror innumerable times and did much foolishness with the powder.

Tullio returned home toward evening, also in a good mood, with a bottle of white wine. Carla threw herself around his neck and kissed him endlessly.

"Be careful not to break the bottle!" said Tullio, laughing.

"Well, let's drink it right away, then," said Carla. She took three cups and filled them and gave one to Tullio and one to Daniele and kept the third for herself. They all stood with cups in their hands, looking at one another and smiling.

"Now we would like a toast, Daniele," said Tullio.

"Yes," said Daniele, "but I don't know what to say."

"You've studied so much, and you can't say two words when it's needed?"

"They hardly taught any toasts, the priests."

Tullio laughed, then said, "Well, I'll make the toast."

He raised his cup to Carla, and arranged his face with great gravity, but he couldn't think of anything to say.

Carla burst out laughing.

"Well—that you might live to be a hundred, Carla," Tullio said.

"Oh, what a toast!" went Carla.

"That we might always be so together and happy as today," said Daniele.

Carla emptied her cup without stopping.

"If you don't go slow you'll end up like that other time," said Tullio.

Carla shrugged her shoulders. "It's sweet."

"Sweet and strong," said Tullio. "It'll betray you for sure."

Daniele laughed stupidly, because he felt happy and saw that things were lighthearted.

Giulia and Daniele and Tullio set the table with solemnity. They spread a tablecloth that Giulia had borrowed, no one knew where from, and they put a tin can in the center with the spicebush, and, next to the flowers, Carla's two candlesticks.

"Now it looks like a funeral, with the flowers and the candles," said Tullio.

And Carla said, "Don't talk like that, Tullio. It's bad luck."

It was already dark outside when they began to eat. Carla had sat down between Tullio and Daniele, and she took care to keep their cups full. Tullio, however, didn't drink much, because he had to go out that night. Giulia didn't drink any wine, and neither did little Maria. The child appeared happy because there were good things to eat, and because the others talked and laughed loudly, and because of her new rabbit-fur collar. She repeatedly rubbed one cheek against the fur.

After two cups, Daniele felt filled with gaiety and laughed more than ever, for no reason.

"Don't let him drink any more, Carla," said Giulia. "He's not used to it, and it'll make him sick."

Carla looked at Giulia's worried face and laughed endlessly. She had drunk more than anyone, and she laughed in the same way that Daniele did.

"Don't think about it, Giulia," said Tullio. "When he gets drunk he'll go to bed and tomorrow he'll be better than ever."

"But there's no need for him to get drunk," said Giulia.

Tullio smiled. "Don't think about it," he repeated.

Giulia said no more, but she didn't lose her worried expression.

At a certain point Tullio stood up. "Now I have to go."

Carla quit laughing suddenly and fixed her gaze on Tullio's serious face. It seemed they were the only ones in the room. "You can't leave it just for tonight?"

"No," answered Tullio, "I'm sorry."

"I'd like for you to stay."

Tullio extended a hand toward her hair and rumpled it a little, as if he were still happy, but he was no longer happy. "I'd like to stay too," he said.

Then he turned to the little girl. "Come, Maria, I'll take you home."

They went out, and in the kitchen there was silence for some time. Tullio always thought of the difficult things in life, and they felt the weight, even while they were half drunk. In any case, it didn't last long, and Carla began to laugh again.

"Let's drink," she said.

There was no more wine in the flask, but Tullio had left his full cup. They drank it together, she and Daniele. First Daniele took a swig, then Carla, then Daniele again, and they had to place their lips always in the same spot, because Carla liked to flirt.

Giulia watched them sadly. Then she suddenly stood up and cleared the table and went to wash the dishes and pots on the floor. Daniele made an attempt to go to help her, but Carla began to shriek for him not to go away. And he remained seated near Carla and was happier to be with her, because Giulia had such a sad face that evening, instead of being happy.

Nevertheless, not even with Carla was it possible to be as merry as before. Carla was having some thoughts now and was preoccupied and a bit depressed. She had taken a candlestick and touched the candle end where it was soft and let some drops of wax fall on the table.

"How stupid we're being," she said. "Do you want me to tell you a story, Daniele?"

"I don't know," said Daniele.

"Yes, I'll tell you," said Carla. She began to tell the story of a girl to whom strange things happened in a strange situation. Daniele didn't follow it very well, because Carla's story was rather confusing, and he wasn't even paying attention to all her words. He just laughed every time Carla laughed. Carla interrupted herself often to laugh.

"We were standing outside that place," Carla was saying, "and suddenly the door opened, and she came out with nothing on."

"Who?" asked Daniele.

"Sara. I've told you before, that girl was named Sara. And the soldier was called Joe, maybe. They're all called Joe, these soldiers."

"Why?"

"I don't know," said Carla. "They're all called Joe, but he wasn't one of those who turn ugly when they get drunk. He laughed, but he wasn't being ugly. And in the meantime Sara screamed and cried, and she escaped outside without anything on, because she was new and scared. And Joe, from inside, yelled like a crazy man, and as for us, no one could understand what he was saying, but clearly it was because Sara had run out. And then we grabbed her by force and took her back inside, and when Joe saw her crying he began to cry too, and then he embraced her in such a way that they both fell on the ground, right there in the midst of us, and then—"

Giulia came over to interrupt her, but without anger. "Enough, Carla."

"Why?"

"Because it's late," said Giulia. "You'd best go to sleep."

Carla laughed in a sly way. "I'm not one bit drunk," she said. "And besides, today I turn fifteen. You'll see how fine it is to be fifteen." She continued to speak similar foolishness, forgetting her story.

Giulia went back to washing the plates.

Daniele had put his head down on the table, and every little while he closed his eyes for a time, and now he was losing track of everything

Carla was saying. Things were getting more and more weightless and they spun around, but his head felt very heavy.

Giulia came over again, as soon as she had finished washing the plates. "Enough now, Carla. Can't you see he's sleeping?"

"Oh, yes?" went Carla, and looked in wonder at Daniele and cuffed him playfully with her hand. "Wake up! You have to help me carry the candles."

Daniele lifted his head from the table, passing his fingers over his eyes. "I must have drunk too much wine."

"Oh, yes," went Carla, with satisfaction. "You're drunk." She kept on laughing.

"Let him go to bed, Carla," said Giulia. "I'll help you carry the candles."

"No, I want him to," said Carla. "Get up, Daniele. We'll have a procession, with flowers and candles, just like two people who are getting married. I should have gotten married, when I was younger."

"Don't do it, Carla," said Giulia.

But Carla took the flowers and put them in Daniele's arms and gave him also a candle to hold. She kept the other candle for herself, and with her free hand she leaned on Daniele.

"Here, just two people who are getting married," she said. "Lift up the blanket, Giulia, otherwise we can't pass through."

Giulia held the blanket up so they could pass. It seemed she wanted to cry. Then she was alone and lit the oil lamp and sat waiting, attentive to every sound.

First, Carla busied herself with the flowers and took a lot of time arranging them in the bowl with a little water. Her expression was serious, and she wasn't moving her hands quickly and competently, as she always did. Leaning against the wall, Daniele watched her, how her hair swayed when she moved her head, and he felt happy because she was so beautiful, and meanwhile he was laughing like an idiot.

Carla suddenly raised her eyes. "What do you have to laugh about?"

Daniele stopped laughing. He remained staring at her with his mouth open, and he saw everything spinning around her, but she was motionless in the center, with a red face and dilated nostrils and dark eyes. Oh, now it would happen like the other time, and he didn't even have the strength to refuse. Suddenly he was no longer drunk, and he understood everything, only he had no strength to refuse.

And now here was Carla, extending her hands to him, without haste, and stroking his neck and his face tenderly, and he felt Carla's damp hands on his neck and his face, and heard her say, "You love me, isn't it true that you love me," words like that, which she kept repeating. She no longer appeared drunk now, and yet she must be drunk to be saying those words.

"Tell me you love me," she was saying. "Why don't you say anything?" And her face came closer all the time.

Finally Daniele found the strength to speak. "What do you want from me, Carla?"

Carla came so close that he felt her words as hot breath on his face. "Stay and sleep with me tonight."

Daniele continued kept staring fixedly ahead, as if he didn't see Carla. She was too close and her features were all muddled. And all his thoughts persisted, thoughts of Tullio and Giulia and of what they should not be doing. He was scared. He trembled with fear.

"Let's let it go, Carla, I beg you."

"You'll wait till Giulia goes to sleep and then you'll come," Carla said. "Tell me you'll come."

He pressed his lips firmly together because she wanted to kiss him. His face was drawn and sorrowful. "It's not possible," he said. "It's not possible."

Carla squeezed her hands harder around his neck. "You'll come?"

He shoved her away with a violent gesture and detached himself from the wall, moving toward the door to leave.

"Tell me, tell me you'll come," said Carla.

From the threshold he turned to look at her but did not reply. He felt a great heat and confusion in his head. He walked to the outer door and opened it. The cold air on his face felt good. He stood leaning against the doorpost, looking out and inhaling the cold air in great gulps. It must be late. Giulia had already said before that it was late. A piece of the moon leaned far over behind the house, and its light cast the shadows of the tumbled walls all around. But none of that was steady in his sight, and he felt a desperate need for something firm.

He searched the sky. There were stars in the sky, bright and sparkling, that had always given him serenity, all the times he had looked at them, and now they offered nothing. Perhaps there was something up there that he should understand, to be so far above everything and to know what one must do. But perhaps there was no right path to follow, where there was good and only good. Because Carla's face was so strange, and repulsive in a certain way, but it also aroused pity and the desire to lose oneself without thoughts of anything.

And not even this was possible. Tullio had gone to work for the night, with a face so serious it was impossible to forget. And Giulia—it would be better if Giulia weren't there. Instead, she was there, waiting for him, suffering and sad, and not even she knew what she wanted from him.

He closed the door again and walked very softly through the corridor. There was a light on in Carla's room, and also one in the kitchen. He did not have the courage to enter there. Then Giulia would see him and would understand what he was thinking in his head and feeling in his very blood. And she would not say anything, only she would see, and would be even more sad and suffering.

"Daniele?" called Giulia.

"I'm coming," he responded, very low. But he still did not enter right away. It felt better to lean against the wall in the dark and to have only himself to deal with.

But Carla had heard their voices and came to the door of her room with a candle in her hand. There she halted and stared stubbornly at him and it seemed she wanted to scold him about something. Then he lowered his head and went into the kitchen.

The oil lamp stood on the table and Giulia could not be seen behind her shelter of blankets. "You were outside a long time," she said.

"I was standing in the doorway. I needed to get some air."

"Don't you feel well?" asked Giulia.

"No," said Daniele. "Just that my head is spinning a bit."

"It's because you drank wine. You're not used to it."

"Yes," said Daniele.

"Go straight to bed, Daniele. You'll see that it will pass off."

"Yes," said Daniele. Giulia did not know and this much, at least, was good. He carried the lamp to the bed and began to undress.

"Remember to turn off the lamp, Daniele," Giulia said again.

He turned off the lamp right away and finished taking his clothes off in the dark. Stretching out on the mattress, he heard Giulia undressing. So she had not gone to bed, and yet she had not let herself be seen when he entered. Giulia understood many things, more than one might think.

He stayed waiting for sleep, but sleep did not come, even though he was so weary. His head was still spinning, and the blood that hammered in a certain place in his head was painful. It must have been caused by too much wine. He was not used to drinking wine.

Each time he closed his eyes he saw faces that shifted around in confusion. The serious face of Tullio, the sad one of Giulia, and Carla's, larger than the others, at once both beautiful and miserable. They all had something to scold him about. And it was Carla who grabbed him from behind in such a way that nausea rose up from his stomach, and he had to open his eyes in the darkness and clamp his teeth to hold it in.

Time passed. Perhaps a lot of time passed, and at first Giulia could be heard turning in her bed and coughing also, deeply, and then nothing more. She must have fallen asleep. He didn't even hear Carla. But he still was wide awake, keeping his eyes closed a little in an attempt to fall asleep, and then he had to open them again to suppress the nausea.

Then Carla came. He became aware of her as she took the last steps right near his bed, and he began to shake. He smelled Carla's perfume and the warmth of her breath. Carla panted a little as she breathed, and he panted also and trembled, and was powerless to prevent that frightening thing that was about to happen.

"Don't talk," said Carla, and she found his face with her hand and pressed his mouth closed. Then, as soon as she was certain he wouldn't speak, she freed his mouth and began to stroke and kiss him. "Don't tremble," she said. "Don't be afraid."

She had put her head down on the pillow and her mouth was close to Daniele's ear. "Give me a little space close to you. Don't be afraid."

He had to summon all his strength not to cry out. "I beg of you, not here. Not here, I pray you."

"Then come to me."

"Oh, that's not possible," said Daniele. "Why do you want us to do this thing?"

Carla began to speak in a louder voice. "If you don't come I'll start screaming."

"Don't speak so loud, please."

"Then come," Carla said, even louder.

"Not so loud, please," said Daniele.

At this point he would do what she wanted. She took him by the hand, and he got up from the bed and followed her. They made no sound, going in their bare feet, and both of them trembled with cold or something else. Right away Giulia began to cough again, but now it was useless. He heard her but he couldn't think about it.

Carla fell asleep, pressing against him with her warm and damp body. He would not have been able to sleep, even if he had wanted to. For him, this was not something so simple that one could fall asleep immediately afterward. He felt a kind of resentment toward Carla, and disgust and remorse for what he had done, and also an ever increasing nausea, caused by the wine. He had drunk too much, he was not used to it. Who knew when the nausea would be gone? Perhaps if he remained with eyes open in the dark and clamped his jaw hard, it would be gone.

In the room he smelled Carla's perfume and the fragrance of the spicebush. He loved that fragrance, which reminded him a little of church, and Giulia loved it also. Giulia must have gone back to sleep. She had coughed a lot, but now after a while he no longer heard her. All was silent in and around the house, except for Carla's breathing. Her breathing was regular and heavy, as if nothing had happened.

He did not want to go to sleep. If he went to sleep, he would stay asleep a long time, and then Tullio, returning, would find him in bed with Carla. Tullio, who had gone out to work with such a serious face. Or else Giulia would come to wake him, early in the morning, probably with a cup of coffee in her hand, and would be full of sorrow and reproach.

He must get up and go away, and yet he did not have the strength. Now his life was all in ruins. With Tullio, and with Giulia, and with Carla, it would never be as it had been, because he had ruined everything. He could not even think of a solution. His brain wasn't succeeding in forming orderly and impossible thoughts as to what remedy there might be.

Only images came to him: Tullio and Giulia and Carla and himself, and everyone was wearing an expression of reproach, even himself toward himself. If only Carla had not gone to sleep! Carla had been so sweet at first, and now also she would be able to do something to relieve his desperation if she did like before, when she had stroked him and kissed him and even talked nonsense. Instead, she was sleeping. Not even for her should it have been something so simple that she could fall asleep immediately afterward.

He had to get out of that bed!

He detached himself from Carla without worrying if he moved too fast, and she did not wake up. She only let out a deep sigh, just like the first time, when the light of the cigarette lighter had disturbed her in her slumber. But that time Tullio was there, and Tullio had said it didn't matter.

The contact of his bare feet with the floor made him shudder all through his body. And the effort to sit up made the blood pound hard in his brain. But he needed to leave. He got to his feet and it seemed to him that he could not stand up straight. The darkness shifted around before his eyes in great red spirals. He made the effort and bumped into the wall, then, leaning against the wall, he made his way to the door. He tripped over an empty jerry-can and it made a never-ending racket. Carla still did not awaken. He could not even hear her breathing anymore. Perhaps the noise had been so loud only in his head. The red spirals spun fast, and he even saw them with his eyes closed, and it must have been the nausea.

He began to move forward. Near the door he smelled more acutely the fragrance of the spicebush that Giulia loved so much. Both of them had been so happy yesterday when he went to gather them for her and had brought them to her. He crossed the corridor, supporting himself on the wall the entire time, and reached the door of the kitchen. He felt bathed in sweat even as he shivered with cold.

Now he couldn't reach the bed by following the wall because there were the table and stools scattered around the kitchen, he couldn't tell where. The effort to think about so many things kept him in dreadful torment. He let go of the door and took one step in the dark. He wasn't able to stay on his feet. Then he got onto his hands and knees, and probing the floor ahead with one hand, he inched forward like an animal, one tiny movement at a time. He had to make a concerted effort not to lose consciousness and to move straight in the direction of the bed.

At last he felt, on his face, contact with the blankets that covered his corner. He had arrived! He reached out an arm until he touched the mattress. He pulled himself up and stretched out on top of the blankets and in that moment the nausea became so great that he couldn't contain it. He had only enough energy to put his head out and vomit on the floor.

Then Giulia came to light the lamp. She didn't say anything. She went to get some water and had him drink it, supporting his head with one hand, and holding the lip of the cup to his lips. But she said nothing. She went to get some ashes from the brazier and covered where Daniele had vomited and swept everything away, into the corridor. She never looked at him directly, and her face wore an inscrutable expression.

And Daniele was desperate, with his head lolling limply on the pillow, and he wished he were alone in the world, without anyone else, even Giulia. And yet he hoped she would return after she had finished sweeping. All his faith in life lay solely in her return. And she came, in fact. She blew the lamp out and went away.

"Giulia," called Daniele softly. She did not answer. Maybe she hadn't heard, she must not have heard. But he did not have the nerve to call to her another time. He had suddenly understood what that confusion of yesterday had been all about, on the bank of the river. And now everything was ruined.

30

As soon as she finished eating, Giulia stood up and set to work in a servile manner, without looking at anyone. During the meal, only Tullio had said something. Then he became silent as well. He rolled a cigarette and began to smoke. Little Maria stubbornly kept her eyes, which were full of sleep, open. Perhaps she sensed that this evening was not like all the other evenings, and she wanted to see what the others were doing. And yet it was like all the other evenings, except that no one was talking. And Carla wasn't there. She must have left right away in the morning, when Daniele was still asleep.

Daniele watched the place where Giulia was washing the plates. The silence weighed on him, and it was necessary to explain himself somehow, as the situation had become unbearable.

Without shifting his gaze he said, "I need to talk to you, Tullio." He spoke the words under his breath so Giulia would not hear.

Tullio continued to smoke without changing his expression. There were two drops of wax on the table. He scraped one of them off with his fingernail. Then he began to scrape at the other one. The short yellow flame of the lamp was giving off smoke.

Daniele swallowed. "I need to talk to you, Tullio," he said again.

"So then talk," said Tullio. He seemed distant.

"Don't be that way," said Daniele. "I need to talk to you, seriously."

Tullio lifted his head toward him and looked at him intensely, and then looked where Daniele was fixing his gaze. Giulia was washing the plates, kneeling on the floor.

"You want to go somewhere else?"

"It would be better."

Tullio shifted his cap a little to scratch his head, but he wasn't being serious. There was even a slight smile playing on his lips, and Daniele tolerated it, because, for him, what he had to say was quite important.

"All right, let's go," said Tullio, standing up.

The drowsy eyes of the child opened wide. "Aren't you taking me home?" she asked.

"Later," said Tullio.

"All right," said the little girl.

"In the meantime, sleep with your head on the table, if you're sleepy," said Tullio.

"All right," said the little girl, and right away she put her head down on the table.

Giulia did not turn to watch them when she heard them leave.

Carla's room was filled with the fragrance of the spicebush. Tullio lit one of the two candles. The spicebush was still on the table, but some of the stems had been taken out of the bowl and put into a tin can.

"Will this take long?" asked Tullio.

"Yes," said Daniele.

"Do you want us to sit down?" said Tullio.

Daniele saw that he still wasn't being serious, and afterward, when they were seated on the bed, he turned his head to look at him, but he couldn't see the expression on Tullio's face, because the candle had remained on the table, a bit behind them. They sat leaning forward, with their elbows on their knees. Some minutes passed. Their shadows made patterns on the wall and danced when the candle flame flickered. From the kitchen came the clatter of plates. Giulia was taking a long time to wash them this evening.

"So then?" said Tullio.

Daniele changed position and then right away turned back again, leaning forward with his elbows on his knees. He said, "Look, I want to go away, Tullio."

Tullio neither moved nor spoke. One couldn't read his thoughts, whether it was important to him or even interesting whether Daniele went or not.

And after a bit Daniele said, "That night when you found me and I came here with you, you said it would be better that I didn't go away right away because of my school uniform. And I've stayed, but by now it's been three months that I'm here. It's not that I'm getting along badly with all of you, on the contrary, but I can't stay here the rest of my life. And anyway, I'm not doing anything to earn my keep. Because keeping the accounts and helping Giulia isn't the same as earning my keep."

He made a long pause, during which Tullio said nothing.

So he went on. "I need to think about my life, Tullio, and it's for this that it would be better if I went to the outside. It might be that on the outside I could set myself up with some good work. If I stay here, you don't give me anything to do, and even then it might be some kind of job that I'm poorly equipped to do. By now I've understood that I'm not succeeding. And so I'm only a burden."

He paused again, waiting for Tullio to say something. But Tullio didn't speak, and it became harder and harder to say those things if Tullio was not going to speak and if a person wasn't able to know what thoughts he was having.

"I'll always remember all of you," said Daniele, "and how good you all have been, since the first day I came here. But now I can't stay. And now the war should be ending, everyone says it will end soon. And also the season will get better later on, and hopefully it might be possible to find work in the fields. I think I'll be able to work in the fields. Those things can be learned quickly."

Again he fell silent. The clatter of the plates ceased, and only the sound of Giulia's clogs was heard from time to time. She was putting the kitchen in order. And she often stopped, thinking something over, as she happened to do many times.

Daniel began to watch his own shadow, and that of Tullio, that were dancing on the wall.

"Why aren't you saying anything, Tullio?" he asked.

"Well . . ." said Tullio, "Well . . ." as if he were searching for something to say and not coming up with anything. But then he asked, "How much does Carla have to do with this business?"

Daniele hung his head. "You know?"

"Yes."

"How do you know?"

"She told me."

Daniele began to twist his fingers nervously. "Where is Carla now?"

"Out," said Tullio.

"Have you sent her away for good?"

"She's out working," said Tullio. "She'll come back tomorrow or the day after, when she's finished. Why didn't you tell me right away that it involved Carla?"

He spoke calmly, as if there were nothing momentous about what had happened, and Daniele did not understand.

"Because I would not have wanted you to know," said Daniele. "I thought it would have upset you to know. I thought of going away, and so it would have ended anyway."

Tullio let some time pass, then he asked, "Is it only because of the business with Carla that you want to go away?"

Daniele continued to twist his fingers and did not reply.

So after a bit Tullio said again, "Listen, I can't get inside your head to see what's in there. It could be that you're also tired of being here with us. It's certainly not the kind of life you thought of having. When all is said and done, you're not used to being with people like us."

"Don't say that, Tullio," said Daniele. "You know it's not true."

"Then why don't you come out with what's in your mind?" said Tullio. "You've said you want to go. You can also do it without saying anything to anyone. Grab your stuff and be off. But if you also want to explain your reason for going, then you have to come out with what's in your mind and not look for excuses."

"It is because of what has happened with Carla," said Daniele.

"Don't you know what kind of work Carla does?"

"Yes."

"Every time she's out at night she goes to bed with someone," said Tullio. "It's her work. Lots of times I'm the one who sends her out, because she's useful to me. So it makes no difference if once in a while she comes to bed with you. Better with you than with someone else."

"Don't joke about it, Tullio," said Daniele. "I know I've done something I shouldn't have. Because I'm here in your house, and you trusted me, and you never even imagined I would have been able to do such a thing."

Tullio said nothing, but he laughed in a sad kind of way.

"You see, you're giving me reasons," said Daniele. "I felt right away that it was a mistake. In front of you, I'm feeling as if I were a bit unclean, and I must go away."

Tullio laughed again, in the same sad way.

"I should have thought before that Carla and I would end up the way we've ended up," said Daniele. "And I should have left before it happened. Instead I ruined everything. Now I don't know how to act, around you and Carla and Giulia."

Tullio raised his head with interest. "Why Giulia?"

"She also thinks it's something I shouldn't have done," said Daniele. "She understands that I'm not clean, and we haven't spoken since last evening, she hasn't said one word to me. Last night I vomited on the floor, and she came to clean up without saying a word. And now she does everything like that, as if she were a servant, and I can't bear it."

"Ah," went Tullio, simply. Then he lifted his left arm so he could see his watch in the light of the candle. "Want to go?"

"Should I get my stuff?"

"No," said Tullio. "We're going close by and coming back. In any event you can get your stuff later."

31

They walked along, all the while in silence. Tullio had taken a path across the ruins of the zone of the dead. There was a sliver of moon high in the sky, and Daniele recognized in many places the way he had gone with Giulia when they went to get water from the river. Then Tullio changed direction, and Daniele immediately became disoriented. The ruins appeared all alike, light and dark under the moon.

At a certain point Tullio made a gesture to stop and went ahead alone, and after a few minutes he returned to get Daniele. He led him behind some huge piles of debris, toward a door that was already open. Above it, the house was entirely fallen down. Tullio entered first and Daniele followed him. It was necessary to bend over in order to pass through. As soon as Daniele got inside, Tullio closed the door and they found themselves in the dark.

"Give me your hand and pay attention, now," said Tullio. "There are five steps."

They descended the five steps one step at a time, holding hands. Then they turned a corner and Tullio turned on a flashlight. He had removed the screen and it threw a bright beam. They were in an underground room, long and narrow, with a low ceiling. Around them were wooden gunracks full of weapons, and on the floor stood cases of ammunition and two huge machine guns covered with hoods. The air was cold and smelled of mildew.

"Here, give me some light," said Tullio, putting the flashlight in Daniele's hands. Then he began to take down some guns at random, bringing them close to the light to examine them carefully. They were almost all submachine guns.

"Every so often it's necessary to take a look," said Tullio. "If the rust begins to eat at them they get ruined right away. Some day the two of us will come to oil and clean all of them again."

"Why are you saying this?" asked Daniele. "You know I must go away."

"Look," said Tullio. "This one is American. It's called a Thompson." Then he leaned the gun against the gunrack, and took down another, heavier one. "And this is German," he said. "It shoots I don't know how many rounds per minute. You should have heard how these things sang when they had the battle in the suburb."

Daniele tried to give him as much light as possible, following him step by step as he moved along the gunracks.

"We have five storehouses like this one," he said. "They are in different places, so if they clean out one they won't get everything. We don't do anything but keep them in order. Some day it might come in handy to have something that sings well."

He had taken down a gun rolled up in rags with particular care. From the rags a shotgun emerged and Tullio broke it open and looked carefully into the barrels under the light. "And this is mine," he said. "My own. Do you like to hunt?"

"I don't know, I've never done it."

"It's what I like best, going hunting. I often went with the owner of the repair shop where I used to work. We went into the marsh where the river begins. Would you like to go duck hunting?"

"I don't know," said Daniele. "I don't think I would like to kill a duck."

"Oh," went Tullio, "you never think about it, when you're there. You shoot and you think only of making a hit."

He went to find a container of grease and generously oiled the gun and began to wrap it up again. "The first day with good weather we'll take bicycles and we'll go to the marsh. We'll take Carla and Giulia too, and a lot of stuff to eat, and we'll spend a nice day together."

"Why are you speaking on purpose as if I were staying with you?" said Daniele. "You know I can't stay."

Tullio gave him a quick look and turned to put the gun back. Then he moved two crates that were stacked one on top of the other, and he looked at his watch before sitting down. "You sit down too," he said. "Here we can talk in comfort."

Daniele sat on the other crate.

"Turn it off now." Tullio said. "We need to spare the battery."

Daniele turned the flashlight off and they were in complete darkness. The moonlight did not penetrate, even slightly, that underground space.

"Was that the first time you went together with a girl?" asked Tullio.

Daniele was reluctant to respond.

"Tell me, was it the first time?"

"How do you mean, together?"

"In bed like that, I mean."

"Yes."

"It's upsetting, the first time," said Tullio. "You don't even know if it feels good or not, isn't that so?"

"I don't know," said Daniele.

"I think you would have been scared more than anything else," said Tullio. "That's how it happens the first time. But this too is needed to become men, and in a way it's just as well it happened to you with Carla. Do you love Carla?"

Daniele hesitated before replying.

"I don't know," he said finally. "I loved her before like a sister, as I already told you. Now I don't know anymore. I'd be afraid to find myself with her again."

"This is something that will pass. And do you love Giulia?"

"Yes."

"As much as Carla?"

Daniele hesitated again, then he said, "More, I think."

"Would you like to do with Giulia what you did with Carla?"

Daniele didn't reply.

"Wouldn't you like it?"

"Why are you asking me these things?"

"Haven't you ever thought about it?" asked Tullio, insistently.

"No," said Daniele, "one doesn't think about those things with Giulia. She's too good. We understood each other so well until now, and now everything is ruined."

"Giulia is becoming a woman," said Tullio.

"More than anything I regret having upset her," said Daniele. "I also regret it for your sake, but you don't take it the way she does. I can't see her working like this, worse than if she were a servant."

"She's becoming a woman," Tullio repeated.

Daniele said nothing. He saw that Tullio had begun to speak seriously now, and he was glad about this in a certain way. At least he had the understanding that for Tullio it meant something similar.

"Hand me the flashlight," said Tullio.

Daniele felt around for Tullio's hands in the dark and passed the flashlight to him. Tullio turned it on and glanced at his watch and then looked at Daniele a long time and turned it off.

"Many times I've wondered if it would not be better if you went away," he said. "We aren't right for you, because we have become too tough through hardship. And Carla has become too tough, even though she is still a young girl. We do things that bother you, and you can't feel comfortable with us. But I think that if you went away, you'd only end up among people like us, or worse, and so it benefits you to stay. At least we all love you, each in our own way, you understand. Are you aware that Giulia loves you?

"I don't know anymore, now," said Daniele.

"She loves you. And Carla also loves you. She did what she did because she loves you, and maybe she doesn't know other ways to show it. And also, I love you. I could have punched you, the first day you came to us, because you understood nothing. Then I ended up loving you anyway."

"Now I've ruined everything."

"Everything will be put right again," said Tullio. "You'll see that in a few days Giulia won't remember anything about it. It's enough that you stay close by, and she won't think about it any longer. She's changed, Giulia has, since you arrived. Before she was always sad, just the way you saw her today. It was always like that, before. And instead, with you, she has changed, and even her health is better.

"Her health isn't very good. Once we took her to the doctor, before winter came, and the doctor said it wasn't anything serious, she just needed to eat better, and cheer up, and get fresh air and sun. But we couldn't do anything for her. We could have had her eat better than we do, but she didn't want that. We began to drink milk every morning, so she would drink some."

He continued, "But as for the rest, Carla and I don't have much time. And anyway, Giulia gets along well with us. She is more like you than like us, in her character, and it was obvious right away that she's happy to be with you. And you can make her do what she needs to do, only you must be affectionate with her, also by now she's no longer a child. If you know what to do, she'll forget easily. Even Carla will forget, you'll see. She'll find some way to let it pass. As for me, don't think you have upset me."

"Does Carla mean nothing to you?"

Tullio laughed in a way that he didn't understand. "By now it's late. Time to go."

They went out into the moonlight and headed off towards home.

The oil lamp had already filled the kitchen with smoke and a bad odor. Little Maria slept with her head on the table. Seated near her, Giulia was mending socks.

Tullio looked at her intently. "You shouldn't be working at night."

"Oh, this isn't work," said Giulia.

"What a one you are," said Tullio and he went over to her and put one hand under her chin and lifted her head, tenderly. Giulia let him do it, but she kept her eyes closed.

"Let me look into your eyes," said Tullio.

Then she opened her eyes and kept them fixed on his, as if adoringly, with her lips slightly parted.

"Don't be so sad, Giulia. Everything's all right. You'll see that everything will be all right."

"Yes," said Giulia.

And Tullio smiled at her, in a wonderful way. Then he approached little Maria and softly took her in his arms and went out with her, asleep like that.

Daniele's heart began to tremble when they were alone. Giulia had taken up her work again and held her head at an angle, and her hair almost covered her face.

"Giulia?"

"Yes," she replied, without raising her head.

"I am sorry about last night. I had drunk too much wine and I didn't know very well what I was doing." He broke off.

Giulia bowed her head even more over her work. "It's not important. It isn't necessary to talk about it."

"You're a good person, Giulia," said Daniele.

She stayed still for some time. Then she said, "It must be late, Daniele. Let's go to sleep." And she stood up in such a way that he couldn't see her face.

Carla returned the next day. She moved through the house rapidly and confidently as usual, but she didn't speak. But as soon as she and Daniele found themselves alone together, she approached him and said quickly, under her breath, "It's my fault what happened the other night. But you'll see, it won't happen again."

Daniele didn't know what to say and lowered his gaze to the floor.

"You have nothing to say?" she asked.

"It was also my fault."

"Well, let's make it as if nothing ever happened."

Then he raised his head to look at her, but she had only a mysterious smirk on her lips, and she kept her eyes focused elsewhere.

arla and Giulia were seated on the edge of the old brick bridge, with their legs dangling above the water. Carla's feet were bare, as she had taken off her shoes. She loved to feel the warmth of the sun on her legs and feet. Below them the water moved silently, and the two women were silent. The only sound was the rustle of some dry leaves. These had stayed attached to the rushes since the previous autumn, and now they made a swishing sound in the light breeze.

Then they heard the report of a gun far off, and both raised their heads at the same time.

"Do you see them, Carla?"

"No," replied Carla.

The whole marsh was immersed in a sweet, luminous peace, and the water silently flowed from the spring holes and moved off towards the sea. The light breeze was coming from the mountains. It had blown away the mistiness of the air, so you could see a long way, to the trees that grew in the fields. And beyond the trees, the hills seemed closer.

"It's three hours that they've been going around through the marsh," said Carla.

"They waited so long for this day," said Giulia.

"But I'm hungry!" said Carla. "I always feel this damn hunger whenever I go out. I remember when we roamed through the fields instead of going to school."

Then they sat again without talking. Giulia turned her head and began to look at the hills. But Carla stayed with her head bowed, and after a while she spat into the water. Two or three little fish rose to the surface and contended to take possession of the spit, as the current carried it away.

"Look, Giulia," said Carla, and she spat again into the water, and more little fish came floating up. "Did you see how they glitter?"

"Yes."

"It's their scales," said Carla. "It's as if they were wearing beautiful outfits, all silvery."

"Ohh . . ." said Giulia.

The bottom of the channel was full of long weeds that bent with the current. But toward the riverbanks the weeds rose to the surface of the water and covered it completely in green.

"I could almost jump in," said Carla. "It would be lovely to bathe here, where there's no one."

"It's not the season yet. And also the water must be cold so close to the source."

"Yes, it must be cold."

Once again they heard a gunshot far away, but they didn't see the boys. A bird with grey plumage burst out of the reeds and flew screeching over their heads. They watched it go off into the distance.

"It's already the third one that's gone by here," said Carla. "I'll bet they haven't seen very many, going in the boat."

Giulia kept looking generally towards the bridge where the bird had disappeared.

"They should be getting back by now," said Carla.

Giulia did not reply, because she was now staring at her hands with a curious interest. The chilblains had disappeared, but some dark marks had remained in their place, and also some marks in place of the cracks. Suddenly she held her hands out in front of herself.

"What do my hands look like, Carla?"

"Why?"

Giulia seemed to regret having asked that question, so she said, "I'd like to have beautiful hands."

"Well, they aren't exactly beautiful."

Giulia pulled her hands back and made them into fists. "Isn't there anything to do to make them beautiful?"

Carla laughed. "How peculiar you are today."

Then they heard another gunshot, close by, and they alertly raised their heads. Two or three birds came out of the rushes and darted off, flying low over the marsh.

"Do you see them, Carla?"

"No."

They continued to watch anyway, because the shots had been nearby. The sun made the water sparkle in some far-off spot, beyond where they were looking. Then the boat came out of the rushes into an open space. It was a small boat, stubby and black with tar, with a flat bottom that moved well through the marsh. Tullio was standing up in the stern and with a long pole he pushed on the bottom to move the boat. Daniele for his part was seated in the bow and was watching the water, in which he trailed his hand.

Giulia's face lit up to see them and, putting her hand to her mouth, she called loudly to Daniele. He pulled his hand from the water and waved. Then he got to his feet and from the bottom of the boat he took something and lifted it up to show them.

"Oh," said Giulia, joyfully. "They must have taken something."

The boat neared the bridge slowly, because it was moving against the current. The water sparkled around it in the sunlight.

"We're coming ashore," shouted Tullio at a certain point, and shoving on the pole he turned the boat into a channel that they didn't see. It disappeared suddenly among the reeds and grasses.

Giulia got up and waited for Carla to put on her shoes.

"I could have bathed here where there's no one," said Carla before they left.

On either side lay the silent marsh, and the road went almost straight along the dike. Now the hills appeared before their eyes, with little houses amid the light green of springtime.

The road along the dike was almost a mile long before it came out of the marsh, and Giulia and Carla walked along slowly to stay even with the boat, which followed the channels without their being able to see it. Two or three times Giulia stopped to call to Daniele, and Daniele responded from the marsh.

"Are you in love with Daniele?" Carla asked, suddenly.

All at once Giulia's face turned red. "Why are you asking me?"

"Just because," Carla said, regarding her curiously. "You don't have to tell me if you don't want to."

Giulia walked on thoughtfully for a few paces. Then she said, "You know I'm in love with him."

"Really in love, completely?"

"Yes, I'm afraid so."

She had a half-smile on her lips, but Carla instead laughed loudly, in an embarrassing way.

"Why are you laughing like that, Carla?"

"Nothing," said Carla. "I just thought that you should tell him. If you wait for him to figure it out by himself you'll have to wait a long time."

Giulia walked along, looking at the ground. "I wouldn't dare to speak to him about these things."

"If you want I can speak to him," said Carla.

Giulia quickly raised her eyes. "Oh, no, don't tell him, Carla, please. If we're meant for each other, he'll understand. And it's not important, even if he knows nothing. I'm happy all the same, this way, so happy. And it could be that he didn't love me, and then it would be worse if he got to know."

"Oh well," said Carla, shrugging her shoulders.

A bit farther along she said again, "A person can see from a mile away that you're in love, Giulia. Whenever he's around you're like a dead cat. I don't know how that dummy manages not to be aware of it."

"But don't you tell him, Carla, please," said Giulia. Now she was looking at the ground once more as she walked, and she seemed sad.

Carla patted her on her hair. "I'll give you a little cream for your hands," she said. "It needs to be put on at night, before going to bed. It's for him that you want to have beautiful hands, right?"

"Yes," said Giulia.

When they arrived at the place where the landing was, Daniele was already tying the boat to the piling, and Tullio was seated on the wooden dock, washing his legs that were dirty with mud up to the knees.

Daniele had seen them arrive, and as soon as he had finished tying up he came toward them on the road. He held in his hand the dead game, and his face was glowing with pride. "Look what we've taken," he said.

Carla watched him with an amused expression, because he was really a little boy. "What are they?" she demanded.

"This is a duck," said Daniele. "And these are two snipes. Ducks of this type are called *marzaiole*, because they come through here in March."

"We're in April now," said Carla.

"Hey, what do I know?" said Daniele. "Tullio said that they're called that. It means they don't know how to tell one month from another very well."

Giulia stood a bit aside, now shy, because Carla knew.

Carla touched the feathers of the duck and she turned it over to see where it had been shot. "Did you shoot it?" she asked.

"Tullio did," said Daniele. "Tullio also shot the snipes. I fired three shots but I didn't get anything. But I had fun anyway."

Tullio came up, carrying the gun on his shoulder, with his pants still rolled up above the knees and his shoes in his hand.

"You can't do anything without a dog," he said. "We lost at least two ducks in the middle of the rushes."

"It's been a good hunt all the same," said Carla.

"Yes, but with a dog there would have been at least two more ducks," said Tullio.

Daniele gazed at the black boat, motionless in the stagnant water of the shore. "Who knows when we'll be able to come back again," he said.

"Maybe soon," said Tullio. "Now the days will be good all the time."

Leaving the marsh behind, the road continued across the fields, between two rows of young mulberries with tiny leaves. But there were few trees in that first strip of land, and the houses of the peasants could seen at the far end, where they had left the bicycles. The fields of grain were a tender green, and they rippled under a light wind. It was good land, recently reclaimed.

Daniele talked the whole way about how the hunt had gone. He was lively in the recounting of it, and the others listened, laughing, except Giulia, who listened seriously. Tullio had rolled down the legs of his pants but he had not put on his shoes, and he walked barefoot in the white dust of the road. Giulia carried his shoes for him.

They entered the barnyard of the farmhouse. A big dog lying by the haystack raised itself on its paws and began to bark without leaving its spot. Then a small child came out onto the porch of the house, a little boy, poorly clothed, with a round, white and red face. He looked and toddled back inside. Then an old man came out, and behind him, a young woman. The baby held onto the skirts of the woman, and put his round face out to watch.

"*Buon giorno*," said Daniele, holding the birds out to them.

The old man came forward on bowed legs. He had white hair and a dark and seamed face, and very worn-out clothes.

"How did it go?" he asked.

"It went well," said Tullio. "We tied up the boat where it was before."

"All right," said the old man, and took the game from Daniele's hands to examine it better. Even his eyebrows were completely white.

The woman went back into the house, pulling the baby behind her. The big dog was once more couched in the sun against the haystack and didn't bark again. The old man gave the game back to Daniele without saying a word; he only made a movement with his head.

"We're stopping here to eat," said Tullio in the old man's direction.

The old man assented with his head. "I won't even ask you to come and eat with us. Times are lean, and extra mouths make themselves felt."

"You're always whining, you peasants," said Tullio, "but you are the ones who are better off than anyone. It always goes well on the land."

"If it were only ours, the land."

"It will be yours. A little while longer and it will be yours."

The old man peered closely into his face. "Are you a Red?" he demanded.

"Yes."

The old man shook his head. "How long has it been that we've been hearing they're going to give land to the peasants? I've heard that ever since I was born. And I've always had a landlord."

Then he lifted his shoulders and headed toward the house on his bowed legs.

"We'll need a little water to drink, Granddad," Tullio shouted after the old man.

"As much water as you want," said the old man, half-turning.

"And after, we'll come find you to work out a deal with vegetables."

"We'll see, we'll see," said the old man.

"And also with eggs," said Tullio.

"You'll have to speak to the women about the eggs," said the old man, and started back toward the house.

Tullio watched him until he saw him disappear through the doorway, then silently he headed to the spot where they had left the bicycles, and Daniele followed him. Giulia and Carla were a little distance away, under a cherry tree at the edge of the barnyard, where they had prepared a place to eat. They had spread a blanket on the grass and had pulled things from the basket. Now they were waiting. The cherry tree had tiny leaves that did not block the sun. All around, the grass looked white with fallen blossoms.

The trailer of the bicycle had a false bottom, and Tullio hid the shotgun and cartridges there and closed it with care, so no one could see anything.

"Just think how one would need so little to live contentedly," he said. "It would be enough just to have a house, honest work, and now and then a day like this one."

The sun sank toward the horizon, and they sped on their bicycles toward the city. The road had plane trees on either side and was asphalted but ruined in many spots. But the small villages they passed through were almost intact, because the war had not done much damage along that road.

Tullio went ahead some yards and pushed hard on the pedals because he was in a hurry to get home. Carla perched on the trailer of the bicycle, on top of the bag of vegetables, and she gripped with one hand the basket full of eggs. Tullio had done a good business with the peasant.

Daniele came along behind, panting slightly along the track, so he spoke little to Giulia. Or perhaps it wasn't easy to say to her things that would go over well in that moment, because they felt a bit melancholy for the day just over, and yet contented with it and with the good things they were bringing back with them. Giulia was seated on the crossbar of the bicycle; she let herself lean back a little, until her head was pressed against his chest. And the breeze stirred by their movement blew a few strands of her hair into Daniele's face, and he let it, hoping she didn't notice. It smelled nice.

Then the road joined with another in the vicinity of the city. This new road was bigger and had many houses along it, and they couldn't see the sun setting. Tullio began to travel at a more leisurely pace.

The streets of the city seemed silent, without the din of trucks. A lot of people were about, because the air was sweet and mild. The gardens between the houses were starting to fill in with green and the trees had new leaves and some wistaria vines had flowering clusters that gave off perfume.

They arrived home, and Giulia and Carla got down, and Tullio carried his bicycle into the shoemaker's kitchen to take the shotgun out of the trailer.

The shoemaker and his wife were eating, and little Maria was sitting off to one side. She seemed happy, just a little, when she saw Giulia arrive.

"Someone came looking for you, Tullio," said the shoemaker. "Around four o'clock."

"Who was it?"

"Don't know," said the shoemaker. "He was one of your people, but I don't know his name."

Tullio lifted the gun from the bottom of the trailer and handed it over to Carla so she could take it home. "And he didn't leave any message for me?" he asked, without looking toward the shoemaker.

"No," said the shoemaker. "I told him you had gone to the marsh, and he said he knew that, but he came by here because he hoped you would have gotten back. That's all he said."

Tullio finished putting the false bottom of the trailer back in place.

"While you go to bring the bicycles back I'll make something to eat," said Giulia.

"What, you want to eat again?" said Tullio, smiling.

"Oh, only for today," said Giulia.

"Well then, make a lot of stuff," said Tullio. "This ride has given me a big appetite."

Then he left with the bicycle. Daniele was waiting outside, and they left right away.

Little by little it got dark, and in the narrowest places the streets were full of shadows. They had to take the bicycles back to Emilio's place. Emilio was the most solitary of the boys, and he lived alone under a sagging tarpaulin on the riverbank. He emerged from a kind of a den when he heard them arrive.

And he said to Tullio, "Antonio and Andrea were here waiting for you for two hours. They said to let you know as soon as you arrived. It's about some business you know about."

Tullio's expression turned very serious. "Has it been long since they left?"

"Must be half an hour."

Tullio was now in a big hurry. They left the tarpaulin, he and Daniele, and took different streets from those they had taken in coming. Daniele didn't ask anything, although he wanted to. That part of the quarter was not very inhabited because a great number of houses had been destroyed in the bombardment.

Tullio walked quickly and silently, and his thoughts must have been troubling him. But when they were farther along, he spoke. "Tonight I have to go out," he said. "You can explain it to Carla. Tell her that I really can't get out of it."

"All right."

Tullio took a few more steps, without speaking. Daniele had never passed through those streets and he didn't know where they were going.

Then Tullio pulled out the canvas envelope that served as a wallet and gave it to Daniele. "When you get home," he said, "put it in the little box that's under my bed."

"All right," said Daniele. "Is something worrying you, Tullio?"

"Why? Because of the wallet?"

"Yes."

"No," said Tullio, "there's nothing. I always leave the wallet at home, every time I go out to these things. It would be stupid to get caught with the wallet in my pocket. Besides everything else, there are some papers in it that they should not see. They wouldn't understand, but it's better that they didn't see them."

"Yes," said Daniele.

"What I'm advising you is, to tell Carla that I'm sorry," said Tullio. "Every time that it would be more beautiful to stay together, it happens that I have to go. There was no agreement to go with the boys tonight."

"Do you have to go far?"

"No. It could also be that I won't find them anymore, and then I'll be home within the hour. And even if I find them, I'll be back tomorrow morning for sure. I'll get back early, before she's up. Tell that to Carla."

"All right," said Daniele.

They walked on a little farther without speaking, each with his own thoughts. Then Daniele realized they had arrived in the Sant' Agnese square. He saw on the right the great dark mass of the church.

"Do you know how to get home by yourself, now?" asked Tullio.

"Yes," replied Daniele.

"Well, see you later, then," said Tullio, and departed toward the wall, and his face was both serious and anxious. The sound of his footsteps faded quickly, and even his outline soon became lost in the shadows of evening.

Then Daniele went off in the opposite direction, and he kept one hand in the pocket of his jacket, gripping the canvas envelope that Tullio had turned over to him. He tried to shake off his sadness over Tullio's departure. He went toward home, where Giulia was, and Carla. He walked across the square, which had mounds of rubble around it.

But he kept his face turned upward, because he liked looking at the moon. The blue of the sky had darkened, and some stars were appearing, but the moon still looked more beautiful to him. It had become luminous and whiter, and even tinged with blue, it seemed.

33

As with the night before, there was in the sky a piece of silvery moon, corroded away on the side where it was broken in half. Carla and Daniele were seated at the door of the house, with their arms resting on their knees, in silence. For a while they had talked of nothing much, but then they had no more desire even to make small talk, and they stayed there, wordlessly. They watched the evening descend. The sun had set behind the house and the shadows of night emerged from the destroyed houses and covered the ground and rose toward the heights to join with the sky. The air was sweet and carried, even into those ruins, the feeling of spring, a feeling of life.

Gradually the night mingled in its shadows everything they could see: the remains of the walls, the piles of debris, the path that ran from the shoemaker's house, and, farther along, the magnolia tree. The magnolia tree was already growing outside the zone of the dead, in the courtyard behind the shoemaker's house. Up in the sky the day died, and the shape of the moon grew ever more distinct.

They watched everything, even the sky, but always their gaze turned to fasten upon the shadows that lay on the path that came from the shoemaker's house.

Giulia arrived from the kitchen, making noise with her clogs, and then, stopping in the doorway, she too looked toward the path that could no longer be seen. "It's ready, if you want to eat," she said.

But Carla said, without turning, "Let's wait a little longer, Giulia."

Giulia stayed to look at the path longer, then she turned and went back into the kitchen.

Time passed, and Carla said, "I seem to have the music of a cricket in my ears."

Daniele was absorbed in his own thoughts. "What?" he asked.

"Nothing," said Carla. Perhaps a cricket was singing in some place among the ruins.

"It's stupid to wait this way," said Carla. "So many times, he hasn't come. He'll come later, and we would do better to go inside and eat."

"He said that he would come," said Daniele. "This morning early, he said."

The sky turned dark, full of stars, and the moon became more luminous and white. Now one could see better into the night, it seemed.

Time passed, and Daniele said, "It's getting cold, Carla. Maybe it's better if we go inside."

"No," said Carla.

They remained seated on the little step, in silence for some time, until Carla said, "Doesn't it seem you can hear a cricket singing?"

Daniele listened, then he said, "No." But he still continued to listen.

Finally, someone came along the path. As soon as they heard the footsteps, they began to tremble, either with hope or with fear, or maybe just because it was by now getting chilly, and their backs felt even colder, hearing those footsteps.

"Maybe it's him," said Daniele.

"No," said Carla.

Slowly the figure of whoever it was emerged from the night and came straight toward the door, halting in front of them. Carla seized Daniele's wrist and squeezed it.

"Greetings, Carla," said the one who had come.

And she said, "Greetings, Marco."

"I've come to talk to you, Carla," he said. He spoke in a low voice.

"Yes," said Carla, "but wait until we go inside."

He waited in silence. And Carla, without haste, stood up and directed her steps toward the kitchen, but she did not let go of Daniele's wrist.

Giulia had lit the lamp in the kitchen. When she saw them come in, she peered into their faces, one after the other, and turned pale. One could smell the odor of cooked food, the meat that Tullio had taken in the hunt just yesterday.

Now Giulia fastened her gaze on the face of the boy called Marco. "Have they taken him?" she asked.

"They've killed him," said Marco.

They stood in silence, each in his own way, with eyes fixed on some spot. Only little Maria continued to observe the others, with her usual expression, serious and a bit dull. Carla didn't let go of Daniele's wrist, but gripped it harder, and so he looked at her and saw her frozen face, with only her lip trembling. It trembled in her frozen face, and after a bit she made a grimace with her mouth to keep it still. Then she said, "Be seated, Marco."

She sat down first, with Daniele at her side, and faced Marco. Giulia remained on her feet.

"Giulia, bring a little food for Marco," said Carla. "Maybe he hasn't eaten yet."

Giulia didn't move, and no one spoke anymore of eating.

"Antonio will come later on," said Marco. "He's the chief, now."

"Yes," said Carla. She had released Daniele's wrist and drew forth cigarettes from the pocket of her dress. She offered one to Marco and also to Daniele, but Daniele signaled no with his head.

"Take one," said Carla.

Daniele took a cigarette, gave it a puff, and then let it alone. The others smoked in silence. Giulia had gone to sit apart, beyond the light of the lamp.

"Marco?" said Carla then, and she raised her eyes to him and saw that he was watching Daniele. Then she said, "This is Daniele. He's been with us five months now."

"Yes," said Marco. "Tullio told me about him."

"Well," said Carla, "tell us how it happened."

"I wasn't there, myself," said Marco. "Antonio got back before it turned light, and he stayed in hiding all day. He'll come here tonight, he said. First he went to Andrea's house, because Andrea had a mother and a sister, and so he went there first. After, he'll come here."

"Have they killed Andrea too?" asked Carla.

"Yes," said Marco. "The three of them went, and only Antonio came back. He was lucky."

"Where did they kill them?"

"On the road," said Mario, "five miles from here. But they've already taken them to the little room at the cemetery, and they'll hold them there for identification. Antonio says that none of us must go to see them. It needs to be done like the other times."

"Yes," said Carla.

"The police won't let anyone through very soon, this time," said Marco. "The strike was too big, with fifteen dead. There were two of ours, and nine of the other band, and four soldiers. Luckily we're not directly involved, because it was the other band that organized everything. They needed someone who knew the streets well, here on the inside, and so three of us went too, but only as guides."

"Yes," said Carla.

"It was the second time that our guys worked with that band," said Marco. "It's a large group, that one. They have trucks and everything that's needed. And American deserters who speak Italian like us are in with them, and they have courage to spare. But this time it went badly. Antonio got away only by a miracle. He was lucky."

No one spoke during the pause after he had spoken. Carla had focused her gaze on her hands on the table, and she waited in silence for him to continue.

"Not long ago this band came into our area," said Marco. "First it was in other places, I don't know where, and they made many strikes, and those always went well. Then they happened to come here, because every so often those who strike the military convoys have to change location. If they don't, surveillance gets too hot, and they're screwed. But around here it was only the second strike they had made, and no one can explain how come there was an escort on the convoy. There has never been an escort on the trucks before. Antonio says that there must be some dirty work in this deal, and anyway, it's really a shame we got ourselves killed. There's no pleasure in losing your skin when someone's playing the spy."

"Who played the spy?" asked Carla.

"I don't know," said Marco. "Someone in the other band. Antonio says it must have been one of those Americans who was pretending to be a deserter and was a cop instead. And then, when the escort began to shoot, someone was shooting also from the sidelines. Antonio says that someone definitely must have shot from the sidelines, if not, there would not have been so many dead on our side. Ours were all sheltering in the ditch, when they began to shoot. Only the two on the truck were up on the road."

Marco paused again, and he looked around at their faces with a meaningful expression.

"Tell us everything you know, Marco," said Carla.

"I wasn't there," said Marco. "But they always make the strikes the same way. They take up a position at a crossroads, along the road where the convoy must pass by, and they stay hidden until the right moment. They put a truck on the road with two of those Americans dressed as soldiers. They pretend to have a breakdown and the vehicle that is coming stops and they pull it to the side of the road. It's almost always toward the rear of the convoy, with the vehicles that follow behind. That way they can take all the trucks they want. And this time also it was going well at the beginning. By that time they had taken two trucks and Antonio was waiting for another to leave, because he had to guide the first three, and Andrea the second three, and Tullio the last three. They wanted to take nine. But when they stopped the third truck, someone started firing from above, because the escort was on it. Still, those in the band began to shoot back, and also someone who was with them began to shoot at them, Antonio says. But the two trucks that were ready left right away, and they didn't take them. So Antonio came home. He was lucky."

Carla had lifted her head. "Then he didn't see them, after they were killed?"

"No," said Marco. "Right away this morning Antonio sent one of ours to the spot, and all the dead were still on the ground, on one side of the road. But there were police who set up a guard and didn't let anyone near. So he wasn't able to see anything. Later they took them to the cemetery in a truck, and then Antonio sent a woman to the police station. She's a woman who had a son who disappeared three months ago, and she told the police that she wanted to see the dead, in case her son was there too. So she went to the little room and saw them. She had never seen Tullio and Andrea before, but she told us how they looked, and how they were dressed, and now we're sure it was them. That woman said that Tullio's belly was full of holes. Those machine guns can make holes really fast."

Marco was still talking when Antonio arrived. No one heard him coming. He stopped at the door and came forward only when Marco was finished speaking. He was a tall boy with a strong face.

"Be seated, Antonio," said Carla. "Have you eaten?"

Antonio sat next to Marco. "I am sorry, Carla," he said. "It would have been better if it had been my turn instead of Tullio's."

Carla smiled sadly. "What's done is done. Besides, he thought he would die this way. Only it was too soon."

"Yes," said Antonio, "too soon."

He, too, eyed Daniele.

"This is Daniele," said Carla.

"Tullio spoke of you many times," said Antonio. "I think he loved you."

Daniele couldn't think of anything to say.

"Don't you want to eat something, Antonio?" said Carla.

Antonio appeared to consider for a moment, but he wasn't thinking about eating. He said, "Tullio and Andrea were the sharpest of all of us. It's a shame that they should both have gone this way. I'm afraid there were some dirty doings in this deal, Carla."

"Yes," Carla said. "Marco has told me."

"And to think it was not even planned for last night," said Antonio. "The strike should have been made Monday or Tuesday. Instead, yesterday they sent someone in a big rush to tell us. There must have been something fishy behind it."

"Don't you want a little coffee, Antonio?" asked Carla.

"Yes, coffee's okay," said Antonio.

Giulia stood up from her place in the shadows and applied herself to making coffee. No one paid attention to her, not even when the stove on the floor began to puff.

Antonio began to scrutinize Daniele again. "You were the one who kept the accounts, right?"

"Yes."

"Do you want to show me the book? I must know what there is now."

Daniele stood up to go and get the accounts notebook that was in Carla's room. Returning, he also brought Tullio's wallet and put it on the table in front of Carla. "He left me with this, before he went," he said.

Without a word Carla pushed the wallet toward Antonio.

"We'll look at this later," said Antonio. He moved close to the lamp and began to turn the first few pages of the notebook, which were full of numbers as well as Tullio's jottings. He set himself to studying them, but he quickly tired of that and skipped to the last pages.

"This here is all we have now, right?" he asked Daniele.

"If you want, I'll explain everything," said Daniele.

"It doesn't matter, it's quite clear," said Antonio.

He continued to study the last pages with an attentive attitude until Giulia came to put the cups of coffee on the table. Then he closed the notebook and put it in his pocket. "I must keep it now," he said.

Each of them took a cup of coffee. Antonio drank in a rush, then he took up Tullio's wallet and emptied it completely. On the table he separated the papers from the money and counted the money. There were almost 50,000 *lire*.

"Didn't he have any other cash in the house?" he asked.

"No," said Carla, "he kept everything in his pocket."

"Everything he should have had is written in the notebook," said Daniele.

"Sure," said Antonio, but he did not look at the notebook. He began to examine the papers closely, one by one. One could see he was very tired. Everyone else remained silent. Little Maria had fallen asleep with her head on the table.

Then, when he had finished, Antonio put everything back into the wallet, except one little folded piece of paper, which he passed to Carla. Carla looked at it, and her face wore a misty smile. She kept the paper in front of her, folded on the table.

"Will you continue to work with us, Carla?" asked Antonio.

Carla shook her head no. "I was doing it for Tullio."

"All right," said Antonio, simply.

"You understand . . ." she began.

Antonio interrupted her at once. "It's all right, Carla."

"I want to be free," said Carla. "Your business for you, and mine for me. I don't like living always with the fear of ending up in prison."

"Sure," said Antonio, and he stood up, and Marco stood up with him.

"Wait, have a little more coffee."

Antonio waited, but he did not sit down. "It's a serious thing this time, Carla," he said. "Up to now there's nothing, but if the police should start to take one of us, it's better to change your location right away."

"All right."

"I'll try to let you know first thing, if there's something," said Antonio. "Meanwhile you shouldn't spread it around, and you shouldn't even be seen around very much. I've spoken to the shoemaker and he has agreed to keep silent. He has his own interests, too."

Giulia came to pass around the coffee, and Antonio drank it standing up. Then he picked up Tullio's wallet, which was lying on the table.

"As for the cash, there's more of it around," he said. "Each one of us has a consigned share. And then there's the goods, that counts more than everything. You'll get your share, now that you don't want to stay with us. And Andrea's mother will have Andrea's share. Tullio's share will remain instead in the communal fund, as we decided in the pact. Only it will take a little time before the accounting is complete."

"Everything's written down in the notebook," said Daniele.

"Yes," said Antonio, "but it'll take a little time just the same."

"That's understood," said Carla.

"I think you'll have something to live on, in the meantime," said Antonio.

"Yes," said Carla, "we'll carry on."

Antonio put the wallet in his pocket where he had put the notebook. "Naturally, Carla," he said, "if you have a need, also in the future, we're ready to help you as we can. And if you want to work with us, we will always be happy to take you in."

"Thanks," said Carla, "but I don't think that will be the case."

Antonio took a step toward the door, then he stopped and stood as if thinking of saying something of importance. He was very tired. He only said, "Good night, then," and he left.

Marco also, before going away, said only, "Good night."

The others remained alone and in silence, the child sleeping at the table, Carla and Daniele seated nearby, Giulia sitting in the shadows as she had all evening, and it was as if she weren't even in the room. Each perhaps was remembering Tullio, how he had been in life, and each thought how he must be now, in the little room, his belly full of holes. They made holes fast with those machine guns and now it was necessary to do the accounts because of his death, the accounts of money and the goods.

"Carla?" asked Daniele. "Did I do the wrong thing to bring out the wallet?"

"No," said Carla, "you didn't do the wrong thing."

"I think Tullio would have done it, in my place," said Daniele.

"Yes," said Carla. She took the folded paper from the table, unfolded it and read it, and smiled sorrowfully. It was a small note, ripped from a page of the notebook. Then she folded it again and put it in her pocket, and the sad smile lingered a long time on her lips.

"Carla?" said Daniele.

"What?"

But Daniele found that he couldn't say anything. Then Carla took his hand and pulled him in front of her, and began to twine her fingers through his, and as she did it, her mind was not on what she was doing, but in some other thoughts that one could not guess at. Finally she let go of Daniele's hand.

"Maybe it's late," she said. "We'd better go to bed."

Daniele asked, "What do you think Antonio will be like, Carla?"

"At one time he was a clever boy," said Carla. "He still is, I'm sure."

"He'll never be like Tullio," said Daniele.

Carla lowered her head. "No one will ever be like Tullio," she said. And after a moment of silence she got to her feet and said again, "We'd better go to bed."

But she didn't move, because she seemed aware only then of the little girl asleep with her head on the table. "Giulia?" she called in a low voice.

"Yes," replied Giulia from the shadows.

"Do you think it would be all right to make her something to eat before we put her to bed?" asked Carla.

"It doesn't matter," said Giulia. "She's already asleep."

"Yes," said Carla, and she approached the child and very gently lifted her, and then went off with her in her arms, to take her home as Tullio had done so many times.

Then Giulia said, "We have to go to get water tonight."

"Yes," Daniele said. "Let's go right now."

34

S tanding in the doorway, Daniele saw the man coming along the path across the ruins. He was wearing an old suit and an old hat. He advanced, watching the ground, but every two or three steps he glanced up towards the house.

The man was already nearby when Daniele suddenly thought that he could only be coming to their house. He hurried to Carla to tell her that a man was coming.

Carla was stretched out on her bed, doing nothing. "What man?" she asked.

"I don't know, it's someone I've never seen before."

Carla got up and rushed to the door of the room, and she right away withdrew. "Sit down on the bed, Daniele," she said in haste. "And don't leave. And don't talk."

When the man appeared at the threshold, Carla was seated on the chair in front of her little table, filing her nails. She appeared calm.

The man entered without removing his hat and stopped next to Carla, muttering a greeting.

Carla lifted her head for a second. "Hello," she said, and immediately went back to filing her nails.

The man glanced toward Daniele. "Is he one of the boys?"

"No," said Carla, "he's a friend of mine."

"Aha," went the man, mockingly, and came straight toward Daniele and sat down on the bed next to him. With two fingers he pushed his hat back a little. "Hello," he said.

Daniele moved to stand up, but then he stayed seated, even though the man had positioned himself a little too close. "Hello," he said in return.

The man had red-rimmed eyes and a long beard, and his clothing stank of filth. Now that he had pushed his hat back, one could see he was bald, at least in front. He wore a pair of military cleated boots, almost new.

"Anything to drink?" he asked.

It wasn't clear to whom he addressed the question, whether to Carla or Daniele. In any case, neither of them replied. Carla remained turned toward the little table, and one could see only her back and the hair on her lowered head.

"Hey, Carla," said the man. "Isn't there anything to drink?"

"No," said Carla. "What are you coming here for?"

"Christ," said the man, "this is no way to receive people. I've only just got here, and already you'd like to send me away. At least give me a cigarette."

Carla took cigarettes from her purse, which lay on the table, and tossed them towards the man. The pack fell near the bed and the man leaned down to pick it up. In spite of that, he appeared satisfied. Carla had remained turned away in the chair after tossing the pack, but she didn't look around.

The man struck a match on the floor to light it. Suddenly he made a face in disgust. "You shouldn't keep cigarettes in your purse. They get to smell like perfume. It's a shame, good cigarettes like these."

"What are you coming here for?" demanded Carla again, in the same tone of voice.

"Oh, to pay my respects," said the man. "Just to pay my respects. Giulia's not here?"

"She's out."

"Good," said the man. "On one hand I'm glad she's out. Because that means she's well, and for that I'm glad. Do you remember how many worries we've had over her health? And anyway, now she's well."

Carla was no longer filing her nails but only looking at her hands, which lay idly in her lap. And Daniele didn't know what to do, seated next to the man that stank.

"I'll bet she's developed now, too," said the man. "The last time I saw her, she was all skin and bones, but it's already been some time since I've seen her. It was difficult for her to come to the outside, poor child. It's too bad when it's hard for a girl to come to the outside. Do you want to guess how much better a girl lives, who has developed? A different life entirely. A girl like Giulia could very well play the lady, now that she's developed."

The man paused to smoke, and Carla asked again, "What are you here for?"

The man continued to smoke in silence until he finished the cigarette. Then he tried to toss the butt out the window, but he missed, and it fell to the floor.

Carla had set herself to watching the man, waiting.

"Why don't you send this young man outside, Carla?" said the man. "It's a shame to keep him inside here on such a nice day."

"He's a friend of mine," said Carla. "You can say whatever you want."

Instead of speaking, the man began to focus on the butt on the floor. A blue thread of smoke rose almost straight up the wall, to the height of the window, then it dissolved in the light air that entered through the open window.

Daniele stayed with his head down, motionless. At first he had dared to give a glance toward Carla, but now he no longer raised his eyes.

"Talk, make it snappy," said Carla.

Then the man said, "I found out about Tullio, poor kid. It's really a shame."

"How did you find out?"

"Oh," went the man, "sooner or later you get to know everything. I knew almost right away. But I waited a few days to come here, until you calmed down. Now you're calm enough, it appears. It's better to remain calm when discussing business."

"What do you want, then?"

"Look," said the man, "I was thinking of you, all these days. All told, it's my duty to think of you, right? Well, I was thinking and I said to myself, Carla has grown up by now, and she's left alone, and now it's only right for me to be concerned for her arrangements. You see, when one is young, one never thinks about arrangements. It seems like one will always be young, who knows for how long. Instead, the years pass, and in the end one finds oneself old with nothing to show for it, and then it's too late. One must think about it now, while there's still time. So I've thought of something for your benefit. At my age, one has a greater experience of life, and one sees better what's best to do."

The man paused a moment, waiting for some sign from Carla.

And she said, "It's pointless for you to continue, since I'll do what I want anyway."

"Wait," said the man. "Let me explain it to you first. It's a good business, even you will understand it's a good business."

"I already know what it's about. It's pointless to talk about it."

The man gave her an unpleasant look. "But you don't really want to spend your life with these . . . little babies?" he said.

"I'll do what I want," said Carla. "You know quite well that I'll do what I want."

The man lit another cigarette and began to smoke. "Well," he said, "then we'll put the question from another angle. I had some business with Tullio, and now it's all fallen through. He told you, didn't he, that we had some business together?"

"No," said Carla.

"What a type," said the man, snidely. "Well, we had some business together. He was someone who understood things, and we were in agreement right away. 'When all is said and done,' I would say to him, 'I have some rights too,' and he understood right away. So he handed me something for the rent and the rest. It worked for both of us."

"How much do you want?" asked Carla.

"Oh, not much," said the man. "It was always about small items.

Cigarettes, stuff to eat, the occasional American bottle of liquor. Hopefully also clothes or linens. Stuff that can be traded easily, in these times. But no cash. I don't know what to do with cash."

Carla was silent for a long time, without ever looking at the man. The man finished the cigarette and tossed the butt toward the window, without even trying to make it fall outside.

"So?" he said.

"I have nothing right now," said Carla.

"What do you mean, nothing? You don't mean to tell me that Tullio hasn't left anything? He was loaded with stuff."

"That stuff doesn't involve me," Carla said. "They had an agreement that it would stay with them. Tullio told me it would stay with them."

The man became agitated. "What a swindle! Didn't you tell him that was a swindle? You're the one who had more right than anyone."

Carla shrugged her shoulders instead of replying.

"It should be protested," said the man. "I'll take it on, myself, to protest it. They need to cough up something."

"Leave them in peace," said Carla.

"Why should I leave them in peace? It's not right what they're doing. Do you think that I don't know how to make them cough up the share that's coming to you?"

"There's no reason for you to get mixed up in their dealings," said Carla. "And anyway, I agree with them. What do you think can do, then?"

"They'll cough it up," said the man, irate.

There was silence for some time. The man lit another cigarette. He puffed in rapid mouthfuls, nervously.

"Listen," Carla said suddenly, "let me finish out this month, and then I'll go back to work. Then I'll pass something on to you. Maybe I won't be able to give you everything Tullio gave you, but I'll give you enough. I'll come visit you one of these days, and we'll make an agreement."

"You are a dope to give up what's coming to you," said the man. "They're all swindlers, those boys."

"Don't think about them," said Carla. "And don't interest yourself in my affairs, either. I'll give you enough but leave me in peace."

The man made a noise that was impossible to interpret. Nevertheless, his resentment was passing.

"And you shouldn't come to this house anymore," said Carla. "The police are still looking around on account of Tullio. You should not come here."

"Oh, the police!" said the man, and having finished his cigarette he threw the butt on the floor, in the direction of the window.

"You can get out of here, right now," said Carla.

The man waited for some time without speaking, then he stood up and said in Carla's direction, "Well, we'll see each other again soon, then."

Carla only made a movement with her head, and the man got to the door, then turned around and regarded Daniele with an unpleasant grin. "Good evening, young man," he said. And he went out, and his step was heard in the corridor as far as the outside door.

Daniele stayed seated on the bed and gazed at the cigarette butts that the man had thrown on the floor. The last one was still lit, and the thread of smoke rose toward the window and dispersed. Then it went out and stopped smoking.

So the time passed, and there was something that had to be done about Carla. Daniele stood up and went over to her, and she remained with her head down. And he, not knowing what else to do, sat down on the floor in front of her, and took her hands that rested in her lap. Carla lowered her head even more, so as not to be seen.

"Carla?"

Carla shook her head no.

"Was he your father, Carla?"

Carla shook her head no again.

"Why should he be my father?" she said with a kind of rancor. "He's someone who lived near us in the old house. He's known me since I was little."

Daniele was unable to say anything. Carla's hands lay inert in his, and he would have done anything for her, but he did not know what to do.

"You mustn't tell Giulia that man came here," said Carla.

Daniele nodded his head.

After a while Carla said, "Go out now, Daniele. I want to be alone."

But Daniele did not move. He laid his head on her knees and began to cry, for the first time.

35

The room had only one window, high above the floor, with some small panes made almost opaque with dirt. On the panes were pasted some strips of paper, now colorless, crisscrossed diagonally. They could have removed those strips of paper, now that the war was over. Beyond the panes was an iron grille, and a bit beyond the grille you noticed something gray that must have been a wall. Scant light came through the window due to the dirtiness of the panes, the strips of paper, and the wall outside.

In the room, in front of the window, there was a bench along the wall. On the bench were seated some women, squeezed in together. One of the women was young and had a small baby, who was sleeping in her arms. All around against the walls were more people, some sitting on the floor with their backs against the wall.

The room had two doors. One entered from the stairs and the other passed into the benefits office. This was printed on the door. The people were waiting specifically to speak to the staff person in the benefits office. He dealt with poor people who went to apply for a subsidy such as charity or an entitlement for someone far away, dead, or even just disappeared in the chaos of wartime.

The room was filled with a bad odor of filth. Each day for many hours, the people waited, dressed in dirty rags, that had an odor you could smell. When they left, a little of that odor lingered in the room. Thus, little by little, the poor people's bad odor seeped into the bench, the walls, the floor, and never went away.

When it was three in the afternoon the room began to get dark. The people spoke little, and with low voices, each one just with his neighbor.

At three-thirty, from the door of the benefits office a man emerged who had entered it a long time before. Everyone's head turned toward him. Even though they appeared so weary and preoccupied, they were paying attention to what was happening.

The man made his way toward the door to the stairs, a bit stiffly, without looking at anyone. It was only when he was near the doorway that someone among those who were sitting around asked, "How did it go?"

The man replied by cursing and slamming the door hard when he left. Then all returned to stillness, as before.

Toward four o'clock the receptionist appeared in the door of the office and said, "Who's next?"

A thin woman emerged from a corner and made her way to the door. Daniele also came forward because he wanted to speak to the receptionist, but the receptionist made a gesture with his hand and hurried to close the door behind the thin woman. Daniele returned to his place in embarrassment. For some time everyone in the room regarded him with interest.

The light entering at the window became fainter and fainter as the sun swung around, outside, and sank toward sunset. Even so, the people could still see well enough, being used to the dimness of the room. An old man who was sitting on the floor hugging his knees had a long fit of coughing. Finally he spread his knees apart and spat on the floor.

For some time yet, nothing happened. Then the little baby who was sleeping in the young woman's arms woke up and began to cry. The woman tried to rock it in her arms, but the baby didn't stop wailing.

"It should stop crying," said someone.

Then the woman uncovered her chest and the baby eagerly latched onto a breast, pushing on it with its little hands. For some moments there was silence, then the baby let go, but before it could start crying loudly again the woman gave it the other breast to nurse.

There was another silence for some moments. Then the baby let go of her breast for good and started to cry again. The young woman looked nervously around. The fussing of the baby was bothersome to everyone.

"What's wrong with him?" someone asked.

"I don't have much milk," said the young woman. In spite of all the efforts she made, the baby continued to cry.

Then the office door opened brusquely, and the receptionist reappeared. The thin woman who had entered half an hour before could be seen inside. Leaning against the post inside the door, she was waiting to talk with the staff person.

"Take it outside!" shouted the receptionist. "Do you think you're in your own home?"

The young woman stood up and went to sit down on the stairs.

Someone said, "They had fun with all the military men passing through, and now they come to apply for benefits."

"Ah, she's one of those?" asked an old woman.

"One of so many," said the man who had spoken earlier. "They get the benefits that others deserve."

From the stairs the baby's crying reached only those who were waiting and did not penetrate the door of the office. Still, even those waiting felt less ill at ease because the little one was outside and didn't face them directly anymore.

Towards five o'clock the receptionist again came through the door of the office and said to the people who were watching him, "That's it for today. Come back tomorrow morning at nine."

This time Daniele caught up with the receptionist before he could close the door. "Have you told him?" Daniele asked.

"Yes."

"And what did he say?"

"Nothing," said the receptionist.

"That's impossible – nothing?"

The receptionist snorted loudly. "Listen, kid," he said, "get off my toe. If you want, come back tomorrow at nine."

Mortified, Daniele passed between all the people. No one had yet left the room, perhaps out of curiosity for what would happen, or perhaps because they had no great need to go anywhere else.

In the street the sunlight slanted through the spaces between the roofs, and the air was mild. Daniele took a few steps under the weight of not knowing what to do. It was difficult to live, too difficult and sad, if goodwill meant nothing. He couldn't return home like this again today, without having tried anything. So he headed toward the square, where the building had its main entrance, the one used by the staff. He would talk to someone at any cost. Leaning against a column of the portico, he waited until he should see someone appear. And someone did, coming towards him.

It was an elderly gentleman, rather well dressed. He made a professional gesture of annoyance as soon as he saw the boy. "Tomorrow," he said. "Tomorrow in the office."

"But I waited all day to talk to you," said Daniele.

The gentleman spread his arms wide. "Too much work. I would have to split into four people to listen to everyone."

He moved to go away, and Daniele held him back. "You must listen to me," he said. "Don't you remember me? You've been to our house so often."

The gentleman regarded Daniele with greater interest. "Of course . . . of course," he said, slowly, in an effort to remember. Then he seemed to remember and said, "Of course!" in a different tone of voice.

Daniele's anxiety resolved itself into a timid smile.

"I'm happy to see you," said the gentleman. "Wait, what's your name?"

"Daniele."

"Of course—Daniele," said the gentleman. "Did you want something from me?"

"I need to find work," said Daniele.

"Work?" said the gentleman. "That's not my area, to find work for people."

"But I need to find work," said Daniele. "You can find me something to do, now that the war is over."

The gentleman laughed. "You people are all alike," he said. "The war ended yesterday, and today you want to find everything in place."

"But I must earn my living, and you have to help me," said Daniele. "You're the only friend of my father that's left. If you don't do it, there will be no one else who can help me."

"I don't understand," said the gentleman. "You have no one?"

"No."

The gentleman stood a moment in thought, then he said, "The only thing I can do for you is get you a subsidy, if you truly have no one to support you. Don't you have relatives?"

"I don't want money," said Daniele. "I want to work. You must help me find work."

An annoyed expression came over the gentleman's face. He drew his watch from a tiny pocket and looked at the time. "Could you come back tomorrow?"

"Listen to me now, I beg you," said Daniele. "I'll make it fast. I don't want to go back home without having concluded anything."

The gentleman was still looking at his watch, mechanically, and he put it back in its tiny pocket. Then he said with indifference, "Just now I have to visit the barber. Come along and that way we'll talk."

Carla and Giulia and little Maria had just finished eating when Daniele arrived home. They were seated around the table, expecting him. Twilight entered through the open windows, brighter than the light coming through the windows that faced the sunset. The lamp was not lit.

They watched him come in and didn't ask him anything, because there was nothing to ask about. He looked discouraged and perhaps desperate, and no one was able to ask him anything when he was like that. One time they had made him cry when they persisted.

He came in and sat down. His place was set with what they had to eat, but he wasn't thinking of eating.

Time passed, and then Giulia asked, gently, "You're not eating?"

"No, I'm not hungry," said Daniele.

"Go on, eat," said Carla.

Daniele didn't answer.

"If you want, I'll reheat the soup for you," said Giulia.

"No. I'll eat later, before I go to bed."

Giulia got up in silence and set to work washing the plates on the floor, under the window that gave the most light.

Little Maria looked around and began to get sleepy.

"Where were you?" asked Carla.

"Around," said Daniele.

Attentive and worried, Carla studied his face. He had a hard, stubborn expression, but beneath it she guessed at a discouragement even greater than previous times.

"You should quit going around looking for work," said Carla. "There isn't any work. So many who have families and more need than you, are without work. If they gave you a job they would take it away from someone else. You at least have enough to live on."

Daniele said nothing. Since he had sat down he had not raised his eyes from the table. Even Carla said nothing more.

Giulia finished washing the plates.

"Giulia," said Carla, "take the little one home, this evening."

"Do you want me to light the lamp first?"

"No, it doesn't matter. It's better to keep the windows open."

Giulia took the little girl's hand and went out.

In the kitchen the light was fading. Crickets could be heard singing outside, in the midst of the ruins. Through the window Carla watched the twilight, and her face, reflecting it, appeared faded.

"Where did you go today?" she asked.

Daniele was sullen and did not answer.

"We can't go on together when you're like this," said Carla.

"And what can I do?"

"Don't be obstinate. What did you do, today?"

Daniele answered after some time. "I went to a friend of my father's. He's the only one that still has his position. I thought he would help me, because he always came by our house. He should have been able to help me."

"What did he tell you?" asked Carla.

"He wants me to go to my relatives in Rome. He says that people like me should not be hanging around the city. It creates more confusion. He says there's already too much confusion."

There were a few moments of silence, then Carla asked, "Will you go to Rome?"

"No."

There was more silence. Something must have been on Carla's mind, that was making her think.

So she said, "Maybe it's better for you to go to Rome, Daniele. This world is not made for you. You are too stuck in your thinking, and anyway it's useless, there's nothing to do. It's like beating your head against a wall."

"Would you be happy if I went away?"

"It's not that," said Carla. "You must understand me. Some people cannot find work in a world like ours. It's not even their fault, in fact they're better than we are. But here we're dealing only with the strong and the weak. You aren't exactly weak, Daniele. You have your ideas, and you're firm in those ideas. But it isn't the kind of strength that is needed to get along in a world like ours."

Daniele said nothing.

"What's that man going to do now?" asked Carla.

"I don't know," said Daniele. "He said he'll write to Rome. At the beginning he wanted to turn me over to the police right away so they could send me to Rome, but then I convinced him to write."

"Then they'll come get you?"

"No," said Daniele. "I gave him a false address."

"You should have known, first of all, that it was useless to go to him," said Carla. "And you did a bad thing, going there. Now he'll get it into his head to look for you, and if he finds you they'll kick us out of this place. And Tullio's dealings are still going on."

"He won't look for me. The whole time I was with him he couldn't wait for me to leave. He has no desire to think about me. Maybe he's already forgotten."

"It's best for you to stay hidden for some time," said Carla.

By now it was dark in the kitchen. The color of the sky had turned dark even toward the west. Daniele was even more disheartened, now that he understood his mistake. But he was also more stubborn. An idea had become stuck in his head. It needed to be said, before Giulia came back and it became more difficult to say it.

"If I don't find work I'll go away."

"To Rome?"

"No, not to Rome," said Daniele. "Somewhere, I don't know where."

Carla reached an arm across the table, until she took his hand. "You shouldn't get these ideas in your head. There is nothing to do, anywhere. Every place is like this one, wherever you go. Stay here with us. Meanwhile times will get better, it can't always go on like this. And then you'll find work suited to you. But for the moment it's not necessary. What I earn is enough for all of us. For me it's less difficult to earn money."

"If I don't find work I'll go away," Daniele repeated.

Then Carla withdrew her hand, and her voice became harsh and bitter. "It's because of my work, right?" she asked, and waited a bit for a reply. Then she said, "Why don't you answer?"

"I don't know," said Daniele. "Sometimes I've thought about it but I don't know what to say. It's not just that. First there was Tullio, and he was thinking of all of you. And now it's me and I myself have to work and get, for all of you, what is needed to live. But, instead, I'm not capable of anything, so then it's better for me to go away. So at least I won't be a burden."

"You are not a burden," said Carla. "What we have here is enough. And even if that weren't enough, it wouldn't matter. Sometimes there might be a shortage, and anyway there'd be a shortage for all of us, but at least we'll be together. I want you to stay with us, and Giulia also wants that. We would do anything for you, because we love you. And you mustn't go away. Promise me that you won't go away."

"I'll go away if I can't find work," said Daniele.

Then Carla stood up, and her face couldn't be seen but her voice was bitter. "All right," she said. "It's because of my work, I know it. Besides, this is the only way you are able to think. But it doesn't matter that much to me, you know. You can do what seems best for you."

And she abruptly left the kitchen.

36

High up, above the door, there was a wooden sign with IV-B printed on it, and a soldier, Bill, was seated on the top step of the entrance, which had three stone steps. From there he could see towards the square. It was a small, isolated square, irregularly shaped, bounded by houses and porticoes and a high brick wall. From his position, Bill could see only that part of the square enclosed by the brick wall.

The soldier was depressed. He was sitting in the entrance to Classroom IV-B, many thousands of miles from the place he wanted to be. In his home town the winter had ended and the prairie had turned green, and the trees on the farms had also turned green. In the square there was nothing that helped him remember that, not even in the courtyard in front of the school building. Here and there grass had sprouted, especially near the wall, but it wasn't like the grass in his home town. There, the prairie seemed covered with green to infinity, high as a horse's belly.

A low wall with two pillars separated the courtyard of the school building from the square. At one time there had been iron grillwork on top of the wall and a gate between the two pillars, but those had been removed. Now, between the two pillars, Joe, another G. I., was doing guard duty, facing the square and carrying a tommy gun.

And a short distance from him stood a group of people. There were thirty in all, but others were continually arriving, and they took up positions seated near the high brick wall. There must have been some sort of pecking order among the people, because when a new arrival tried to take a spot that wasn't his, the others protested and forced him to the far edge of the group. The hot May sun beat down on the people sitting there. The sun was already lowering toward sunset behind the school building.

Bill became interested in the group of people. In fact, he wanted to talk to someone about them, even though he already knew quite well what they wanted. But there was no one to talk to about it. Luke, another G. I., seated lower down on the stone steps, didn't want to talk. He was already fed up with Bill's earlier questions, or for some other reason, and he didn't want to talk. He stayed sitting there, bent forward, keeping company with his own thoughts.

A tanker truck arrived carrying water. The negro driver leaned out the window, and Joe stepped to one side and signaled for it to pass on. The vehicle drove to the end of the schoolyard, to the corner where a kitchen had been set up. The whole schoolyard was hemmed in by a high brick wall, like the one Bill could see in the square. There were even small trees planted in rows a short distance from the wall, with leaves of light green. The leaves on the trees closest to the kitchen were withered from the heat and smoke.

The tanker had begun to unload water into some drums. Some soldiers came over from the other side of the courtyard to fetch water in jerry-cans. The other men of the unit were resting inside the school building. Not much sound could be heard. Not even the people who were waiting outside made much noise, except when some new arrival insisted on taking a spot that wasn't his.

At a certain point Luke stood up and without speaking passed close by Bill, to go into Classroom IV-B. He had to arm himself, as his turn to stand guard had come. The corporal, who was sleeping on a layer of straw, stirred at the sound he made but didn't wake up completely.

Luke went to relieve Joe, and he seemed small between the two pillars, with a helmet that looked too big and even covered his neck.

The group of people now numbered about fifty.

Bill waited until Joe got closer, then he asked, "What are those people, Joe?"

"Sons of bitches," answered Joe, and went into Classroom IV-B to put away his weapon and helmet.

He also made some noise and the corporal woke up and went drowsily to the doorway, with traces of sleep on his face. He saw the tanker parked next to the kitchen. Then he took a jerry-can and went to get it filled, after which he washed his face in the schoolyard, using his helmet as a basin.

Joe had come outside to sit on a step. He seemed bored, his hair was sticking up with sweat, and he had a red mark on his forehead where his helmet had pressed on it. When the corporal finished washing, Joe also washed his face in his helmet and went back into the classroom.

The tanker drove off, leaving a large wet spot. The negro driver waved as he passed, and Bill returned the wave.

The shadow of the school building lengthened on the ground, reaching to the people who were waiting next to the brick wall. Luke was by now completely in the shade.

The corporal sat down on the second step and looked toward the people who were waiting. There were over fifty of them by now. Each held a container for carrying food.

Bill studied the corporal's face. It was an expressionless face, but Bill wanted to talk. "The first ones have been there for three hours," he said. "I was still doing guard duty when the first ones came."

The corporal and Bill watched the group of people in the square. There might have been seventy or eighty now, and the shadow of the school building inched ever closer to them.

"When will we be sent home?" said Bill.

"Don't worry about it. It's worse if you worry."

"We should be going, now that it's over," said Bill. "Why aren't they letting us leave?"

"It's pointless to worry about it," said the corporal.

The shadow of the school building stretched closer to the people.

Then activity was observed in the area of the kitchen. The sergeant put a whistle between his lips and went around, blowing it, to the other side of the schoolyard, as far as the interior of the school building. The cooks took the cookpots off the fire and lined up in the courtyard.

This produced movement among the people in the square. Many got to their feet to see better what was happening in the schoolyard, and all of them became restless. There were now more than one hundred people.

"Go get something to eat, Bill," said the corporal. "It's time to relieve Luke."

Bill went to get his food with his mess kit and his cup. He sat down to eat on the step and stopped watching the people. Many eyes were fixed on him as he ate. They counted each bite he put in his mouth.

"I'm going to get something to eat too," said the corporal, getting up. Joe also stood up, with a bored expression, and went with the corporal.

Soldiers began to gather from the other side of the courtyard and passed with their mess kits in front of the cookpots. Among the people who were waiting, others got up off the ground, and together they all began to move toward the low wall, almost imperceptibly.

Then Luke planted his feet wide apart and shouted, "Hey! Get back!"

The people didn't understand what the soldier was saying. They spoke in a different way. But they stopped, because it was clear what the soldier wanted. But they didn't turn back.

One man said, "We aren't doing anything. We only want to see."

The soldier didn't understand what the man had said. He shoved the butt of the tommygun under his armpit and pointed its barrel at the people. "Go on, back!" he shouted.

Everyone's eyes were full of fear, but as a group they gathered courage. They retreated a few steps and remained on their feet to watch the soldiers who were passing in front of the cookpots, getting food.

The corporal and Bill and Joe chewed slowly and did not take their eyes off the people after they heard Luke shout. They had gone to get their weapons and kept them ready at hand.

The corporal watched but said nothing.

Standing among the cookpots, the mess sergeant supervised the distribution of food. His name was Appiano, and he was from Jamaica, New York. At a certain moment the officer who commanded the unit billeted in the school came up beside him. The soldiers had almost finished getting their food, and only some latecomers were arriving. The others who had finished came to the cookpots to dump the leftovers they had not wanted to eat.

"Those people are waiting for something," said the sergeant.

The officer had seen the people. There were now perhaps two hundred people, grouped along the wall, and Luke was holding them at a distance at gunpoint. "Let them wait," he said.

"But later, can we give them whatever is left?" asked the mess sergeant.

The officer seemed undecided. "If we do it today," he said, "tomorrow we'll have all the damn beggars in this damn city in our face."

The sergeant remained quiet until the officer was on the point of leaving. Then he asked again, "Can we give them what's left?"

The officer still seemed undecided. Then he said, "I don't want any disturbance. Above all, tell those people not to come back tomorrow. I don't want to have these damn beggars in front of the barracks."

"All right," said the sergeant.

As soon as he finished eating, Bill armed himself and went to relieve Luke.

"Watch out," said Luke. "There is sure to be some dirty bastard among them."

"Okay," said Bill. He stood with his feet wide apart, with his tommygun in position under his armpit, aimed at the crowd.

The shadow of the school building had reached the people. The sun still beat on the wall, turning the old bricks red. The people on their feet kept their eyes fixed on the kitchen in their desire to see what would happen over there. Nevertheless, nothing was happening to reward their hope for a little food. Bill took his turn calmly.

The school building had its main entrance on the square. From there soldiers began to emerge, in small groups. They had eaten and they were going into the city center in search of entertainment.

From the group that was waiting, a boy stepped forward and went toward the soldiers who were coming out of the main entrance. Some people followed him with their gaze as he went.

The boy approached a soldier, and the soldier kept walking, as if unaware of his presence. But the boy continued to walk beside the soldier, with his hand out, and meanwhile he tried to say, in English, that he knew a girl with whom the soldier would be able to have a good time. The soldier proceeded halfway across the square, then he stepped aside and threw the cigarette he was smoking at the boy. The boy caught the half-smoked cigarette and bumped into another soldier, still with his hand out and trying to say some words in English.

Two or three other people stepped out from the group and went toward the soldiers to beg. Some soldiers gave them nothing. Others gave cigarettes or cash. Then many other people broke out of the group to go to the entrance to beg. Those who had more confidence that food might be forthcoming stayed waiting along the wall, because begging for money or cigarettes was not the same as waiting for food.

The shadow had mounted the wall, and only the tallest houses on the square remained lit by the sun.

Sergeant Appiano ordered all the various kinds of food that had not been distributed to be returned to a cookpot. Finally, the cookpot was half full. Then, with two cooks, he carried the cookpot toward the two posts. The people, seeing the arrival of the cookpot, lost their fear of Bill's weapon and started perceptibly to advance.

The cookpot was deposited on the ground inside the schoolyard, and Sergeant Appiano climbed up on the low wall to address the people. The people composed themselves to listen.

"The food that I'm going to distribute to you," said the sergeant, "is food you are getting from the American government. There will not be enough for everyone, because there are too many of you. And tomorrow it will be useless for you to come and wait. Tomorrow there will be nothing for anyone. Now I'm distributing a little food to each one, until it's gone. But you need to get into line, so the distribution can get done without any trouble. Until you get in line, I won't begin to distribute."

There was confusion among the people as they got in line. Those who had gone off to beg ran back and began to argue to get their old places back. Everyone shouted and pushed to get a place in line, as there would not be enough food for all.

Finally, a man emerged from the group, who was wearing an old pair of gray-green army trousers. Yelling and pushing, he succeeded in establishing a measure of order in the first rows of people.

Then Sergeant Appiano had the cookpot brought outside the posts and he stood behind it, with a ladle in his hand. At his side stood two cooks. Behind was Bill, with his weapon ready and an odd smile on his face. Everything proceeded with sufficient decorum, and he barked at the hungry people, keeping them in their place.

The first people came forward in an orderly fashion, one at a time. The sergeant flipped a ladleful of food into each can and they went off. Around twenty people came by turns to get the food.

Then the man in the gray-green trousers became afraid he would be left without and came forward with his can to get food. Behind him the people fell out of order and at once began to shout and push. The sergeant continued to ladle out food randomly into the many cans that were extended over the cookpot. Finally, when there was still a little food left, he could no longer move, jostled on all sides by shouting people. So he stopped, with his ladle raised. The people began to scrape around in the cookpot with their cans, but they didn't get much result, because then those behind tried to grab the cans from them, and the food spilled.

The sergeant shouted something at the top of his voice, and no one was able to understand him, because in his excitement he was shouting in English. But he and the two soldiers were in agreement. Pushing back against the pressure behind them, they broke out of the circle of people who were pushing them. The cookpot overturned on the ground, and a few people fell over it.

The sergeant and his men withdrew, cursing, from the schoolyard, and at the entrance they ran into the corporal and Luke and John, armed and helmeted. They all yelled at the people, who could neither understand nor hear them. Bill still wore that unreadable smile on his face.

But Joe glared at the frenzied people with disgust and hatred. "Do I shoot?" he asked the corporal.

"Leave it to me," said the corporal. He raised the butt of the tommygun under his armpit and aimed the barrel at the sky and let off a couple of prolonged bursts. The people scattered, screaming, and fled from the little square. The cookpot remained upside down in front of the corporal with some food scattered on the ground, and many trampled cans, and one woman who was screaming and trying to escape, dragging herself along the ground. She had a bad leg and couldn't walk.

The corporal laughed.

"Sons of bitches," said Joe.

The sergeant with the two cooks came forward to recover the cookpot. They were perspiring and cursed the people for causing the fracas. The two soldiers took the cookpot and carried it back to the kitchen.

But Sergeant Appiano walked toward the woman. She was filled with terror, and screamed and dragged herself over the ground. She looked ridiculous, but the sergeant wasn't laughing.

The woman scrabbled with her hands on the ground, trying to get away. She was terrified that the sergeant would kill her.

"I'm not going to do anything to you," said the sergeant in Italian. "And quit screaming."

The woman stopped screaming, but her face remained contorted in fear.

"Where did you get hurt?"

The woman pointed to her right leg.

The sergeant bent down and as soon as he touched the ankle she began screaming again. "Damned bunch of animals. Do you see what can happen to create chaos?"

The woman began to feel somewhat safer. "It wasn't me," she whimpered.

The sergeant straightened up, by now his ire had cooled. "There shouldn't be anything broken," he said to the woman. "Try to stand up."

He had to help her and then she stayed leaning against him, standing on only one leg. "Try to walk."

The woman cautiously put the other foot on the ground, but she quickly pulled it back, trembling. "I can't walk."

Then the sergeant said in the direction of the guards, "Hey, one of you come and help me." In saying this he raised his eyes to them and was somewhat disconcerted to see other soldiers with them, and also an officer.

Bill came forward and took the woman on the other side and together they carried her to a seat on the low wall. Then the sergeant released the woman and went to present himself to the officer, saluting him.

"They caused a bit of a ruckus," he said.

The officer had a stern expression on his face. "I heard," he said. Then he nodded with his head toward the wall. "And those, what do they want?"

The sergeant looked in that direction and then he noticed two people who had remained seated against the wall. One was an old man who was holding a can for food between his knees. The other was a boy, who did not have a can.

"I'll go see."

The old man and the boy were not together. They were sitting a short distance apart, each by himself. The sergeant spoke first to the old man, and the officer went with him. The old man had skin darkened by the sun and a ragged shirt and a pair of ragged trousers. He wore an old pair of military boots from which his bare toes protruded, for the toes of the boots had been cut off. Possibly the boots had been too small for him and for that reason he had cut them off.

"What are you doing here?" demanded the sergeant to the old man.

The old man raised his eyes with a faraway gaze. He did not answer, but with one hand he held out his can, and his hand was shaking.

"Tell him that if he doesn't leave, I'm going to order him shot in the back," said the officer.

"Get out of here, old man," said the sergeant. "If you don't leave, they'll shoot you in the back."

"Why? You can't."

"Get out of here, old man," repeated the sergeant.

The old man put his can back between his knees and lowered his head. Anyone could see that he was not leaving.

"He must be very hungry, sir," said the sergeant to the officer.

The officer didn't say anything. That old man must be crazy, or else he didn't have much longer to live and didn't care what could happen to him.

"Do you want to talk to the boy too?" asked the sergeant.

"Ask him what he wants," said the officer.

As they approached, the boy got to his feet. His face was tired, and his clothing was untidy but not ragged.

"What do you want?" asked the sergeant.

"Nothing."

"Then why are you here?"

"I don't know."

"Do you always do things without knowing why?"

"I saw people and so I came too," said the boy. "I didn't know what else to do."

The sergeant looked straight into the boy's face. "Are you hungry?" he asked.

"Yes."

"And why didn't you say you were hungry?"

"I want to work."

"This one wants to work," the sergeant said in English.

"What do you mean, work?" asked the officer.

"That's what he said," said the sergeant.

The officer studied the boy thoughtfully. Then he said, "We can't do anything for him."

But the sergeant asked the boy, "Do you know how to wash cookpots?"

"I can do that."

Then the sergeant said to the officer, "We could put him in the kitchen, sir. We've already had boys to help us out in the kitchen before."

The officer remained in thought for a moment. He turned to look at the boy, then at the old man. He said, "Give the old man something to eat. And the woman too. Then she should be taken to the hospital. There must be a hospital in this damn city."

The sergeant almost smiled. "What about the boy?"

"Try him out to see if he does well in the kitchen," said the officer. "If he's willing to work, we can keep him with us while we're staying here."

"Yes, sir," said the sergeant.

The officer went off and the sergeant turned to the boy and to the old man, who had remained seated. "Come on," he said, "I'll give you both something to eat."

They went together toward the kitchen. The old man walked with effort, very bent over, and his head shook continually as he walked.

"What's your name, kid?" asked the sergeant.

"Daniele."

"We'll try to keep you with us. If you're willing to work, you can stay as long as we're here in this city. Maybe we won't be here for very long, but until we leave you can work and eat with us."

"Thanks."

"But only if you are willing to work."

Arriving at the kitchen, the sergeant told the soldiers, "This boy is going to work with us. He can help with the cookpots or some other thing. Meanwhile give him something to eat."

"Better make him work first, Sergeant," said one soldier. "These people don't want to work anymore once they've been fed."

"Let him eat," said the sergeant.

They gave the boy a mess kit full of food and a large slice of white bread. He ate, sitting on a chest. Beside him sat the old man, and the sergeant watched them eat. The old man never said a word, intent only on eating. He scraped his spoon noisily inside the can to get the last bits of food.

At the far end of the schoolyard two or three soldiers were singing. One also had a guitar, but it could be heard only occasionally. Little by little it got dark. A small vehicle moved into the schoolyard and then left in the direction of the square, taking with it the woman who couldn't walk.

The old man gripped the empty can between his knees and put the dirty spoon into a pocket in his pants. "Do you have a little tobacco?" he asked the sergeant.

The sergeant pulled out a pack of cigarettes, shook one out, and tossed it to the old man. "Now get out of here," he said.

The old man got up and went to light the cigarette with a piece of wood he took from the fire. His hands shook with a slight tremor. "Thanks," he said to the sergeant.

The sergeant said, "Don't come back tomorrow, old man. And tell the others they shouldn't come either. It creates too much chaos."

Without saying more, the old man went off in the direction of the pillars. He walked with difficulty, as before, and his face wore the same expression as before, resigned and distant.

The soldiers at the end of the schoolyard stopped singing for a bit. Then they began a new song, and this one was sad also.

The boy got up from the chest. "Tell me what I must do."

"Why didn't you eat the bread?" asked the sergeant.

The boy turned away his eyes in embarrassment. He had hoped the sergeant would not notice he had put the bread in his pocket instead of eating it.

"It's white bread," he said. "I'd like to take it home."

"Who do you have at home?"

"Two sisters. They're younger than me. They'll be happy if I bring some white bread home."

"And you have no father?"

"He died in the bombardment," said the boy. "My mother also died in the bombardment."

The sergeant came closer to the boy and put a hand on his head, then sat down on the chest where the old man had been sitting. "Sit down."

The boy returned to his seat. The sergeant didn't speak, and the boy felt a bit embarrassed. "They're singing," he said.

"Yes," said the sergeant.

The soldiers' sad song finally reached them, along with some accompaniment by a guitar.

"It's because they want to go home," said the sergeant.

"It's beautiful," said the boy.

In silence they listened to the song until it was finished.

Then the boy asked again, "Tell me what I must do."

"Nothing," said the sergeant. "Nothing for tonight. Tomorrow you will come here at seven."

"All right," said the boy. He was still holding the dirty mess kit, and he asked, "Should I wash the mess kit?"

"Yes, wash it," said the sergeant.'

The boy went to the place where the cans of water were and washed the mess kit, rubbing it with dirt. A soldier who saw him gave him a piece of soap, and he washed the mess kit again with soap. Then he turned to the sergeant.

"I'd like to dry it," he said, "but I don't have anything to dry it with."

"It's not important to dry it," said the sergeant. He seemed preoccupied, as if thinking of other things.

The soldiers at the end of the schoolyard were still singing.

The boy stood and waited; then he said, "Thanks for the food."

The sergeant seemed to return from his meditation. "You'll come back tomorrow morning?"

"Yes."

"Good," said the sergeant, and seemed to become preoccupied again.

"May I go home now?"

"Yes."

The boy made a move to go, but the sergeant stopped him after a few steps. "Wait," he said and went off, and after a bit he returned with another slice of bread and two round boxes.

"Hide these under your jacket," he said. "It's better if the guards don't see them."

"Thanks," said the boy.

He walked toward the two pillars with growing anxiety. Inside Classroom IV-B a light was on, and he saw the figures of two soldiers seated on the top step. They said nothing as the boy passed by. But the soldier on duty between the two pillars noticed the bulge under his jacket and said something to the boy that he didn't understand.

The boy halted a second, with his head lowered, but then he had the courage to lift his eyes, and as the soldier had his face turned toward the dying twilight, he was able to see his expression. He was smiling, that soldier, in the same mysterious way, and it was clear that he wasn't going to do anything about the stuff hidden under the boy's shirt.

Then the boy smiled too and said something the soldier didn't understand.

So he went off across the square, and the soldier between the two pillars followed him with his gaze as long as he could, smiling that indefinable smile. And the boy also smiled as he walked, and touched his hands to the bulge under his jacket.

37

One day the first magnolia blossoms opened, and Giulia climbed up into the tree and gathered them to take into the house. There were three blossoms, and two of them were not open all the way. But they would open later, standing in water.

She put them on the table in the kitchen. It was pointless to put magnolias in Carla's room, because Carla was almost always out, sometimes two or three days in a row. Now the magnolias smelled sweet in the kitchen and were beautiful, white flowers and bright green leaves. She had been very careful not to touch the white petals, because they spoiled quickly when they were touched.

Daniele would be pleased when he returned. One day, as they had walked along the river, he had said how he liked them. "They have a good scent," he had said. Giulia remembered every word he had said.

Then Daniele arrived. Giulia wasn't expecting him yet; he never got back so early ever since he had begun working with the soldiers. The sun was still shining through the window facing the sunset.

Daniele stopped at the threshold of the kitchen and ran a restless glance over everything inside it, and he didn't seem to notice the magnolias. And he also avoided looking directly at Giulia. He glanced at her clothes, her legs, her bare feet, but not her face.

Then he came forward, all the while trying to appear unconcerned. His gaze flitted from one thing to another.

"Carla's not here?"

"No."

Something was once again broken in him, and Giulia felt her heart contract in sympathy.

Right away he had turned his back to her and he took out what he had brought and laid it on the table. And the magnolias were also there on the table; perhaps they might have spoken about them. It would have been enough for him to say, "Look at the magnolias," preferably in that tone of voice people use when speaking of nothing much, and immediately the twinge of pain in her heart would have melted away.

Instead, he said nothing and retired behind the blankets in his corner. The food he had brought remained on the table, white bread and boxes, more stuff than other times. And it seemed to Giulia that for some reason he had lost his job with the soldiers. Now, once again, he would roam the city in search of other work, and would always be tormented by his thoughts, and many nights he would not have come home.

Daniele had sat down on his mattress, doing nothing. Then he noticed the crickets were making music outside the window, and he lost himself in listening to them.

Giulia moved about doing things in the kitchen, noiselessly in her bare feet. But her thoughts were elsewhere, not on what she was doing. Then she went to the window and stopped to look at the ruins against the lowering sun. A little distance away, a wild vine was forming into a great mass of green above a heap of debris. She listened to the crickets singing and shifted her gaze to the spots where she heard them.

The sun turned red and sank behind the rubble. Then she turned back into the kitchen and called softly to Daniele.

"Yes?" Daniele answered.

And after he had answered, she didn't know what to say. Perhaps she didn't even expect that he would answer. But then she asked, "Is something not right, Daniele?"

"It's nothing," said Daniele. "Nothing."

He waited a moment to hear if Giulia would say something more. She remained silent. All was silence, except for the trilling of the crickets outside the window. Then he took his suitcase and put it on the bed and opened it very slowly, taking care not to make a sound with the latches. First he looked for his books. One by one he took them in his hands and looked at them, thinking it over, then he set them aside without opening them. Books were no longer of use to him.

He took in his hands a journal album in which he had written some thoughts, during the time when he had been in school. He began to read, turning the pages. They were stupid thoughts. Only a few months had passed, and yet they were already stupid thoughts.

Outside it was night, and not enough light reached the place where he was sitting. He put the journal in his pocket. Later, he would burn it.

The books were placed apart, in a row on the mattress. Now he needed to pull out the stuff he would need. He picked up a shirt. It had torn once, near the collar, and Giulia had mended it. Giulia was so sweet when she sewed, with her hair almost covering her face, and her intent expression. Everything would have been simpler now, without Giulia.

All the difficulties were on account of her—he felt so more strongly every moment. Coming home, he had done nothing but think of her, and then doing all those things like listening to the crickets and taking his books from the suitcase and searching for a mend in his shirt. Up until the moment he read in his journal, Giulia had been somewhere in his thoughts.

"Daniele?" Giulia's voice called again.

"Yes," he answered.

There was a pause, then Giulia asked, "What's the matter?"

He turned his face in her direction, as if he could see her, and said, softly, "I have to go away."

She felt suddenly cold throughout her body, as if she were dying, and she couldn't speak. Daniele didn't speak either. The crickets seemed to go mad with trilling and covered the silence between them and the even greater silence they kept inside themselves.

Then Giulia felt the cold pass off, and she got hot, and her temples and hands began to perspire. Still, now she could speak, and her voice didn't shake, even though she felt weak.

"When are you going?"

"Tomorrow morning," said Daniele. "I'm going away with the soldiers."

"Are you going far?"

"I don't know," said Daniele. "They haven't told me where they're going. They're leaving with the trucks."

There was a moment of silence.

"Are you going away for good?" asked Giulia in the same voice.

"I don't know."

"Maybe the soldiers will return to America, now that the war is over," said Giulia. "You aren't going to America, right?"

"No," said Daniele. "Maybe even the soldiers won't be going to America."

"But you'll go far away all the same, isn't that right?" asked Giulia.

"I don't know," said Daniele.

Once more there was a moment of silence and then Giulia asked, with the same voice, that was weak and slow and monotonous, "Are you getting your things ready to leave?"

"Yes."

The twilight was dying on the horizon, and the kitchen became darker all the time. By now only the brighter objects could be seen well, and the magnolias on the table better than anything else. They were a light patch suspended in midair, and perhaps one wouldn't have known they were magnolias if one hadn't seen them before.

Time passed, and they remained motionless and without speaking. Then Giulia moved, making no sound in her bare feet. She went into the corridor to take down some handkerchiefs that were hung up to dry and went into Daniele's shelter. Inside, nothing was visible. "Where are you?"

"Here."

"I brought you these handkerchiefs. I washed them today."

Daniele felt for her hands to take the handkerchiefs. He barely touched her hands and he let them go at once. Giulia's hands were too warm, and in any case he couldn't stop to touch them.

"I'll help you get your things together," said Giulia.

"No, don't do that," said Daniele hastily, afraid to be with her.

"I'll help you," said Giulia. She ran the blankets aside on the cord that held them, but hardly any light fell on the bed.

"You don't have to," said Daniele again, without conviction.

"Are you taking everything?"

"No."

Giulia knelt on the floor in front of the suitcase. "What do you want to take?"

"My grooming things," said Daniele. "And a little underwear, just one change."

"Yes," said Giulia.

"The sergeant isn't allowed to take me away, but he's taking me anyway," said Daniele. "He's the one who asked me, and I said yes. But I have to hide inside the truck, and so I can't take many things. I think they'll give me something to wear if I stay with them."

Giulia began to take things out of the suitcase. By now it was so dark that even white objects could only be seen with difficulty, including her hands and face, which were so pale. In any case, she recognized the things solely by touch.

"I'll take care of the things you leave here, Daniele," she said. "And if you happen to come back, you'll find everything in order. It may be that you'll want to come back to us, in time."

Daniele didn't reply. He would have preferred that Giulia didn't say anything, at the very least. Her voice was so slow and monotonous, and he knew that it was only an effort for her to say those words that were useless anyway and only caused unhappiness.

"Here's the big sweater," said Giulia. "It's better that you take it. Later, winter will come."

"Winter's far off."

"You should take it. You might go into the mountains. It gets cold in the mountains, even in summer."

"Yes," said Daniele.

The suitcase was empty by this time, and Giulia remained motionless in the dark, kneeling in front of the empty suitcase. Time passed without either of them saying anything. The crickets sang outside the window. Daniele felt as if they were inside his head, giving him a headache with their noise.

Then he began to fear the dark, and also Giulia, who was staying so silent in the darkness and not moving.

"Do you want me to light the lamp, Giulia?" he asked.

"Wait a little longer."

Now her voice was no longer monotonous but warm and trembling and full of fear. But he had a bad feeling. He was seized with a sense of anguish.

"Giulia?" he cried out.

"Why are you going away?" said Giulia.

Oh, she shouldn't stay so still in the darkness! "Giulia, let's light the lamp," he pleaded.

"Wait," said Giulia. "First tell me if you're going away because you're fed up with us."

"Don't say such things, Giulia," said Daniele. "Let's light the lamp. I can't stay in the dark any longer."

"You must tell me if you're fed up with us."

"No, it's not that."

"We've always treated you well," said Giulia, "and if sometimes we didn't, it wasn't on purpose, but just because we made mistakes. I've always tried to do what you wanted. I was always happy to do what you wanted."

Daniele said nothing.

"It's only because of the work that you're going away, is that right?" said Giulia. "Only because here you'd be left without work, now that the soldiers are leaving?"

"Yes."

"Swear to me that it's only because of the work."

"I swear."

Then she turned toward him, still on her knees on the floor, and felt for his hands in the dark and began to kiss them. Daniele couldn't tolerate her remaining like that, on her knees in front of him and kissing his hands and wetting them with her tears. It was senseless for her to tremble and weep, and he couldn't bear it.

"Don't do this, Giulia," he said. "I don't have much strength left, don't take it from me."

"Have pity on me," she said.

Then he took her head between his hands and lifted it, and her face was hot and wet with tears. She let him lift her head, and it seemed she had no more strength.

She repeated, barely audibly, "Have pity on me." Then she stayed as if dead between his hands, only trembling.

He stroked her hair very gently a bit above the temples, and it seemed to him he had never wanted anything else, in all his life, but to stroke her hair. But since she continued to stay there as if dead, he was afraid and slapped her and called her name.

She heard but could not say even a word.

"Get up, Giulia. Get up, please!" Daniele was saying.

Giulia made an effort to stand up but couldn't, because she had no more strength. She leaned against him helplessly. Then he lifted her and held her up straight. He felt her thin body trembling under his hands. She yielded completely to him.

"Don't tremble anymore," he said.

She still trembled. Then he took her in his arms—she weighed so little—and carried her to her bed. Even lying down, she continued to tremble, and he didn't know what to do other than to stroke her hair and her face, which was too hot and wet with tears. After some time, he called out to her again. Giulia took one of his hands and pressed it to her face with what little strength she had.

"You can't go away," she said.

"No, I won't go away anymore."

"And we'll be together always, for all of life."

"Yes," said Daniele.

She trembled and wept, and she was too hot.

"Let's light the lamp," said Daniele.

"No," said Giulia, "I'd be ashamed, because I love you so very much."

"And I love you so very much, too."

38

When it was ready, Giulia gave little Maria something to eat and then stayed to wait for Daniele. He arrived late, but the days were so much longer now, and there was still a lot of light before night came. They ate in a hurry, without speaking. He had brought home with him the discouragement of another fruitless day, and he did nothing to conceal it.

Right after they had eaten, Giulia got up and washed the plates and came to dry them on the table. "Don't be this way, Daniele," she said. "It hurts me too when you're like this."

He raised his head an instant and then lowered it again. "How could I be any different? Every day it's the same thing, try and search and never succeed with anything. They don't even ask me what I can do. They only say there's no work."

"There's no work?" said Giulia.

"Well, some people do succeed in finding work," said Daniele. "It must be my fault that I'm not good at anything."

"You shouldn't think like that," said Giulia. "You're better than the others, that's why you're not successful. There's still so much poverty around and then everyone tries to shove arrogantly ahead, and those who are actually better than they are don't get anywhere."

Daniele didn't answer right away. Then he said, "I've decided that I'll go to Antonio, Giulia. He'll give me something to do for sure."

"What?" asked Giulia.

"I don't know. Something or other. At this point nothing matters to me anymore."

"Don't I even matter to you?"

"But I must find a job."

"You know they've changed, now," said Giulia. "They aren't like they were before, when Tullio was here."

"When a person can't move ahead by the best road, he must take whatever road he can," said Daniele.

Giulia had stopped drying the plates. Now she began again and finished in a rush and put everything back in its place. Then she came to sit down near Daniele.

"You cannot go with them," she said. "They would for sure give you work you're not suited for. They might send you into more danger, and I won't be able to stand it, thinking that you're in danger."

Daniele said nothing.

"You cannot go with them," Giulia repeated. "Promise me you won't go."

Daniele still didn't respond, and Giulia became discouraged whenever he got so stubborn. She didn't have much influence, by herself.

Still, she said, "Wait another month before you go to them. Tullio always said that there would be new times coming, with the war over. He said that then everyone of goodwill would be able to live by his own labor. *Honest* labor, he meant. It's a matter of waiting only a little longer and having faith. Promise me that you'll wait at least a month."

"All right, one month."

Giulia slipped her arm around his neck and squeezed him close, face to face.

"And now let's not think any more of such things. At least not until tomorrow. If not, there will never any time left over to be a bit contented."

She pressed against him tenderly, and then she realized that little Maria was watching them, and she let go.

"You are too curious!" she said, playfully. She did it mostly to dispel her sadness.

But Daniele continued to be despondent.

"She's watching us because she's jealous," said Giulia. "At first, I loved only her, and now I love only you. I love you so much that there's not even a little left over for other people."

Daniele forced a smile. "Really?"

"No," said Giulia, "I love her too, but with you it's not the same. You don't know how much I love you."

"How much?"

"This much," she said, and she kissed him hard, with no regard for the child who was watching. Then she added, "Carla's not jealous."

"Does she know about us?" asked Daniele.

Giulia nodded yes.

"And has she said anything?"

Giulia bit her lip, with an expression both playful and shy. She again nodded, with an air of mystery. "I can't tell you what she said."

"Was it something so bad?"

Giulia hesitated uncertainly for a moment and then she shook her head no.

"Tell me, then."

Giulia rolled her eyes toward the little girl, who was paying close attention. "Not now. I'll tell you another time."

"Later?"

"Maybe later."

"Let's take the little one home," said Daniele.

They left the child at the shoemaker's house and returned alone along the path.

"Tell me what Carla said," said Daniele.

"You're too curious."

"Tell me, Giulia."

"I'll tell you later," said Giulia. "Let's not go inside just now, if you want. It's too warm inside."

They went to sit behind the house, facing the twilight, and he once more became silent and morose. And even Giulia became like him, with a heaviness inside and a great sorrow, because loving served no purpose, if life was always so sad.

A strip of light could still be seen on the horizon, as if that summer day would never end. But various stars were already appearing in the sky, and one was more lovely than the rest. And if she had asked him what that star was named, he would have answered that it was named Giulia, because it was more beautiful than all the others.

And then she would have asked: "And what's that one named?" And he would have answered: "Saturn." And then she would have asked: "And what's that other one named? And that one?" And he would have answered, Jupiter, or Mars, or some such name, because he knew the names of many stars, or else he would have answered "I don't know," and then he would have kissed her, and they would have gazed at all the marvelous things in the world, joyfully and because they saw in each other such marvelous things . . . and now none of that was possible, because they were too sad.

Night came, and there was no remaining hint of twilight in the sky. They sat somewhat wordlessly, thinking over what had been said. Then they stood up and went into the house, and at the door she gave him a kiss.

"Don't you want to tell me what Carla said about us?" asked Daniele.

"Wait," said Giulia, "wait a little longer."

They didn't light the lamp but they began to kiss, and it was wonderful to kiss so completely, without fear and without shame, even if their blood did surge inside them, and it seemed that something mysterious and momentous must be about to happen. Never had Giulia been so sweet and warm and uninhibited as she was that evening, and her hands never stopped caressing him.

"Tell me what Carla said," said Daniele.

Giulia's breath came in gasps. "She said . . ."

"What?"

Giulia pressed against him, trembling. "Oh, Daniele," she said, "maybe you don't have the nerve to ask me to, but if you want, we could be together all the time, even at night."

Daniele couldn't speak right away, for his heart was pounding inside his chest. Then he asked, "Do you want to, Giulia?"

"Yes," Giulia said, "with all my heart."

39

The big market square came alive at dawn. In the freshness of the morning, people began to set tables up and set out their wares. They were busy but still very sleepy. More people arrived, who were going about in search of something to eat.

At one time any kind of food would have been found at the city market. The peasant women also would come from the countryside to sell chickens and eggs and cheeses, and they would all set up together in one corner of the square. And it was possible to find every kind of thing other than food: fabric and sewing notions and shoes and tools. Now there were only a few fruits and vegetables and lots of old things, things that people pulled out of houses in an attempt not to starve to death.

Vendors were there in great numbers but almost timid and insecure, each one having little to sell. They were almost all new vendors. Those from before had already become rich and conducted commerce in a big way, and in any case, they preferred to sell their things outside the marketplace.

When the sunlight reached the square, it began to get hot. Little by little, the market reached its peak. For some time the square was full of voices, activity, tables of merchandise, and people who were anxious to find something to eat. Then the activity slowly diminished. Vendors without anything left to sell departed. Later, people who had given up hope of finding food also began to go away. After noon the marketplace appeared almost deserted, with only the tables of those who offered things that were difficult to sell. The big square was neither paved nor cobblestoned, and it was white under the hot sun.

Daniele found a spot in the shade of the houses, where the square gradually narrowed until it became a narrow and crooked street with low porticoes at the sides, like the others. There was little shade, the sun being high. There was a tavern in front, under the porticoes, and beyond that, a doorway that looked completely dark. From the tavern came the sounds of voices, and intermittently the sound of an accordion, and also the odor of frying onions.

Daniele sat down on the ground with his shoulders against the column of a portico. A bit ahead of him, in the sun, a man was seated on a crate, with a big straw hat on his head. That man had nothing more to sell, but all the same he sat behind his table, which was made of some planks resting on two sawhorses. Beyond him was another man who sold old books and paintings with gilded frames. Two barefoot children kept watch over the paintings, heedless of the strong sun. The man had made himself a shelter with some sacks.

After a while the man who had nothing more to sell got up, picked up the crate on which he had been sitting, and came toward the shade. He studied the position of the sun in the sky and chose a location near Daniele.

"Oh," he said, as a kind of greeting.

"Hello," said Daniele.

The man put the crate against the next column and then looked at Daniele. "If you're not doing anything," he said, "come give me a hand to carry the table."

Daniele got up to help the man carry the planks and the sawhorses. They reassembled the table in the shade, as it had been in the sun.

"Why don't you go home?" asked Daniele. "You don't have anything more to sell."

"I'm waiting for merchandise," said the man. He sat down on the crate, leaning his back against the column. "Do you know what time it is?"

"I don't know," said Daniele. "Maybe two o'clock."

"No, I don't think it's two o'clock," said the man.

"I don't know," said Daniele.

The man looked off toward the far end of the square, where one could see a short stretch of wall, as well as the San Tommaso gate. Perhaps the merchandise would arrive through that gate, and as he looked he squinted his eyes, as the light was very strong. The end of the square shimmered in the heat that rose off the ground. Then the man got tired of watching. He pulled his hat over his eyes and leaned back with his head also against the column. He seemed to fall asleep right away.

Daniele observed with interest this man who was perhaps asleep. He was like all the other men who sold vegetables or some other thing in the market: poorly dressed, with a long beard and skin baked by the sun. Yet there was something about him that inspired trust, the way in which he had spoken before or his looks, that was hard to pin down. At least Daniele made himself believe it, and for this reason he would ask him for work as soon as he woke up. It might be that this man might bring him luck.

Daniele made a motion to shoo away the flies. He was barefoot and wore a pair of short pants that had been Tullio's, which Giulia had cut down for him because they were worn out at the knees. They were good like that for summertime. But the flies bothered his bare legs. There was a great number of flies in the square because of the filth. The refuse of the day before remained in heaps in two or three places, and there was new garbage and horse manure scattered on the ground.

The odor of frying onions faded in the air and no longer issued forth from the tavern. The sound of the accordion also stopped. A while before, a man with that instrument on his shoulder had come out and had headed toward the city center, keeping to the shade of the porticoes. The air was hot and drowsy, and the short shadows made by the houses seemed to stay always in the same place.

Then two patrolmen came out of the tavern. Standing quietly

under the porticoes, they surveyed the square with the tables of goods that people were not buying. One of them noticed the man who was apparently asleep against the column, and he spoke to the other one, and they both came toward the man. Daniele was afraid because he didn't know if the patrolmen were coming toward him or toward the man.

In any case they went over to the man and one of them gave him a swat on the shoulder. The man stayed seated, but he took off his hat and lifted a sleepy face.

"What are you doing here?" demanded one of the patrolmen.

"I'm waiting for merchandise."

"What merchandise?"

The man rubbed his hand over his face. "My partner has gone to get it. He's late. He should have been here before noon."

"What are you selling?"

"Fruits and vegetables," said the man. "You know that very well."

"Let's see your license," said the patrolman.

The man fixed his eyes on the patrolman for an instant, then lowered them. He had to get up to pull his wallet out of his back pocket, and he stayed on his feet. He produced the license out of the wallet and handed it to the patrolman who had spoken.

The patrolman examined the license and said, "You need to pay the fee for your booth."

"I paid it," said the man. "I paid it directly to you this morning. Possibly you don't recall. One-time payment is good for the whole day. Do you want to see the receipt?"

He searched for the receipt in his wallet and it appeared he couldn't find it. The patrolman who had not yet spoken watched attentively, with a supercilious and stupid expression.

Then he located the receipt in his wallet and showed it to the patrolman who had spoken, but the guard gestured toward the spot where the man had been before, in the sun. "You paid for that spot," he said, "not this one."

"But isn't it the same, here or there?" said the man. "I moved over here because it's in the shade, and when the goods arrive, I can sell them here in the shade."

"You took a spot that wasn't assigned to you."

The man rolled his eyes with an exasperated expression. "You all want to mess with people," he said. "You're always finding something wrong. And you always want to see the license and you know very well that I have it. I'm here every day and you see me."

"Hey, enough with the smart talk," said the patrolman who had not yet spoken.

"It could end badly for you," said the other patrolman. "You've taken a new spot without authorization, and you're putting up resistance."

It appeared that the man might rebel, but instead he made a gesture of defeat, hanging his head. "I'm not resisting," he said. "I'll put the table back where it was before."

He picked up the crate and carried it into the sun, and as he returned he looked at Daniele. Then Daniele got up, in spite of the fear he felt toward the patrolmen. Together they carried the table, and the patrolmen stayed to watch them do it.

The man watched as they then went off, and on his face was rage and despair, and so Daniele didn't dare ask him for work, not even after they were once again seated on the ground, both of them leaning against the column. But he felt a kinship with that man, the same humiliation in an unjust world.

Just then it occurred to him that he loved the man. "They should not have done that."

"I can't do anything about it," said the man. "I have a wife and kids at home, and they have to eat. Those guys are capable of pulling my license if I don't stay under their thumb. Maybe even haul me in, too, they would be capable of it."

"But it isn't fair what they're doing."

The man regarded him with the shadow of a suspicion. "Who can say what's fair or not fair?"

Daniele would have liked to overcome his mistrust. "A person can tell when things are fair."

"Well," said the man, "what does it matter to me even if I can tell? I can't do anything about it. Those at home must eat, that's all."

So said the man, and then was silent, and Daniele didn't have the nerve to talk to him for some time.

But then he asked, "How does a person get a vendor's license?"

"It requires an application and lots of documents," said the man, "and then you wait. They make the rounds of the city offices and the magistrate, and you wait. It also depends on what you're able to pay. I waited three months before I got my license."

"And after three months they give it?"

Again the man regarded Daniele before replying.

"It's not a sure thing," he said. "My brother-in-law has been waiting for six months, and they haven't given it to him. Before, he was a high-school teacher, my brother-in-law was, and they threw him out for political reasons, so they aren't issuing him a license. They say it's because there are too many people around selling stuff. But every day someone new arrives here with a license."

"But if there are no political reasons, do they issue a license?" asked Daniele.

"Perhaps," said the man.

Daniele let some time pass while he thought, then he turned brightly to the man. "Do you think they'd give me a license?"

"You're too young," said the man. "They want you to be eighteen years old to have a license, or maybe twenty, I'm not sure."

Again Daniele fell quiet for some time. Then he asked, "And your brother-in-law doesn't work?"

"He goes around buying vegetables from the peasants," said the man. "We have a bicycle, and so he can go around."

"I could also go and buy vegetables," said Daniele. "Would you sell my vegetables if I brought them to you?"

"Do you have a bicycle?"

"No," answered Daniele.

"So what do you want me to do, give you the bicycle?" said the man. "We have just the one, and it breaks down every day. Even today it must be broken down, that's why he's so late."

Daniele held his tongue a moment in confusion. Then he said, "I could go in your brother-in-law's place, since he's a schoolteacher."

"Oh sure," said the man, "and he'd end up here, doing just what you're doing right now, right? There's no difference between teachers and non-teachers."

After a bit Daniele asked, "If I found a bicycle and went around buying vegetables, would you sell them?"

"Yes, anything sells," said the man. "It's good enough if it's something to eat."

Daniele stood up. "Then I'll come back," he said. "I'll come back as soon as I've found a bicycle."

He went off toward home. At first he walked fast, almost running, then little by little more casually, because as he thought over the news that he would bring to Giulia, it seemed less and less attractive. Nevertheless, when he entered the kitchen Giulia noticed right away that he was not like at other times.

"Do you have any good news?"

"I don't know," said Daniele. "I've met a man at the market. Someone who sells vegetables. He said he might be able to give me work. If I bring him vegetables, he'll sell them and collect half the earnings. Wouldn't that be a fine thing?"

"Yes. It would be a fine thing."

"But it requires a bicycle, to go and buy the vegetables," said Daniele. "I thought I could ask Antonio for one just on loan. Tullio had so many bicycles, and now they have them, and they might lend me one. I'd put a box on the front, and one in back, and I could carry enough vegetables. Oh, Giulia, do you think they'd lend me a bicycle if I asked them?"

"Maybe it's better if Carla asks for one," said Giulia.

"Do you think they'll give Carla one?"

"Maybe so," said Giulia. "Carla still has some business with them."

"They'd also want some money," said Daniele. "It would only take a little, to get started. Then I would pay them back, as soon as I began to make money."

"It's easier to get the money," said Giulia. "Maybe Carla has enough to help you out."

"Just think how fine it would be," said Daniele.

40

Daniele carried the bicycle into the courtyard behind the shoemaker's house and leaned it against the wall. There were two racks attached to the bicycle, one in front and one in back, with boxes fastened to them. From the front box he took the basket where he had put the eggs, the vegetables, and the peaches.

The shoemaker was in the courtyard, seated on a crate in the shade. He didn't say anything to Daniele, and so Daniele went on home, thinking to find Giulia there. Instead, he found only little Maria in the kitchen. She knew that Giulia had gone to do the washing at the river.

"She said to tell you she's gone to do the wash at the river," Maria said.

"Isn't Carla here either?"

"No."

Daniele pulled the things out of the basket and and put them on the table, and left the peaches in such a way that Giulia would see them right away when she came in. They were big, pink peaches, the first big peaches of the season. He offered one to the little girl, but she was slow-witted and couldn't decide to take it in her hands.

"Don't you want it?"

"All right," said the child, still hesitating. Then she took the peach and began to eat it.

Daniele sat down and tried to read a book, and he couldn't. Suddenly everything was different, when he missed Giulia. There was no desire left in him to do anything. And Giulia should not have gone to do the washing. In the morning she had not even thought of doing it, otherwise she would have told him before he left for work.

Meanwhile, it was getting hot in the kitchen. The sun entered through the west window, blazing hot, even though it was already low.

Daniele watched the little girl. She had eagerly eaten the peach, and her face was sticky around her mouth. Now she was becoming absorbed with her own thoughts. She and Daniele had never succeeded at becoming good friends.

"Do you want for us to go and sit outside?" he asked.

"No," said the child.

"It's too hot in here," he said.

The little girl kept her eyes raised, dully, and didn't say anything.

Then Daniele went to sit by himself on the front step. There was no breeze at all outside but there in the doorway it was less hot, because that whole side of the house was in shade. Giulia should not be long now. He waited to see her appear at any moment, in the sunlight along the path that came from the river. But she didn't arrive.

He got up and took a few steps toward the shoemaker's house and then returned to sit down. It would be stupid to go to that man and ask him why Giulia had gone to do the wash. He wouldn't know, of course. And even if he did know he would have made a poor reply or would not have answered at all. It was no longer the way it had been at one time, when Tullio was alive.

The shadow of the house crept along the ground and reached the ruins farther away. Then the path also was in shadow, and also the magnolia tree, as the sun set behind the house.

Finally Giulia came along the path, and as soon as he saw her from afar he began to smile. She made her way slowly, too slowly. She carried the washing on her arm. She was wearing her big winter dress.

The smile got brighter on Daniele's face, but then it froze and vanished. Because Giulia was unwell, he could see at once she was unwell. There were circles around her eyes and her lips were bloodless, and her entire face was pale and damp. Her gaze avoided his, and yet she smiled. "I went to do the wash," she said quickly.

"You're not feeling very well, right?"

"Yes."

"You should not have had to do the wash," said Daniele.

"Maybe it's the heat that's making me sick," said Giulia. "Before, I felt all right, and then I went to do the wash. Instead, I got tired out. It's been too hot today."

She was speaking rapidly but with little strength.

Daniele took the washing from her arm and right away she sat down on the step.

"You washed everything," said Daniele. "Even your dress."

"It was because of the coffee," said Giulia. "I wanted to tip the pot of coffee and I missed, and it spilled on me. That's why I had to wash everything."

Daniele went into the corridor and hung the wet things on the cord and then returned to her. She seemed to be slightly better now that she was sitting down.

Daniele sat down on the step also. "I felt empty when I didn't find you at home," he said, and took her hand, and her hand was too hot. "You have a fever," he said.

"It must have been the heat."

"I'll go to find you a doctor."

Giulia smiled, in an attempt to seem unconcerned. "There's no need for a doctor. It's of no consequence, tomorrow I'll feel better. I'll certainly be better, don't be so worried."

He also tried to smile. "I'm not worried."

They waited a little longer, sitting there, while the shadow began to climb the ruins. The summer evening arrived, slow and hot.

"Daniele?" called Giulia under her breath.

"What?"

She hesitated a little. "Nothing," she said. Then she nodded vaguely at the sky or the ruins. "It's beautiful, isn't it?"

"Yes."

"It's because we two are alive, that it's so beautiful," said Giulia. "We're alive and together."

"Yes."

"We two should always be together."

The crickets trilled, scattered in the shade, and a mosquito flew close to Daniele's ear, and he chased it away with a movement of his hand. "There are mosquitoes," he said. "It makes you think of autumn."

"Right now it's still summer," said Giulia.

In silence they waited a little while longer, watching the things of the evening. Then they got up to go inside, and Giulia stood up stiffly, because she was very weak. She got to her feet in front of Daniele, leaning on him, and wrapped her arms around his neck. "Will you carry me?" she asked.

"Give me a kiss first."

"Not tonight."

Daniele made a glum face. "Why?"

Giulia kissed him on the cheek. "There, that's enough."

Daniele lifted her in his arms to carry her in, and she clung to his neck with what little strength she had.

"I'd like to always be like this," she said.

He lowered her to the floor when they were in the kitchen, and Giulia saw the peaches on the table.

"How fine they are," she said, appreciatively.

"They're for you," said Daniele. "The finest that I found today."

Little Maria came from the spot where she had been sitting. "He gave me one of them," she said.

"Did you eat it?"

"Yes."

"Good girl," said Giulia, and stroked her face, and she looked pleased. "Let's make something to eat before it gets dark," she said then to Daniele.

"You sit down and tell me what I should do," said Daniele. "Do you want to make eggs with vegetables?"

"Too late for vegetables," said Giulia. "Cook the eggs and get a box of meat. You can mix them together, if you want."

In a short time Daniele prepared the food, but then Giulia didn't want to eat anything or drink any milk. "I'll just have a peach," she said.

She took a peach and bit into it listlessly and then put it aside.

Daniele started feeling sadder and more worried. "We should find you a doctor," he said.

"No, tomorrow I'll feel better."

She raised a hand and with her fingers she brushed his hair from his forehead, tenderly. "You've gotten dark from the sun," she said. "And more handsome and stronger, as well. It does you good to go around on the bicycle."

"You'll come too, before summer ends."

"Sure, I'll come."

They fell into silence and each of them felt a profound worry that would not go away.

"Go take Maria home," said Giulia. "Then we'll talk a bit, before going to sleep."

"Yes," said Daniele, and right away he got up and went to take the child to her house.

When he returned, Giulia was already in bed, but with the blankets of her shelter drawn to one side, so she could see the last light of day. "Come here," she said. "Sit here on the bed. Let's talk awhile."

Daniele regarded her anxiously.

She appeared wan in the half-light of dusk, with only her eyes lively and bright.

"Are you feeling worse?" he asked.

"Just tired," said Giulia. "Because it was so hot today."

When he was seated on the mattress, she lifted a hand and stroked the hair on his forehead as before. And her eyes focused on his face and were full of a desperate love. "Tell me what you did today."

"I went to get the peaches."

"Far?"

"Not far. Five miles on the road. I made four trips with the schoolteacher. Now there will be work for a long time with the peaches."

"That's good, then," said Giulia.

There followed a heavy silence. Giulia closed her eyes, and kept them closed for a long time, and then opened them. "Keep talking," she said.

"The schoolteacher promised me he would help me study," said Daniele. "He won't give me lessons exactly, but he said that if I don't understand something I can ask and he'll explain it to me."

"I'm happy you've found that schoolteacher."

"He must be clever, you know," said Daniele. "Before, he taught high school in some city, he didn't tell me where. When they threw him out of school he had no way to survive, and then he came to his brother-in-law's. He was ashamed to display his poverty in that city where he had been a schoolteacher."

In the pause that followed, Giulia nodded yes with her head. She had taken his hand and held it between hers, but without strength.

"He knows so much about commerce, but of course he can't do business," said Daniele, and he had no desire to continue on, because he saw that Giulia wasn't paying attention to what he was saying. A heavy thought must certainly be occupying her mind and frightening her.

The room had gotten almost dark, and he couldn't make out the expression on her face very well, not even in her eyes, which she kept closed. He waited a long time for her to say something, and she neither spoke nor stirred.

Then he thought she must be asleep and tried to withdraw his hand that she held closed in hers, but she held onto it. "Daniele," she said weakly.

"Talk to me."

But Giulia said nothing.

"What is it? Tell me, what is it?"

She opened her eyes again. "I wanted to tell you," she said, and made a long pause, and then continued, "I wanted to tell you that when we're together at night, there is nothing more beautiful to me, and then I'm sure we two are one thing only, and nothing more can separate us. But I'm not very well, and so we can't sleep together for some time, until I get better."

"You'll get better soon."

"Yes, tomorrow I'll feel better," said Giulia. "But even afterward, for some time, we shouldn't be together at night. Only for a while."

"It makes no difference, this thing."

"No, it's important, and you should understand that if I could, I would. Nothing would make me happier than that. But now I can't do it anymore for a while, because it makes me sick. But you're not to think that it's because I love you less than before. I love you with all my heart, every moment I love you more. You must believe me, even if we can't be together at night."

"I believe you."

"And you won't get tired of that, right? You won't think of going away because we can't be together at night?"

"My place is here," said Daniele. "I couldn't live anywhere else without you. And even if we had to be always like brother and sister, I would keep loving you and I'd stay with you until the end of our lives."

"No," said Giulia. "It will only be for a while." And she brought his hand to her mouth and began to kiss it and was not ashamed to let him know she was crying.

iulia coughed often during the night, and Daniele sometimes heard her and sometimes he didn't, being accustomed to that sound. But one night, after a fit of coughing, Giulia began to rasp, as if she couldn't get a breath, and then he found himself violently awakened.

He called to her, shouting, and ran to her and kept calling, but she wasn't able to respond. She was dying, and he didn't know what to do. He couldn't see anything in the dark and he had forgotten where the matches were.

Giulia was still rasping, so she wasn't dead. He put his hands down to feel for her, and he found her hot and wet. Everything he touched, her face and the blankets, was hot and wet. He froze in fear and anguish and trembled all over, uncontrollably. Her rasping ceased, and began again, and then it turned into labored breathing. Once more he called to her and, worse than anything else, he couldn't hear her or see her.

Then he decided to go and find the matches. Outside the open window he saw the pale glow of the stars. But inside the kitchen it was dark, and he wasn't able to find the matches. He went to get some from Carla's room, on the little table.

He struck one with trembling hands. Then he saw only the color red, on her face and on the blankets. Everything was smeared with bright red, and he could see it was all blood. The match went out in his fingers. He stood bewildered and paralyzed in the dark, with the huge red stain remaining before his eyes.

Giulia's breathing continued, laboriously.

He struck another match. She lay with her eyes closed and mouth open in the attempt to draw a breath.

The flame burned itself out. He was left again in the dark, without the courage to strike another.

After a bit it seemed that Giulia was breathing with less difficulty. Then he lit the lamp and carried it to the bed. With a handkerchief he cleaned her lips of the blood. She opened her eyes and focused for a second on his, and they didn't even seem to be her own eyes, they were so dilated and terrified.

"Giulia, do you feel pain in some place?" he asked.

She closed her eyes again. Miserably, she attempted a smile and shook her head no. Then she lay immobile, in her faraway world.

And he in desperation searched for something he could do for her, so she wouldn't drift away. He could have her drink some water, perhaps. He went to get a cup of water. "Giulia . . . drink a little water, Giulia," he said.

She reopened her eyes and made a gesture as if pushing the lamp away.

"Why? Does the light hurt you?"

"It smokes," she said.

Daniele carried the lamp outside to close it down in the corridor. Then he returned with one of Carla's candles.

"Do you want to drink some water?" he asked.

Giulia answered yes with her eyes.

He helped her to drink, supporting her head, and after she had taken barely a swallow, she didn't want any more and fell back, worn out. She drifted away again, where he could not follow.

He sat down next to the bed, waiting. Giulia's hair was spread over the pillow. He touched its ends with dread, and then took up a handful and squeezed it, but he didn't dare to touch where her hair was hot, so close to her skin.

Now Giulia would die, like this. Her breathing was a bit calmer, but it had become too weak. Then even that weak breathing would end, and then she would be dead. He watched and waited to see her die. Her blood was drying around her mouth and turning dark, but the rest of her face, where there was no blood, appeared alarmingly pale in the light of the candle. Meanwhile he caressed her hair, but he was afraid to touch her anywhere else. It was a fear as if she were made of something that could dissolve if he touched her.

Still, Giulia regained strength, little by little. She kept her eyes open longer now, although she focused them on the ceiling. Suddenly she said, "It's passed now." Her voice was so weak it was almost inaudible.

"Yes, it's passed," said Daniele.

"Then go to bed, Daniele," she said.

"No, I'm not leaving you here alone."

She remained in silence for a bit and tried to smile. It hurt to see her smile, with her face so stained with blood. "Go . . . to . . . bed . . . please, Daniele," she said. She paused between the words to swallow and take another breath.

"Why do you want to send me away?" asked Daniele.

Again she remained in silence. When she replied, she said, "I'm ashamed to be so sick."

"You aren't sick. Now it's gone. Only, you shouldn't make an effort to talk."

"I'm sick on the inside," said Giulia.

Daniele was unable to say anything. If he had tried to speak he would have started to cry, and he mustn't cry.

"Go away for a little while," said Giulia. "Just let me wash and then you can come back."

"Doesn't it hurt you to wash?"

"No," said Giulia. "I want to wash."

"Then I'll heat a little water. It's better for you to wash with warm water."

"Yes, please do," said Giulia.

Daniele got up and lit the stove and put on a pot of water. Then he came once more to sit by Giulia. She then turned her head toward him and moved her lips, speaking, but he couldn't hear anything because of the noise of the flame. Daniele lowered his head to her mouth.

"I'm going to die pretty soon," she said.

"Don't talk, Giulia," said Daniele. "Don't make an effort to talk."

"I'm going to die pretty soon," she said, again. Then she closed her eyes and stayed a long time without opening them. Daniele didn't know what to do except to stroke her hair and watch her with a desperate intensity, as if he hoped that what had happened would reverse itself and the blood would disappear and Giulia wouldn't be so terribly sick.

After, Giulia made a sign that she wanted to speak, and he leaned his head lower. "The water," she said. "It must be ready."

Daniele went to shut off the stove and brought the water.

"What time is it now?" asked Giulia.

"It's still nighttime."

"It's a long night," said Giulia, and closed her eyes.

When the water was hot, Daniele poured it into a basin, then helped Giulia to sit up in bed.

"Now go out," she said.

"Why? I'm washing you."

"No, you aren't."

"Are you ashamed? Once you said that you felt no shame with me."

"I didn't think I would be so sick, then."

"It doesn't matter that you're sick. You shouldn't feel ashamed."

She didn't put up resistance. She was so weak that she accomplished only with difficulty those few movements Daniele asked her to do. He removed her nightgown and washed her with a towel. Everywhere—on her face, her chest, and her arms—her flesh appeared frighteningly white, as if all her blood had left through her mouth and none remained beneath the skin. He washed her and dried her, then he took her in his arms and carried her to the other bed.

She stayed motionless for some time, exhausted. But at least she was barely able to say, "You shouldn't have brought me to your bed, Daniele. You could get this sickness. I don't want you to get sick."

"I won't get anything," said Daniele. "And you'll recover. I'm going to find a doctor, and you'll recover."

Giulia fastened frightened eyes on him and grabbed his hand to hold it. "Don't go."

"No, not right now," said Daniele. "When day comes."

Giulia's eyes implored him. "Don't go for a doctor. And don't tell anyone I'm sick. Not even Carla should you tell. No one can do anything for this sickness. I just want to die here by you."

"Don't speak, Giulia, please," said Daniele.

"You must just take care you don't get this sickness," said Giulia. "And wait a little while. After I die, then you can leave. It's better that you don't stay here anymore once I'm dead."

"Don't talk of dying," said Daniele. "You won't die. But you must be good and go to sleep. Now close your eyes and try to sleep."

"Yes," said Giulia, and she closed her eyes, but she wanted to keep Daniele's hand between hers. The activity and the effort to talk had wasted her and she began to breathe laboriously again. It took a long time for her to become peaceful. Then she remained still and once in a while she seized Daniele's hand with a compulsive squeeze.

The night passed slowly. Daylight filtered through the window. Daniele blew the candle out.

Giulia opened her eyes right away, because she wasn't sleeping. "It's day."

"Yes."

"Open the windows."

Morning light and cool air entered through the open windows.

"Open the blankets wide, too," said Giulia.

Daniele slid the blankets open on the cord. Giulia was enraptured to see bright sky through the window. She was at peace now, and resigned. "Daniele?" she called, without looking at him.

"Yes," answered Daniele.

She couldn't speak right away. Her eyes appeared bright from the tears that were forming in them. "If you want to go away," she said, "I can't keep you."

"I'm not going away, you know that."

"I know," said Giulia. "And maybe I'll recover. I already feel better."

"Yes," said Daniele.

"I could get up, too, if I wanted to."

"Wait," said the Daniele. "First the doctor will come, and afterward you can get up if he says you can."

Giulia got upset again. "I don't want the doctor. By now I feel better. What could the doctor do?"

"This isn't the first time you've gotten this illness, isn't that true?"

She kept looking at the bright sky beyond the window. She appeared even more faded and bloodless in that light.

"How many times have you had it before?" asked Daniele.

"One time."

"It was that day you went to wash your dress, right? Why didn't you tell me then?"

"I thought it would not come back," said Giulia.

"It was because you were afraid I would know, right?"

"Yes."

"You shouldn't be afraid. I love you even if you are sick. I love you even more, now that I know. But you must get well. Maybe your illness isn't so serious. You just need to take care of yourself and you'll get better, it's an illness one can recover from. The doctor will tell you what needs to be done, and the medicine you need to take. You'll recover, for sure."

Giulia withdrew her gaze from the window and looked him in the eyes. Two or three tears slipped down her cheeks.

"You must recover for me, just for me," said Daniele.

"Yes," said Giulia.

"And you must let me go and look for a doctor."

"The doctor can't come here."

"He'll come. When a person's sick, the doctor must come."

"But he can't come here. If he sees we're living here he'll make us leave."

"I'll take you to the shoemaker's. First, I'll go and tell the doctor to come, then I'll take you to the shoemaker's."

Giulia shook her head no. "He won't want me. It's an illness that no one wants in the house."

"We won't tell him that you had blood coming from your mouth," said Daniele. "We'll just say that you're not very well and the doctor must examine you."

Giulia said nothing, and Daniele started to go. But she held him back. "Wait," she said. "You can go later, when Maria comes. Don't leave me alone."

"I'll go and call her," said Daniele.

"Wait a little longer," said Giulia.

Daniele remained sitting.

Again she directed her eyes toward the sky outside the window, with a pensive expression. "Listen, Daniele," she said. "If this blood should come again into my mouth, it could happen that I might die without being able to speak. Already last night it seemed I might die, and I wasn't able to say anything to you. Or it could be that I might die when you were out. I need to talk to you right away before I die."

"Don't talk anymore about dying. You won't die. I know you won't die."

"Maybe I won't die," said Giulia. "But in any case, I need to tell you what I'm thinking, because I could miss the chance if I don't do it right away."

Daniele remained in silence.

"So many times I've thought of these things," said Giulia, "and I had them all clear in my mind, and now that I must tell you they aren't as clear as before. But I'll try to tell you all the same, and you must understand me. It's important for you to understand me well."

"Yes," said Daniele.

"It has to do with how I love you," said Giulia. "I can't tell you how much I care for you, but it's so much that it will never end. Not even if I were to die would it end. Do you believe there must be something after we're dead?"

"I don't know," said Daniele. "My mother always said there was another life. The priests said so, too. And Tullio said there was nothing."

"I believe there must be something," said Giulia.

Daniele hesitated a little, because they had never spoken of such things.

Then he asked, "Do you want me to go and find a priest, Giulia?"

"No," said Giulia. "It's not what I want to say. I just want to say that if there's something in the hereafter, maybe the same feelings will continue when we die. So then I'll continue to love you always, and wait for you until you come. And you, while you live on this earth, would need to continue loving me as if I were here, and then when the moment comes you will pass over to where I am waiting for you, and you'll come with the thought of joining me, and we will be together without end."

"You know I'll love you always," said Daniele.

"Yes, I know," said Giulia, and smiled peacefully toward the sky.

The day was at its end when Daniele knocked on the door of the room. From inside the old man answered for him to enter, but he did not get up from his armchair. He turned his head toward the door and right away he recognized Daniele, even though he had seen him only that time when he had come with Tullio.

"Ah, it's you," he said.

"Yes," said Daniele. He stopped on the threshold before closing the door. It seemed that he did not want to come any farther.

"Have a seat," said the old man.

Daniele advanced a few steps and stopped again in the middle of the room. He didn't see where he could have sat down. The furniture from before had been taken away, and now there was a military-type folding cot along the wall, and a big chest in one corner.

"Sit down on the cot," said the old man.

Daniele sat down. He felt bone-tired.

"Did you come about Tullio, perhaps?" asked the old man. "Did they learn that you were together?"

"I've come about Giulia," said Daniele. "She's sick."

"Sick in what way?"

"She had blood in her mouth. It's the second time she's gotten blood in her mouth."

The old man dropped his head onto his chest and closed his eyes as if he were asleep. He had no topcoat on but otherwise he was dressed as before, with a jacket and tie and his brimless hat on his head. It was impossible to know what he was thinking.

"Something should be done for Giulia," said Daniele.

The old man didn't move.

"Something should be done for her," Daniele repeated.

The old man raised his head. "What can be done? It's an ugly disease. So many things would have to be done, and at the same time maybe she would not recover."

Daniele began to wring his hands. This was no longer the same old man. The other time when he had been there with Tullio, he had had the impression that there was some vibrancy in him. He had confused ideas, but he had vibrancy, or at least an interest in other people. Instead he, Daniele, had been wrong. Or else in the meantime things had happened to the old man, things that had made him so apathetic and self-pitying.

Because he started talking about himself, and he complained about being alone and useless, and Daniele almost didn't listen to him because his misfortunes didn't matter, since he had become so desperate as to lose concern for his fellow man. He shouldn't be like this, with Giulia so sick.

She was really sick, Giulia was. It could be she was already dead. Twice when Daniele had gone home during the day, he had found her immobile, lost in a kind of dream, worlds away, from which she could not return except with great difficulty. Maybe that was the agony, the moment that precedes death, and there he was, without a plan to find help for her.

By now the old man had stopped talking, and Daniele stayed sitting on the folding cot, twisting his hands. He wanted to leave.

But all of sudden the old man asked, "What can I do for her?"

Daniele brightened with hope. "It is necessary to find a doctor for her. All day I've gone around to find a doctor and wasn't able to. They send me from one to the next, and no one wants to come. They say they have too much to do."

"There are so many sick ones," said the old man.

"But they shouldn't be that way," said Daniele. "When the sick are poor they leave them to die like dogs."

"The world put itself on this path," said the old man, "and it's not my fault. What do you want from me?"

"You should help me find a doctor," said Daniele. "Surely you know some doctor. Tell him to come. We can't let Giulia die like a dog."

The old man repeated his words thoughtfully. "No, we can't."

Daniele jumped to his feet in anger. "Why are *you* this way, too?" he said. "You know it's not right. You can't say they're right."

"I don't say they're right," said the old man. "Only one loses one's grip, from staying alone and thinking. There comes the moment when one loses one's grip."

"*Do something for Giulia!*" Daniele demanded.

The old man dropped his head, closing his eyes as before. And Daniele moved to leave. But before he could reach the door the old man stopped him.

"Wait," he said. "I'll write you a recommendation to a doctor. At one time we were good friends."

"Why don't you go and talk to him?" said Daniele.

It seemed the old man was laughing. "How would you have me get there? It's months since I left this house. And I'll never go out anymore until I die, if they don't take me away first. But by now that time shouldn't be far off."

Daniele felt a fresh surge of anger. Now that the world the old man believed in had vanished, he didn't want to go out anymore, not even to do what bit of good he could have done.

"I'll write you a note," said the old man. "Maybe it won't serve any purpose, but it's all I can do." He got up and went out of the room.

Then Daniele no longer felt hostility toward him, but only compassion, because he saw how he had changed over those few months. The time must not be long now before he would be gone, for sure.

He went to the window to wait. In the garden below some grass had grown up, and also there were some blossoms on the few plants that had survived.

And now it was nighttime. No doctor would go to them at night, and Giulia meanwhile could die, if she wasn't already dead.

The old man returned with a folded sheet of paper on which he had written an address. "Try him," he said. "But don't expect him to come. Not right away, anyway."

He stood holding himself up with his hand on the wall.

"Thanks," said Daniele.

"Return soon," said the old man. "Come back and tell me how Giulia is."

"I'll come back," said Daniele.

As soon as he was on the street he tried to run but he couldn't. He had eaten nothing since the night before, and he had not slept much during the night, and a scary thing had happened that had taken away his wish to keep on living. Giulia could die, and he wasn't finding help for her anywhere in the world. Each person thought only of himself, even the old man thought only of himself in his fear of being alone.

Still, Daniele's hope returned when he arrived at the doctor's house. A woman looked out of the upper window and said right away that the doctor wasn't at home.

"I have a note," said Daniele. "It's a note from a friend of his."

The woman closed the window and shortly appeared at the door. "Give me the letter," she said.

"I need to hand it directly to him," said Daniele. "I also have to speak to him."

"Very well, but he's not at home," said the woman. "What do you want me to say?"

"I can wait," said Daniele. "It's important. I need to talk with him."

"Is it for you?"

"For my sister. She's very sick."

"Well, come tomorrow, then. Tomorrow morning at eight."

Daniele headed home. The streetlights lit the streets and they no longer had blue screens. Many windows were open and lighted, also, because there was now peace in the world.

Daniele walked slowly. Twice he changed streets, and then he stopped in front of a café, where some people were listening to the radio. A man was announcing the news with a clear, strong voice, but Daniele couldn't understand him.

Instead, he was weeping without knowing it. And then one of the people listening looked at him strangely, and so he realized he was crying, and began to walk slowly once more. He didn't want to arrive there.

43

At home, Carla was waiting. She was sitting in the kitchen, and one of the candles was lit on the table. The blankets in Daniele's corner were closed.

"How is she?"

"Asleep. She waited for you, but now she's sleeping."

They went to sit on the bed in Carla's room. Before sitting down, she closed the window and lit another candle on the little table. She had done everything rapidly and confidently, as usual. But her attention often drifted to some nearby object for no reason. However, he felt better when he was close to Carla.

"All day I looked for a doctor," said Daniele. "No one wants to come. But tomorrow I'll find one, I've already agreed to go at eight."

"A doctor came."

"You brought him?"

"Yes."

"I wasn't able to."

"It was easy for me. I knew him before."

Daniele waited while she spoke.

"It's tuberculosis," said Carla. "Her mother died of tuberculosis, and it was to be expected she would end that way herself."

"Does she have to die?" asked Daniele.

"The doctor didn't say that," said Carla. "He said maybe she could get better. But now she's weak because she's lost too much blood."

Daniele set himself to looking at the candle. "She will die."

"Maybe she won't die," Carla said. "And we shouldn't let her see that we're afraid she might die. We need to deal with her always as if we were sure that she'll get better soon. The doctor says that this way we can help her stay alive. It's to give her courage."

"Did the doctor do anything?" asked Daniele.

"He gave her shots," said Carla. "And he prescribed medicine, and cold packs need to be put on her chest. And she needs to stay quiet in bed, too. But he says the most important thing is that she has the will to live and has faith that she will live. You can do a lot for her, Daniele."

"I'm scared," said Daniele. "I'm scared that if she talks about dying I'll start to cry."

"You must have courage," said Carla. "You must have courage if you want to help her to live. We must behave around her as if she isn't sick."

"I'll try," said Daniele.

There was a long pause, then Carla said, "The doctor said that he'll make out the papers for the sanatorium, Daniele. Maybe they won't serve any purpose, because there's no room in the sanatoriums. But even if things go smoothly, it will be necessary to wait many months for a place."

Daniele turned his eyes toward her. "She'll recover, going to the sanatorium?"

"They sent her mother to the sanatorium, and it was totally useless. But other people recover, for a little while."

"She could recover?" said Daniele.

"Yes," Carla said. "But what I wanted to tell you is that you shouldn't let her know that the doctor's making out the papers for the sanatorium. I'm sure she would not want to go there. The only thing that's important to her is not to be separated from you, for that reason she would not want to go to the sanatorium."

"She must go there, if she's to get better," said Daniele. "I'll find a way to convince her to go."

"Well, when the moment comes you can try to convince her," said Carla. "But for now, don't talk about it. Maybe the doctor won't succeed in doing anything with the papers, and so it would be useless to talk to her about it. You would cause her suffering for nothing."

There was another long pause, as each remained with lowered head, thinking his own thoughts.

At length Carla asked, "Do you love her truly?"

"Why are you asking me this?"

"Then you're not thinking of going away, right?"

Daniele lifted his face. "How can you believe such a thing?"

"I don't," said Carla. "But she's afraid. She said only a few words in the time I was with her, and I understood that she's scared and thinks continually about that. When someone's sick like that, it seems they take comfort in thinking the worst. And you should do everything you can so she doesn't have those thoughts. Even if it should happen that you were afraid, or felt disgusted by her illness, you must not let her know. I'm sure she would die right away if she lost her trust in you."

"You don't understand how much I love her," said Daniele.

Carla had a curious, almost pained, smile. "I know," she said. "But what's important is that she feels sure of it. So then what's wanted is a way of making her feel that way, and it's hard to make her feel these things in the right way, for someone as sick as she is. Even without wanting to, people make mistakes."

"How can I do better?" asked Daniele.

"I don't know," said Carla. "Up to now you've done fine with her. You need to continue to be good, like before, and do everything she wants, only you should consider her illness, and then don't kiss her or go to bed with her. You must not do this even if she wants you to."

"It's she who doesn't want to anymore."

"Yes," said Carla. "She understands a lot of things. Besides, it would damage her health if you went to bed with her."

"I know."

"But above all you should never talk about going away," said Carla. "Even if it crossed your mind at some moment, she must never know. This is important. Because, you see, she could last a long time, even sick like this. She could even get worse and yet keep on living for a long time. Then you could get tired of being with a dying woman who keeps on living."

"Don't talk that way, Carla."

"I said it in a manner of speaking. I don't believe it would happen with you. But sometimes things happen that a person could never have imagined before."

"I'll never leave her. And if she must die, I'd wish to die in her place."

Carla smiled, again with a pained expression. "Well, I'm glad you think that way."

Once more, each lapsed into private thoughts. The house was silent, and even outside it was silent, except for the intermittent chirping of a cricket. In a corner of the room, on the floor, Carla had placed the jar with some magnolias, a bit faded, that previously had been in the kitchen.

"We have to decide what should be done," said Daniele after a moment. "Now it's necessary for one of us to be always close by her and never leave her alone. In any case, you should be with her. You're better at these things, and you're never lacking in nerve, and you know better than I do how to take care of her. Don't worry about anything else, for now. There's no more need for you to go out to work. What I make is enough for all of us, and even if medicines are required that cost a lot of money, I know how to find them. And Antonio can help us if necessary. I'm sure he will help in a case like this. For the rest, all I need is the bicycle. At this time of year I can earn enough with my work."

Carla had listened thoughtfully. "We'll do it so that one of us is always with her."

Daniele turned his head and looked severely at her. "It's you that should stay with her. Don't you really want to quit that work?"

Carla rebelled. "Why are you talking to me this way? You don't have the right to interfere in my business. What difference does it make to you?"

Daniele's face crumpled. "Well, I have no right," he said, and got up and began to leave.

Carla also stood up. "Wait," she said with a changed voice that was trembling.

She approached him, looking straight into his eyes. "Wait," she said again. "You don't have to be mean. You always have a way of getting off on the wrong foot with me. And I love you."

She paused and moved one hand to caress him, always looking right into his eyes. "I don't want to do anything to upset you," she said. "As far as that goes, even if I could, I wouldn't do it. You must believe me."

Daniele didn't answer.

"Why don't you believe me?"

"There is no need for you to do that work," said Daniele, obstinately.

Carla bent her head and it appeared she had nothing to say. Then suddenly she raised her eyes to his, pressing her lips together with exasperation. "What makes you think the four cents you earn are enough?" she said. "You saw what you got into today with that doctor. And just try to go and buy things on the outside. And ask the shoemaker what he wants so we can stay here. You'll see how far your pennies will go."

Daniele's face wore an expression of sorrow, or perhaps disbelief. He moved away from her. "I'm sorry," he said, and he didn't know precisely what he meant to say.

He left abruptly, and she sat down again on the bed and stayed there, staring at the floor for a long time with a fixed and almost numb look. Then she got up and blew out the candle. She went toward the kitchen. But her face had already become expressionless.

44

Daniele leaned the bicycle against the wall and hurried toward home, carrying the basket with the vegetables and eggs and a bottle of milk for Giulia. He left the shoemaker's courtyard through the breach in the wall, and as soon as he got onto the path he started to look toward the house. Every night he did the same as he came home, anxiously.

The house was silhouetted against the sunset light, and he couldn't see it well. Only when he was closer did he notice Carla on the step.

She was seated on the threshold, looking down, and she didn't realize he was approaching. But when she heard the sound of his footsteps, then she raised her head without surprise, as if she had been waiting to see him there.

Daniele stopped. Carla's face appeared stunned, her eyes fixed and wide, and her mouth rigid and slightly open. It was a face that didn't want to reveal anything. But then one lip began to tremble and she—not right away but after a bit—grimaced to hold her face still, and again lowered her head.

So Daniele knew that Giulia was dead.

He went on and passed close to Carla without saying anything and reached the kitchen. The windows were open and the kitchen was filled with the glow of sunset. He put the basket on the table and drew from it the eggs and vegetables and the bottle of milk for Giulia. He placed each item in order on the table. The blankets in Giulia's corner were closed. The silence struck him, and the sense of immense emptiness that was there in the silence.

He advanced as far as the corner and gently moved aside the blankets to see. Giulia was lying on the mattress, on top of the blankets. She was wearing her white summer dress, and her feet and legs were bare, and by her head were Carla's two candles, one on each side. Little Maria was sitting on a stool next to the bed.

She raised her eyes as soon as she noticed Daniele. She had the usual expression, serious and a bit dull, and her eyes were dry. "She's dead."

"Yes," said Daniele.

He came close to see Giulia better. Carla must have washed her and combed her hair and closed her eyes and mouth, and this way she looked sweet and serene, as if she were still alive and sleeping. Only, her features were a bit stiffer and her face was whiter and more drawn. Daniele lowered a hand to touch her forehead, and it felt cold, and he could not take his hand away.

The little girl kept staring at him. "Is it true that she won't talk anymore?"

"Yes," said Daniele.

"And she won't move anymore?"

"She won't move anymore."

The child turned her gaze to Giulia, quietly. "They'll put her under the ground."

Daniele said nothing for some time, but then suddenly he leaned down to take the child's face between his hands and raised it to look into her eyes. "Aren't you sorry she's dead?" he asked. "Aren't you sorry they'll put her in the ground?"

The little girl thought and then said "Yes" quietly, but her eyes remained expressionless.

Then Daniele released her face and left the kitchen.

He took a few slow steps in the corridor. Carla was still sitting on the little step and she didn't turn when she heard him coming. He had no desire to go to her just now. He had no desire to do anything. He leaned against the wall, waiting for some thought to come, and none did, perhaps because his stomach was hurting, and all he could think of was this pain in his stomach.

He went into Carla's room. He looked in the mirror and saw his eyes and face, and it was as if they were the eyes and the face of someone else. He didn't want to see himself in the mirror. On the little table there was a basin filled with water. He lowered one hand in the water and held it there for some time. Then he passed his hand over his hair and once again put his hand in the water and once again passed it over his hair, and he did this until his hair was completely wet.

Then he left the table and went out to sit on the little step next to Carla. "Do you have a cigarette?" he asked.

She turned and they looked at each other. She reached out a hand and brushed a drop of water from his temple. Then she produced the pack of cigarettes from the pocket of her dress. She took one for herself and gave the rest to him. She lit her own cigarette first and then his, but as they did this, they avoided meeting each other's gaze.

Daniele inhaled deeply once or twice. But it didn't help anything. The pain in his stomach got stronger. It seemed that all the sorrow over Giulia's passing was centered in his stomach, and it was useless to smoke. But he continued. And quickly his mouth filled with the bitter taste, and his whole being was flooded with nausea. Then he threw the cigarette down and stood up and staggered away a few paces. Leaning against the wall, he vomited on the ground.

Carla turned her gaze toward him, but she didn't move. He finished vomiting, then went to the kitchen to drink a little water, and he couldn't stay there. He had the impression he couldn't stay anywhere. He went back to sit on the little step, next to Carla.

"Has it gone away?" she said.

"Yes."

Both of them remained sitting there the same way, hugging their knees and staring at the ground in front of them. Carla still held the cigarette between her lips, in a corner of her mouth. And right after she finished it, she lit another.

"Can you give me another, Carla?" he said.

"No," said Carla. "It's not good for you."

Daniele didn't ask again, but said, "It seemed she was getting better, and instead she's dead."

"It was her illness," said Carla.

"But she didn't have to die," said Daniele, despairingly. And right away he asked, "Didn't she say anything before she died?"

"Nothing," said Carla. "She couldn't say anything. She got another mouthful of blood, and she was all full of blood, in her mouth and her lungs, and she died of suffocation. The doctor had told her she could die in just that way."

Daniele held his tongue, thinking of that. After a bit he asked, "Was it you who washed her, Carla?"

"Yes."

"I would have done it. I did it the other time, too."

Carla turned to look at him. "You shouldn't take it that way. When things like this happen, it seems that it's all over and there's no more hope in life. But instead, it's necessary to let time pass and meanwhile other things will happen, and a little at a time everything will settle down. Just give it time."

"She didn't have to die," said Daniele.

Carla continued to study him for a little while, but she said no more.

The sun had set some time ago, and evening was coming on. The days were much shorter than in summer, and twilight arrived sooner. The part of the sky that they could see already had a few stars.

"We should go and tell the shoemaker, also," said Carla. "Maybe he will have to fill out some papers, now that she's dead. There will be papers to fill out."

"He doesn't know yet?"

"No."

The crickets hummed in the silence, but in spite of their music you could also hear the silence. Daniele had never experienced that silence so acutely before, the silence of all those dead. And evening was coming on quickly. "Do you want me to go?" he asked.

"Where?"

"To the shoemaker's, to let him know," said Daniele.

"Maybe that's better," said Carla. "You're a man."

Daniele got up and went off toward the shoemaker's house. Carla lit another cigarette. She stayed still, making only the small movements that went with smoking.

After a bit Daniele returned, accompanied by the shoemaker, and it was almost dark.

"I'd like to see her," said the shoemaker. "You both are really sure she's dead?"

"She's dead, for sure," said Carla.

"I'd like to see her," said the shoemaker again, and he entered the house.

"You go too, Daniele," said Carla. "Go close up the windows. It's already dark."

Daniele entered the kitchen to put the cardboard pieces on the windows. The man stood behind the shelter of blankets. When the windows were covered, Daniele saw the shadow of the man's head on the ceiling, and occasionally, also, the shadow of his arm as he moved it. Maybe he was touching Giulia, but Daniele had no desire to look.

Then the man came out. "Now we're going to have a lot of bother with the city," he said. "And with the priests too, for the funeral."

"I don't know," said Daniele.

"*I* know it," said the man. "It will be necessary to take her to my house and think about the funeral. Maybe a doctor should come and see her."

"Will that require cash?" asked Daniele.

"Sure. But not just cash. There is also the fuss."

"I don't know," said Daniele again.

The man looked at him and started to say something but then went out without saying anything. Daniele also moved to go outside. Still, at the door he stopped and turned back. "Maria?" he called.

"What?"

"Are you afraid to be alone with Giulia?"

"No," answered the child.

Then Daniele went again to sit down on the step next to Carla. The man was still there, he could see his shadow in the dark.

After a while the man said, "There could be a way to avoid everything, the expense and the bother."

"What way?" asked Carla.

"Giulia had no one who might come and look for her, right?"

"There's no one."

"Not even the doctor, right?" asked the man.

"I don't think he'll come," said Carla. "He only came once, maybe twenty days ago now. He must have forgotten about her. He was supposed to make out the papers for the sanatorium and he hasn't done them."

"Are you sure he hasn't done them?" asked the man.

"Yes, I'm sure," said Carla.

"Then it would be possible to do what I'm thinking," said the man.

"What?"

"Bury her inside the zone," said the man. "Here there are already so many dead, that one more won't make any difference. The important thing is that no one comes to look for her."

"I don't think anyone will come to look for her," said Carla.

"It would be better also because of the ration cards," said the man. "If we don't report that she's dead, those in the town hall will keep giving me her ration cards. They still give me Tullio's ration cards, and no one says anything."

"But what if later they find out about it?" asked Carla.

"If no one comes looking they won't find out," said the man. "Worst case, we'll say she left without saying anything. How many girls go missing these days, and no one knows where they end up? So we'll say that was also the case with her."

There was a moment of silence, then Carla asked, "What do you think about that, Daniele?"

"I don't know," said Daniele, and there was more silence.

Then Carla said, "Maybe Giulia would not be unhappy to be buried close by."

"Maybe she wouldn't be unhappy," Daniele repeated, mechanically.

Carla raised her head toward the man's shadow. "We'd want something to dig the hole with."

"Do you want to bury her right away?" asked Daniele.

"If it must be done, it's better to do it right away," said Carla.

"Sure, better do it right away," said the man. "Right now it's dark enough to do it, and later there will also be the moon. I'll go get a pick and a shovel and we'll dig a hole. We'll choose a good spot in the middle of the ruins, and afterward we'll put some stones on top, so no one will see anything more than that. And if they do find her, they'll think she died in the bombardment."

"It can be done this way," said Carla.

"I'll go and get the tools, then," said the man, and at once he went off toward his house to fetch the tools.

They stayed both alone and together in the dark.

"The moon will rise later," said Daniele, looking at the serene sky.

Carla looked at the sky too, toward where the moon would rise.

"Carla," said Daniele, "doesn't it seem to you an ugly thing to bury her like this in secret?"

"It's the best we can do," said Carla. "She would be happier to remain near us."

Daniele continued to watch the sky. Then he said, "If some part of us lived on even after we were dead, the others there would know it, isn't that so?"

"I don't know," said Carla.

"To me it seems as if she ought to come out and sit with us here," said Daniele. "So many times we sat here, she and I, on this step. She told me everything that was going on in her mind. She had a way of saying things that I understood immediately, and so we were right for each other."

"Yes," said Carla.

"And now that she's dead, I'm afraid," said Daniele. "I would have been able to do so much more for her. Now my mind is full of the things I would have been able to do or would have been able to say. It seems that I wasn't capable of making her know how much I loved her."

"You did everything you had to do," said Carla.

"No," said Daniele. "There was always something inside me that I was not able to make her know. Now, instead, I could make her understand everything. I think this must be so, only because she's dead. If she were still alive, I wouldn't be able to tell her anything of all this."

"She understood everything about you," said Carla. "She could understand everything because she loved you, and it happens that way when two people truly love each other, that they understand even those things that don't get said. I know she understood everything. And with you she was as happy as anyone can be on this earth. You don't know what she was like before you came to us."

"But she shouldn't have died," said Daniele. "She was so good, she didn't deserve to die."

"Everyone dies," said Carla. "The good ones and the bad ones."

"But she shouldn't have died so soon," said Daniele, and then he stopped because he heard the footsteps of the man, returning.

The man came and dumped on the ground the tools he had brought. "It's too dark now, we need to wait for the moon."

"The moon should not be long in coming," said Carla.

The man turned to look at the sky over his house. "No sign of it yet. It's best to go inside. It's too damp for me here outside."

"Yes, let's go in," said Carla, getting up.

On the table the eggs and the vegetables and the bottle of milk for Giulia were still arranged in a row.

"Do you want to eat something, Daniele?" said Carla. "You haven't eaten anything since this morning."

"I ate out," said Daniele. "I'm not hungry anymore just now."

The man and Daniele sat down. Carla brought to the table some bread and a cup and a spoon. Then she called Maria to come and eat.

The child came to sit down at the table and began to eat the bread, soaked in milk.

"You drink at least some milk, too, Daniele," Carla insisted.

"No," said Daniele, "I don't feel like it."

"We need a flask of wine," said the man.

"We don't have any wine," said Carla.

"Oh, I know that," said the man. "I just said it because every time it's happened that I kept vigil for a dead person there was wine to drink."

No one spoke after that. The air was warm in the room. The candle flame made the shadows of the blankets dance on the ceiling.

When the child had finished the bread and milk, Carla made two holes in an egg and had her drink it. Then she started to smoke. The man also began to smoke, taking a cigarette from Carla's pack.

"You're lucky, you are, that you always have tobacco," he said. As he smoked, the man regarded Daniele with curiosity. "You were her friend, isn't that right?"

"What?" said Daniele.

"Weren't you the friend of Giulia?"

Daniele looked off somewhere else without answering.

"It's sure disappointing when someone dies like this," said the man.

"It should disappoint everyone when someone like Giulia dies," said Carla.

"Sure," said the man.

"May I take the child home, Carla?" asked Daniele. "It's already her bedtime."

"Yes," said Carla. "Go if you want."

Daniele jumped up hastily. "Do you want to go home, Maria? It's time to go to bed."

"All right," said the little girl, and she got up, ready to go.

"Don't you want to say good-bye to Giulia first?" asked Daniele.

The child appeared uncertain and looked at Carla.

"Go and say good-bye," Carla said. "Tomorrow she'll go away and she won't come back anymore."

Daniele went with her behind the shelter of blankets. The two candles were almost burned down. One was shorter than the other, and the wax had dripped all down one side. Daniele adjusted the wick so it wouldn't burn down so fast. The child waited, not knowing what to do.

"Do you want to give her a kiss?" asked Daniele.

The little girl looked at Giulia and then at Daniele, hesitating.

"Give her a kiss on the forehead," said Daniele. "She'll be happy if you kiss her."

The child bent down to kiss Giulia's forehead, then Daniele took her by the hand and together they went off to her house. Now the moon had risen low over the ruins.

Daniele walked slowly, holding the child's hand tightly. "Don't you ever cry?" he asked after a while.

"What?"

"Why don't you ever cry?" said Daniele. "Don't you ever feel like crying?"

"Yes," said the girl.

"When do you feel like crying?"

The child thought a long time before answering. "When I hurt myself." she said.

Daniele asked her nothing more. Entering the courtyard he let her go on ahead by herself, and stood waiting until he heard the door of the house opening and closing. Then he went back, but he didn't go into the kitchen. He sat down on the threshold and gazed toward the moon.

45

The moon was rising above the ruins in a golden mist. It was a large moon and was missing only a thin sliver on one side. The night was a bit humid and not too warm. By this time the nights were like this, because summer was at an end.

When the moon was a bit higher, Daniele went into the kitchen and said to the man, "We can go. The moon's up now."

"Yes," said the man and he got up.

Carla wanted to stay in the house. "I'll make you both a little coffee," she said, "for when you will have finished."

The man and Daniele took the tools and went some distance from the house, toward the center of the zone of the dead. The man selected a spot where the ruins ended in a collapsed wall. "Let's lift the stones and dig here."

"All right."

"Then we'll put the stones back on top and no one will see anything."

"Yes."

They cleared debris from an expanse of ground, then the man thought about measurements. "She was tall. Tall and thin."

"She was almost as tall as me," said Daniele.

The man began to strike the ground with the pick, and he cursed because the ground was too hard. "If it isn't softer underneath," he said, "we'll still be digging here tomorrow morning."

Daniele didn't speak, waiting for the man to loosen the earth with the pick. Then he would dig in one spot with the shovel.

"We can do this in one of two ways," said the man. "Put her just under the ground, in such a way that if they find her it will seem that she died under the ruins. Or dig down at least a couple of feet, so they won't find her, not even if they come looking for all these dead."

"It's better to put her down deep," said Daniele.

"Because of the stink?" asked the man.

"No, I wasn't thinking of that."

"You should have smelled what a stink there was here, right after the bombardment," said the man.

The moon was quite high in the sky when they quit working and went back to the house. Carla was sitting close to Giulia. She had lit two new candles, in place of those that had burned down.

Daniele went over to her and then she asked, "Is it ready?"

"Yes," said Daniele.

Carla got to her feet and with one hand she brushed his hair off his forehead. "Do you want us to go?" she asked.

Daniele looked at Carla. "Will you let me be alone with her for a bit, Carla?" he asked.

Carla delayed for an instant with her hand on his forehead, then she left in silence and made coffee for the shoemaker.

The man was tired and grumpy. "It must be after midnight by now," he said.

Carla looked at her watch. "Yes."

The man drank a cup of coffee, and Carla poured him another. Daniele's cup was on the table, still full.

"But what's he doing inside there?" asked the man.

"He'll come now," said Carla.

The man drank the second cup, then he said, "It's better that we get a move on, now that everything's ready."

"There's no rush," said Carla.

"Why wait?" said the man. "I'm sleepy."

"If you want to go, we'll do it ourselves," said Carla.

"No," said the man. "I want to see this, I do. It's me that'll go to jail first, if they notice something."

Carla entered the shelter of blankets. Daniele was sitting on the mattress, gazing at Giulia.

"Daniele," Carla called softly.

He turned his wide eyes to her.

"There's coffee, Daniele."

"Fine," said Daniele, and went back to gazing at Giulia.

Carla lowered one hand and put it on his forehead. "Now you must be brave."

Daniele raised his face once more to her, and he was calm. "Yes, not afraid."

"So then, we have to go. That man is tired, he doesn't want to wait."

"All right," said Daniele, getting up. "I'll carry her. Tell him to go ahead."

"You won't get tired carrying her yourself?"

"She weighs so little," said Daniele. "Tell him to go ahead."

Carla went out to talk to the man, and when she returned, Daniele was still sitting on Giulia's mattress. He was stroking her hair with the tips of his fingers, a bit above the temples.

"Let's go, Daniele," said Carla.

He didn't turn, but said, "Look. This is how she was the first time, when we first knew we loved each other."

Carla waited a moment, then she said again, "Let's go, Daniele."

"Yes," said Daniele, and he got up and put his hands under Giulia's body. "It's all hard," he said.

"It's because she's dead for several hours now," said Carla.

Daniele made an effort with his arms and lifted Giulia's body. Her legs dangled and one arm fell, inert, and her head dropped back a bit. Blood dribbled from her mouth and stained her face.

"Look, Carla," said Daniele. "Clean her mouth."

Carla cleaned Giulia's face with a handkerchief.

"And the arm," Daniele said. "Lift up the arm."

Carla took the arm and bent it over the body. Then Daniele began to walk with Giulia in his arms. Carla blew out the candles and followed close behind.

The man was waiting impatiently, close to the hole. "We need to make it quick."

"Hold her a moment, Carla," said Daniele.

Carla took Giulia in her arms, and Daniele climbed down into the hole, which was not very deep. "Now lower her down," he said.

The man and Carla lowered Giulia's body into the hole, holding it by the arms. Daniele took it and laid it out on the bottom.

"We've forgotten, Carla," he said. "We should have brought some magnolias too."

"It's late now," said Carla. "We'll do it tomorrow."

"Yes," said Daniele. "She liked magnolias so much."

Then he climbed out and with the shovel began to fill the hole with earth. And when it was filled up, they stepped on it to flatten the dirt, and then with the stones they covered the place where the earth had been disturbed. And when everything was done, they stayed to keep vigil by the faint light of the moon.

"A rainfall, and you won't see anything," said the man.

The other two said nothing.

Then the man gathered up the tools and loaded them onto his shoulder. "Alright, I'm going," he said. And he went off.

46

As soon as he heard Carla stirring, Daniele lit the stove and made coffee. He put the cup on the table in anticipation of Carla's appearance. For a little while steam continued to rise from the cup, then it stopped. From time to time Carla made sounds, moving around in her room. Then she came into the kitchen. She was wearing her good dress and her hair was nicely combed and her lips were painted, and clearly she was ready to go out. She busied herself absentmindedly with some object that wasn't in its proper place.

"If you want, I'll reheat the coffee," said Daniele.

"No, it doesn't matter." She took the cup and carried it near the window. She began to drink in small sips, looking outside.

"Daniele," she said. "Maybe I won't come back tonight."

Daniele turned his face toward her, but he could only see her back and her hair. "All right."

Slowly Carla finished drinking and she turned and came to put the empty cup on the table. She didn't look at him but said, "Why aren't you going back to work, Daniele?"

He seemed to be searching for the answer. "I don't feel like it."

Carla moved to take her handbag that was hanging on a nail. She turned it over and began to clean it out, without haste. "I'm not telling you to go to work for money," she said. "But I think it would do you good to work, just for something to do. A person can't keep living the way you're doing."

"No, a person can't," said Daniele.

Carla paused to focus on him, and her gaze became sharp. Still, when she spoke her voice was almost expressionless. "If I shouldn't come home tonight, think about making something to eat for yourself and Maria."

"All right."

"There's still something to eat in the food chest."

"All right," said Daniele and raised his face toward her, and their eyes met for an instant and right away both of them looked away.

"Water needs to be fetched also, tonight," said Carla. "I can tell the shoemaker to come and help you."

"No, I'll take care of it," said Daniele.

Carla left, carrying her handbag, and he sat down on a stool and remained seated like that for a long time. Then he got up, and after looking around he decided to wash the cup that Carla had left on the table. He washed it and put it in its place on the shelf and returned to sit on the same stool as before.

The bells in the belltowers of the city began to ring the noon hour, not all at once, but some at first and then others, closer or farther away. When they stopped, Daniele got up and changed position, going to sit down on the small step of the threshold. He stared a long time at the ground, then at the ruins, then at the sky. White bands ribbed the sky. Maybe the weather would change.

He experienced a kind of mental blackout as he observed the sky, so immense, and then he came back to earth. He appeared to take an interest in his shoes, the soles of which were worn out. He touched the leather at its thinnest spot and felt it soft and flexible. Those shoes wouldn't last much longer. Even above the soles, on the uppers, they were cracked. Then he abruptly lost interest in the shoes and leaned his head back against the wall and closed his eyes. His hands and arms lay completely limp. And his mind wandered, without his controlling it or following it, along its own path.

Unexpectedly a thought gave him a quick feeling of joy, and just as suddenly he forgot that thought, and as much as he might meditate on it, he wasn't able to recapture it. Then he opened his eyes again. He began to focus on a spot on the ground, and doggedly considered all the thoughts that would have been able to create joy: that his mother was still alive, and that Giulia was alive, and that the war had never happened.

But no joy resulted from his effort to think those thoughts. That first one hadn't really been a thought, just a fantasy, as if his mother and Giulia were just around the corner and were doing something and humming. He closed his eyes again and tried to bring images into his mind. His mother and Giulia were seated together on a flowered couch that was in the flat on the fifth floor of the skyscraper. They were sitting together and speaking to each other softly, and they appeared happy. And all that was worthless, because a bomb had made the skyscraper fall and Giulia was dead of tuberculosis, and his mother and Giulia had never known each other. No joy could come of those nonsensical thoughts. Once more he opened his eyes and returned to focusing on a spot on the ground and chasing other thoughts.

He needed to do something. He delved into his mind to find what it was that he needed to do. He remembered that he needed to make something to eat for himself and Maria. Carla wouldn't be coming back that night. And water should be fetched. But these things had no importance. They would have been done in any case, even without thinking about them. Something else should be done, and it wasn't coming to mind.

The sun had passed over the house and a strip of shadow fell across the ground. Some white streaks stretched across the sky. Maybe for this reason it was possible to think that the weather would change.

He felt hungry. It must be due to hunger that his mind went its own way so numbly, without obeying him. He got to his feet and went into the kitchen. From the food chest he pulled bread and cheese and ate greedily, and greedily drank a lot of water. Then he returned to his seat on the step. Now he felt better. Bit by bit the important thing that he had to do took shape in his mind. Then he got up and went onto the street, passing through the shoemaker's house, and walked without haste through the streets of the city, straight to the market square.

The man who sold vegetables was at his place, seated on the crate behind the table. He smiled as soon as he noticed Daniele coming, but when he got closer his face changed expression. "Have you been sick?"

"No, not sick."

"It's been almost a month that you haven't shown up."

On the table were only some stalks of celery to sell, not very good ones. Almost no one was around the square at that hour, because it was hot. Daniele looked around the square as if lost.

"I came to say good-bye," he said. "Tomorrow I'm going away."

"Where are you going?" asked the man.

"To Rome," said Daniele. "Those relatives of mine in Rome found out that I ended up here, and they wrote to me to come."

"Better that way," said the man.

A woman came to buy celery. She was a small woman with a flimsy, threadbare dress and a pained face. She looked for a moment at the celery and checked the price and hesitated before selecting five stalks.

Daniele looked around the square again. "Is your brother-in-law away?"

"If you'd come half an hour ago you would have found him," said the man. "Now he's gone out."

"Yes," said Daniele.

The man looked around the square also, now. "Maybe the weather will change. It's too hot for this time of year."

"Yes," said Daniele.

Then the man's voice became more lively all of a sudden. "It's better for you if you're going to Rome," he said. "You won't have so many worries about living. And you can go back to school. Staying here you'd have become a vagabond."

"Yes," said Daniele.

The man peered at him attentively. "Aren't you happy about going to Rome?"

"Yes," said Daniele, "I'm happy."

The man could see it wasn't true, but he said nothing more on the subject. Instead, he said, "I still owe you some money from the last time."

"It doesn't matter about the money," said Daniele. "I don't think I'll need it, at this point."

"I'll give it to you in any case," said the man. "Money is always useful."

He found in his wallet a scrap of paper with numbers written on it. Then he took out some money and gave it to Daniele. "It's not much."

"I didn't come here for this," said Daniele. "I didn't even think of it. I only came to thank you. You helped me by giving me work."

"We helped each other," said the man. "Your labor benefited me, and I'd be glad if you could still work for me."

"Now I can't anymore."

"Fine. It's better for you this way."

"Yes," said Daniele, in a hurry to leave. "Tell your brother-in-law that I was happy going around with him. He taught me so much."

"I'll tell him," said the man.

Daniele still stood there somewhat absorbed in thought, then he suddenly held out his hand and the man squeezed it.

"Good luck," the man said.

"Good luck to you," said Daniele, and he turned away at once to cross the market square in the direction of the gate of San Tommaso.

The man watched him go, touched inwardly with emotion. Then someone else came up to buy celery and he thought no more about the boy for a few minutes. Afterward, when he returned to thinking about him, it was no longer with the same emotion as before. By now the boy had gone.

47

Daniele went out through the gate of San Tommaso and passed along the big peripheral road, and then he took an avenue to the left, that had some two-story cottages lining it, each with a little garden in front. Now he had to go to the old man's house. At least, it seemed he must go. Things presented themselves one by one in his mind, and the rest of the world remained murky or unknown. Now it seemed necessary to go to the old man, and so he walked along the avenue, straight to his house. Every so often he glanced up at the sky with its white bands. The weather was about to change, as it was hot. He had not realized it before, but it was hot.

He found the old man in his armchair, and nothing had changed in the room.

"Sit down," said the old man, and Daniele sat down on the folding cot.

They remained in silence a long while, but unself-consciously, as if each were alone in the room. Only a bit later did Daniele begin to take an interest in the old man. His hands, resting on the arms of the chair, with such large veins, bothered Daniele. It also annoyed him that the old man seemed so absent, staring out the window. Daniele felt the desire to wound him somehow.

"Giulia's dead," he said.

"I know."

"Who told you?"

"Carla," said the old man. "Carla comes to visit me sometimes. But you never come. One does want to stay connected to life somehow."

Daniele still stared at him. He had been stupid to come. There was no obligation to come to say good-bye to the old man; they had never gotten on well together. He felt an even stronger wish to wound him. "Did you sell it, the furniture that was here before?" he asked.

The old man turned his head, startled. "Yes."

"Did you sell it so you could eat?"

"To survive," said the old man.

Daniele made a face. "Is it really important to live?"

"We must live," said the old man. "We come into the world with some duties to accomplish, for ourselves and others. Everyone should make the effort that is expected of him for the benefit of others."

The sneer on Daniele's face became more pronounced, as if he were laughing. "Why do you say things you don't believe?"

The old man didn't answer, and once more he turned to stare steadily out the window.

"I'm sorry," said Daniele.

"You understood me," said the old man.

Daniele sat there with his head down. He didn't mean to hurt him, truly he didn't.

"It's because we're alone," said the old man. "And you are all alone like me, now. Carla has told me how you spend your days. It seems easy to find someone, among all the people in the world, who might love us, and we don't find it. Or else it is we ourselves who are incapable of loving others, I don't know. But this way one stays all alone and as if dead, even if one doesn't have the courage to kill oneself."

"I'm sorry," said Daniele again.

The old man turned his head toward him, and his eyes were bright. "It's you who should pardon me," he said. And after some time he asked, "What did you come here for?"

"I came to say good-bye. I'm going away."

"Where?"

"To my relatives in Rome," said Daniele. "There are some relatives of my mother in Rome."

The man regarded him at length, attentively. "Come closer."

Daniele got up and approached the armchair.

The old man took hold of his arms and looked him straight in the eye. "You have no intention of going to Rome," he said.

"No," said Daniele.

"Where do you want to go, then?"

"Somewhere," said Daniele. "I don't know where."

"Why are you going away?"

"I don't know. I can't stay here any longer."

"But there must indeed be some motive for your going away."

"Giulia's dead."

"That's not a reason. If Giulia's dead, here or somewhere else is the same thing. You'll never get her back by going somewhere else."

"No," said Daniele.

"And so then, why are you going away?"

Daniele made a sharp movement with his head.

"But I must go," he said. "I don't know how to explain it, but I must go. Before, when I was in school and my mother was alive, I was able to stay in school. And afterward I could not stay there any longer. I did everything I could to stay there. I knew that in whatever other place I might have gone, I would have been worse off. But I really couldn't stay there any longer and I ran away. And it's the same way now, since Tullio's dead and Giulia's dead. I feel I can't stay in that house any longer. It doesn't matter if it'll be worse where I end up."

"Well, so it's like that," said the old man thoughtfully.

"Yes, it's like that," said Daniele. "And you can understand it better than anyone else, yet you're being the opposite way on purpose, as if you're trying to confuse me."

The old man raised sorrowful yet mild eyes. He observed that Daniele was still standing on his feet near the armchair. "Sit down."

Daniele returned to sit on the folding cot and he began to gaze out the window. He saw a bit of sky with those white streaks, indicating perhaps the weather would change.

Suddenly the old man began to speak, and clearly he was making an effort to say the things he said. Daniele listened, all the while gazing out the window.

"You're desperate, now," said the old man. "You're just as desperate as I am. But there's a difference between us, because you are young and it's not right for you to cut yourself off. So maybe it's not so bad that you should leave. Afterward you can come back, or go to Rome, or stay somewhere else, but in the meantime you will discover the strength to overcome this moment by moving. It takes a lot of strength to continue to live, because you and I are not the only ones who are alone, but everyone is like us, alone and lost, and there's no one who can help us. This is the result of the war, and not finding support in anyone."

Daniele listened without moving, and it seemed to him that the words accumulated slowly in his mind. Yet he understood everything.

"But humanity cannot move ahead amidst the evil of this world," said the old man. "Humanity must rediscover itself one day, and then a greater good will come to all, to the poor and the rich, to those who have lost and those who have won. I think constantly about these things, and I'm certain a better time will come. I don't know when, but it will come. And if I don't have the strength to reach that day, it isn't important. But you must reach it, and all those like you, young people with goodness in your hearts. You all should not give up. You have your mission to fulfill in the world, so that men might become better and forget violence and hate, and so they might know how to forgive themselves for the evil that they have done to each other."

"I never did evil to anyone," said Daniele. "Neither did Giulia. And Tullio stole only to help others, only for that. And for all that, they're dead."

"The evil is not in you or me," said the old man. "It's in everyone together. And we all must endure the evil in everyone, even those who are without blame."

"That's not right," said Daniele.

"I know," said the old man. "But for this there is no solution, other than to wait. There is both bad and good together in people. When they get tired of evil, maybe the good will come forth. This is the faith that one needs to have in humanity. It's not a big thing, a faith like this, but there should be at least this much, lacking something better—at least you young people must have it and must do what you can toward the times that are coming."

Daniele said nothing in the long pause that followed.

"You must not let desperation conquer you," said the old man.

"I'm not desperate," said Daniele. "I'm only confused."

"Then wait for time to pass," said the old man. "And try to believe in something. You'll see, everything will become clear."

"Yes," said Daniele.

Then the wish to leave suddenly overcame him. He jumped up from the folding cot and went over to the armchair. "I have to go now."

"We won't see each other ever again," said the old man. "At this point not much time remains for me to live. But I'd be happy if you remembered some of my words. They'll help you."

"All right," said Daniele, and extended his hand, as he had done previously with the man who sold vegetables.

But the old man lifted his hands and clasped Daniele's head. It was as if he wanted to kiss him on the forehead, but he didn't.

"Good luck," he said.

"Good luck," Daniele said, and he went out.

48

Daniele walked slowly through the streets. For a while he kept thinking of the old man, and almost laughed to himself. He wanted to give him courage, the old man did, and meanwhile he had spoken only of things that were meaningless to both of them, things they didn't believe in. Tullio would have been able to say things like that and speak of the grand day when goodness would have come to the world for everyone. But Tullio was not one of the lost. And anyway, he was dead, instead of someone else.

Daniele chased from his mind thoughts of Tullio and the old man. He continued to wander through the streets without taking an interest in people or things, without even knowing where he was going. He allowed himself to be guided by some inner impulse, and he had no awareness of it.

He came out finally in the square of the cathedral and looked toward the ruins of the skyscrapers. All right, if it was there that he should go, it was still too soon. Now he had only to go to the house and prepare something to eat for himself and Maria. And then fetch water.

Passing through the shoemaker's house, he collected little Maria. Arriving at the house, he had her sit down. "Carla won't be home tonight," he said.

"All right," said the child with a serious face.

It wasn't possible to talk with her, and it was better that way.

He looked in the food chest for things to eat. There was some bread and two tins of meat with vegetables. He lit the stove and put water on to heat in a pot. He could feel the gaze of the little girl following him as he did these things. Twice he tried to smile at her and she didn't respond. Then he paid attention solely to his tasks.

He took one of the tins, punched a hole in the lid, and placed it in the pot to warm up. There wasn't much water, so the tin was not submerged up to the perforated lid. He sat down next to the stove, turning his back to the child. The water began to steam and, in a while, to boil. The sound of the boiling water could not be heard due to the sputtering of the flame. But he watched the water bubble and the steam rise. After a short time he turned off the stove and took the tin and opened it. He put some bread on the table, and also two forks and two plates. He divided the meat in equal portions with the vegetables. They ate without speaking, soaking the bread in the juice from the meat. Then Daniele washed the plates with the hot water and put them away on the shelf.

In the meantime, the sun had set outside, but the air was still bright. He chose from the jerry-cans the one that had the white crosses on it. The little girl got up, seeing him pick up the canister. They went together toward the outside door, but in the corridor Daniele stopped and put the canister on the floor and knelt beside the child. Kneeling there like that, their faces were at the same height, and close together.

"Now we have to say good-bye, Maria," he said.

The little girl regarded him dumbly, without saying anything.

"Do you remember the magnolia tree?" asked Daniele.

Still the girl did not answer.

"The magnolias," said Daniele. "Can it be that you don't remember the tree with the magnolias that's in the courtyard behind your house?"

"I know . . . the tree," said the child.

"Well," said Daniele, "now it has no more flowers because summer's ended. But summer will come back another year, and there will be flowers again. Then, you must pick the flowers and bring them here and put them in some jars with water, as Giulia did."

The girl nodded yes. "Like Giulia did."

"You won't forget?" asked Daniele.

"No," answered the girl.

Daniele seemed to think a bit, then he asked, "Do you know my name?"

"Daniele."

"You won't forget my name?"

"No."

"Say it again."

"Daniele," said the girl.

Daniele smiled. She had not forgotten. It was an effort for her to understand things, but then they didn't fly out of her head.

"Good," he said. "Now give me a kiss."

The child circled Daniele's neck with her arms and gave him a kiss.

"No, not like that," said Daniele. "Harder."

The girl squeezed with greater force and kissed him again. He held her close a long time and kissed her more times, on her hair and face. She was warm, and he liked feeling the life in her, even though it might be a futile life, caused only by blood that was pulsing somewhere.

He let her go and said, "Well, that's all right. Let's go now."

He got up and took the empty jerry-can and with the other hand held tight to her hand and led her to her house. The shoemaker and his wife were eating. The other door was open onto the street.

He put the empty canister in its place next to the door. "I'll come pick up the full one later. Right now I have to go out."

"Don't be away long," said the shoemaker. "We want to go to bed early."

"I won't be away long," said Daniele.

The streets were immersed in the shadows of twilight, and in the sky streaks of clouds could still be seen. The air was stuffy, too hot for the season. For this reason, too, it seemed sure that the weather would change. He turned this thought over in his mind continually, and he found a measure of contentment in that, even though it wasn't important.

He arrived too early at the cathedral square, while it was still light, with a low band of sunlight along the horizon. He sat down on a step of the entrance portico, waiting, and meanwhile he gazed towards the mounds of ruins. Someone was sitting not far from him, but they didn't speak to each other. Even down low, the sky was darkening bit by bit. And the evening star was already big and bright.

Then he got to his feet and walked toward the first pile of ruins. He went behind it, to where his house had been. Maybe they had been in bed, his father and mother, when the bomb fell. And now they were dead right on that spot, under the debris. He sat down and concentrated hard on them and appealed to them for the strength he needed.

When he got up it was already night. He returned home, walking fast through the streets now lit by streetlampswithout screens.

The shoemaker was waiting for him, but the woman and the child were already in bed, in the big double bed against the wall. He took the full jerry-can and carried it to the kitchen.

Then he sat down and remained sitting a long time. Now the thing to do was to go to the river and get the water for washing. He had to fill all four jerry-cans. It could be accomplished in two trips, perhaps. But he felt tired, especially in his mind. Nevertheless, he was unable to rest, even sitting down. The preoccupation with the need to go and get water seemed even more tiring than actually going and getting it.

So he stood up and went to get the water, two jerry-cans at a time. He stopped repeatedly with the full jerry-cans and listened to the silence, the silence of all those dead, a silence he had feared so much since Giulia had been buried in their midst. She was buried under some stones, and it would rain and then no one would see anything.

When all the jerry-cans were full, he didn't rest. Now he had to go to Giulia.

He easily found the spot and the biggest stone, where he was accustomed to sit. He tried to talk to her, but perhaps what Giulia had said, that something of her would remain afterwards, was wrong. Nothing of her had remained on earth, otherwise he would have known it by now. Or else in order to hear her one must become like her, passing beyond life with the intention of loving her.

He searched the sky. That star was no longer there, having already set, but there were so many others. Not all of them, because of the streaks of clouds, but there were so many, and they were already the stars of winter, and he knew some of them: one cluster of little stars were called the Pleiades, and three lower and brighter, in a row, were Orion's Belt. His mother had taught him their names, and he had taught them to Giulia, in the evenings when they stopped along the path while carrying water. He had been the bond that had united his mother and Giulia, in infinite time. He had united them with his love, and it had been useless, because they had gone away and had left him alone and lost on the earth.

He stood up wearily. Now he needed to go to sleep. He looked once more at the scattered stones under which Giulia lay, and he asked her for the strength he needed. Much strength would be needed for the big thing he must do.

The kitchen windows were open, but the air inside was still warm— too warm for the season. He lay down on top of the blankets and went to sleep. He woke up once in the night and felt cold. He got under the blankets and went back to sleep right away.

49

He woke up again when it was daylight, and then he got up. Carla's purse, which she had taken with her the day before, was in its place, hanging from a nail on the wall. He looked into the food chest. There was some bread and some tins of milk and some biscuits, and the glass jar where they kept the sugar was full. Carla had earned those things with her work. Things that were useful to eat. Or for living, the old man had said, but it was the same thing.

But that didn't make any great difference by now, because it was the last time. Later, he would be gone.

He went to sit on the small step of the threshold. The sky was overcast, and he was glad about that. It had no importance for what he had to do, whether the sky was cloudy or fair. Just the day before, he had thought the weather would change, and now he was pleased to see that it had. Maybe it would rain also before evening, because the air was still too warm for the season. Rain had great importance for a certain thing, and that was that no one would notice where Giulia was buried, not even when passing nearby.

Any sign of the sun was missing, so he had no idea what time it was. The whole time he sat there, he waited for bells to start pealing from some belltower. Nevertheless, the bells didn't ring. Perhaps noon had gone by while he was still asleep.

Then he heard Carla stirring in her room, and he returned to the kitchen to make the *caffè-latte*. As soon as the *caffè-latte* was hot he drank a cup and ate some of the biscuits.

Carla came into the kitchen ready to go out, like the day before. And, like the day before, she took a drink of *caffè-latte* looking out the window, and said, as if distracted, "I might not come back tonight, Daniele."

Daniele asked, "What time is it, Carla?"

"Three," said Carla.

Daniele said, "It's late."

Carla finished the *caffè-latte* and took her handbag, and before leaving the kitchen she said, "See you later, Daniele."

He followed her into the corridor. He called her back when she was already by the door. "Carla," he said.

Carla stopped, turning back. He advanced with slow steps. "Carla," he said, hesitantly. "We need to say good-bye, because I'm leaving."

Carla didn't say anything for couple of seconds. She looked down at her bag, made of gray fabric with two iron rings for handles. She twisted one of the rings. "When are you going?"

"Today. I have to go."

"For good?"

"Yes," said Daniele.

Carla closed her eyes and dropped her arms, which hung limply by her body. Then she opened her eyes and slowly returned to the kitchen. Daniele stayed there without moving, leaning his back against the wall of the corridor. Carla came back right away, and he didn't know what she had gone to the kitchen to do.

"Let's sit down," she said.

They sat on the small step and Carla started to smoke. "You want a cigarette too?"

Daniele seemed undecided, but then he shook his head no.

Carla smoked a cigarette and right away lit another, and when she had finished the second one she lit a third, and never said a word the entire time.

"Aren't you going out?" asked Daniele.

Carla shook her head no.

More time passed, and they remained in silence.

"It's getting late," Daniele said suddenly.

"Why late?"

Daniele didn't answer.

Suddenly Carla turned toward him. "You're going away because of me, right? Because of what I do for work?"

"No. That has nothing to do with it."

"Why are you going, then?"

"I can't stay here any longer. Every minute I stay here is full of despair, because Giulia isn't here anymore. And I can't get anything done, in this despair. I'm not even able to think."

"You need to let more time pass," said Carla. "Let time pass and you'll heal. Try to go back to your job. You can't let go. Everyone is like you, and everyone does nothing but suffer over their sorrows and miseries, but they don't let go. Tullio always used to say that there was something marvelous in the strength that people have, to hold on. And he said that as long as people were like that, not even he could let go, and he found a purpose for being in the world."

Daniele shook his head disconsolately. "You think I'm like Tullio," he said, "and you think I'm the same as you. Why do you go and see that old man?"

"What old man?"

"That retired schoolmaster. Why do you go and see him?"

"Because," said Carla.

"You're like Tullio too," said Daniele. "Full of strength and life and concern for others. I, instead, am not able to feel the troubles of others. That's not a nice thing, but it's just how I'm made. All I know is there were some things I loved and they've taken them all away, my mother and my father and my home, and Tullio, and Giulia. And so I'm left empty inside. I can't do anything about it."

"Do you think it will be different somewhere else?" asked Carla.

"I don't know," said Daniele. "Maybe it won't be different, but I have to try. As long as I stay here, it's as if I were dead. Since Giulia died, it's as if I died also."

He was quiet and looked down at the ground, hugging his knees. Carla looked at the ground also, in an absorbed and sorrowful way.

Then Daniele said again, "It's late."

Carla nodded. "Listen, Daniele, if I quit my work and took up a different life, then would you stay with me?"

Daniele didn't answer.

"We could leave this house," said Carla. "Go to another place, hopefully another city. And you would find work, and we could live together off your work. It wouldn't matter to me if we lived poor."

"Would you be capable of that?"

"I could try. I know I could be capable of anything, if you helped me."

"With my work?"

"No," said Carla. "Not only with work."

Daniele turned his gaze to her. "How, then?"

Keeping her head down, Carla said softly, "You should love me the way you loved Giulia, Daniele."

Daniele returned his eyes to the ground. "How could I?"

Carla stayed a long time in silence. Then she said, "It doesn't matter, Daniele. I said that because it seemed like a lovely thing, but it doesn't matter. By this time I'm no longer used to such lovely things."

"It's not that," said Daniele. "It doesn't depend on what you do. It's because I'm empty inside, that's all. I won't be able to love anyone again."

"Yes, that's so," said Carla in a low voice.

"You must believe me," said Daniele. "It's not what you think. If it were not for all these misfortunes, and if I weren't so empty, I could love you, I'm sure I could love you."

"Thanks," said Carla. "But it doesn't matter."

"You must believe me," said Daniele.

"I do believe you. Only I should not have spoken of these things, because I know it's useless. Even if you did love me, it wouldn't lead to anything, maybe. When someone begins a job like mine it's hard to break out of it. A person doesn't even think about it. Only sometimes I do think about it, whenever things happen like this with you. But then one falls into it again."

"Tullio thought that, too," said Daniele.

"Did you speak of these things with Tullio?"

"Yes."

Carla raised her head. "When?"

"One evening, maybe two months before he died."

"Was it that time when I had my feast day?"

"Yes."

Carla stayed somewhat immersed in her thoughts. "I made a mistake that time."

Daniele said nothing. After a bit he asked her what time it was, and she said it was past four o'clock.

Time passed and Carla asked, "Have you decided where to go?"

"The place doesn't matter."

"You're not going to Rome?"

"No."

Carla was quiet once again for some time. Then she said, "I should get you a little money. If you wait for me, I'll go look for someone who might lend it to me. I won't be away for very long."

"Money serves no purpose," said Daniele.

Carla studied him a long time, as if trying to understand something. Or maybe she wanted to look at him just to remember him better, afterwards, to remember what he was like, with his face that was so sweet and hair that was always a bit messy, that fell over his forehead. His hair was too long on his neck.

"Maybe you could buy a train ticket with the money," she said.

Daniele smiled listlessly. "I'd have to know where I was going, to buy a ticket," he said, "I don't know where to go. I could take any freight train. Where it takes me, it takes me."

"You'll need to get your stuff ready," said Carla. "Maybe you have things to wash, and it won't dry today, with this sunless weather."

Daniele hadn't yet considered his things. "I'll wash them where I'm going."

"You can't stay one more day? Only until tomorrow."

"One more day serves no purpose. When someone has decided to go, it's better to go right away."

"Sure," said Carla. She was no longer watching him, now, but she shifted her gaze at long intervals to things around her. Her face wore a bitter expression.

All of a sudden he said, "You were ready to go out, before. Maybe it's best that you go out, Carla. We can say good-bye that way, and it will be easier."

"Are you scared?"

"No. But it will be easier for both of us."

"It will be easy anyway, not being scared."

"But you shouldn't ask me to stay anymore. It upsets me too, to tell you no."

"I won't ask you anymore," said Carla. And then she began to gaze at him again, but now with an alert look, not dreamily as before. "You should cut your hair before you leave," she said.

Daniele shrugged his shoulders, but he smiled in acknowledgement.

Carla continued to observe him. His suit was still good enough. It was chestnut-colored, of a heavy fabric, good for the season that was about to arrive. But his shoes were too old and worn-out.

"The shoes!" she said, and got up.

"Where are you going?"

"Wait a moment." She went into her room and returned a short time later with a pair of low-cut shoes, almost new.

"What are you doing, Carla?" said Daniele.

She smiled and sat on the ground in front of him and began to untie one of his worn-out shoes.

"Leave it, Carla," said Daniele. "Let me do it."

"I'm happy to do it," she said.

He let her do it, yet he felt uneasy.

Carla took off the old shoe and prepared to slip on the new one. "Let's hope they fit you," she said. "They were Tullio's before."

Daniele's foot slid easily into the new shoe.

"How does it fit?"

"Well," said Daniele. "Just a bit big."

"It's better if they're a bit big," said Carla. "That way you can put on two pairs of socks, when it gets cold."

She began to untie his other old shoe. "Tullio didn't want to wear these shoes," she said. "He said they were too tight. I think it was because they were too new. And anyway, they are a gentlemen's style of shoe. He didn't want gentlemen's things."

Daniele smiled, not knowing what to say.

"He was so odd about certain things," said Carla, and meanwhile she was lacing up the new shoes on Daniele's feet.

"Try to walk now," she said when she finished.

Daniele stood up and took a few steps.

"Do they fit?"

"Yes," answered Daniele. Then his eyes went to the old shoes, and he compared them with the new ones.

"It's not necessary," he said.

"You have to have new shoes to walk around in," she said.

Daniele looked as if amazed. "That's true. I didn't think of that."

Carla came to take him by the hand, and it was clear that she was trying not to be too sad.

"Let's go inside," she said. "It's better to get the things ready before it gets dark."

"Yes, it's better," said Daniele.

They went into the kitchen and together they got his things ready on Daniele's mattress. First, they emptied his suitcase, and Carla looked over the underwear carefully. The clothes were dirty by this time, but there was nothing to do for it, because the things Tullio had left behind were dirty also.

"Now tell me what you want to put in the bottom," said Carla.

"I'm not taking the suitcase," said Daniele. "Not even the books. I want to take just a bundle, with a little underwear and my toilet articles."

Carla went into her room and returned carrying a kind of sack of coarse gray canvas, like a soldier's haversack. She began to put the things into it. She moved with just enough casualness and at times she laughed, too, a bit strained, and talked almost continuously.

But Daniele didn't feel like talking. And so she also, when she had finished getting the things ready, no longer tried to conceal her sadness. They sat on the mattress next to each other, without speaking.

Outside it was rapidly getting dark because there was no sun. And each of them remained with his own thoughts, and Daniele in his mind recalled the other time, when his things were by then almost ready, and then Giulia came in, and he no longer had any desire to leave, but to stay with her for always, however life might turn out, and instead it was over so fast.

They heard the footsteps of little Maria who was coming to eat, and Carla got up. "I've got to prepare the meal."

Daniele then stretched out on the mattress and closed his eyes, listening to the sounds. He heard the puffing of the stove and the sound of Carla closing the windows, and her footsteps on the floor, and the few words she exchanged with the little girl, some words or other that she forced herself to say and then suddenly became tired of saying. The air filled with the odor of cooking food. He opened his eyes and saw the yellowish glow of the lamp on the ceiling. And his stuff was all ready in that canvas sack. It seemed to him he would not need that stuff. Yet he should be appreciative toward Carla for that and for the shoes, and for her efforts to appear cool and make everything easier.

"It's ready, Daniele," said Carla.

They ate little, speaking little and of nothing in particular. The sadness within them grew ever heavier, and not even Carla had the strength to conceal it. The little girl began to watch with sleepy eyes. No one made a move to wash the plates.

"Put your head on the table and go to sleep, Maria," said Carla.

The child hurried to obey.

Daniele asked, "What time is it, Carla?"

Carla looked at her watch. "Almost eight," she said.

"It's getting late," said Daniele.

"No," said Carla.

They lapsed into a long silence.

Then, suddenly, Carla said, "You must promise me something, Daniele."

"What?"

"You're going far away just to recuperate, right? Just to get healed."

"Yes."

"It's not because you're ashamed to be with me."

"You shouldn't think like that anymore."

"Good," said Carla. "Then it may be that after you're away for some time, you'll feel better and then you should come back. It doesn't matter even if you don't love me. For me it's enough that you're close by me. I'll do everything you want, if you're close by me."

Daniele sat without responding.

"Do you promise?"

"Yes."

They once again fell silent. The child slept with her head resting on one arm, and she breathed peacefully with her mouth open.

After that Carla said, "It may be that you might realize that it's useless to go away. When we have pain like this inside, we always carry it around inside us, and it's pointless to change location. It may be that you'll realize this soon. It may also be that as soon as you've left here, you'll feel more desperate than before. Then you should turn back. You should not be ashamed to turn back right away. I'll understand."

"You do understand," said Daniele.

"Then you promise?"

"I'll do it, if that's the case."

"Thank you. This way I'll be able to wait for you. Now it seems important for me to wait for you."

Daniele said nothing. He stared fixedly at the table and felt that any attempt to say anything, or even to look at Carla, would have started him crying, and he desperately did not want to cry. Crying would have ruined everything. Then, as soon as he felt strong enough to speak, he said, "It's getting late, Carla."

"No," said Carla.

There was such pleading in her voice that Daniele still remained silent for some time.

Then he said, "It's getting late, Carla. The shoemaker will want to go to sleep. Now I'll carry the little one home, and I'll leave from there."

"You can get out through the barbed-wire fence."

"I don't know the way."

"I'll accompany you that far."

Daniele remained undecided.

"I'll accompany you, don't be afraid," said Carla.

Daniele stood up. "All right, then," he said. "Meantime I'll carry the little one home."

He took up the little girl in his arms, very gently so she wouldn't wake up. He walked slowly out of the house. The darkness was dense, and the child felt good in his arms, and she was light to carry, in any case not cold and rigid like Giulia the last time. Instead she was warm, in spite of her pointless life. He stopped to kiss her hair, and he did it at first softly, then harder, until the child whimpered a little. Then he stopped kissing her, but it was by then too late to prevent himself from crying. The tears fell from his eyes without his being able to stop them. Soft tears, without hope. He arrived at the house and leaned against the wall, waiting until they stopped.

Then he went up to the door and knocked by tapping it with a foot. The shoemaker came to open it, and a stripe of yellow light came through the doorway. Daniele didn't want to step into the light. He put the child down on the threshold, supporting her until she was able to stand up by herself.

The shoemaker was in a hurry. "Go on, go to bed!" he said.

The child took a few steps on unsteady legs.

"Maria, Maria!" called Daniele.

She stopped, turning halfway around. With her fingers she rubbed her eyes, because of the light and her drowsiness. Then right away she continued to go towards the bed on her unsteady legs.

"Maria," called Daniele again.

"What is it?" demanded the shoemaker.

"Nothing," answered Daniele.

Then the shoemaker closed the door and Daniele found himself alone in the dark. He waited a long time before returning to the house. He didn't want to let Carla see the evidence of his tears.

When he entered, Carla was on her feet, leaning against the table, with her back to the lamp. They didn't look at each other. On the table his things were ready to go, the sack and his cloak.

"I put the gloves and the scarf inside the sack," said Carla. "And also something to eat, what there was."

"You shouldn't have, Carla," said Daniele.

"Why?" said Carla. "I can find more again. There are two pieces of soap in the sack. One to wash with and one for the laundry."

"Thanks," said Daniele.

He had stopped in his tracks after entering and had not moved from there.

"Sit down for a while," said Carla.

He sat down.

For a long time they found nothing to say.

Then Daniele asked, "What time is it?"

Without turning, Carla raised her arm to see her watch in the light. "Ten," she said.

Daniele didn't speak. He fastened his gaze on the lamp flame, yellow and very smoky. Whenever you blew your nose, the handkerchief would be all dirty with soot.

Carla didn't move at all. She stayed with her head down and her face in shadow. There was no sound.

"What time is it?" Daniele asked again.

"Almost ten thirty, now."

"I should go. It's getting worse and worse, waiting."

"Yes," said Carla, but she didn't move right away. She stayed still with her head down, thinking.

Then with a jolt she pushed away from the table. "Let's go," she said.

Daniele looked around, as if startled. Then he put on the cloak and took from the table the sack with his things. Carla blew out the lamp, almost as if she were in a hurry to be in the dark. Absolutely nothing could be seen.

"Where are you?" asked Carla.

"Here," answered Daniele. He heard her walk cautiously toward him, and then he felt her hand on his body. Both of them were trembling a little.

She put one arm around his shoulders. "Let's go, if you want."

They moved together that way as far as the door of the house. Outside one could see better, even though there were no stars.

"Walk behind me, now," said Carla.

She moved away along the path in the middle of the ruins. There were still a few scattered crickets singing, not numerous like in summer. When they got close, the crickets quit, and you could hear only those farther away. Perhaps it was the same path that Daniele had taken with Tullio the first time, but he couldn't tell. Ruins and remnants of houses emerged as vague silhouettes, and the night immediately enveloped them again in a uniform darkness.

At length Carla stopped. "Here we are."

Daniele looked around for evidence of the barbed-wire fence, without seeing it.

"The barbed-wire fence is a little bit ahead," said Carla.

"All right," said Daniele.

Now it was necessary to leave, and it would have been good to say something to her, but he didn't know precisely what. He wanted the words to be right, in that moment. He felt Carla move away two or three steps.

Then she called to him. "Come here, let's sit down a moment."

Daniele went over to her.

"Careful, there are some stones here," said Carla.

He touched his hands to the ruins before he sat down. Carla sat down next to him.

"I . . ." Daniele began, then fell silent.

"Don't say anything, Daniele," said Carla. "It's not important, even if you don't say anything."

He made no attempt to say more. Whether she understood anyway, or whether she didn't, it didn't count for much with respect to how they would be tomorrow, or in a week, or in a month.

Carla wrapped one of her arms around his neck, tenderly, and he let her do it and rested his head on her chest. He could hear her heart beating and also feel her warm breath on his face, and both her heart and her breath were slightly labored. Gently Carla began to stroke the hair on his forehead, with a slow movement of her fingers, and then she stopped making even that movement, remaining just with her hand on his forehead, at the hairline, and it was something that made no sense, for two people who were leaving each other as they were about to do.

And it was painful to bear, because of his desire to go. Because, resting against her chest like this, he no longer felt any worry, but only the peace that he yearned for, and at the same time he understood that it would not have lasted. Only for a few seconds would it have lasted. Indeed, if she had asked him to stay, now, he would not have had the strength to leave.

But Carla didn't ask. She stood silent and motionless, just gently squeezing him in her arms.

Suddenly he was afraid of crying and losing control. He liberated himself. "I must go."

"Wait."

"No."

"All right, then," Carla said, meekly.

Daniele got to his feet, and she also stood up.

"Take your things, Daniele," she said.

Daniele picked up the sack in his hand. They walked as far as the barbed-wire and stopped to listen. No sound could be heard. Carla bent over and lifted the barbed wire at the pass-through. He put the sack and his cloak on the ground and dragged himself through. He looked around and listened before standing up.

"Everything alright?" asked Carla.

"Everything's alright," he answered.

She passed the things to him under the fence. "Walk to the right and you'll arrive at Sant' Agnese square," she said.

"Yes, I know," said Daniele. He had put his cloak over his shoulders and stood still, with the sack of things in his hand.

"Hurry now," said Carla.

"Yes," said Daniele, and began to walk away.

"Good luck, Daniele," said Carla.

He stopped and turned toward the place where she was standing, and looked, even though he was sure he wouldn't be able to see her.

"Good luck, Carla," he said, and began once more to walk.

50

He walked along the fence without thinking about anything, as if in a daze. He encountered no one on the path. Then he reached the big square. There were four streetlamps at the corners of the square, and others along Via Sant' Agnese that led to the walls. The realization of what he was doing suddenly struck him. He went ahead cautiously, and every so often he stopped and listened, as Tullio had taught him to do. Each time he looked up at the sky he saw blackness: the layer of clouds must have gotten thicker.

There was more than a mile to go, to reach the railroad crossing outside the station, where the freight trains stopped. Leaving the walls behind, he walked faster. Two or three times it happened that he heard other people, and he hid until they were far away. He guessed that it must be past midnight.

Then a light, not very cold rain began to fall. He covered himself up better with his cloak. He abandoned the road and walked into the fields. Already he could see the far-off lights that marked the railroad line. When he got closer, he chose a point between two lights, and walked straight toward it.

Suddenly he noticed up ahead the railroad embankment with a line of train cars stopped on a siding. He listened for a long time. A train was moving far away, on the other side of the station, then it stopped. Now he heard nothing but some crickets, and some frogs, too, that were singing and calling in the rain.

Cautiously, he moved forward and crawled under the train cars on the siding, and he crossed the main tracks as well. Beyond was a meadow, and a bit farther on, another track. He stopped at an equal distance between the two tracks, in the middle of the meadow. Now he would take the first train that came by. Looking toward the station he watched the red semaphore lights at the crossing and the rows of streetlamps that appeared to quiver in the distance.

It was raining lightly but steadily, and the rain made no sound on the grass of the field. He waited a while on his feet, and then he felt tired and sat down on top of the sack. The cloak was still keeping the rain out.

A bit later, a train came out of the station and passed on the tracks to his right, but it didn't stop. The locomotive puffed heavily to move away. It must be a passenger train or military train, because the cars were lit up. The silence lasted a long time. At some point the cloak no longer kept the water out.

He could have taken his scarf out of the sack to cover his head or put it on completely under the cloak. But that wasn't important. He was glad, rather, to feel the rain on his head, because somehow it helped him to keep his thoughts in order. It wasn't a heavy rain, but all the same, if it lasted a long time, it could erase the traces where Giulia was buried.

And Carla must have reached home before the rain. Certainly more than an hour had passed since he and Carla parted, and she was in bed now, and whether she was asleep or not, not even that had any importance.

Meanwhile, no train was coming, and at six o'clock a new day would begin.

Then he heard a train approaching behind him. He didn't turn to look at it, but in his mind he prayed it would stop. The semaphore lights at the crossing were red. The train came along slowly and whistled several times and came to a stop in front of the semaphores, which remained red. It kept whistling, insistently.

He was already waiting at the tracks and he walked along in search of a car he could get onto. Toward the tail end of the train a white light was moving along. It was certainly the switchman; still, he would not have been able to see Daniele.

Daniele tried the doors of some covered cars and always found them closed. Then he arrived at an open car and got on by climbing up the side. The car was empty. He went to sit down in a corner, on top of his sack. The surface of the planks was all wet and also dirty, but he couldn't see what made it dirty. The locomotive whistled at brief intervals to request right of way, with annoying persistence.

Then the semaphore clicked, and its lights turned green. He felt the locomotive strain and the train made several long jerks as it lurched into motion. The lights of the semaphore slowly passed over his head. Every so often the light of a streetlamp reached into the car. The bottom was dirty with a black powder, maybe coal. Against the light, the rain was falling thicker than it had seemed in the dark.

Still, the train didn't pull ahead strongly, and it seemed it would be stopping a bit farther on. The locomotive stopped puffing for a while, and the train of cars lost speed bit by bit, and there was a long shriek of brakes toward the end as it stopped. He couldn't succeed in seeing out, being seated as he was, nor was he able to stand up or they would have seen him. There were many streetlamps around there. Perhaps the train was in a station.

Distant voices were heard, and a man passed along the cars shouting something. Then he heard again the sound of a moving locomotive, but the train remained stopped. It would be day soon, and he would be thrown in prison.

The cloak was now soaked. He remained seated, without feeling afraid or worried. He had already forgotten they would put him in prison. He was completely without thought, and he watched the lines of rain, bright against the light. Someone shouted again, close by. Then the sound of a whistle repeated at length. And finally the train started to move, not in the direction he thought it would, but in the opposite direction, as if turning back. Still, that wasn't important as long as it was going, it didn't matter where.

The locomotive strained again, and the semaphores once more passed over his head. Suddenly he felt the urge to look out. He might have been able to see the lights on the city side. A row of streetlamps would have marked a peripheral road, reflecting on its wet asphalt. Hopefully there would have been a lighted window even though it was so late, now that the war was over.

He resisted standing up to look. It was useless to look. The city was as it was: he had it clearly in his mind, with the towers and belltowers that projected above the rooftops, and many wrecked roofs, and light and dark mounds of debris where the bombs had fallen.

He even knew what the people were like, he had seen them clearly in the streets and the market: people who were struggling just to procure food so they would not die, and who fell into greater and greater ruin because they had no other reason to live except to find food so they would not die. It even seemed like a joke. It was useless to think of the people.

The clacking of the wheels on the joints sped up, and every so often there was the different sound of the switches. Now the rain was hitting him in the face.

He got up and staggered toward the other end of the car. Up ahead he saw the glow of a fire that was reflected in the sky. Even against that glow the drops of rain seemed bigger. Maybe it was raining harder than before. The fireman was loading coal into the engine. And it was a good thing that it should rain harder, since it served to wipe out the evidence of a tomb that should disappear.

The train passed over more switches, to get onto its nighttime route. He sat down against the side of the car, the only possible shelter from the rain, and he drew the drenched cloak tightly around him, covering even his head. It didn't matter what route the train took. His path lay anywhere. He focused his mind on that thought, adjusting it to the rhythm of the wheels . . .

When he uncovered his head, he saw that the sky was dark gray, and from that he understood that day was coming on. It no longer was raining, but the air was damp and cold. He felt himself in a stupor and numb with cold. Perhaps he had slept a long time, amid the roar of the moving train. He must be a long way from the city, by this time. Perhaps a hundred miles. Perhaps even two hundred, if the train had kept traveling all night.

From his position he couldn't see anything other than the gray sky that streamed past. The bottom of the car was filthy with black sludge, coal dust mixed with rain. He gazed a long time at his dirty hands, with a sense of increasing sorrow. The locomotive blew its whistle. The train went on, and he didn't know where.

Suddenly he realized that he had not resolved anything by leaving. He felt empty and alone, desolate as he had never felt before. It must be that something wasn't going right. He tried to put his mind in order, considering thoughts one at a time. Giulia was dead, and also his mother and father were dead. If it depended on them, he would never find resolution, because they no longer existed. And Carla was lost, also without remedy. He had had nothing to do with Carla, other than that moment of weakness. He could not return to her and tell her that together they would find another reason to live, with himself being so empty. It didn't make sense.

And the old man had said so many words—words that would help, he had said. There should be faith in humanity, he had said, and he had spoken of the great day when goodness would come on earth for all people. Daniele had no wish to wait for that great day, he didn't believe in it. Not even the old man believed in it, and in any case it wouldn't come for him, because by now he had sold even his bed in order to eat. Now he might be dead, and for him to die would be a good thing, since he was so alone and lost. And besides, it wouldn't have mattered to him, Daniele, even if the old man died of starvation. He, Daniele, would have felt no remorse. He was indifferent, like all the rest of the world besides himself. He felt mean toward all the rest of them.

The locomotive up ahead blew its whistle again. Something still remained for him to do. But meanwhile he felt too cold. He got up. The wind, rushing over the sides of the car, struck his face and whipped his hair. He shuddered with cold. The day was already just light enough.

The train ran along the foot of a range of mountains. Wads of thick white clouds clung to the flanks of the mountains.

Once more the locomotive whistled. He leaned out to look ahead. He saw a small, yellow-painted signal house with a number painted in black. Outside the signal house stood a disheveled woman, with some kind of big stick in her hand. He wasn't afraid to let her see him. As his car passed, the woman made a gesture with that big stick, either in greeting or threateningly. He stared at the woman as long as he could. And she kept shaking the stick and he didn't understand what she wanted. He thought of the other human beings who were nearby: the engineer, the brakemen, the soldiers who were on the train, perhaps as guards. If they had seen him, they would have put him in prison, without caring how he felt, so empty and alone and desolate.

There was no remedy for such things. He looked down. The grassy shoulder of the tracks rushed along underneath him, appearing as a green stripe. The world had no remedy for the evil in people, for the lack of understanding and the solitude and the indifference. There was no remedy, so that you got pushed away from other people, far away. Suddenly he knew what remained for him to do. It was an immense thing, but he felt calm enough to do it.

He sat down to think, but in his mind now there was no room for anything but that thought. He began to untie his shoes; he took them off, and he also took off his socks, and sank his bare feet into the black, cold sludge. He tied the shoes together and threw them away. He took off his cloak and jacket and threw them away. That stuff would be useful to someone. It was hard to find shoes and clothes and underwear. He also took off his pants and threw them away. And now he felt good toward the rest of humanity.

It no longer mattered to him what the men might do to him if they found him on the train. He carried out each act mechanically and deliberately, afraid of losing that sense of inner calm that he had found in the big thing that remained for him to do. And here, he felt a great coldness, now that he was naked out of love for humanity. Like Jesus and also other saints—just now he couldn't remember who they were.

He faced the end wall between his car and the other. Everything was flashing by below, and there was a gray stripe between the two wheels. He felt gloriously calm. Now the important thing was to fall right onto the rails. He climbed over the wall and got down onto the post of a bumper, holding on with his hands to the wall of the car. The train swayed, and a fearful racket rose up from below, but by this time he could feel no fear. It just needed to be done quickly, because he was feeling too cold. He dropped down, clinging to a hook that stuck out. Then, he let go.

51

It was toward the end of September when it rained on the city. The sky was cloudy for several days. People pulled out their rags, left over from the preceding winter, and went around gray and sad, in a frantic search for their daily food. Tired faces roamed the streets of the little city. Listening to the drumming of the rain on the roofs and the cobblestones, feeling the cold and dampness of the rain penetrate their houses and their bodies, people had developed a terror of the coming winter.

A year had passed and misery prevailed, continually worse. People still had no other aim other than to procure food so as not to die. Everyone had to struggle for that food and carry on in such a way that if anyone were to go without, it would not be oneself. And meanwhile another winter was coming, and they all knew that in this new winter many more would die of starvation, and hardship, and sickness that they could not cure. To be sure, the war was over, by this time by several months. And to be sure, it was often spoken, at first, of the good that would have come after that war.

Little by little people understood. There was no longer a war to endure; it was a war of betrayal. Notwithstanding all that was said, what was needed was to consider that it was a war of betrayal. And they had been left to bear the weight of betrayal by themselves, a weight that was too heavy for an impoverished populace, in a town devastated and cleaned out by war. And no one could foresee when the weight of betrayal would end. Perhaps it would not end within a person's lifetime, and then all those people who lived and thought would never again have been able to be content with their lives, having enough food and clothing and shelter against the cold, and enough hope of being still alive the next day.

But then the clouds went from the sky, and the air became more translucent than even in summer, and the sun more radiant, even if less warm. By now its rays penetrated deep among the south-facing porticoes, and the shadows along the ground were long, even when the sun reached the zenith of its range.

Looking around them after the rain, people knew that summer had gone, and autumn had come, the season of harvest and a sort of melancholy mildness and also the terrible anxiety about the winter that would arrive afterward. Everything was more beautiful, but with a slightly diseased beauty. The colors of the city came back to life along the avenues and in the little gardens, in the clothes hung out to dry, even among the oldest houses and the heaps of debris.

Along the great roads of the plain, dried-up foliage from summer fell from the trees and landed on the asphalt or on the grassy roadsides or in the dry ditches. Along the ring of the walls, and wherever the horse chestnuts still remained, nuts with spiny husks fell and broke open on the ground, and someone would come by to gather the husks and the nuts, which were good for starting fires.

People, sitting in the sun, waited in weary resignation.